"How come you've never—"

Radar, intuition, whatever he wanted to call it, Leif knew exactly what she was asking. "Remarried? Because I can't imagine ever replacing her. I don't see how anyone can ever measure up. No woman wants to settle for replacement status."

"So your alternative is to keep yourself locked up in this gorgeous prison of a house."

He didn't like where this conversation was going. "I have a job. I go out every day. I'm hardly locked up here." Why did he feel so defensive?

"True, but not convincing." Marta leveled her gaze to his, and he wanted to squirm out of it. "The difference between you and me is that I've never turned my back on love. Loving comes easily for me. It always has. Isn't that the point of being on this planet? We're here to share love with each other."

He wanted to get her with the constant urge to arms and let alone.

* * *

Home in Heartlandia:
Finding home where the heart is

FALLING FOR
THE MUM-TO-BE

BY
LYNNE MARSHALL

All rights reserved including the right of reproduction in whole or in part in any form. This edition is published by arrangement with Harlequin Books S.A.

This is a work of fiction. Names, characters, places, locations and incidents are purely fictional and bear no relationship to any real life individuals, living or dead, or to any actual places, business establishments, locations, events or incidents. Any resemblance is entirely coincidental.

This book is sold subject to the condition that it shall not, by way of trade or otherwise, be lent, resold, hired out or otherwise circulated without the prior consent of the publisher in any form of binding or cover other than that in which it is published and without a similar condition including this condition being imposed on the subsequent purchaser.

® and ™ are trademarks owned and used by the trademark owner and/or its licensee. Trademarks marked with ® are registered with the United Kingdom Patent Office and/or the Office for Harmonisation in the Internal Market and in other countries.

Published in Great Britain 2015
by Mills & Boon, an imprint of Harlequin (UK) Limited,
Eton House, 18-24 Paradise Road, Richmond, Surrey, TW9 1SR

© 2015 Janet Maarschalk

ISBN: 978-0-263-25143-2

23-0615

Harlequin (UK) Limited's policy is to use papers that are natural, renewable and recyclable products and made from wood grown in sustainable forests. The logging and manufacturing processes conform to the legal environmental regulations of the country of origin.

Printed and bound in Spain
by CPI, Barcelona

Lynne Marshall used to worry that she had a serious problem with daydreaming—then she discovered she was supposed to write those stories! A late bloomer, Lynne came to fiction writing after her children were nearly grown. Now she battles the empty nest by writing stories that always include a romance, sometimes medicine, a dose of mirth, or both, but always stories from her heart. She is a Southern California native, a dog lover, a cat admirer, a power walker and an avid reader.

This book is dedicated to my readers.
Thank you for giving a new author a chance.
I've poured my heart and soul into the Home in
Heartlandia series and loved writing the Whispering
Oaks duo before that. I have felt so fortunate to be a
part of this wonderful line over the past five books,
and to be introduced to loyal readers like you.

Chapter One

The last place Leif Andersen wanted to be was the Portland airport. An avowed loner, he didn't look forward to sharing his home—his sanctuary—with a stranger. But that was what he got for owning the biggest and emptiest house in Heartlandia, and it was the imposition he'd accepted on behalf of the town mural.

The absolute last thing he expected to find was this woman sporting a female version of a bolero hat, black gaucho boots and a sunset-colored wrap waiting beside the baggage claim. That had to be her—who else could it be? In all honesty, what should he have expected from an artist from Sedona? She was probably dripping with turquoise underneath that poncho, too.

Attitude adjustment, buddy. This is for the greater good. You volunteered.

Approaching the conspicuous woman, he called out, "Marta Hoyas?"

She turned her head and nodded demurely. All business, or plain old standoffish—he couldn't tell from here. Maybe she thought he was a chauffeur, but he worried about a long and awkward ride home in either case.

He approached and, seeing her more closely, was taken aback by her appearance. The term striking came to mind. He offered his hand. "I'm Leif Andersen." She'd already been notified by Elke Norling that she'd be staying at his home for the duration of her mural painting.

Marta had olive skin with black walnut eyes, the color of his favorite wood for woodworking projects. They tilted upward above her cheekbones, accented by black feathery arched brows. A straight, pointy-tipped nose led to her mauve-colored lips. *Nice.* Rather than smile she made a tense, tight line, jutting out a strong chin. Her raven hair was pulled back under the hat brim in a low ponytail that hung halfway down her back. She'd qualify for beautiful if she didn't look so damn stiff.

"Good to meet you." Marta said the words, but combined with her weak handshake, Leif had a hard time believing them. However, years in construction had left him unaware of his own power. Maybe he'd crunched her fingers too hard.

"Just point out your bags and I'll get them for you," he said, focusing back on the task at hand and not the unsettling woman to his right. Again, she nodded. Hmm, not much for conversation, and truth was, that suited him just fine. He wasn't looking for a friend or female company. Having lived alone for the past three years in his five-bedroom, three-thousand-plus square foot home that he'd built, well, having another person around was going to take major adjustment. So far, she seemed as much of a recluse as him, and she'd probably get lost in that great big house just like he did. They'd probably never even run into each other. Good.

She pointed at a large purple—why wasn't he surprised?—suitcase rounding the corner on the carousel and he pulled it off. Then another. And another. Had she moved her entire wardrobe?

"Let's take these to the curb, then you can wait while I bring the car around. Sound like a plan?"

"Fine. Thanks."

He rolled two suitcases. She rolled the third, plus her carry-on bag to the curb. Then he strode off, vowing not to feel compelled to get this one to talk. She wasn't here to talk. She'd come to Heartlandia to paint a magnificent mural on the city college walls, one that would depict the city's history and live up to the beauty of her great-great-grandfather's beloved town monument.

Making the trek to his car, he decided Marta wasn't exactly standoffish. He'd only just met her and shouldn't make a snap judgment. She was definitely distant and quiet, but something in the way she carried herself portrayed pride. Maybe taking a mural-painting job for a small town was a step down for her?

He'd studied her website when the college had made their final decision. She had a solid reputation and did art shows across the country but mostly in her home state of Arizona. Some of her work hung in modern-art museums and at US universities. The kind of painting she did, as best as he could describe it, and he definitely wasn't an expert, was Postimpressionism. She liked large canvases and big subjects. The style seemed well suited for their historical mural needs.

In a world of pop and abstract art, he appreciated her use of vivid colors and real-life subject matter. Hers were paintings where he knew what he was looking at without having to turn his head this way and that, squint to figure it out and then make a guess. What he liked most was her use of intense colors to make her point. In that way she was bold and unrestrained, unlike the quiet woman beneath the bold and unrestrained clothing he'd just met. Bottom line, this style would stand out on a wall at their local college, and that was all that was important.

As he drove toward the curb to pick her up, it occurred to him that beneath her cool exterior, deep under the surface, maybe all was not right in Marta Hoyas's world. This was one of the traits he'd developed since he'd lost everything he loved—an uncanny ability to read people, especially in the pain and suffering department. He could spot sad people anywhere. Saw the same look on his own face every day when he shaved. Yep, he'd go easy on the woman, and maybe they'd work out a compromise for living under the same roof for God only knew how long it would take her to paint that mural. This, too, he would survive.

He stopped at the passenger pickup curb. She got in while he put all three bags in the bed of his covered pickup truck. Being in construction since he was eighteen—he still couldn't believe it had been twenty-four years since he'd joined his father's business—there was just no point in driving a nice car.

"You ever been to Oregon?" he asked once he got back into the cab.

"Not in many years."

"Ever see your great-great-grandfather's monument?"

At last, a little sparkle of life in her dark eyes. "Yes. When I was fifteen. Beautiful."

She removed her hat, and he was struck again by her beauty. An uneasy feeling, one he hadn't experienced in years, demanded his attention, and it rattled him.

You're a man, damn it. You've always loved women. Quit thinking like a priest.

Too bad he was hell-bent on living with a dead heart. Didn't matter what this woman did to his pulse. Losing Ellen to cancer had left him devastated. The thought of ever again going through anything close to that—loving someone with all of his heart and soul and losing them— had shut him down. *Never again.*

So how the hell could he explain the humming feeling under his ribs and down to his fingertips when he looked into her dark and mysterious gaze? She crossed one booted leg over the other and stretched forward to adjust the seat belt, jutting out her chest in the process.

"Can I help you with that?" he asked, trying his damnedest not to notice her breasts.

"I've got it. Thanks."

He focused back on driving, vowing to only look straight ahead from that moment on.

Typical of Oregon weather in late September, it drizzled as he exited the Portland airport and headed toward the freeway. Being three o'clock, it would be after five before they got back to Heartlandia this Saturday afternoon. And because she had yet to utter more than ten words, and he didn't exactly feel like playing twenty questions, Leif gripped the steering wheel a little tighter and hunkered down for what he'd expected since first laying eyes on her—an extralong drive home, punctuated by awkward and strained silence. *Like right now.*

He swallowed. Fine with him.

Marta stared out the window, struck by how green everything was. What should she expect from a place that got more than forty inches of rain a year? Compared to her red-rock desert home, anyplace would look green. She glanced at Leif's profile. If he ground his molars any tighter, he'd break through his jaw. His weathered fair complexion, darkened by his outdoor work—she'd been told his was the construction company that had built Heartlandia City College—made him look in his midforties…like Lawrence. She shook her head, trying to ward off any more thoughts about her benefactor, and wasn't that all he'd wound up being? Her ex-benefactor… and ex-lover.

For five years she'd given up everything for him. Five years she'd traveled with him, met the people he thought she should meet for her career. Respected his boundaries and accepted his terms. Evidently Marta was only worthy of being his significant other. It had suited their relationship well for the first year. Hell, she'd even set up the rules. She'd rebelled against her parents' traditional marriage. Pooh-poohed her father's favorite saying: "A love like ours only comes once in a lifetime." Heck, she'd been through half a dozen boyfriends by the time she was twenty-two, and not a single one had been interested in anything beyond the here and now. That kind of love was passé. She hid behind her rebellious facade, the edgy artist, and tried to believe it didn't matter that no man had come close to loving her the way her father loved her mother. But they were so old-fashioned. Old school. She was a modern woman.

It had worked well with Lawrence at first, what with her traveling and long hours in her art studio—the studio he'd financed and built for her. But surprise, surprise, she'd fallen for him anyway, and celebrating her thirtieth birthday had made her long for something permanent. Something that said he held her above all others, that she wasn't replaceable. For three more years she'd settled for focusing on her art and waiting, but then her mother died and put a whole new perspective on love, one Lawrence could never measure up to. By then their relationship seemed more like a habit than a love affair. Even now with her leaving him, he hadn't protested…much.

Think it over, my dear, he'd said. *Nothing needs to change.*

Wrong! Everything had changed eight weeks ago, and if he thought she'd hang around forever waiting for him to propose marriage, he'd been terribly mistaken.

She attributed her change of heart to losing her mother so suddenly last year. They'd been estranged over Marta's chosen lifestyle when an aortic aneurysm had suddenly taken her life. She'd never even gotten to say goodbye. Losing her mother had cut to the core, and she'd been determined ever since to honor her mother's memory with Lawrence. He, however, wasn't on the same page— that was the phrase he'd used when she'd first brought up the subject.

Even now, with the new situation and her world turned upside down, he hadn't budged in offering marriage.

She glanced at Leif again. Dark blond hair cut short, the kind that stuck up any which way it wanted, not the carefully styled spikes of younger men. His crystal-blue eyes had nearly drilled a hole through her head when he'd introduced himself. The guy was intense and focused on one thing—getting her where she needed to be for the next couple of months. That was fine with her. She needed this break, and the job had popped up at an opportune time. She needed the money. Granted, she'd been quite sure she had an edge in the final decision, being the great-great-granddaughter of Edgardo Hoyas, the Heartlandia town monument artist. This job would allow her to get away from home and her problems and regroup, to put a little money in her bank account so she could focus on the only thing important to her right now, the...

"You okay with staying at my house?" Leif broke into her thoughts.

She'd been told she would have her own wing in a large and beautiful home.

"Oh, yes, um, that should be fine. Thank you for offering."

"Normally my guesthouse in the back is available, but I'm remodeling a house and the homeowners needed to store some things, and well, the woman had been renting the cottage from me for a couple of months—"

"I understand." She cut him off, not needing to hear another word of his long and rambling explanation.

He glanced at her, then quickly returned his gaze to the highway. "I work long hours, so I won't be around to bother you. And I keep to myself. So—"

More explanations. "We'll work things out." She should give the guy a break, since she could feel the sliceable tension in the cab.

She smiled, then noticed his poor excuse for a smile in return, but at least it softened his eyes. It also made a huge difference in his appearance. His wasn't a bad face. Not by far. He had a ruggedness that appealed to her artistic instincts. The kind of face she'd like to paint, especially when he grew older. Craggy with character. That was what it was—he had character. She suspected that something besides working outdoors had stamped those premature lines in place. Being near him made her wonder—*how would I depict this man on canvas?*

The thought struck her. Even though Lawrence was profoundly handsome, she'd never desired to paint him. Photography was how she dealt with his classical good looks. The man belonged in pictures, not paintings, a subtle difference to most, but a deep divide in her right-dominant brain.

Why did Leif live in a huge house by himself? He didn't wear a wedding ring. Was he yet another man unable to commit? But why the big house, then? A man wouldn't build a big house without the intention of filling it with family, would he?

Quiet, brain. She'd been up since the crack of dawn to meet her driver to Flagstaff to catch her flight, then, because it seemed impossible to get a nonstop flight anywhere anymore, she'd spent more than six hours, including the layover, making her way to Portland. This highway was long and tedious, except for the lovely green pines. Her eyes grew heavy and she rested her head against the cool windowpane. She'd been far more tired than usual these past two months. Whirling emotions could do that to a person. And other things…

The silence in the truck and the vibration of the road soothed her, and soon she drifted off to sleep.

Leif pulled into his driveway and around the side of his house to the circular portion where he parked. Marta had slept contentedly for the past hour, which was fine with him. It gave him the opportunity to look at her without being obvious. She was hands-down beautiful, but even in sleep she tensed her brows. What was bothering her? Having to live with him? She'd said it wasn't a problem, and these days most thirty-four-year-old women, especially an independent artist like her, would be fine with that. He tilted his head, his hunch about all not being right with her world growing stronger by the moment.

Stopping the car woke her up, which was just as well because any second now his dogs would come barreling around the corner making a happy racket.

"We're here."

She stretched and shook her head to knock out the sleep. "Oh, thanks. Wow. This is lovely," she said, glancing across the yard toward the house.

He opened his door and jumped outside, and just as expected, Chip and Dale, one blond and one black, came running full out to the fence, barking as if they'd seen a wild turkey. "Hi, guys. Hush now." They didn't listen, just kept tossing those loud Labrador barks into the wind.

Marta crawled out of the cab, squinted and smiled. Good. She was okay with dogs. Because chances were they'd eventually break into her room and lick the living daylights out of her. Though he planned to keep them out of her studio. What a mess that would be.

He pulled her baggage from the back and they made their way up to the back door. Entering through the kitchen, he asked, "Are you hungry or thirsty? I can make you a sandwich or something to hold you over until dinner, if you'd like."

"Water would be great, thanks." She held her hat in her hand, and because the house was warm, she took off her poncho and folded it over her arm. Form-fitting black, straight-legged slacks hugged her curves with a simple white blouse tucked into the waistline. He'd been wrong—there wasn't a turquoise bobble in sight. As he filled a glass with filtered tap water, she pulled the clasp from her hair and down came thick black hair curtaining her shoulders. He looked away and swallowed quietly.

"Here you go," he said, handing her the water. "I'll take these bags upstairs to your suite." The sight of her standing in his kitchen made him need to put some distance between them.

Marta drank the water heartily and looked around. The kitchen was big enough for a staff of four. The huge granite-covered center island had a second sink in it, plus a food warmer and an enclosed temperature-controlled wine rack. Lawrence was rich and she was used to the finer things in life, but seeing this *Architectural Digest*–style kitchen in a contractor's house surprised her.

She walked through a marbled entryway and into a grand room, again meticulously decorated, with a magnificent stairway and beautifully crafted, ornately carved dark walnut newel posts and railings. He'd made the wise decision to leave the matching hardwood steps uncovered, and the wood shone in what was left of the daylight radiating from the huge midceiling domed skylight.

Figuring she'd be sleeping upstairs, she took the steps and, once at the top, glanced around the wide and long upper-floor landing with accent tables and chairs, vases and paintings carefully chosen, not haphazardly picked from a decorator's warehouse. Over the balcony a huge living room was tastefully furnished in relaxing sage and beige with pops of deep red and purple here and there. Wow. Impressive.

"I'm over here."

She heard Leif's voice coming from her left and followed it to the French doors filled with thick etched milky glass. Quality surrounded her.

"Here's your room."

He swung the doors open to reveal a huge bedroom complete with a fireplace in the corner with a chaise lounge in front of it, long sliding doors to an outside deck and several windows.

"But this is obviously the master bedroom. I don't want to kick you out of your own room."

"I sleep down there." He pointed to the opposite end of the landing, to a single closed door. "Haven't slept in this bedroom in three years." He walked across the thick wool area rug to another set of French doors and opened them. "Besides, this can serve as your studio while you're here. What do you think?"

It was an amazingly big studio with a high ceiling and three skylights, along with several other arched windows. It brought in as much light as the Oregon weather allowed in early fall.

"This space was used for quilting, reupholstering and furniture repair. You name it."

Was?

Even with two long workstations and a sink area, there would still be plenty of room to sprawl out. The space was perfect for her planning and mapping out of the mural.

"It's phenomenal—better than my studio at home. I love it." She stared at him, searching for a reason for him to be so generous to a complete stranger. "Are you serious about this wing sitting empty?"

"Yes. I don't even use three of the bedrooms. I probably should have sold and moved a couple of years ago, but I built this house, and it's a part of me. I couldn't bring myself to leave it behind." He stood, knuckles on hips the way men sometimes do. Masculine as hell. Thoughtful, too. "You probably think I'm crazy living in this big place all by myself."

"I don't judge." Who was she to comment on his choice of living? "I'm sure you have your reasons."

His almost white brows lifted and his chin came up, as if he had something further to say, but he didn't make a peep. Okay, so he had his reasons, and he wouldn't be sharing them with her today. Besides, if she pried into his life, he might want to pry into hers, and that was definitely off-limits for now. She was damned if she'd share her latest news with him. They were strangers living in the same house for a time. End of story.

Besides, he'd find out soon enough.

He studied her as she checked out the studio, but from the corner of her eye she noticed him, too. He looked to be around six feet tall, lean yet solid, the kind of body a man earned from hard labor. His hand had felt rough when she'd shaken it earlier, and the naturally cut muscles lining his forearm and bulging beneath his sleeves hadn't gone unnoticed. There was a term for a guy like him—a man's man. The kind many women went crazy for.

Not her. She had other things to concentrate on for the next several months, and men had been kicked to the bottom of the list.

"Well, I'll get out of your way so you can unpack if

you want. The dresser is empty, and there's a walk-in closet." He turned to leave, then swung around again. "I'm starving, so I'll be cooking dinner. If you'd like to join me later, I'll give you a holler."

She wasn't hungry, but she knew she needed to eat. "That would be nice. Thank you."

With that, he left her standing in the center of a bedroom big enough for a princess, wondering what had happened in his life three years ago and assuming it had something to do with a woman. Didn't it always with a man like that?

Probably a broken heart.

That was something Marta could definitely relate to.

Leif caught himself humming while he cooked dinner and sipped wine. Cooking was one of the few things that brought him contentment. Well, that, his dogs and building houses, oh, and his favorite pastime, woodworking. See, his life wasn't nearly as empty as he'd thought. Building was the one endeavor that he felt came anywhere near to being *creative* in Marta's sense. He wouldn't dare call his woodwork artistic, but he liked what he saw whenever he finished his mantels and built-in bookcase projects. He'd done all of the woodwork for his home, right down to the posts, and was proud of it. Ellen had loved his special touches throughout the house, and her being an interior designer, he'd loved hers, too. He hadn't changed a thing since she'd died.

He took another sip of wine, then used clean hands to mash together the fine bread crumbs, parsley, minced fresh garlic and ground chicken with egg. He formed it into small meatballs and put them into the frying pan lined with olive oil. Not knowing what Marta's eating habits were, he'd taken the safe route and used chicken instead of ground beef for the meatballs.

He couldn't get Ellen out of his mind, maybe because of the new woman in the house. A dozen years ago, when he'd worked for his father and was still a bachelor, he'd make excuses to go back into the model homes they'd completed, knowing Ellen would be there. Her job was to stage the homes before the open-house events. He loved her style, and, more important, he liked the way he felt whenever he was around her. The first time she'd smiled at him, well, his world had changed forever.

He washed his hands, tossed the diced mushrooms into another pan, began to sauté them and took another sip of wine.

He'd taken a shower and thrown on fresh clothes after taking the dogs for their long afternoon walk through the hills. He'd put on his broken-in nicer pair of jeans instead of one of the dozens of work-worn pairs in his drawers. In lieu of a sloppy sweatshirt, his usual go-to, he'd chosen a polo shirt, one without any visible holes in it.

And he'd said he wasn't going to let having a woman in his house change how he lived. Right.

The dogs had been fed, but they still sat expectantly behind him praying for fallout, no doubt. He added the sliced zucchini and diced sweet red bell pepper to the simmering mushrooms, threw in some salt and stirred. The water had started to boil in the third pot, and after he moved the meatballs around to brown on another side, he put the angel-hair pasta in the boiling water. And took another sip of wine as he hummed another nameless song.

Moments like these were the only remaining shadows of joy he once knew. Feeling good, he tossed each dog a cooked chicken meatball after blowing on it to cool.

The table had been set and the pasta was about ready. He'd told Marta he'd holler when dinner was served, but somehow that didn't seem right. He'd given her plenty of time to unpack and get organized, so he turned everything down to simmer, quickly covered the distance from the kitchen to the stairway and took the steps two at a time to tap on her door. The dogs followed and beat him there. Just as he was about to knock, he saw her shadow behind the thick milky glass and the door swung open.

"Oh," she said.

"It's time for dinner." The dogs watched her curiously. So did he.

She'd changed clothes. Had put on lounging-type pants and a bright green patterned tunic over a black tank top, which dipped low enough to display cleavage.

"Thanks," she said. "I could smell the cooking up here."

As they descended the stairs he said over his shoulder, "I hope you're hungry." He got a murmured response.

They entered the kitchen. She held back a little bit, but he pretended he didn't notice.

"I'm having wine. It's a blend of three whites and is pretty good. Would you like a glass?"

"Oh, no, thank you. Water will be fine. Actually, make that milk if you could."

Okay, so she wasn't a drinker. No problem. "Kent, my doctor, has me on fat-free milk. Is that okay?"

"Yes. Fine. Thanks. May I help with anything?"

"You can take the plates to the table while I get your drink. How much pasta?"

He used a pasta spoon to measure the cooked angel hair for her plate.

"A little less, please."

They made eye contact so she could direct him on the portions for the sautéed veggies and meatballs. Either this one was a small eater, or she didn't care for what he'd prepared. Either way, he wasn't going to let it bother him. Then he served his own plate with generous portions and handed that to Marta, as well. She carried them to the table as an idea popped into his head. He'd wired the entire house for sound and rarely used it anymore. So he flicked a switch, and they had music to dine by. But then he quickly worried she'd get the wrong impression—like this was a date or something.

"Is music okay, or do you prefer silence?"

She listened to the light classical sounds and nodded. "It's fine."

He poured her milk, topped off his glass of wine and brought them both to the table. The basket of whole-grain sourdough bread was already in place. So was the butter. It had felt dumb for them to sit one at each end of the long dining table, and he thought it would be too casual to sit at the breakfast bar for their first dinner together, so he'd sat her to his left, like he and Ellen used to do.

They ate for a few minutes with the soft music in the background but without conversation. After a bite of the chicken meatballs, she complimented him on his cooking. She seemed to mostly move her food around the plate, eating very little. She did drink her milk and managed half a piece of bread, though.

He enjoyed his meal and decided not to worry about this grown woman. She could and would take care of herself. Maybe she was nervous about this new project. Or, even though she'd said she didn't have a problem staying here with him, maybe she was uncomfortable about the living arrangements. He could make guesses all night.

"You're a good cook," she said again. "I wish I could eat more, but my stomach has been giving me fits lately."

She did look a little drawn, but because of her olive complexion it was hard for him to tell if she was paler than usual.

"Sorry to hear that. I've got antacids if you need—"

"No. No. I'll be fine. Thanks."

There she went again cutting him off. His impression so far was she only tolerated being around him. He'd make a point to stay out of her way from now on.

But a meal was meant to be accompanied by conversation, and damn it, he couldn't enjoy this delicious dinner—if he did say so himself—nearly as much in silence. Leif racked his brain for an ember to spark a conversation.

"So tell me about your work. Your studio. Your home in Sedona."

She took a small bite of zucchini, then smiled. A genuine smile, and it almost pushed the wind out of his lungs. "Are you familiar with my work?"

"I've been to your website. You're very talented. Obviously."

"I've lived in Sedona for the past eight years, though I grew up in Phoenix. My father is still there. I was fortunate enough to acquire a benefactor who believed in my painting. Without him, I don't know…well, I doubt I'd be nearly as successful." She took a sip of milk.

"You seem to like to do landscapes. Do you paint outdoors?"

"Sometimes, but it gets terribly hot in Sedona several months of the year, so mostly I spend a few days taking photographs of what I want to paint at different times of day. I try to capture the perfect lighting, then I blow them up, cover my studio walls with the pictures and go from there."

He thought of a few more questions to prod her along, but his mouth was full so he waited.

"I have an art showroom downstairs and I live upstairs where my studio is. I'm fortunate to have a small staff working for me so I can concentrate on painting."

"You're not married." It sounded matter-of-fact, and maybe intrusive of her privacy, but he'd had a glass and a half of wine and just sort of blurted it.

"No." She looked at her plate, but just before she did, the subtle crinkle of her brow made him wonder if he'd hit a sensitive nerve.

She was what, thirty-four? Did women these days still get touchy about being single after a certain age? What did he know? He'd lived in a cave for the past several years. At forty-two, he'd often felt his life was over in that department. Now, that was one hell of a pill to swallow for a perfectly healthy man, but, nevertheless, that was how he felt. He took another sip of wine; the glass was almost empty. He could save this sorry excuse for a conversation. He used to be good at it. *Think back, Leif. Or, here's an idea—pretend she's a man.*

"Well, I've got to tell you," he said. "I think your painting will be perfect for the mural."

"Thank you." She still looked at her plate, moved some pasta back and forth.

"So walk me through this mural-painting process. I'm a novice."

She popped a small piece of bread into her mouth and drank a sip of milk. Then she said, "I have to be honest and tell you I've never painted an entire mural before."

Now, that was a surprise. Maybe that was what she

was nervous about. Come to think of it, he'd only seen her huge canvas paintings at her website. She'd also submitted a preliminary mural design, which had helped the committee make their choice.

"But I've put a lot of thought into this project, and I've studied how it's done. First, I lay my idea out on a grid. Since this is the biggest painting I've ever tackled, I'll go about the process one step at a time. I've already started the grid and plan to paint it in the one inch to one foot scale first. After that I'll transfer it to the wall one section at a time."

So that was why she had three suitcases. One was probably filled with supplies.

"Will I need to prepare the walls for you?"

"Oh, good question. Yes, please."

"Just tell me what you need and when and I'll get her done."

"Great, thank you. That won't be for a while, though."

They continued chatting about the steps to undertaking this project, both engaged and distracted from whatever other cares they had. He promised to take her to the college to see the outdoor walls soon. After she explained what needed to be done, he planned to remove the stucco and prep the walls to her specifications while she painted her smaller-scale grid.

After dinner she helped him wash the dishes, then she went on and on about how beautiful his house was and how extraordinary her living quarters were. Suddenly the day, and meal that had gotten off to a rocky start, was ending on a much better note.

Because she'd eaten so little, he showed her where the leftovers would be and several other choices for snacks, making sure she understood the *mi casa es su casa* philosophy they needed to agree on. It was called Scandinavian hospitality or the Viking code and the god Odin had originally laid down the law in the poem *Havamal*: "Fire, food and clothes, welcoming speech, should he find who comes to the feast."

She thanked him again and said good-night, then quietly went up the stairs. He planned to take the dogs out for one last quick walk, but before he did, he watched her hair sway as she ascended the stairs and, to his surprise, he also noticed the twitch of her hips. But what man wouldn't?

Having a woman in the house had already changed things. A life force was again coming from that end of the second floor. The often overbearing emptiness of the house seemed tamped back a bit, and it felt…well, it felt damn good.

Later, when he laid his head on the pillow, he tried to remember the last time he'd engaged a woman in a conversation for more than two minutes. Not counting women trying to engage him in conversation, like his guesthouse renter, Lilly, who was always full of questions about the town. But what could he expect from a reporter? Or little old ladies at the market with single daughters or granddaughters.

Nope, he'd initiated this conversation tonight, and somehow he'd managed to draw Marta Hoyas out of her shell, even if only for a little while. The thought made him happy, a foreign feeling for him. Well, he'd had a couple of glasses of wine, which probably helped that along.

Yeah, that had to be the reason for that goofy-feeling grin pasted on his face.

Not the beautiful woman from Sedona.

Chapter Two

"Ellen?" Leif rolled over in bed, mostly asleep. "Ellen?" No flash of a dream came back to him like usual. What had driven him out of deep sleep thinking of his dead wife? And what time was it? He looked at the bedside clock—quarter to five. Almost time to get up anyway.

Leif sat up, gave a quick shake of his head and pulled on his jeans for the short walk to the hall bathroom. Another inconvenience of having a woman in the house. As he woke he understood he must have been dreaming about Ellen, but usually when he did he remembered it. He didn't remember anything about this dream. If that was what it was.

He heard a sound and stopped. It was very faint but undeniably a sound he remembered.

He stood quiet and listened harder. There it was again. Retching.

The old and familiar heaving from when Ellen had suffered through chemotherapy came rushing back. He must have heard that unmistakable sound in his sleep.

Retching? What was up?

He squinted and listened. It had gone quiet again, but the puking sound had come from Marta's room. Had she gotten food poisoning from what little she'd eaten last night? Damn, that would be horrible. He felt fine, so why would she get sick?

After he finished his quick pit stop and washed his hands he heard more retching and fought off a wave of terrible memories. *Oh, God, Ellen, what you went through.* He strode to the end of the hall, not wanting to be nosy but unable to let this lie. It was quiet again.

Marta was curvy—not ultrathin like anorexics or bulimics tended to be. What a crazy thought to even entertain, that she might have an eating disorder. That couldn't be it. But she'd picked at her meal and looked queasy during dinner, even said her stomach had been giving her fits.

She'd also refused alcohol.

A lot of people didn't drink. But a warning thought planted inside his brain and made him back off as he heard one more round of intense dry heaves. He wanted to help her out, but it could prove embarrassing for her, and that wasn't his intent. She needed—deserved— privacy. If she was sick, he'd gladly take care of her, but not without an invitation. She was a grown woman and he assumed she wouldn't hesitate to ask for help. Unless she was one of those superproud ladies who couldn't ask for anything.

He ran his hand through his hair, torn. *Let it be, Andersen.* He listened to his intuition stemmed from the fact she'd refused any wine last night. A troubling thought of what a woman throwing up first thing in the morning usually meant made him step away from the door, then he headed back to his bathroom for a shower.

Later, Leif had eaten and was feeding the dogs, having decided to take them with him over to the job for the day. He'd promised to finish the add-on to Gunnar Norling's house in six weeks, and Gunnar had offered to help as much as possible. That meant today, before the sergeant's shift at Heartlandia PD, they'd install the triple-paned windows that had arrived yesterday. Even though he'd been driving his crew hard on this project, no way would Leif ask them to work on Sunday. The guys needed at least one day off. He and Gunnar could handle it.

After both dogs took a quick whiz, he whistled for them to jump into the bed of the truck. He'd removed the cover and had thrown in his window installation tools. Just as he finished closing the tailgate, he noticed Marta standing in the kitchen doorway in a robe that looked like a Native American blanket. With her hair parted down the middle and not brushed, it tumbled over her shoulders in a wild mess. The vision moved him in ways he hadn't felt in years. It also bothered him to react so viscerally to a near stranger. She might be pregnant, for crying out loud.

"Where are you going?" Curiosity knit her brows.

"I've got a job today. I left you a note in the kitchen. Sorry, but I didn't want to disturb you."

"Oh, okay." She folded her arms. "That's all right, then. I'll wait to talk to you later."

"Is there anything you need?" He thought back to the noises emanating from her suite earlier.

"Besides a good night's sleep and peace of mind?" She offered a wan smile. Her pained look made him want to wrap his arms around her and tell her everything would be okay, and what was up with that impulse? But other than having a pretty solid hunch, Leif didn't know what her problem was. He really didn't have a clue if things were okay in her world or not. Obviously, something had robbed her peace of mind.

"Do you want me to stick around? Take you anywhere?"

She shook her head. "No. I'll be fine. I'll work on the grid." She glanced down at her slippers, then quickly back up. "I would like to talk to you about something when you get home, though."

"If it's urgent, I'm all ears."

"Not really urgent. I'll talk to you later." She started to back away from the door.

"Okay, then." Leif opened the cab door and started to get inside.

"Oh, hey, what time will you be home?"

"Gunnar's got to be at work at three, so I'll see you before then." It felt eerie having a woman ask when he'd be coming home after all these years. "Do you want me to bring some lunch or anything?" *Saltine crackers?*

"You've got plenty of food here. Thanks. We'll talk later." With that, the beautiful, straight-out-of-bed vision disappeared from the door.

As he backed out the truck, Leif was certain Marta was going to tell him she was pregnant, and he chided himself for having already developed a little crush on her. *On a pregnant lady. How desperate is that?*

Seven hours later, Leif returned home and put the dogs in the gated backyard and pool area. He went in the back door, took his dirty shoes off in the laundry room, then headed to the kitchen. The house was quiet enough to hear a drip of water in the sink. As he turned the faucet completely off, he noticed a bowl in the sink. She must have eaten cereal, so at least that was something.

He headed up the stairs in his stocking feet. Not wanting to come off as a sneaky surprise, he cleared his throat and made a fake cough, preparing to hear her news— *I'm pregnant.*

"Marta?" he said, taking a turn for the studio.

"I'm in here."

He entered the bright white room, thinking maybe he'd overdone it with three skylight panels, but Ellen had always loved it, saying it was the perfect natural lighting for intricate stitchery. Maybe Marta would like that, too.

She was hunched over a table, a long piece of white paper spread along the entire length. A second piece of paper was laid out on the other worktable.

"Come here and have a look," she said. "Tell me what you think so far." She glanced up, her hair pulled back into a low single braid, though a few wavy tendrils had broken free around her face. He fought the urge to tuck one behind her ear. She wore a teal-colored plaid flannel shirt with the sleeves rolled up and holey old jeans. He couldn't help but notice she still wore her slippers.

"You could have turned the heater on, you know," he said, worried she'd been cold all day.

"I've been fine. The skylights bring in a lot of warmth."

Good to know. He stepped closer, her dark eyes and olive skin quickly reminding him he was still a man. She used a graphite pencil and a yardstick to draw the final sections of grid over her mural sample.

"This is the tedious part," she said, then stood. "Come and look at this. Let me know what you think."

Long sections of Heartlandia history were sketched and laid out before him, beautifully depicted with her natural and flowing artistic style.

"Notice something?"

How beautiful you are?

Actually, something besides the fact she smelled like cinnamon and ginger did draw his attention. He pointed to a blank area at the beginning of the mural. "That?"

"I've been concerned about this project from the start. All the information the college provided me was exceptionally helpful, but when I began my sketches, I kept feeling blocked right here." She pointed to the beginning.

"I wound up having to work backward because this strange sense of darkness stopped me from advancing. I got the Chinook and fisherman part just fine, but something—pardon me for sounding overly dramatic, but *forbidding* is the only word I can use to describe it— tugged at me to start even before then. Yet no one sent any information about before that point."

Ah, jeez. Was this woman a psychic? Were artists more in tune with secrets?

For the past few months a private panel had been meeting at city hall to discuss this exact matter. Sleepy little Heartlandia hadn't been founded by the Scandinavian fisherman with the help of the native peoples—the Chinook—as they'd always assumed, but by a scurrilous pirate captain named Nathaniel Prince, also known as the Prince of Doom.

The perfect little tourist town had been thrown into a dither over this newly discovered fact, in no small part thanks to Leif. While breaking ground for the new college, he'd dug up an ancient trunk filled with journals. The pirate captain's journals. After authenticating the captain's accounts and having Elke Norling, the town historian, decipher them, their worst fears had proved true. There had been a concerted effort somewhere back in time by the people of Heartlandia to suppress the truth, and now it was time to come clean.

Plans were in place for a town meeting, where the information would be revealed by mayor pro tem Gerda Rask, with Elke by her side. And Lilly Matsuda, the new journalist at the *Heartlandia Herald*, had agreed to run the entire historic findings in a three-part story. But that only solved the first problem; the second was even worse. Captain Prince had alluded to a second trunk filled with gold coins and jewels…buried at the Ringmuren. Which happened to be sacred burial ground for the Chinook. Even now, the thought of dealing with this town-wide problem made his head want to explode, and because he was the guy who'd kicked off the whole mess and he'd been on the secret panel from the start, he couldn't avoid the predicament or the fallout.

The bigger question, right this moment, was how much should he tell Marta. And how crazy was it that she'd sensed a problem without knowing about Heartlandia's dark side? One thing he did know—he'd wait a bit, feel things out more, before saying a word to her.

"The problem is—" Marta watched him as she spoke. Was she trying to read his reaction? He went still, willing his face not to give anything away, afraid he already had. "The problem is Elke gave me scant information before this shipwreck where the Scandinavian fisherman first arrived in these parts. I think that's the issue. What about the native people, the Chinook? I need more information to do the mural justice."

He inhaled, not having a clue what to say or how to handle things right this instant.

"I hope you don't think I'm crazy. I assure you I'm not a woo-woo type at all. It's just this dark feeling I keep getting has clouded my vision of the project from the start. Once I'm past this initial area, I'm fine." She pointed to the beginning, the blank part of the mural, tapping her finger. "But this part right here, well, something isn't right."

"I'm sure there's a logical reason, and we'll find it while you're here." *A cop-out for sure, but the best I can do right now.*

The only thing Leif could think of at the moment was to distract her. Because he sure as hell couldn't give her a truthful answer, not before the mayor made her official announcement about this very thing to the people of Heartlandia. And not before all hell broke loose. Man, maybe he *should* give her a heads-up first.

"So is this why you've been all keyed up? Not able to eat? I think I heard you throwing up this morning." May as well come clean.

She took a quick surprised inhale, then nailed Leif with open, honest eyes. "I see I'm not the only one gifted with intuition." She smiled. "Look, since you're being direct, I will be, too. I'm pregnant. Eight weeks. Sick as a dog most mornings. Can't wait for this first trimester to pass. It's my first pregnancy, so all I can do is believe the books."

Leif had been right, but hearing the words from her mouth took his breath away and made him suddenly want a drink. He strode to the sink, opened a cupboard and found a glass, filled it with filtered water, gulped a few swallows. "Would you like some water?"

She nodded, probably more to be polite than for any other reason. He filled a second glass for her, handed it over, then engaged her eyes. He saw questions in hers, and realized this moment would speak volumes about his character.

"You want to talk about it?"

Marta took a sip of water, apparently thinking, then sighed quietly. The expression on her face seemed to communicate, *I may as well.* "I've recently broken up with a man I'd been involved with for five years." She looked resigned, not brokenhearted.

Leif was already stuck on the first sentence. Didn't people usually get together when they got pregnant, not break up? Was she waiting for this guy to show up and take her home?

"I wasn't trying to trap him or anything. The pregnancy was definitely an accident. But when I told him, I thought maybe he'd ask me to marry him." She put the glass on the counter, folded her arms, paced toward one of the windows and gazed outside. "He wasn't exactly happy with my news, but at least he didn't say he didn't want me to have it or anything." She glanced at Leif over her shoulder, then back outside. "I got the feeling he just didn't give a damn. 'Things don't have to change' was all he said." She swung around, suddenly animated, an accusing expression on her face, as if Leif was a representative for all of the lousy men in the world. "What was that supposed to mean? Of course things would change. Everything had *already* changed. We'd be parents." Out of nowhere she'd found a tiny cuticle on her index finger to bite and went for it with gusto. "I'd given him five years of my life. I'd given him everything I had. And now I'm pregnant and he isn't particularly interested in that part." She used the back of her hand to brush the air. "'Just take care of it,' he said. 'Get this pregnant part over with, then things will be back to us again.' How self-ish of him. How foolish of me to think he'd ever want to marry me." Rather than say more, she curled her bottom lip inward and bit it.

At least she wasn't crying. He wouldn't know what to do if she started sobbing.

Leif had been right. He'd recognized a fellow traveler on the broken and hurting road. Turned out he wasn't the only person in this house whose spirit needed some mending.

"I'm very sorry to hear this. Uh, not that you're preg-nant, but about your breakup. That things didn't work out for you."

"I understand. Thanks. I guess that's life, right?" She lifted her chin.

Yeah, he knew about "that's life." It had kicked the spirit out of him, too.

"Maybe he'll come to his senses while you're here."

"I no longer care if he does. It's over."

"What about the baby?"

"Look, I'm sorry to drag you into my problems," she said.

His first response was to say, "That's what friends are for," but they were practically strangers. "For the record, I'm glad you opened up."

She tossed a surprised glance his way. "Thank you."

He needed to do something to change the mood, to move away from the heavy subject, to keep himself from walking over and taking her into his arms for a tight, long and comforting squeeze. He hardly knew her, yet he already felt the urge to protect her.

"I've got an idea," he said, glancing at his watch. "It's only two-thirty. Why don't we get outside and take in some fresh air? I'll show you the City College and where your mural walls are located. What do you say?"

She glanced back again, as if his idea wasn't half bad.

"Who knows, maybe it will help you get unstuck."

Her face brightened at the suggestion. "You're on. Just let me change my shoes."

Marta enjoyed the distraction of driving around the quaint and colorful city of Heartlandia. She looked out the window, taking it all in.

"We're heading north past Heritage, the main street in our downtown section. That's the Heritage Hotel, oldest building in town. Now we're heading toward our hill that we like to call a mountain, Hjartalanda Peak. It's not exactly Saddle Mountain, over there—" he pointed eastward toward a large pine-covered mountain range off in the distance "—but it's good enough for us." He smiled at her, and a weird fizzy feeling flitted through her chest. Those eyes. Must be those crystal eyes.

"Heartlandia City College is halfway up the hill between the Ringmuren wall and downtown, which took a lot of campaigning to approve clear-cutting a large section of our pines. In the end we agreed that we needed the jobs, the incentive for our kids to stay home to go to college instead of leaving the area and the influx of new blood the school would bring into town. Plus, I promised not to cut down one more tree than necessary and to plant a whole lot of other trees somewhere else." He looked at her and smiled again. "I'm not going to lie—I'm very proud of the college."

"Your company built the entire college?"

He nodded. "My father started his construction company fifty years ago from scratch. He built half of the bungalows and sloping-roof Scandinavian log houses you see scattered across the hills. When he was fifty and I was twenty he developed rheumatoid arthritis and asked me to take on more responsibility for when the time came he couldn't do the hard work himself. I learned the business from the ground up for the next ten years, and when my dad moved to Arizona at sixty, I took over. I'm glad to say the business didn't fall apart when I stepped in." He flashed a smile she could only describe as charming, and there went that fizzy feeling again. "I've actually brought the company to a new level but only because of the foundation my father laid down for me. And the work ethic he instilled in me."

"That's very impressive," she said, meaning it.

"Thanks."

They pulled into a large lot and parked close to a long and low building to the left of the main three-story administration center and a cluster of other one- and two-story structures. They'd gone the clean, midcentury modern route with a definite Scandinavian influence in architecture.

He opened the door for her, and she followed him toward the long, low bungalows.

"This is the history quad," he said. "We thought this would be the best place to put your mural. See those walls over there?"

She nodded and sped up her pace to keep up with him.

"Those are your walls."

She liked the sound of that—her walls.

"The mural will be visible to everyone as they enter the campus. Pretty good, huh?"

"Fabulous. Now I'm getting excited but nervous, too."

"No need. You're very talented. I'd say quit stressing about your artist's block. Things will work out in their own way. You may be surprised. Just keep getting your grid together."

She walked ahead of him and followed the long twelve-foot-high walls, imagining what her mural would look like when she'd finished. "Wow, this is great. See, I'm getting goose bumps."

He politely took a look at the raised hair on her arms. "I'll get right to work prepping these walls for you. When you're ready to start, nothing will hold you back. I guarantee."

"I wish I had as much confidence as you do." What if she couldn't break through the mental block about the beginning of Heartlandia's history? What would she do then? She'd been hired based on two reasons, and she was sure the first carried the most clout. Her great-great-grandfather had designed and built the town monument. Also, the mural committee liked her style of painting. She'd only done extralarge canvas paintings so far and they were much smaller than these walls, but the committee had chosen her once she'd submitted her preliminary vision for these walls. They must have seen something they liked.

"Are you kidding? You're a fantastic artist. Listen, if it will help I'll arrange with the school librarian and the history department chair to get you more books and photographs from our town. We have a great Maritime Museum with loads of old pictures, but it's undergoing renovations after a recent fire. There's all kinds of stuff for you to look at right here."

"That's really nice of you. Thanks." It meant a lot to her to hear Leif praise her work.

"I want to help in any way I can. I built this college and I want to see it at its full potential. Your mural will make all the difference in the world."

If she could only believe in herself half as much as he did. She couldn't let her personal circumstances and disappointment hold her back on this project, or let the insecurity of not being wanted by the father of her child spread to her art, and she silently vowed to make this mural her best work yet. She needed the job for financial security and the recognition it would bring for her and the baby's future.

"So what will you need?"

Lost in her thoughts, she glanced at him blankly.

"For painting," he said.

"You mean paints?"

"Yeah, and brushes and drop cloths and any other supplies."

"Acrylic mural paints are a must, and I'll be needing gallons and gallons of the colors. It might be tough on the city budget."

"Do you have a list of your colors yet?"

"I have a good idea what I'll need."

"Then, let's go shopping."

"Are you serious?"

"Dead serious. It's four o'clock, so we better hurry because our hardware and paint store closes at six on Sundays."

With that they rushed back to the truck and hopped

inside. Marta hadn't felt this excited and full of energy in weeks.

"Tell me about your family," she said as they drove, deeply curious about the man, a near stranger, who had so much faith in her abilities.

"My people came here in the 1800s. They were fisherman, like most of the other Scandinavians in this area. I think my first relative might have been an indentured servant on a fishing boat from Denmark. I'm Danish, by the way. Well, I'm actually an American of Danish descent. I guess you'd say that is more accurate."

She understood. "My ancestors are from Argentina, but like you, I think of myself as American with Latino roots." Her mother had always been too traditional for her taste, and overprotective, but that was to be expected and it was her way of showing she loved Marta. But they'd argued constantly about her free-living lifestyle, and it had driven her away. Now she wished with all of her heart she could have mended their differences before her mother had died. Family had taken on a whole new meaning eight weeks ago.

Leif ran down his brief genealogy chart while they headed for the paint store, then he suddenly hit a bumpy patch in the story. "My father died eight years ago, so we moved my mother back here from Arizona where they'd retired. I'd originally built the guesthouse for both of them to come and visit whenever they wanted. Five years ago, Mom had a massive stroke and died on the way to the hospital."

"I lost my mother last year and can only imagine how tough it must be to lose both parents."

"Yeah, I guess that makes me an orphan."

"I believe you're right." So who had he built that big gorgeous house for? "Were you ever married?"

"Yes."

Of course he was a traditional kind of guy. The kind of man she'd never run into while living her sophisticated artist's life.

"I built my future wife's dream house as a wedding gift. I had to do something to get that woman to marry me." He worked at a smile, but it came off as wistful and far from his eyes. "My wife was Norwegian, since we're talking about Scandinavian ancestry."

"Are you divorced?"

"No." He grew quiet for a moment. "She died from ovarian cancer three years ago."

Things suddenly added up—why he'd offered her the master bedroom and studio, why he hadn't slept in that room for three years, why he stayed in the big house by himself rather than sell it. "I see. I'm very sorry to hear that." Not only was he an orphan, but he also was a widower and had lost everyone he loved. "That's a lot of people to lose in a very short time."

"You're telling me." He inhaled as he parked and cut the engine. "But losing my wife was the hardest thing I've ever been through in my life." He gazed solemnly out the windshield. "Ellen... She was the one who suffered the most."

The thought sent a chill through her. "You don't have children?" She turned toward him rather than move to get out of the car.

He faced her, too. "That's how we found out about her cancer. We wanted to be a family. A big family. Decided to have a bunch of kids. We tried for that first baby for a couple of years and finally decided to go the fertility clinic route, first checking out my plumbing, then hers. That's when they found her cancer. Already too late."

His distant glance over her shoulder was tinged with agony. It nearly broke her already raw heart.

Overcome with compassion and respect for this man who'd lost everything he'd loved, making her own situation pale in comparison, Marta leaned across the bucket seat, reached for his forearm and squeezed. "You suffered, too, Leif. I can only imagine."

Their eyes locked for a couple of moments. New understanding passed between them. He studied her as if he was trying to figure out if he appreciated her concern, or if he resented the pity. It wasn't pity, as far as she was concerned. This connection was an honest desire to offer him comfort. She wondered how he'd managed to survive losing his entire family. How lost he must be all by himself. In such a short time, she'd already figured out he deserved much more than this lot in life. And she had nothing to complain about. She had her health, a baby on board and a profession she loved. She almost had everything…except a man.

"If it wasn't for the business, I think I would have gone nuts."

"You're a survivor. A person can tell that about you right off." She started to remove her hand, but he reached for it and squeezed, holding tight for a moment before releasing her. His warm touch surprised her. In twenty-four hours it had already changed from their initial mechanical handshake.

"What do you say we go shopping?" He'd obviously had enough of this heavy conversation. His story was probably the last part of Heartlandia history he'd wanted to dig up today, but she was glad he had. It helped put so many things in perspective.

"Let's do it." She smiled and he returned it, in obvious relief. They'd come to a realization—they'd both been knocked in the teeth by life. The major difference was his love had died, and though she'd broken off with the person she once thought was the love of her life, she had a new life growing inside her. She wasn't about to complain about that, especially when all Leif had been left with was an empty house.

With masks firmly back in place, they got out of the cab and she followed him into the store for some major distraction.

An hour and a half later, ten minutes shy of the hardware closing time, they rolled two shopping carts filled to overflowing to the checkout. Gallon after gallon of top-quality mural paints in a dozen different colors plus protective clear varnish to ward off the effects of weather. Primer, which Leif would apply after preparing the walls for her. Every size and shape brush she could possibly need, drop cloths and plastic basins for mixing colors. Thinners. Thickeners. On and on and on the supplies piled up on the counter.

"Oh, we can't forget these," Marta said adding several packages of paint odor valved respirators to the pile.

When the total rang up, Leif didn't blink. Marta tried to not look but noticed anyway and was surprised by the total. "Put it on my account," he said.

Both pushing a cart back to his truck, she couldn't ignore where her thoughts had been heading since they'd walked into the store. "So you're the town benefactor for this project?"

He tried to look surprised but did a poor job of it and immediately came clean. "I made a bundle building that college," he said while opening the tailgate and beginning to unload the supplies. "When the topic came up about the mural, the committee balked at the expense. I volunteered to see it through. That's all."

"I'm being paid very well. You must be a rich man."

"Like I said, I've been blessed with a successful family business."

"That you've obviously grown into a mega business."

He nodded, playing down the blood, sweat and tears that must have gone into the process. "True."

She tapped his chest. "You're far too humble, Leif Andersen."

He laughed. "Not that humble. Truth is, I want this mural to be a kind of legacy for my family. For my father, who added so much to this community, and my mother, who'd always been a patron of the arts. And for my wife, who believed in the community college from the start, when everyone said it was a crazy idea."

"Like I said, you're too humble." As she handed him another can of paint, their gazes clicked with perception and they finished unloading in silence.

One more unsettling thought occurred to Marta as they emptied the carts. There was a huge similarity to his position of benefactor and her recent personal history with Lawrence. Hadn't she vowed to never let that happen again? The difference was, this was a job. She'd been hired. There was nothing personal between them. Though they'd definitely reached a new understanding this afternoon. She'd opened up to him, and he'd opened up to her. They'd shared a special moment in the car.

Something had come over her after hearing his heart-wrenching story, and she couldn't help herself. She'd reached out for him in the parking lot and they'd connected. Spending the afternoon with Leif had been the highlight of her day, and how crazy was that for a pregnant woman?

She was in Heartlandia for a job, and though the city had hired her, Leif was writing the paychecks. No matter how appealing he was, she'd keep everything between her and Leif from here on out strictly professional.

She had no choice.

Chapter Three

It had been four days since Leif had told Marta about his wife and she'd told him about the pregnancy—and they'd shared a special moment. But she'd pulled back. He'd gotten up each morning and left for work before she was awake, though a time or two he'd heard her losing her cookies before he'd left. When he came home, he'd walk the dogs. Inevitably, by the time he'd gotten back she'd have left a note on the kitchen counter saying she'd already eaten and not to cook for her.

Mostly, she'd stayed in her studio. He knew she was working hard at placing the grid on her preliminary mural, but wasn't she getting cabin fever? The most surprising part was how he'd already missed what little interaction they'd had those first couple of days. Here he'd been living as if he didn't need anyone anymore, yet her presence made him hungry for companionship. What was that about?

He didn't think less of her because she was pregnant, but did she think he did? Maybe it mattered to her that he was a man who'd never managed to get his life back on track once he'd lost his wife. Or maybe she felt as though she'd told him too much and wanted to keep things on a different level. He couldn't figure out the change in her by guessing, that was for sure.

One thing he did know—he owed her some kind of explanation about why she was blocked with her painting. It wasn't her imagination; there was a reason and she deserved to hear it, yet he'd kept her dangling in the dark. Sure, there was going to be a town-wide meeting tomorrow morning breaking the news, but why let Marta think she was a little cuckoo for having those weird feelings about the beginning of Heartlandia's history for one more day? Besides, it would give him an excuse to draw her out of the artist's cave.

She was one perceptive woman, and he hoped his reason for asking her to take a ride with him right now wasn't nearly as transparent as he suspected it might be. He missed her and wanted to spend some time with her. Was that a crime? Something about her, besides her good looks, called out to him.

Whatever the reason, it was only three o'clock on a beautiful day. Why not take advantage of it? He rushed up the steps and tapped on the studio door.

"Come in," she said softly.

"Haven't seen you in a while." He entered the studio, aware of the huge mess. "How are you?"

"Doing well."

That was not how she looked. Weren't pregnant women supposed to have some kind of glow or something? She looked pale and tired and maybe even a little thinner than when she'd first arrived. How long was morning sickness supposed to last?

"The grid almost done?"

She nodded. "I'll be ready to go by next week. I'm going to work backward with the painting, like we talked about, and see what happens when I get to the beginning."

"Sounds like a solid plan."

"I'm just not sure how much space to leave."

"I guess that's something to take into consideration."

Her eyes drifted back to the grid with a fretful stare. Maybe he could make her day a little better.

"Oh, hey, I was just thinking it's really nice out and you've kind of been cooped up in here for a few days, and the dogs and I are going to—"

"Sure, I'd love to." She went to the sink and washed her hands.

He cocked his head and suppressed a smile. "How do you know what I'm asking?" Did she always cut people off?

A light, teasing laugh trickled from her lips. It was really great to hear it. "I'm sorry. It's a bad habit, but I was pretty sure you were going to invite me along, right?"

"You happen to know where we're going, too?" He couldn't resist teasing her, and when she laughed at his playful dig, he grinned.

"Maybe I am psychic after all." She smiled for him and the bright studio got even lighter. "Let me get my purse and I'll be right with you."

It felt great to talk to her again, and he looked forward to spending time with her. He planned to take her to his favorite place, a small park just before the Ringmuren where the view of the river was spectacular.

"I'm ready," she said a couple of minutes later, popping out of nowhere, a baggy olive-green sweatshirt over her white work shirt and worn jeans. She'd run a brush through her hair, too, and the sun from the skylights cast a bright sheen over the raven-colored waves.

"Let's go, then."

The view of the Columbia River was magnificent from this vantage point. Marta would have believed it if Leif told her it was the Pacific Ocean because the opposite bank was nowhere in sight. And farther south in the distance, the Astoria-Megler Bridge looked as if it was a hundred miles long. Wow.

She inhaled fresh air and felt less queasy than she had in days. The dogs frolicked around the park without cares, and their antics made her laugh. "Do they ever get tired of chasing that Frisbee?"

"Never," Leif deadpanned and tossed it again.

He struck her as a solid guy, one who carried on no matter how tough the going got. He'd already been through hell; anything else must seem trivial.

"Let's sit over here." He pointed to a bench at the end of a pretty walkway surrounded by flowers. Though it was hard to tear her gaze away from the river, she followed him.

When they arrived, Marta realized the bench was a memorial to Leif's father. "You put this here?"

He nodded. "Dad always liked this view."

After only knowing Leif for a short time, Marta suspected there were a couple other perfectly placed benches in Heartlandia for his mother and wife, too. A pang of sorrow over her mother caught her off guard. Maybe she'd call her father later to catch up. "Well, it certainly is fantastic. This is a lovely part of the country."

"Agreed."

"You've never wanted to leave?"

"I considered it in my late teens, but then my dad offered me the apprenticeship and I had the good sense to recognize a solid future when I saw it. Then after Ellen died, I thought I'd get the hell out of Dodge, but something held me back." He'd been facing the vista, but now he turned and engaged Marta's questioning stare. "All my memories are here, you know? If I left, I'd feel like a huge part of me was missing. Where's a guy supposed to go from there?"

How different that was from her need to break the chains of her overbearing parents when she was a teen. She'd left home for college and never looked back. She'd thought of her mom and dad as old-fashioned and wanted nothing to do with their lifestyle. Leif honored his parents and their memories. She loved and missed her mother and decided right on the spot that when she finished the mural she'd paint a series of pictures dedicated to her. Some might say it was too little too late, but hopefully her father wouldn't be one of them.

"So you get comfort knowing your loved ones once existed here," she said.

He agreed, then tapped his chest. "And here. Always."

"But you take your heart everywhere you go."

"True. But there's actual evidence of my mother and father and Ellen here. I guess I'd worry my memories would fade faster if I went somewhere else."

There was that urge again to reach out and touch him, to take hold of his hand and squeeze, to let the man know he wouldn't always be alone, but could she guarantee it?

At this point in her life, she felt completely alone, too, and the fact she was staying in Leif's house helped smooth out those rough feelings, but there was no guarantee she'd ever find anyone to love again, either.

Something about Leif called out to her. He deserved so much more than what life had dealt him.

"Listen," he said. "I wanted to clear the air about something."

That got her attention. They needed to clear the air already?

"We've recently come to find out our town's story isn't exactly the way our history books tell it."

"What are you talking about?"

"I'm saying there may be a reason you've been artistically blocked at the beginning of your project."

Okay, now he was making the hair on her arms rise, and not in a good way. "Go on."

He proceeded to tell her the whole sordid tale of the Prince of Doom discovering Heartlandia. How he'd shanghaied sailors from Scandinavian ports and forced them to come here. How his ship had sunk and, though it had never been found, may very well still be somewhere off the coast of Heartlandia in the Columbia River.

Then he explained how none of this would have been known if he hadn't discovered the buried trunk when building the City College.

"If the Chinook and Scandinavian fisherman hadn't joined forces to overthrow the pirates, Heartlandia might have been named Princetown."

She could hardly believe her ears. What a wild story! And what a relief it was to know she wasn't crazy, that there really was a reason for her hesitation to start the mural with the Chinook and Scandinavian fishermen working in harmony to build a storybook town.

The bigger questions was, how had the information been suppressed all these years?

"For the past few months I've been involved with a special committee looking into the contents of the trunk and following up with where the journals led. We'd chosen to keep the information to ourselves until we authenticated the journals, dated them and figured out what exactly they meant. We've finally decided the time is right to move ahead with informing the locals, and tomorrow is our first community meeting. Lilly Matsuda, our new journalist, will follow up with a three-part story, explaining everything."

"This is amazing," Marta said, working very hard not to let her jaw drop.

"Tell me about it. Anyway, I hope you'll come with me tomorrow. I'll introduce to you the mayor and city council and show you around the rest of the town, too."

"I wouldn't miss it for the world."

"Okay, then, it's a date. Hey, feel like grabbing something to eat? Oh, wait, I already know the answer to that."

She offered a sad-faced smile. "I wish I had an appetite."

"How about if I make us omelets?"

She tried to look enthusiastic but only managed a wan smile. He read right through it. "I'll make yours as bland as water. You should be able to get some of that down, right?"

She screwed up her face, unsure how the food would affect her. "Sometimes it's more about texture than taste or smell."

"I make great toast, too." The guy was persistent, and

his effort made her want to at least try to eat. He snapped his fingers. "Oh, hey, how about a fruit smoothie?"

She lifted her brows. Ah, now he was on to something. "That has merit. I'll give it my best effort," she said with deep appreciation for his concern.

"That's all I can ask." For one quick moment, his everyday good looks stood out against the backdrop of the darkening sky and the deep river below; the fact that she noticed threw her for a second. She had absolutely no business enjoying his appearance, not in her condition.

His sharp whistle for the dogs snapped her out of the thoughts, and they headed back to the big lonely house on the hill that she could spot all the way across town from the memorial bench at Leif's special park.

The next morning the town was buzzing with interest and maybe a little concern. What could merit a town meeting when they hadn't had one since last year when their former mayor announced his early retirement? Leif considered that some of the businesspeople might wonder if the town was in debt or, worse yet, failing. He'd overheard another group whispering about the effects of the financial downturn on tourist towns such as theirs nationwide.

After introducing Marta to Lilly and Desi Rask, Gerda's granddaughter, he planted her on the adjacent chair to Desi and headed to take his place on the podium with the rest of the committee. Marta was wearing the same black slacks and white blouse she'd worn the day she'd arrived. Looking at her from the podium, there was no way anyone could suspect she was pregnant. Both artists, Desi and Marta, appeared to chat easily while waiting for the event to begin. It made Leif happy to see her connect with new people. He worried he kept her locked up in his empty castle like Rapunzel or something.

Gerda, the mayor pro tem; Elke Norling, the town historian; Gunnar Norling, her brother and local police sergeant; Jarl Madsen from the Maritime Museum; Adamine Olsen, president of the Small Business Association; and Ben Cobowa, the only Native American of Chinook ancestry on the committee, all sat in a unifying row.

The interested crowd grew by the minute, and by ten o'clock, the appointed time for the meeting, the city college auditorium was packed to standing room only.

The mayor stepped to the microphone, her usual white bun twisted so tight, Leif wondered if it would give her a headache. She cleared her throat. "Thank you all for coming." She waited for the chatter to die down, but it didn't.

Gunnar, in his police uniform, stepped forward. "We'd like to get started," he said loudly. "Let's pipe down, okay?" He nudged Gerda back to the podium microphone as the auditorium grew quieter.

"We've called this town meeting to announce some rather startling news we've recently discovered."

Her use of the word *startling* caused the few remaining talkers to go quiet.

"I know you're all anxious to hear why we called everyone here today, so we'll get right to the point. When we broke the ground for the college, Leif Andersen discovered an ancient trunk. The contents were priceless and we have spent the past several months making sure everything was authentic. Elke Norling has done a wonderful job, and we wanted to share the information with you."

From there Gerda went on to tell the story of Captain

Nathaniel Prince to the obvious disbelief of many in the crowd. Several times, Sgt. Norling had to ask the auditorium to pipe down again, and glancing around at the faces, Leif realized the magnitude of this disconcerting news about their beloved town roots.

Adamine Olsen then stood and explained how the local businesses could capitalize on this new information, that the allure of a one-time pirate outpost turned solid small town and sleepy little tourist attraction could be a boon for the local shops and restaurants.

Gerda stressed what mattered most was not how they'd begun but how they'd turned out, and there was nothing to be ashamed of.

Then came the questions of why they'd waited so long to come forth with this information. Gerda tried her best to explain that the committee had wanted to be completely sure about their findings before addressing the town. Leif was grateful she hadn't included the fact he'd sat on his findings several months before bringing it to the town's attention.

Everyone knew Gerda had only stepped in to the mayor position when the town needed a fill-in after their mayor had had a heart attack. She'd done so willingly. What they didn't know was that almost immediately Gerda had gotten slapped with the crazy possibility of the pirate discovering what everyone knew as Heartlandia. The stress had made Gerda sick, but she'd struggled on and led the committee in an honorable way.

"We realize there must be hundreds of questions." Gerda spoke over the grumbling. "And that's why the *Heartlandia Herald* will be running a series of articles beginning this afternoon in a special edition and continuing through Saturday. We want to stress that it's not how you begin that counts, but how you end up, and Heartlandia is still the wonderful place we've all known and loved all of our lives. None of that has changed. So please bear with us. This committee has worked hard to make the best of a troubling situation. If after the series of articles your questions are still unanswered, please feel free to submit any and all questions to the newspaper. We vow to answer each and every one personally as well as in the newspaper.

"The most important thing to take away today is that our town hasn't changed. We are still the great town of Heartlandia. The only change is how we got started. Please continue to be proud to be a citizen of the best little place on the Oregon coast."

The questions flew from the curious and agitated crowd, but there was no point in sticking around because the first newspaper article would hit the stands that afternoon. Lilly had done a phenomenal job of writing the articles, and the entire committee had approved them. They'd printed triple the usual copies, expecting a run on the newspaper.

As far as Leif was concerned the meeting was over. He left the stage, grabbed a stunned-looking Marta by the arm and took her out a side exit.

"I had no idea how this would affect the citizens. It didn't seem like such a big deal to me," she said. "Wow. This is crazy."

"All we can do is move forward. Paint your mural from present day to the beginning. I'm sure you'll figure out how to portray this part when you get there."

"I certainly hope so." She didn't look the least bit confident, and Leif decided distraction was the key to helping her relax.

"Come on. I'm going to rent you a car so you can have more freedom. You must be going bonkers being stuck in my house all day."

Her eyes lit up. "That's a great idea, but I can rent my own car."

He gave her a "don't argue with me" look, the kind that imparted there was no way in hell she'd win this debate. She inhaled, ready for a fight, thinking how her parents used to give her ultimatums all the time, but wasn't Leif completely different, only thinking of her welfare? *Hmm, maybe that's all they'd been thinking about, too.* Mentally shaking her head at her old headstrong self, wishing she could turn back the clock, she accepted his offer.

Using the GPS, Marta spent the next few days exploring the city and getting to know some of the townsfolk. Though everyone, and she meant everyone, was in an uproar about the crazy news—she'd kept up with the three-part story like everyone else, and found them extremely well written, informative and to the point—she was still enchanted by Heartlandia. What a wonderful place it was. Who cared if some crazy pirate discovered the land?

The Chinook and the Scandinavian fishermen had worked together to build the town…after they'd joined forces to overthrow the pirates. What city worth its salt didn't have a dab of violence in its past? She chuckled quietly and shook her head. Who'd believe this from looking at the city today?

Rethinking what Mayor Rask had said—what mattered most was how the town had wound up, not how it had begun—Marta scouted out a parking space. Wasn't that a lesson for everyone? She'd been calling home just about every night talking to her dad, sharing what was going on in her life but conveniently leaving out the part about being pregnant. That was something she preferred to tell him face-to-face. If she kept up these calls, maybe she'd work up the courage to tell him how sorry she was for the way she'd treated them way back then. Sure, she'd been a royal pain to her parents, but what mattered most was how she'd turned out—pretty darn well, thank you very much. Hopefully her father would understand that point. She just wished her mother could be around for the long-overdue apology.

The scent of fresh bread wafted through her opened window, and fond memories of her mother's kitchen piggybacked along. There went another pang of sadness and loss. Being pregnant made a woman think about her own mother a lot. The inviting smell continued to invade her nostrils as she parked in front of a little bakery with a blue-and-white canopy. She took a deep breath and realized for the first time in three months she wasn't queasy. Rushing out of the car she went inside and, seizing the moment, she ordered a fresh croissant, then slathered it with butter and jam. She nearly inhaled it. God, she was hungry.

And not the least bit nauseous.

Thinking *what the heck* because she didn't know how long her reprieve might last, she ordered a second croissant. Once she'd wolfed that down, she asked for directions from the clerk and headed to the nearest market. A huge weight had lifted from her. She was almost through with the first trimester, and could the loss of nausea possibly be ahead of schedule? All she knew for sure was today, this hour, her appetite had returned, and, boy, had she missed it.

After two weeks of Leif cooking for this very picky eater, it was about time for payback. Because she still felt great, she decided he deserved a special dinner prepared especially for him.

Off she went to buy the ingredients to her favorite Tex-Mex, Sedona-style meal, hoping Leif would enjoy every bite. Fingers crossed she'd keep her appetite through dinner.

Leif came home from a long hard day of construction to the most amazing smells. Meat, onions, spices and corn tortillas. He entered the kitchen to a busy and beautiful Marta wearing a forgotten apron and whisking around his kitchen with three pots simmering on the stove.

"Hi!" she said brightly.

"Wow. What's all this?"

"I'm finally hungry, and this is my way of saying thank-you for taking such good care of me."

He couldn't help the smile as he lifted one of the lids and took a deep inhale. "This smells great."

"I was hoping you'd say that. It's beef and wheatberry chili, just like my momma used to make. Now wash your hands, pour yourself a glass of wine and grate some cheese for me, okay? I had to improvise with Colby-Jack since the clerk gave me a blank stare when I asked where the queso was."

"What do you expect from Little Scandinavia?"

"Good point."

How could a guy refuse a beautiful lady with a wooden spoon in one hand and a small plate of diced green chiles in the other? She had poured herself a tall glass of lemonade and it looked so good, he decided to forgo the wine and join her. As Leif poured his drink, the fatigue of the day lifted, and because of Marta's contagious happy mood he thought he might be smiling all through dinner.

And so went the next few days—Leif came home to meals already on the stovetop or in the oven. One night she'd surprised him after dinner with mint-chip ice cream sandwiched between two extralarge homemade chocolate-chip cookies.

Another night she'd made pasta sauce that tasted as good as his own. After they'd washed the dishes together, like a carefree kid he'd picked up three tangerines from a bowl on the counter and juggled for her—a trick he'd learned in high school specifically to impress girls. Then he memorized the surprise and joy on her face as she clapped and tolerated his out-of-character antics. Since when had he enjoyed himself enough with anyone to let part of his old self sneak out?

One night, deciding to have a glass of wine with dinner—another excellent meal from his houseguest— he was surprised when his mind wandered to a quick fantasy of cooking a meal with Marta.

That wasn't where those thoughts ended, either. Night after night he'd torn up his bed in fitful sleep, once waking in the middle of a hot and sexy dream where he was wrapped in the body of a faceless woman. It had to stop. He couldn't let himself become a sad and foolish bore pretending that this "thing" going on with Marta was anything more than a business proposition. One she'd agreed to take for pay.

The fact he'd spent several nights restlessly staring at the ceiling, wanting things he'd forced himself to forget and imagining how empty the house would feel again after she left, nearly sent him over the edge. He needed to get hold of himself. There was nothing between them beyond two people learning to cope with what life had thrown at them. They'd achieved a comfortable rhythm in their day-to-day life, and the last thing he wanted to do was ruin it.

Thursday night, Leif sat at Cliff Lincoln's bar nursing a beer after a long day. He inhaled and chewed his lower lip, trying his damnedest to get Marta's face, her sculptured nose, cheeks and chin, and especially her soft, plump lips, out of his mind. He'd purposely avoided going home tonight after the crazy, sexy dream he'd had last night. In it, he was making love again, and this time he'd seen her, couldn't deny who it was. Her long artful fingers had stroked his skin, driving him to wake up hard as cement.

He downed the last of his drink, dreading coming face to face with her later, and by the time he got home, she was already upstairs. He presumed it was for the night. An odd mix of relief and regret circulated through his brain. Nowhere near ready for bed, he considered lighting a fire, but the thought of just having the dogs to share it with seemed all wrong. Instead, he decided to take Chip and Dale for one last moonlit walk.

An hour later, he headed up the stairs.

"Leif? Is that you?"

Pleasantly surprised she was still up at ten o'clock, he wandered to her studio. "Yeah. It's me." It was great to see her in her loose lounging pants and with a colorful purple scarf tied around her head.

"I'm heating some water for some herbal tea. Want to join me?"

"Sure." He wasn't about to refuse an invitation to spend more time with the woman he'd been trying all night to get out of his mind. Because he really was a sap.

"I'm glad you're here. I wanted to show you something."

He walked closer, trying his hardest not to notice her cinnamon and ginger scent.

"What do you think?" He glanced at her and liked what he saw. Oh, wait…she was asking about something else.

She'd filled in the blank, as it were, and added a front portion to her mural. It was mostly a striking landscape of the Columbia River, cliffs, rocks and all. In the center sat a ship painted to scale. It looked small compared to the raging river but was big enough to figure out Neptune's Fortune belonged to Nathaniel Prince. Subtle yet telling, the perfect balance of truth and suppression.

"I like it."

"Do I need to get approval from your committee?"

"It would be a good idea to run this by them, but I can't think of any protests. It gets the point across without hitting anyone over the head."

"That's exactly what I was going for." She looked appreciatively at him and they shared another one of those instants where the tension tugged between them, the kind of moment that seemed to happen more and more often. Her expression changed quickly from mere appreciation to something more, and there went that longing, straight from his gut. Again. Thank God the kettle whistled and broke things up or he might have done something he'd regret.

Soon, she was sipping her piping hot tea and studying him, while he blew on his. He wasn't the least bit comfortable under her scrutiny. "What?"

Caught in her obvious stare, she smiled. "You, that's what. I'm glad to see you, that's all."

Well, because she was sharing, he felt compelled to be honest. "I have to admit, for the first time in ages, all this past week I've looked forward to coming home." Except for tonight when he wasn't ready to face her after having such a lifelike erotic dream about her.

"Because the house isn't empty."

Was that the reason? "Maybe."

"Did you have to work late tonight?" So matter of fact. He wasn't used to people being this straightforward.

"Had some things I had to do." It wasn't a lie if what he'd "had" to do was sit in a bar, have a beer and think about what he should do about all the crazy feelings he'd developed for Marta.

"I have to admit I like it better when you're here at night. This place is so quiet otherwise." She went back to studying the latest section of the painting.

"You can always bring Chip and Dale in to keep you company, you know." She seemed to enjoy the dogs, but maybe she wasn't a dog person like he was.

"That's a good idea. Next time you work late, I'll do that."

Things changed. She'd shown him the new part of the mural and maybe that was all she wanted. Aware she was deep in thought, he felt as if he needed to leave, but it was the last thing he wanted to do, so he stood there staring at her, thinking how lovely she was, watching her long slender fingers measure and sketch within the grid. Enjoying her hips as she bent over to draw. He forced himself to look away and blew over the tea again. It wasn't just the tea that needed to cool off.

"Is that what your wife used to do?"

His mind had wandered far from the subject, and the insertion of his wife into the conversation threw him. Was she making a point? "Pardon?" Had he been too obvious? Great going, idiot.

"When you worked long hours, did Ellen use the dogs for companionship?"

Obviously, Marta was reminding him he had a wife he still mourned. Or was she challenging him? "She had a lot of friends and also kept busy with her projects. Though the dogs were always good company. The good part about owning your own company is you can set the rules and hours."

Marta had gone still, as if she'd had far too much time to think this evening and was thinking extra hard right now. Anyone in their right mind could figure out he was way out of practice with women. She'd also lived in this house long enough to sense it was a huge mausoleum instead of a home. He was stuck here and couldn't move forward. And wasn't that why he was so damn mixed up about the sexy dreams and the desire to spend time with this outsider, the artist from Sedona?

She stood with her freshly brewed tea, walked around the worktable, balanced a hip on the edge, then took a sip. "How come you've never—"

Radar, intuition, whatever he wanted to call it, he knew exactly what she was asking. "Remarried?" She wasn't the only one who could read minds and cut people off midsentence. Hell, he'd only taken off his ring last year. "Because I can't imagine ever replacing her. I don't see how anyone can ever measure up. No woman wants to settle for replacement status." His tea was still too hot to drink easily, but he forced a swallow, roof of mouth be damned.

"So your alternative is to keep yourself locked up in this gorgeous prison of a house."

He didn't like where this conversation was going and made no bones about showing Marta his negative reaction. "I have a job, and I go out every day. I'm hardly locked up here." Why did he feel so defensive? Because she was challenging him.

"True, but not convincing." She leveled her gaze to his, and he wanted to squirm out of it. "The difference between you and me is that I've never turned my back on love. Loving comes easily for me. It always has. Isn't that the point of being on this planet? We're here to share love with each other."

Oh, yeah, here she went with all that free spirit Sedona mumbo jumbo. He looked at her differently now, wondering how many relationships she'd been in during her adult life. "The thing is, you have to find the right person to share love. Otherwise it's not really love, is it?"

"That may be true, but sometimes jerks, if given the chance, turn out to be the most wonderful people." She glanced wistfully up through the skylight, where a gibbous moon was rising. "And sometimes the most wonderful men turn out to be jerks," she said softly, with a resigned tone.

He wanted to get angry for her broaching a tough topic at the drop of a hat, but instead he fought that constant urge to comfort her, to wrap her in his arms and let her know she didn't have to be alone. He was here for her.

Yet he didn't move. Couldn't.

Because wasn't that crazy? He'd just assured her that any woman in his life would merely be a replacement, that he'd closed the door on any future relationship because it wouldn't be fair. He shouldn't be having these kinds of feelings. He wasn't ready. Would probably never be.

Aware he hadn't uttered a response, she nailed him with those dark, inquisitive eyes.

"You might think of me as a fool, but even now I'm optimistic I'll love again. I wouldn't be alive otherwise."

Wait a minute—had she just lobbed a sly attack? "So because I'm not in love or planning to fall in love, that makes me dead?" He was distracted by her beauty and at the same time irritated she was hitting him with tough reality. And the last thing he wanted to do was have this conversation.

"I'm not calling you anything. I'm just sharing how I feel about love and life. I make no judgment on you."

She was digging too close to raw nerves, and he ground his molars rather than spit out the first thought in his head. *You have no idea what I went through.* But he did wonder what she was getting at, and for some crazy reason it mattered what she thought. "You think I'm a ghost? You think I don't feel?"

She shook her head widely. "I know you feel. I've been around you long enough to know you are a kind and sensitive man. You've opened your home to me. You've made me feel like a special guest." She bit her lower lip and with soft, inquiring eyes she probed. "I'm just thinking it would be such a waste to never love again. As brokenhearted as I am right now, I still look forward to the opportunity to fall head over heels again. It gives me hope." She set down her tea, then on an inhale she must have formed one more thought. "Knowing that I'm open to new relationships helps me through the rough places. There's something out there waiting for me. All I have to do is find them."

Still bristling from her earlier comments, now reeling from this revelation and all mixed-up inside, he shifted uncomfortably from one foot to the other. She stood before him beautiful, radiant, filled with life, and that naked dream with her straddling him, touching him everywhere flashed in his brain.

She was open to love. What the hell was that supposed to mean?

"I'm just wondering what helps you survive," she said.

He'd barely been surviving, as it turned out, and the first woman forced into his life had quickly become a fantasy driving him crazy. He wanted her, and he couldn't utter a sound or she'd figure it out.

"Are you just surviving?" she prodded.

What was with the interrogation? Who was she to point out how badly he'd handled his losses? He ran a business. Had a home. Owned dogs. He lived and breathed.

Damn it. He *was* just surviving.

"There's more to life than surviving, Leif."

That was it—she'd crossed the line. She viewed his life as mere survival. She talked as if she knew him and understood his circumstances, which she didn't. No one could. How could he pick up the pieces and move on when they'd been scattered so far he could never find them?

So why in the hell was he still so damned attracted

to Marta, even though she'd pried far too deep and kept pushing and pushing?

Instead of feeling furious, as part of him felt he had the right be, he got waylaid by the growing desire that had kept him awake the past week simply by having Marta under his roof. That feeling finally hit full force. If he was going to feel guilty as hell for lusting after her, he may as well have a damn good reason. In the next second, as if a dam of pent-up feelings, building and battling for release, had sprung a leak, he lost it.

Completely confused but driven by his gut reaction, Leif put down his tea with a thud, hot liquid splashing over the lip, burning his hand, but he didn't care. If she wanted to know what surviving looked like, he was about to show her. With three long strides and a boatload of determination, he grabbed Marta by her arms, pulled her close and kissed her.

Marta felt the intensity coursing through Leif's pulse. All passion without a hint of finesse, his mouth pressed hard and ragged against hers, and she let him. Didn't even consider fighting him. Stunned into submission, she allowed the kiss to pound through her, deeper and deeper still, bewildered by the stirring he'd set off inside. His claiming lips made her knees weaken and her insides quiver. She put her arms around his solid shoulders and held on tight for the wildest kiss of her life.

Yes. She kissed him back. She wasn't ashamed to admit she was as attracted to him as he obviously was to her. Her philosophy in life had always been things happen for a purpose.

But as abruptly as the kiss had started, he ended it, his eyes dancing over every part of her when he did, heat flaming inside them, communicating two perfect thoughts.

You asked for it. Had she?

And *I bet you didn't see that coming, Miss Psychic.* No. She definitely hadn't.

Oh, but there was so much more in that burrowing stare. He'd lost his battle for control, and he wasn't sorry. His kiss had made her brain mush and left her body tingling.

Before she could think one more thought, and long before she could ever hope to form a single word, he bid her good-night, turned and left the studio, closing the door with a thud behind him.

Standing perfectly still, catching her breath, taking stock of her full-bodied reaction, she realized she'd moistened her underwear...from one rough and heady kiss.

She tried to swallow but couldn't, so she reached for her tea and lifted it with trembling fingers. "My God," she whispered after taking a sip. "What just happened?"

She'd taunted a beast out of its cage and the result had been indescribable. Could she even call that a kiss? His hungry mouth had clamped onto hers and sent her parasailing through the skylight. She wrapped an arm around her stomach, trying her best to regain some balance.

She'd lectured him, a man who'd chosen to shut himself away from that part of his life for three years, about not giving up on love. Used herself as an example. Dangled the higher, mightier approach in the face of an emotionally starving man, knowing full well he'd been traumatized by loss.

Had she bullied him into kissing her?

And now that she'd unleashed his sexual outburst, where did they go from here?

Marta inhaled a shaky breath, knowing without a doubt she'd be up all night trying to figure out the odd yet powerful chemistry she and Leif Andersen most definitely shared. Plus the fact she'd promised herself to keep this relationship purely professional. Still knowing without a doubt that if he ever wanted to kiss her again, she'd let him.

So much for promises.

Chapter Four

Six o'clock Friday morning, Leif stood in the kitchen making a pot of coffee, the only light from filtered rays of frail early Oregon sun. He hadn't slept most of the night, warring with the onslaught of feelings he'd unleashed. He and Marta couldn't continue to stay under the same roof after that kiss last night. If he couldn't control a kiss, there was no telling what might happen next. How must she feel? Hopefully not violated. He wouldn't blame her if she asked to move out, though.

If only things were different.

A quiet rustling behind him drew his attention. He turned. It was Marta. And there went that same tiny implosion he experienced every time he saw her.

"I'm sorry," they said in unison.

"No," he said. "It was all my fault. Forgive me."

"I was equally responsible." She was wearing that

Southwest-patterned robe again and her hair hadn't come near a brush, and the effect made him immediately lose his resolve to steer clear of her. "And honestly, I'm not sure apologies are even in order," she said, tossing her hair and lifting her chin. "We may have been thrown together for a specific purpose with the mural, but who knows why else?"

Her logic evaded him. He didn't think in such esoteric ways. *Why else?* Sounded like Sedona mumbo jumbo for that meant-to-be baloney spouted by romantics. One thing was sure—he was not a romantic. At least she wasn't taking the sexual harassment route. What a mess.

When in doubt, play dense.

"Your point being?" Suddenly dying for his first taste of coffee, anything to distract him from her, and needing fortification to make the slightest bit of sense out of her "who knows why else" statement, he poured and drank.

"Sometimes things are meant to happen. Maybe we've met for a reason." She kept her distance and leaned against the door frame with her arms folded, studying his face as if preparing to sketch him.

With her explanation the world seemed far too complicated to navigate. "It's way too early for me to think, let alone wrap my brain around that, Marta."

A quick smile creased her lips. "I'm pretty sure thinking had nothing to do with what happened last night."

Wasn't that the truth! That moment of insanity, kissing her as if it might be his last kiss ever, thrummed through him. He had to make things right.

"Look, I can arrange to store Gunnar and Lilly's things and move into the guesthouse if—"

"Not at all necessary on my account. Please." Those

pleading chocolate eyes made their point without further words.

She was okay with what had happened.

There was no need to ask if she was sure or not; the tilt of her chin settled it. He drank her in with the next sip of coffee. She was fine with things as they were. "Okay. But keep in mind you may be too intuitive for your own good."

He poured more coffee into his travel mug and headed out the door to take the dogs for a quick walk. Once he'd let off steam, he'd go right on to work. The less he saw of Marta right now, the more in control he'd feel, and he definitely needed to take back some control.

But as the day wore on, his strategy didn't pan out. He thought about Marta spending too much time on her project. He worried about the baby. Was Marta eating the way pregnant women should? Was she getting enough rest? And though they'd apologized to each other that morning, it didn't feel official enough. He should do something more. To distract himself from the barrage of thoughts, he worked hard right along with the crew putting the finishing touches on Gunnar's house. As he did, an idea for multitasking occurred to him.

"Rick and Dexter, I want you guys to head over to the college and start scraping off the stucco on those bungalows we talked about in the history quad." The only way to keep Marta out of his hair—and mind—was to keep her busy and out of the house. The sooner he prepped those cement walls for her, the sooner she could begin painting her mural and—though he hated to think about the next part, it was necessary—the sooner she would leave town.

End of problem.

The intuitive artist made him squirm with feelings that for three years he'd managed to keep at bay. She could recite all that "meant to be" business as much as she wanted, but he wasn't buying it. Nope. She was a beautiful woman and he'd fallen for her looks. That was all. He was nothing but a shallow man and her beauty had done him in.

But what about her quiet ways and how it calmed him knowing that she was at work in the studio? What about the energy she'd added to the big empty house? Ack. He pounded a nail into submission, then used a framing nail gun to zip through the rest. The loud and distracting compressor tools were his friends today, as they had been on many rough days in his life.

By lunch, the demanding physical activity had drained the tough-guy barriers right out of him. He felt raw and real, and as he ate a sub sandwich, Marta crept back into his thoughts.

Not the sexy-vixen Marta, but the pregnant, fresh-from-a-broken-relationship version. His vulnerable and appealing houseguest. That line of thought needed to stop. He jutted out his jaw, took another ravenous bite of his sandwich, then put his lunch away and went back to pounding nails and using his drill and power tools, thankful they required his undivided attention to detail.

It didn't work.

Marta's unguarded, wide-eyed expression, bordered with bed hair, planted itself into his mind. Sage or seductress? And why was everything about her so damn appealing?

He tossed his hammer on some nearby grass. "You guys finish up today. I've got an errand to do." He grabbed the towel he kept with his gear and wiped his face and neck. Then, secure in his handpicked crew finishing the job without supervision, he headed to his truck.

He'd become a pro at shopping for healthy groceries when his wife had first been diagnosed. He also knew the perfect power-food soup that, if good for a cancer patient, must be guaranteed to increase a baby's IQ and boost a mother's vigor. Off he went to the supermarket with a mental list already prepared.

By four o'clock he was cleaned up and standing in front of the stove stirring vegetable stock, adding chopped this and that and finally the skinless, boneless chicken he'd cut into bite-size pieces and browned in a pan. He'd also stopped by the bakery and bought some fresh dark rye bread, which was still warm and smelled great.

Forty-five minutes later, Marta hadn't stirred from her studio, so he carried a tray with two bowls of soup and a basket of bread with butter up the stairs. Nothing said "I'm sorry *and* I hope you're taking care of yourself" like a healthy home-cooked meal.

Testing a new color, Marta heard a faint tap on the door. "Come in!"

Leif used his shoulder to push through the door. He emerged with a tray of food, and because Marta hadn't eaten in a few hours, the aroma set her stomach juices to dancing. Well, that and the natural-born male delivering it. "What's this?"

"My special power-play soup. You're gonna love it."

"If you say so." She'd always liked confident men, and on so many levels Leif fit the bill—except when it came to venturing toward her. What a sweet gesture, though. "Wow, it looks great."

He put the tray on the kitchenette sink and delivered both bowls to the small table in the corner. "Let's eat, then."

Blowing over her spoon with the first bite, watching Leif do the same across from her, she was touched. His thoughtfulness seemed so different from the crazed-with-lust man who'd kissed the air out of her last night. This was the Leif she'd first found so appealing—the earnest, caring guy who'd been dealt a lousy hand in life. But the man she'd encountered last night was what'd sealed the deal for her on the concept of Scandinavian lovers. Roll both men together and, wow, she felt like the luckiest girl in the world…that was, the luckiest single pregnant woman in Heartlandia.

Maybe she needed to put a little more thought into this. Besides her being in the family way, the man was an emotional landmine, which until last night she'd only suspected, and now she knew for sure. She wasn't doing so great in that department lately, either, and she was definitely in no condition to deal with *those* feelings right now. She had a job to do—a big job. The biggest job of her professional life. And the most important.

So much for her meant-to-be philosophy. Not this time. She'd said it to him without realizing the extent of Leif's issues, and in that regard, boy, had she been wrong for so many reasons. The two most obvious being she was pregnant and he was still mourning his wife.

Their timing was colossally off for any kind of potential relationship. Sad but true.

"You should market this soup. It's fantastic," she said, hoping to put her mind back on food instead of the overwhelmingly appealing man across from her. Especially after her compliment when his proud, sexy grin nearly undid her.

"I told you. This is going to make that baby do somersaults."

"Oh, gosh, I hope not. I've just only gotten my appetite back." She gave a self-deprecating smile, knowing how much they'd shared over nearly four weeks and how generous he'd been throughout. "The last thing I need is my baby rolling around inside."

He grinned again, genuine and handsome, and it cut right into her heart.

What in the world was she going to do for the rest of the time it would take to paint the mural?

After another bite, she sat straight. "I've been thinking about your offer of the guesthouse."

She could have sworn there was a flash of disappointment darkening his gaze, but he covered it well and pasted on a smile. "You stay in the house. I'll move out there. It will only take a couple of days before Gunnar and Lilly are ready to take their furniture back to their new house anyway."

"That isn't necessary. This is your house. All I have to do is move my suitcases."

"The suite and studio suit you. You should stay and I'll—"

"You know what? That's just a bad idea. Neither of us should go. Forget I ever said anything."

"But the last thing I want is to know I've made you uncomfortable or that I've kept you locked away in this house if you don't want to be here."

The way you keep your heart? "You've rented a car for me, remember? I can come and go as I please. I don't feel the least bit like a prisoner. I've just been concentrating on the mural preparation, that's all."

"Good." He looked down to the last of his soup, which he sopped up with a chunk of brown bread.

This man was so honest and real. So thoughtful even under fire. Overcome with sweet feelings, she reached out and touched his arm, his gaze quickly finding hers. Then, overcome with his vulnerable side and wanting more, she stood and walked to his side, bent down and delivered a gentle kiss on his stubbled cheek. "Thank you for everything," she whispered.

He looked up, an entire story written in those aqua-blue eyes, yet his mouth was set tight, as if trying not to respond to her kiss.

She couldn't help but suspect his thoughts and repeat them out loud. "If only things were different, right, Leif?"

He cleared his throat and on an inhale stood, wordlessly gathered the dishes and placed them on the tray. In a completely different manner from last night, he solemnly left the room, his response to her query left unspoken.

Three days later, after barely making contact with each other over the weekend and his treating her respectfully but only as an acquaintance whenever they did pass in the hallway, she'd had enough. Early Monday afternoon, he was out back with his dogs filling their water bowl, having just returned from a walk. She rushed out the kitchen door, leaving it flapping behind her, and approached him.

"Hi!"

He turned, looking surprised. Had they made a silent

agreement to keep clear? No! Not her, but it certainly had been his recent approach to their relationship.

"What's up?" he said, affably enough but far from personal.

"I was wondering if you'd take me somewhere."

His brows came together, and he surreptitiously glanced toward her rental car with a puzzled expression. She couldn't let on how angry she'd been with him for completely withdrawing after they'd forged a pretty decent friendship. So what if a couple of kisses confused things? They could still be friends, couldn't they? Truth was, she'd missed his company.

"After reading all of those great articles and learning about the Chinook burial ground in Heartlandia's changing history, I want to see the Ringmuren. And who better to see it with than a town native? Will you take me?"

"Sure." With his chin tucked, he didn't exactly look enthusiastic, but it was a start. "How about tomorrow? I'll let the crew know I won't be around."

She stood straight, unfolding her arms with palms up to communicate she really wanted to spend time with him. "I'd like that." She wasn't sure whether or not her thoughts or actions fell on fertile soil or desert, but she'd done her best to make her point. *Let's spend more time together.* And that would have to be good enough for now.

Tuesday morning, meeting at the agreed-upon time, she'd dressed in her favorite jeans, which were beginning to get too tight around the waist, and a colorful loose top to hide the fact she'd left the top snap on her jeans undone. She'd combed her hair and twisted it around off her neck and splashed an extra drop of her favorite fragrance, a combination of lavender and pumpkin-pie spices, on her shoulders and nape.

He'd also cleaned up nicely, freshly shaved, hair still damp and close to his head, a button-up tailored shirt in a minty green wreaking havoc with his blue eyes and broken-in jeans showing his long, solid legs in all their glory. All man. The grooves on his cheeks deepened with his genuine, greeting smile.

"Ready?" he asked.

"Absolutely."

They drove in companionable silence. The higher up the mountain they went, the greener things got. She spotted Hjartalanda Peak, and he verified it when she pointed it out. Maybe it was the fresh air or the gorgeous scenery, but Marta felt her heart lift and suddenly she had an overwhelming desire to open up to Leif. Hey, they'd known each other a month already, hadn't they? In her opinion it was well past time.

"When I was a little girl, my grandfather used to make a big deal about my drawings." She did her best to imitate how he puffed out his chest and made his eyes big as teacups. "'You are going to be an artist, *mi hija*.'" She also copied his accent, then lightly laughed. Leif turned and smiled along with her.

"Maybe because my grandfather didn't inherit the gift his father had for art, he always encouraged any little attempt I made at drawing and painting. He probably hoped the talent had skipped a generation or two. Whatever. But I believed him and from then on, that's what I wanted to be."

"He was right. You're a gifted painter."

"Thank you. I've worked hard at my craft."

"I can't wait to see the finished mural at the college. And, oh, I've been meaning to tell you the walls are all prepped and you're free to start any time you want."

She wondered if it was because he wanted the assignment completed so she'd get out of his life, but she pushed the thought away. Negativity wasn't her style. Yet she kept waffling back and forth whether she had met Leif for a reason or not. Sometimes she was sure of it; other times she couldn't imagine him ever letting someone into his life again. Why bang her head against his proverbial wall? But he'd offered his house to a stranger, and once that door was open, it was anyone's guess what their ending might be. Today, instead of dwelling on the "not gonna happens" in life, she opted to go with hope. Who knew how things might turn out?

A few minutes later they pulled off the road into an old parking lot covered in gravel, with weeds and flowers growing through jagged cracks in areas of ancient asphalt, a huge expanse of bright green grass just on the other side. A few rocks and boulders erupted through the pristine lawn here and there, giving it a rugged appearance. Gentleman as always, Leif helped her out of the truck cab and they began their trek to this side of the Ringmuren. In the distance she glanced at the long rock-and-stone wall that demarcated the park side from the sacred side. She couldn't wait to get close enough to see the three-hundred-year-old workmanship and what lay beyond. She'd definitely add this wall to the mural.

"Wow, this is gorgeous."

"It is something, isn't it?"

"I can almost feel the history that must have taken place here." The fine hair at the back of her neck stood straight. "This is amazing." Drawing closer, the wall became even more impressive. "They didn't even use mortar to hold this wall together. How has it withstood the elements all these years?"

"Good question. Our Chinook citizens are positive the spirits from the sacred burial ground watch over this wall. We've had some fierce storms over the years, but the wall always stands strong. It's kind of a mystery, when you think about it."

"You're giving me chills." She skimmed her palms over her arms.

"I don't mean to scare you or anything."

"Oh, no. On the contrary. I find this fascinating." She walked on, exploring the wall and peeking over it from the beautifully manicured side to the other rugged and left-to-its-own-resources side. The sacred burial ground. For several moments she stood there, studying and wondering. Leif courteously gave her space to go inward and she imagined the past, how the Scandinavian sailors had joined forces with the Chinook to delineate hallowed from natural ground. How the endeavor must have forged new respect and cooperation between the two groups. How they'd used that respect to go up against the pirates. To fight for their lives and their families.

When she'd thought long and hard enough, adding new vision and a few extra details to her mural, she turned and smiled widely at him. "Thank you for bringing me here. If I ever run out of inspiration, I'll come here to refuel."

"Sounds like a plan."

They walked together toward a group of trees and a small clearing where another bench sat. This one turned out to be dedicated to Leif's mother, Hannah. It was exquisitely carved from a huge tree stump, and the workmanship both touched and impressed her. It made her think of her own mother, Gabriella, and there went that usual pang in her heart for her.

They sat in silence for several minutes, Leif with his legs outstretched and his feet crossed at the ankles, his arms lounging across the back of the rugged bench.

A few moments later he cleared his throat. "You know, I've always envied people who could put their feelings into art."

"And I've always envied people who could build beautiful houses." She shared another smile with him, his eyes picking up the color of the distant Columbia River, and felt warmth spread across her chest. "By the way, who carved the intricate work on your mantel around your fireplace?" She already had a hunch about the answer.

He used his thumb and index fingers and touched the edges of his mouth. "I did."

"Uh-huh, and what about this bench? It looks similar in style. Is this your work, too?"

He dipped his head.

She tapped his thigh. "How can you not consider yourself an artist? Your work is beautiful and like nothing I've ever seen."

He quirked a brow. "You really think so?"

"I know so, but it doesn't matter what I think. What matters is how you feel about it. You need to shape up and admit that you, Leif Andersen, are a gifted craftsman and wood artist."

Obviously trying not to show his pride, he still looked tickled and a little doubtful. "I do enjoy it. I like to leave a special touch in every house I build. Like the bookcase I'm installing at Gunnar's house. It's kind of like my signature."

"It's a good signature. An artist's signature." She smiled just before a somber veil dropped over her expression.

"My mother used to worry being an artist was not the right kind of profession for a young woman. I fought her on it, pushed for my independence. Pushed her away." Marta glanced at her folded hands in her lap. "I wasn't at her side when she died, and to this day I regret all the thoughtless things I said to her. She couldn't understand how I lived. I bragged I never wanted to get married, that it would hold me back." She quietly shook her head. "How that must have hurt her, a woman who wanted nothing more than a loving family, could only have one child, and she got me."

Leif comforted her with a squeeze of her folded hands. "I'm sure she was proud of you."

"I hope so, but I'm afraid all I ever brought her was shame."

"I don't believe that for a minute."

"If she knew I was pregnant and unmarried now, I think she'd roll over in her grave."

He laughed gently at her absurd remark.

"Forgive me for getting all dramatic, but sitting on your mother's bench, well, it made me think of her."

Leif glanced at Marta, happy she appreciated his brand of creativity yet sorry for her complicated, conflicted feelings about her mother, especially not being able to say goodbye before she had died. The sun glinted off her dark hair, making it look silky and touchable. He fought the urge to reach out and roll a loose lock of her hair through his thumb and fingers. How good it used to feel to touch his wife whenever he wanted, to have free reign of her body. What was it about Marta that always led his mind in that direction?

He pulled back his thoughts, worried that Marta really

could read them, but evidently not soon enough. Before he realized what she was doing, she'd scooted closer on the bench, her pupils wide and round, her hand reaching for and soon caressing his cheek. Maybe she'd read his thoughts after all. Without thinking further he tilted his head and, boom, she kissed him.

Her mouth settled on top of his, spreading warmth and a gentle invitation to kiss her back. Her sweet, spicy scent combined with the feel of her plump lips made for a heady swell. He returned the kiss and soon pressed his tongue into her welcoming mouth. Her slick, wet tongue tasted like mint and honey.

He'd missed this part of his life. Being with a woman, sharing natural responses.

Her sweet, innocent gesture quickly changed to something more. Something about Marta, having her in his arms, made him come alive. His hands gripped her shoulders and wandered around her back, sizing up her softness and strength. He wondered about how right this could be. A quick, fanciful thought.

As though sensing his discovery, she responded to his touch and kissed more eagerly, her fingers pulling his neck and head closer, the tips pressing into his skin. It felt great to be wanted. Beyond great. It had been far too long. But the moment of closeness also brought back a rush of memories, both good and bad. Opening up had become too hard, forgotten even. He couldn't allow himself to get involved. His loss with Ellen had been too much. He couldn't go there again. It was too painful.

Her sweet kisses were an invitation to heartache and devastation, and he'd already had more than a lifetime's worth.

Allowing his torn thoughts to ruin the moment, he

backed away from the kiss, an old, familiar deadness taking hold inside, and he slowly withdrew.

Her puzzled expression soon turned to concern.

She lowered her head, unable to look him in the eyes, his detached attitude shattering her normally straight-forward approach. He hated himself for doing that to her but was nowhere near able to explain why he'd done it, knowing without a doubt the old "it's not you, it's me" routine would fall on deaf ears. She'd never buy it. She expected too much of him—expected him to be normal again. Didn't she get that he couldn't?

"It's because I'm pregnant, isn't it?"

What? No! He hadn't even allowed himself to get past the point of kissing a new woman, let alone to think about anything else. The pregnancy hadn't entered his mind. But she *had* given him an out...because they'd gotten too close and it freaked the hell out of him.

Unknowingly, she'd handed him the perfect excuse he was grappling for to keep her safely at a distance. Low blow as it might be, he'd take that pretext and use it. Anything to keep from opening up his life to someone again. Anything to avoid being vulnerable.

Hating himself even as he took the easy way out, he nodded, strongly suspecting her being rejected over the pregnancy would sting to the core. And he hated himself for it. Hated to face how messed up he still was. Hated to impose that on her.

"I'm not looking for a husband, if that's what you're thinking."

"I know that." But hadn't she been disappointed when her ex hadn't offered marriage?

He dared to look into her eyes to see the broken-hearted expression he'd put there and quickly realized he may as well have taken a knife to his own flesh.

Chapter Five

Leif suffered through his attraction to Marta over the next couple of weeks, suspecting she loathed him for rejecting her over the pregnancy. It hurt like hell, but there was no point in pursuing their attraction, so he let her think the worst of him.

He watched her get up each day decked in overalls and a T-shirt and head over to the college to paint the outdoor mural. On the first day, he'd loaded his truck with the supplies and cans of paint, wondering how she'd manage to do the hard labor on her own. Painting to the scale of the walls, one inch to one foot, seemed a daunting task for a lady barely five-feet-six-inches tall.

Once at the college he delivered her supplies and was surprised to find a team organized and waiting to help. Desi Rask, a new enrollee in the art department, had arranged the group, which included Elke Norling, Ben

Cobowa and a handful of other art students. Anything Marta needed, they jumped to the task, making it happen. Honestly, Leif felt a little useless. So after he delivered the combination ladder/scaffold work platform for the higher-up painting, he'd left and hadn't gone back.

To make up for the fruitless feeling, he dived into his private project to find a way to remove what they suspected to be buried treasure from the sacred ground, hoping to do the least amount of damage in the process.

The town was already in an upheaval over the news about their distorted history. There seemed to be two clear factions—those who embraced the pirate story and those who were horrified by it. Personally, it wasn't an issue for him; there was nothing they could do about it so they may as well make the most of the attention it would bring. As the local small business folks said, the influx of tourists would be good for everyone.

The committee knew they couldn't keep the buried treasure a secret much longer. Leif needed to complete and present his report ASAP. As a result, he worked long hours with the engineer consultants reviewing the infrared thermal study findings. What they came up with was the best, nondestructive way to positively identify the trunk and its contents. He knew where to get the equipment to do the job. Removing it with a straight-down dig would only disrupt a tiny fragment of the entire burial grounds. And that was the sticking point. He hoped it would be considered a compromise.

The special committee was divided over his report at the Thursday-night meeting. Ben and Elke were firm on not disrupting the sacred ground for any reason. Even the lure of potentially millions of dollars in ancient coins and jewels, which could benefit the college and the entire town, wouldn't change their minds. Jarl Madsen waffled between the benefit to the Maritime Museum the findings would bring and the principle of respecting the Chinook spirits. The rest of the committee voted to move forward with the plan, and though Leif admitted to being uncomfortable with the task, he felt it was necessary.

Division seemed to be the term of the day and the theme of their meeting, and when Leif arrived home with a pounding headache, the last thing he wanted was to be taunted by Marta. Yet there she stood at the base of the staircase, wearing a silky, long, flowing, cream-colored dress with a wide leather belt that matched her open-toed shoes and a linen bolero jacket that had a collar more suited for a bathrobe. Her hair hung loose over her shoulders, and with large gold hoop earrings, she looked gorgeous as always, even while nailing him with a serious stare.

"How'd the meeting go?" she asked.

"As to be expected. How is the mural coming along?" Maybe he could divert the line of questioning.

She raised a brow as if he'd asked a loaded question or had dodged her question. He should have known the tactic wouldn't get by her.

"The mural's great. We're moving along really well. At this rate I should be out of your hair within another month to six weeks."

Did she really think all he wanted to do was get rid of her? Was that why she'd dressed to slay him with that getup and those red toenails? "That wasn't my point."

"I understand." No she didn't, but he was too tired and wiped out to argue. Though seeing her had instantly revived a basic part of him. "Listen, I overheard Elke and Ben talking about more bad news at school today.

Is that why you've been so busy lately, why you had this meeting tonight?"

He nodded. Why deny it? Everything would come out within a week after the citywide vote because the committee had decided to go public again. "Yep. This pirate business seems to be the gift that just keeps on giving."

With folded arms she stepped closer, and even from this distance, his body reacted to her.

"How so?"

He inhaled and rubbed his jaw. "You mind if I pour myself a drink?"

"Of course not. It's your house." Now she looked downright curious. "What's going on, Leif?"

He strode to the wet bar in the corner of the living room and poured two fingers of Glenlivet Scotch whiskey straight up, swirled the liquid in the glass, took a drink and plopped down on the nearest chair beside the fireplace. If she weren't pregnant, he would have offered her a snifter. The liquor burned its way down his throat, with a welcomed woodsy taste accompanying it. Due to his empty stomach, he almost immediately felt the relaxing effect.

Marta had followed him into the room and primly sat on the edge of the adjacent wing-back chair, catching her hair and putting it all over one shoulder, making her look sexy as hell. She took off her shoes and dug her toes into the fluffy faux-animal-fur rug. Man, she was driving him crazy. Was it intentional?

"So part of our findings from the beginning were these journals. You know the story." She'd read all of the newspaper articles, so he knew she was aware of the facts. "We also found a map made by Captain Prince, and the journal indicated a second trunk, which he'd buried. I hired a company to provide an infrared imaging of the area in question, and the consensus is this alleged second pirate trunk is buried on the wrong side of the Ringmuren."

"Seriously?" Her eyes were wide, and under the recessed ceiling lights they looked the color of his whiskey.

"So once again, we're in the middle of a mess. Do we dig for it or respect the grounds?" A rhetorical question.

"Respect the sacred grounds," she said without blinking.

"It's not that easy."

"Yes, it is."

He shook his head slowly and took another drink, rolled the liquid around in his mouth for the fullest effect, then swallowed. "Nothing is ever that easy."

And that could be the metaphor for his life. Already the drink had worked its wonders, making him go all philosophical as part of the process. For Marta, everything seemed easy-peasy. How different they were.

"Heartlandia could benefit from the treasures in the trunk on more levels than we can count. The citizens will vote on it."

"It would be disrespectful and nothing good would come of it."

"You don't know that."

"I guarantee it."

"How can you be so damn sure of everything?"

She tossed her head. "It's a gift, I guess."

She sounded sarcastic, and Leif suspected things weren't over yet. He decided to put the topic to rest for now by pointing her in another direction. "So any questions you have can get answered at the next town meet-

She wasn't suggesting forever. She was offering now. And it shook his world down to the root.

He was tired of dropping out of his personal life. Sick and tired of wanting but not taking. On instinct, he put down his glass, stood and walked toward Marta. Pulling her up and into his arms, he took control of the moment, drawing her close, fitting his mouth to hers, kissing her as he'd wanted to for days. Like the first time he'd kissed her, she responded to his touch with the passion she'd just hurled at him, along with those challenging words to knock him out of his rut.

She'd done more than that.

Her mouth had already become familiar, and he captured it with the lunge of his tongue. He held her close and tight, aware of her full breasts pressed to his chest, her hips flush to his, the energy that arced between them. He inhaled that crazy cinnamon-spice scent and whatever the hell else it was. Exploring her lips and tongue, the kiss set off threads of heat and longing that laced a twisted path to his groin. Losing control with each kiss, he deepened it, pulled back and dived in again. And again.

Lost in her, his fingers dug into her hair, loving the thickness and satin feel, and keeping her mouth exactly where he wanted it. They breathed each other and made out like randy teenagers, enjoying a clandestine moment outside of time. This wasn't forever, she'd said. That concept had clicked, and for whatever crazy reason, he'd come to a point where he could deal with that. The right now.

Long heady moments passed as they kissed, caressed and explored, his body waking up kiss by kiss from its extended sleep, hungry for more. And more.

Marta bracketed his face with her hands and, revealing her flushed cheeks and swollen lips from his over-enthusiastic kisses, pleaded with her eyes. "We can do this, Leif. It's ours for the taking. Just for now. I promise I don't come with strings."

He fought for focus, his ears ringing, his body zinging with impulses. "You've got to understand something first."

She watched and waited.

"I don't know about healing or right now or being good for each other," he said. "I don't understand any of it. All I know is you make me want to do things I've tried to forget, and you're driving me crazy."

Concern flashed in her eyes. Did it finally compute how hard she pushed his defenses? "We don't have to rush it, then," she said, dropping her hands and edging out of his arms. "As long as we know we're on the same page."

And that was the problem. Was he on the same page as her? An affair? Short and convenient. While they just happened to be living under the same roof. Could he separate emotions from a physical relationship with the snap of a finger? Could he be with someone new after the twelve years he'd devoted to Ellen? Right now it seemed like forever since he'd been with her. Tension crept back into his body.

"It's been a long day," Marta said, her palm skimming the length of his chest, taunting him without effort. "You're welcome to join me in my bed…" Before he could open his mouth she lifted her hand. "Or think about my offer awhile longer." Her serene smile indicated it wasn't a test, that in some way she understood. "No pressure. Honestly. I'm good either way."

Still looking flushed, with her hair messed from his hands, she gave the hint of a smile, turned and left the room with her head held high. After taking the stairs quickly, she disappeared.

Half in shock—he'd never had a woman be so blatant before—Leif drank the last drops in his glass and closed his eyes while it curled down his throat. Then he poured more.

If he needed fortification to make love to a beautiful and vibrant woman like Marta, he still wasn't ready. Sad but true.

But he wanted to be ready; God, he wanted to be. He'd finally admitted it—well, she'd forced him to—but even that was progress.

He finished off his glass, then climbed the stairs, his legs feeling like sandbags yet his mind whirling with desire and possibilities. At the top he glanced toward Marta's room, his old bedroom. The final stumbling block between them. The thought of making love to her in there, where he and Ellen had shared the bed, mixed him up beyond belief. When he took her—and after her come-on just now he would, he was sure of that—it would be in *his* bed, in *his* room, under *his* conditions.

Taking Marta up on one more of her offers—to think things over—he turned right instead of left and headed for the smaller guest room, his room. It was definitely time to quit being a guest in his own house; Marta's suggestion had made that clear. His father used to say a man needed to be the king of his castle. Damn right.

Whoever this woman was, pregnant or not, he wanted her...just for now. She'd promised, no strings. He could deal with that.

That night, surprisingly, he went right to sleep, and

whether or not fueled by whiskey, Ellen came to him in his dream. Healthy Ellen, not his wife from their last months together. She looked so real he wanted to touch her, but she stayed beyond his reach. Her beautiful smile nearly made him cry. *Stop it*, he could have sworn he heard her say. *Quit waiting.* Her form drifted closer, her face near enough to kiss, but he couldn't make his head or hands move to touch her. Without uttering a sound she communicated with him. *Live your life. I'm the one who died, not you.* And then, long before he was ready to lose her again, she was gone.

Leif woke up, raising to his elbows, searching the room as if expecting to find her hiding in the corners. His heart raced. Ellen. God he missed her.

Slowly the words she'd said in the dream repeated in his mind. *Stop it. Quit waiting. Live your life. I'm the one who died, not you.*

He lay back on his pillow and rubbed his forehead. Had she released him? He pinched his temples and thought. Or, after three years had he finally released himself? He'd mourned her long and with all of his heart. It was okay to move on, the dream seemed to say. Wasn't that what Marta had said, too?

He got out of bed and paced his room. The large fanlight window above the French doors let in a trickle of moonlight, intensifying the shadows. He was alive and Ellen was gone, yet he'd been living like a dead man, a ghost. Opening his house to Marta and her persistence had finally forced him to face it.

He thought about the lady down the hall, so open and willing to share her affections, and how he'd shut her down. He hoped he hadn't lost the chance to show her that blood actually ran through his veins. Tomorrow was another day, and it was filled with possibilities. Hell, what about tonight? Right now? The thought drilled a path right to his gut and put a smile on his face. He could carry her to his room and make love to her under the moonlight until morning.

Heading for the bathroom to freshen up he heard loud moans quickly followed by a sharp, pain-filled groan.

"Leif!" Marta called out, and he sprinted toward her room.

Chapter Six

Marta tossed and turned in bed with discomfort. The ache had started an hour ago, and it suddenly had escalated. At first she'd thought it was an emotional response to taking that risk with Leif and putting herself on the line. Again.

The offer had drummed up memories of old arguments with her mother, too. How they'd fought over Marta's carefree ways with men. Gabriella had tried every trick in the book to restrain her daughter, but that had only made Marta more determined to prove she didn't need traditional marriage or commitment with men.

The joke had been on her, though, because Lawrence had let her down. She'd promised to be a woman without strings when they'd started dating. He'd been married once already, with young-adult children ready to fly the nest; the last thing he wanted was another marriage…

another child. She'd said she was fine with that. He'd offered travel, parties, hobnobbing with the important people in the art world. Everything a young artist could hope for. He'd given her all of that, then spoiled her by supporting her and her art.

Her mother had accused her of being a kept woman, but Marta made excuses. *No. He's my benefactor. He believes in my talent.*

He pays your rent and you give him sex, her mother had shot back. Insulted by what she'd insinuated, Marta stormed out.

They'd never ironed out their differences, had never said they were sorry, and Marta hadn't spoken to her mother the last year of her life. Now she was dead. And Marta was pregnant. Lawrence didn't want to marry her. And she'd just offered Leif a "no strings" fling.

Would she ever learn?

Would she ever honor her mother's biggest wish for her?

The answer hurt. God, it hurt to remember.

The pain in her gut never settled down, either.

Now a sharp pang cut through her side, making her cry out.

"Leif!"

Within seconds he came rushing into the room, flipping on the light, looking mortified. "What's wrong?"

"I'm not sure." She squinted at him through the harsh light.

"Where do you hurt?"

"Here." She uncurled her body and moved her hand around her lower abdomen.

His eyes went wide, and a shocked and concerned expression covered his face. "You need a doctor." He rushed to the phone beside her bed and punched in some numbers. Having never been pregnant before, and to be honest, unnerved by the intensity of her pain, she didn't protest.

"Kent? Sorry to call so late, but it's Marta. She's doubled over in pain, and honestly, I'm worried for the baby." He pinched the bridge of his nose, closed his eyes and listened. "Thank you!"

Leif hung up, immediately returned to Marta's side and took her hand. "He's on his way over."

Though Sedona had many small-town qualities, this selfless attitude seemed unique to Heartlandia. Did doctors even make house calls anymore? Evidently they did here.

Having Leif beside her helped settle the nerves coiling through her. He'd verbalized her greatest fear—he was worried for the baby. So was she. She was just getting used to the life-changing circumstances, but she'd embraced the thought of becoming a mother. Wanted to be a good mother like hers had been.

And the craziest part of all was, she wanted to go about it the same way her mother did, even if the cart had gotten before the horse.

Was this a cruel joke from the universe? Dangling motherhood before her. Forcing her to admit she wanted a more traditional life, including marriage, only to yank it away from her?

As if reading her mind, he gathered her close and held tight. "What can I do for you?"

"Just hold me." She snuggled in, feeling curiously safe and secure through the waves of pain.

He gently rocked her, helping the gripping to back off

a little. Then he kissed the top of her head. This from the hermit? Even in pain, she felt his tenderness.

Earlier she'd been stunned when Leif had admitted he hadn't backed away from her because of the pregnancy. She'd fibbed about knowing otherwise, recalling how deeply his candid confession had struck that day at his mother's memorial bench. But she'd held out, thinking the best thoughts, that he'd come around, see the light. Negativity wasn't her style.

Knowing his honest feelings—that the pregnancy wasn't an issue for him—renewed her hope. He was a good, solid man worth knowing. Loving even? Who knew? Their circumstances were anything but ideal, and that worried her, but nevertheless, she'd only offered him "just for now." What man in his right mind wouldn't accept?

In her world, that was the only way to truly get to know a man. Turns out old habits die hard. *Sorry, Momma. I'm a work in progress.*

Not more than fifteen minutes later the doorbell rang, rousing the dogs who'd been hovering around the bed since sensing something was wrong.

"It's okay," Leif said to quiet them as he took off down the stairs.

Marta immediately missed his warmth and the comfort he gave. Even though she still hurt, his being there had made it bearable. Another wave of cramping built, and she curled back into a ball.

Heavy footsteps soon ascended the stairs and Marta came face to face with Desi's fiancé. Desi had said he looked like a Viking, and she hadn't been lying. She'd even shown Marta a picture on the cell phone, but it hadn't done him justice. Well over six feet tall with a build to match, the big man had nothing but concern on his kind face.

He reached out to take her hand. "I'm Kent Larson. So tell me what's going on."

Leif left the room as the good doctor began his examination. He couldn't help but recall the many times Kent had come to the house during Ellen's final months. Remembering the pain and suffering she'd gone through made his skin crawl. How he'd felt helpless and angry and wished he could be the one dying, not his wife. God, he couldn't go through these memories right now.

How could he ever let himself care that much for anyone again? And if he couldn't ever care that much for anyone, it wouldn't be fair to get involved. That had been his mantra for the past three years. But earlier Marta had offered "just for now" and it had thrown him sideways. How could he even think these thoughts now? The woman was in pain. Possibly losing her baby. Now wasn't the time to think about anything but her well-being.

Damn it. Where Marta was concerned, he already *was* in over his head.

He tried to talk himself down from the growing panic of the caring-losing cycle. This was a completely different situation from his wife's. Marta was not dying from cancer. From his personal experience, he'd probably always overreact in situations like these. He worried about the baby and whether Marta would need to be admitted to the nearest hospital forty miles away. Would they need to call an ambulance? The memory of an ambulance coming to his door, taking his wife away, never to return home again, sent a shiver down his spine. Damn. Damn. Damn it all.

He paced outside the room, then went to the kitchen and made himself a cup of herbal tea—the kind Marta had been drinking for weeks now, the kind that was supposed to have a calming effect—and paced some more.

A few minutes later, he stared out the kitchen's dark window but only saw his reflection in the glass. That freaked-out expression made him flinch as memory after memory haunted his thoughts. No, he couldn't let himself be in that situation ever again.

Kent called his name from the top of the staircase.

"Yo! I'm coming." He rushed up the stairs and took his first deep breath when he saw the relaxed expression on Kent's face.

"What we have here is a pregnant lady taken out by the current intestinal flu. I've seen no less than a dozen patients in the past two days with the exact same symptoms."

"The baby's okay?"

He nodded. "Did a thorough examination and everything checks out. The bad news is, there's no shortcut or treatment for this flu. It'll have to run its course for the next two to three days. The intestinal pain should subside within twelve hours, with lingering digestive symptoms after that. You know the drill. Keep her hydrated and call me if anything unusual develops."

Leif slapped Kent's shoulder. "Thank you, man. What do I owe you?"

"Your crew just painted my house for barely the price of the cans of paint. I say we're even."

No point in arguing.

"Thanks." That was how the community had always worked, each person helping the other, and it went all the way back to the fisherman and native Chinook, just like the town monument depicted.

"Any time."

Their respect being mutual, the men walked in silence down the stairs as Leif showed Kent out.

Immediately back on task, Leif rushed the stairs and found Marta asleep, her face occasionally grimacing but otherwise looking peaceful. Rather than go back to bed, he turned the dimmer to night-light level, sat in the bed-side chair and rested his shoeless feet on the corner of the mattress.

"Thank you," she whispered.

He grasped around in the shadows, found her forearm and squeezed. "You're welcome."

Over the next couple of days Leif saw the worst of Marta, which wasn't bad at all, and the best of himself. He'd stood guard outside the bathroom door whenever she'd made a mad dash or while she cleaned up. He'd fed her when she was too weak to lift her soup bowl. He'd memorized every freckle on her face and the thickness of her eyelashes when she slept, and he'd learned how to braid her hair. He'd been through this drill before, knew how to care for a sick woman—a dying woman.

But Marta wasn't dying. She was very much alive, and every day she looked and felt better, and that made all the difference in his attitude.

"I can't stand another day without a shower," she said on Sunday, day three.

"Let's do it."

"Let's?" She cast a questionable glance, sitting at the bedside, gingerly lowering her feet to the floor.

Caring for her had given him a false sense of intimacy, but she'd cleared that right up. "I'll be nearby if you need me," he said.

She tried to stand but her knees went wobbly. "Maybe I better take a bath instead."

"I'll run the water. Wait here."

Back in a jiffy, the bath filling with warm water, he assisted her into the bathroom. Wearing loose pajamas covered in cartoon owls, she sat on the edge of the extralarge soaking tub and smiled. He'd even lit some scented candles to help her relax.

She gazed up coyly. "You can go now."

He lifted one corner of his mouth in a smile. "If you say so."

She tossed a "seriously?" glance. "I say so."

With his smile stretching into a full-blown grin, Leif turned and left but hovered nearby, changing the sheets on her bed while she bathed.

"Leif?" she called out after several minutes. "I need to wash my hair. Can you bring my shampoo?"

He finished plumping the pillow and went to the bathroom door. "Knock, knock. Is it in there?"

"Yes, in the shower."

To be polite he covered his eyes and walked past the tub toward the sink and on toward the shower stall, feeling his way along the walls. She laughed. "I'm covered."

Disappointed, he looked, hoping she really wasn't, but found she'd added bubbles to the tub and had put the washcloth across her chest. A beautiful sight, her hair piled high on her head and her dark eyes striking the perfect balance of bashful yet sexy.

"I'm a great hair washer," he said, sadness striking like an electric jolt with the quick memory of the two of them in the tub washing his wife's hair before it had started falling out.

Marta picked up on the brief mood change, but instead of letting the moment pass, she surprised him. "I could use your help."

He knelt beside the tub and turned on the water, letting it trickle over his fingers until it warmed. She turned away from him and sat, shifting through the water so her head was closer to the handheld shower sprayer, affording him a glance at her back. She stayed sitting with her back to him, and he ran the water over her hair. After adding shampoo he lathered it up, careful not to get soap in her eyes, loving the feel of his fingers entangled in the suds and hair. She arched her neck, and he rinsed, glancing over her shoulder and taking in all her femininity, down to the curve of her throat and the top of her breasts. Through the waning bubbles he could see the heart-shaped swell of her hips and bottom where she sat, the intimacy nearly undoing him.

When he was done he wrapped her hair snugly in a towel, handed her a second bath towel, activated the drain and left her to dry in privacy. Walking out the door while wanting to see her standing and fully naked proved to be one of the hardest things he'd done in the past three years.

He wanted her, and things would never be the same between them.

Seeing her, touching her, caring for her had cracked through the last of his armor, gripping his heart and forcing him to feel again. Closing the bathroom door, Leif realized there was no going back, and he was incapable of doing "just for now." He was crazy about Marta, wanted only the best for her, and if she was just looking for a fling, he had a big surprise for her.

* * *

By the fourth day, Monday, Marta felt 90 percent better physically, but one thought plagued her conscience. She'd become completely dependent on Leif—he housed her, fed her, even took care of her when she was sick—and she'd promised she'd never be in that position again. She'd learned the hard way with Lawrence. Yet she felt grateful for everything Leif had done for her during her bout with the flu. She cringed thinking there was almost nothing she could hide from him now.

What a crazy relationship they'd forged in seven short weeks.

In her postflu weakness, she worried about jumping from one failed relationship into another superficial one. From one rich and powerful man to another...one who also signed her paycheck. Leif had made it quite clear that the city council couldn't afford her, and he'd stepped in to get the mural painted. It was a legacy he wanted to leave for his family as well as himself, she knew it. In this regard, he was just as much her benefactor as Lawrence had been.

Hell, before she'd gotten sick, in that moment of nearly unbearable sexual desire, she'd invited Leif into her bed. Did she want to repeat the pattern with him, or break that promise of independence?

Yet she'd been the one to suggest they help each other heal, and at the time she'd meant every word. She missed the closeness of making love with a man, believed it would be good for her and the baby, too. The truth was hard to take, and lying in bed for days had forced her to think through things. Being near Leif, the different way he made her feel, honored and cherished even, she'd realized the spark had died between her and Lawrence long before she'd gotten pregnant. What could she expect from accepting his offer—just you and me and the world of art? His underwhelming response when she'd told him about the baby had dashed out the final embers. There was no room in his life or heart for a child. Which meant there was no longer room for Marta, either.

Seeing Leif at his best, an open, giving and tender man, had sharpened the contrast. As she looked back with a clear eye, she could see Lawrence had maintained a cushion of distance for five years and had subtly made it known who had the power. As far as she was concerned the only thing the men had in common was the first letter of their names.

As her strength returned, so did her resolve to think of Leif as a transition. He was her now, not her future. She could and would deal with that. Besides, she couldn't expect any man to accept another man's baby before it was even born, could she? Hell, the baby's own father couldn't. Leif said he did, after saying he didn't. That left just enough doubt to keep her guessing. And she couldn't live or think like that anymore. She had a bigger job to do—being a future mother.

No, she and Leif would have whatever they had while she was here, and that would be it. She couldn't hope for more, even though, when she was completely honest, she did want more than that. *I get it now, Momma. Okay?* But when? And with who?

Ack, maybe she'd take just this one last day to rest and straighten out her thoughts. Because from where she lay, everything that had seemed so logical and sophisticated before she'd gotten ill—just for now—was suddenly a jumbled-up mess and a gamble with her heart she wasn't sure she could or should take.

Leif had stayed home from work on her account, so at the end of the day she put on her long, flowing lounge dress, the same one she'd worn the other night. She noticed she'd lost a little weight, so she tightened the belt around her waist. Before she left her room, she threw on a golden-threaded slate-colored shawl and some gold sandals and headed downstairs for her first dinner out of bed in days.

"Something smells fantastic," she said, entering the kitchen.

Leif turned his head while stirring a pot of bubbling water. "Someone *looks* fantastic, too. You'd never know you'd been sick."

"You lie, but thank you anyway."

"You don't believe me? Come here."

She stepped closer and he put his hand on her waist, pulled her near, looked her straight in the eyes with a mischievous gaze and kissed her. Wrapping her arms around his neck, returning his affection, she marveled over this changed man and how natural they felt together. Even knowing him for such a short time, she felt completely comfortable in his embrace. As if they belonged together. With all the confidence in the world he kissed her lips, her neck, took her hair into his hand and lightly tugged on it. When the kiss ended, he made a soft sound in his throat; she was covered with tingly bumps and he had fire in his eyes. And her resolve about "just for now" had definitely melted into "maybe something more."

The boiling water frothed and splashed over the top of the pot, taking his immediate attention. With a wooden spoon he fished out one piece of corkscrew-shaped pasta, blew on it, then tossed it into his mouth, eyes wide from the heat.

Blowing out while chewing, he grinned. "Al dente. Perfect."

Her hands flew to her mouth in a prayer pose while she lightly laughed. Such a silly and fun man, not afraid to be himself for fear of coming off uncool or out of control…unlike Lawrence.

"You like beef stroganoff?"

"Love it."

"You and the baby need the protein, and you can use the calories. Want to grab those rolls for me?"

She followed his orders and put the basket of bread on the already set table while he dished out the noodles and covered them with stroganoff sauce. Her mouth watered—another positive sign the curse of the flu had passed.

With Marta and Leif both being ravenous, dinner became a series of contented sounds and food-lover faces, plus occasional glances that imparted so much more. Two people who knew how to enjoy food. Could it be a metaphor for enjoying sex together? They'd definitely reached a new level of closeness since she'd had the nerve to invite him into her bed, and it was obvious he wanted to take her up on it—though he'd chickened out originally. Then she'd gotten ill and had allowed Leif to care for her, and she couldn't run or hide from him. Only one thing more was needed between them: complete intimacy. She'd felt bold and worldly when she'd called Leif a hermit and dangled the carrot of making love before him. Now? Considering everything they'd built between them, like friendship and trust, making love with Leif would change that, and that bold and worldly part…she wasn't feeling so much anymore.

When dinner was finished, together they carried the

dishes to the sink. As she turned on the water to rinse them, his hand joined hers under the stream, testing the temperature. As their fingers touched, her temperature definitely went up.

"I'll get this," he said.

"I want to help."

He reached behind, then handed her a towel, gently drying her fingers first. Their gazes connected for a second and a tiny bubble of adrenaline popped in her chest. "You can dry."

She stood too close when he turned to hand her the first plate and their shoulders bumped. "Oh, excuse me," she said.

He gave a quick peck to her cheek. "I forgive you, but what for?"

His ice-blue eyes melted any doubt she'd allowed to build up tonight. And if her sudden willingness to be with him wasn't proof enough, her charging pulse was the final clue.

She found the only remaining forks on the counter and put them into the sudsy water, his hand quickly finding hers in the water, running his thumb over her knuckles. "So how are you feeling?"

Pretty damn fine. He obviously waited for a sign, and here was the kicker—Ms. Bold and Modern suddenly felt nervous. Leif wasn't like any man she'd been with before. He didn't play games or need to prove anything or flaunt his position of power. Wasn't he the richest man in Heartlandia? Couldn't prove it by her.

His strength, character and sense of permanence rattled her to the core.

"I'm all better." Her voice sounded softer than usual,

tentative even. What was coming over her? *Momma, don't mess with me now. Please.*

To distract herself from the odd insecure reaction, she got busy opening a cupboard, ready to put some dishes away, but he stopped her. She shifted her glance to his. He shook his head. *Not now.* Then he dried his hands and turned off the water, took her by the palm and led her toward the stairs.

Mute, she followed, out-of-the-blue jitters budding in her center. Where had her worldly woman confidence gone? The thought of being with Leif had made her blood run hot, yet now the reality of it threw her off balance. Theirs could never be a fling, and that was all she'd been used to with men. What would it be like to find that "once in a lifetime" love her father always talked about? Her head spun with the thoughts as Leif guided her toward the stairs.

Was she ready to throw away this chance to know Leif in the truest sense because of imperfect circumstances?

Chip and Dale eagerly romped up the steps with them but Leif sent the dogs away. Obeying their master, sensing he had something planned that didn't involve them, the dogs lowered their heads and tromped off to their downstairs beds.

When Leif and Marta reached the top of the stairs, his hand tugging her to the right instead of left, she let doubt creep back in full force. Leif was completely different from the man who'd let her down, but the current situation of being dependent on him rang too familiar. Though she'd agreed to a business arrangement, it smacked of power and dependence, one over the other, a subtle but steady struggle that she couldn't quite get a grip on. The circumstances were too similar; she was supposed to learn from her mistakes. She stopped.

"Maybe this isn't such a good idea after all," she said, nowhere near convincing herself, yet edging her hand from his until only their fingertips touched.

He looked at her with a probing gaze, as if asking, "Now who is afraid?" Then, calling her out, he gave the most confident smile she'd ever seen.

"Like hell it isn't," he said, sweeping her up and carrying her toward his bedroom.

Chapter Seven

Marta sank into Leif's powerful arms as he carried her to the bedroom. He used his foot to open the door and she soon realized he'd planned this seduction well in advance. The fragrance of musk disguised in sandalwood from scented candles permeated the atmosphere of the room, which looked damned sexy with the turned-down covers and shiny sheets. The bed faced French doors covered only by sheers. Dusk provided enough light to see his face, rugged and craggy from hard outdoor labor and sexy, so, so sexy. His was the face that had quickly become her measure for handsomeness against all other men.

Tingling sensations began coiling through the soles of her feet to the insides of her thighs and upward. Her breath slipped out of sync as she gazed up at Leif and anticipated making love with him for the first time.

He dropped her feet lightly to the floor, pulled her close and, holding her face, kissed her gently, arousing a stronger reaction than any hot, wet and wild kiss would. His timing was perfect. Start slow, build from there, though she sensed his overwhelming struggle to contain himself. It taunted and energized her and, because her hands were free, she began fumbling and thrashing away at the buttons on his shirt.

The kisses deepened, their sounds luscious and hungry, nearly torturing her. The deep coiling throughout her body turned warm and itchy as she matched his probing tongue. Woozy from the heightening need, she held on to the shirt fabric as his hands gripped her shoulders, then skimmed her upper body, feeling her every curve, releasing chills along her skin. She stripped him of his shirt and ran her palms over his muscular chest and flat stomach. The feel of his skin, surprisingly smooth, nearly sent sparks up her arms.

Obviously wanting her naked, he pulled the skirt of her dress all the way from the floor to over her head in record time. That left her glad she'd worn her favorite lacy peach-colored underwear, though the small baby bump made her feel a twinge of self-consciousness.

His urgent gaze scanned her head to toe but soon settled on her chest, passion and longing so obvious any insecurity disappeared and her nipples pebbled beneath the lace. Had she ever felt so needed before? She stepped forward and he unlatched the front clasp of the bra, the weight of her breasts released and free to the cool evening air. With his face expressing amazement and desire, first one hand explored her tender skin, then the other, lifting, caressing, lightly passing a thumb over the sensitive tips. A faint admiring curse escaped his lips. He bent forward and kissed first one then the other breast, inhaling her scent while the beauty of his touch rolled through her. Cradling his head, she kissed the crown of his hair, surprised by the softness, then leaned forward and nuzzled his ear and neck, his shower-fresh scent similar to the candles. On a deep inhale he rose and pulled her close to his chest, flesh to flesh, heat fanning from every point of contact, his mouth devouring her neck, earlobe and jaw. Then, placing a palm on each of her hips, in a hungry move he pulled her closer, and she found the strong erection beneath his jeans. Nothing short of electricity arced between them as they caressed and explored each other.

He lifted her again and placed her on the cold, silky sheets. On her elbow, she waited to welcome him as he dived next to her.

"Hold on," she said, unzipping his jeans.

He flashed a quick look of chagrin, then gladly let her do the honor. The man's neon green underwear both surprised and delighted her when she got on her knees and pulled the jeans off from the leg cuffs. The boxer briefs fit snug over those thickly muscled thighs and outlined his erection. The sight of him crashing through her.

Her breath caught. *So gorgeous.* How could he live like a hermit when women probably had been beating down his door? He didn't give her near enough time to enjoy the view as he tugged her up by the waist and lightly tossed her onto her back. She laughed, then got serious, watching as the urgency shifted gears while he removed her lacy thong as though unwrapping a delicate package. Then, much quicker, he removed his own underwear, freeing that full erection. The vision branded her brain. She wanted him. Without a doubt.

She reached for his thighs, ran her hand along the powerful muscles and took him into her grip, skimming the silky skin over solid strength, her thumb pressing over the head.

Would she ever forget this moment?

Then all her thoughts left as he shifted and took her into his arms. Starting at her head and mouth, then covering all points south, he fought his own need, solely concentrating on her, thoroughly and desperately making love to her body. Wanting nothing more than to please her.

Her breath ragged, her skin burning with desire long before he was finished showing her how he needed her, she bucked beneath him, ready, so, so ready for him. Snapping out of his enthralled sexual haze, he got down to the business of sheathing himself from the tiny package he'd removed from his bedside drawer. Quickly back on task, little by little he entered her, and more quiet oaths and prayers tumbled out of his lips.

Soon molding to each other, closer than seemed humanly possible, they rocked together, finding the rhythm that was exclusively theirs. Discovering what worked and what drove the other crazy. Marta felt as starved for this moment as Leif must have been, as she followed his demanding pace, nearly burning up the sheets beneath her one moment, then slowing to draw out the exquisite pleasure the next.

Rolling on top, she took control, loving the sublime expression on his face when she did. His verbal outbursts as she frantically made love to him prodded her on. She wanted to drive him wild and, from the tense muscles and desperate expression on his face, she was. Every nerve ending in her body vibrated with the energy buzzing through her because of him.

His jaw clenched and he grabbed her hips, holding her firm against him as he, amazingly, increased the speed, spiraling the tension, whisking her to the edge of release and dangling her there. Her elbows gave out, landing her face to his neck, and she tasted the salt of the sweat they'd worked up together. Willing herself back up, gasping for air, she bucked on top as he pounded into her and kept her suspended so close to heaven she could barely breathe. After what seemed like blissful eternity, he set off an implosion at her center so intense, she moaned and cried out and, unable to hold herself up another second, she collapsed onto his chest again. The orgasm rolled through every cell in her body, drenching her. He rode out the waves of her release, extending them on and on, and only when she'd finished, he finally let himself come.

Several seconds later, still breathing rough and ragged, she could hardly get the words out. "You're amazing."

He panted, too. "We're amazing."

Now realizing what she would have missed if she'd let her better judgment take over, she thanked whatever wisdom had stopped her from backing out of making love with him. Grateful Leif hadn't let her. He was a sexual force to be reckoned with, a man who had a lot of lost time to make up for, and she was the exceptionally lucky woman he wanted to be with.

For now.

The citywide vote had taken place on Wednesday and today, Friday, the results were going to be revealed. The meeting was set for 10:00 a.m. at the college auditorium. Leif swung by the mural to pick up Marta on his way over.

He hadn't seen the mural in a couple of weeks since they'd steered clear of each other for part of it, then he'd gotten super busy with new projects after that. But each day he arrived home eager to see her, and from the usual welcome he got, the feeling was mutual.

"Wow, you're really clipping along, aren't you?" He squinted, the autumn sun bright and assaulting, yet the vivid colors on the college wall stood out, one lively scene transitioning into another. He spotted a perfect rendition of the Ringmuren and a growing city in the distance in her latest panel, and the Heritage Hotel and the town monument sketched out in the next. She had to be halfway through already. His chest tightened at the prospect of what that meant.

From atop a ladder, Marta put the finishing touch on one of the pine trees in the forest on Hjartalanda Peak. "Hi!" She turned, removed her painting respirator mask, her face beaming. "Yeah, so what do you think?"

"It looks fantastic." And so did she. Even in overalls and a plain white T-shirt, both splattered with paint, with her hair pulled back and covered in a large scarf and not wearing a stitch of makeup, she looked fantastic. Even wearing that mask she looked great. The woman who'd been keeping him and his bed warm for the past week had quickly become the object of his undivided attention. Sometimes when his guard was down, like right now, the thought squeezed the breath out of him. And it reminded him of how he'd first felt about Ellen when she'd finally started dating him. "I didn't realize how fast you painted."

"Preplanning does that for you. Plus I've had a lot of

help from Desi and the crew. All I have to worry about is painting my scenes since they take care of everything else. It's been great."

He glanced down the wall to the two students applying the protective varnish to the finished sections. The viselike pressure around his chest tightened. Everything was moving too fast.

Could she read the caution in his expression? To avoid her scrutiny, he smiled harder than necessary. "Fantastic." He seemed to be stuck on the word.

She cleaned her hands and took off the scarf. "Time for the meeting?"

He nodded. They'd avoided the topic since their argument the night she'd gotten sick. She probably assumed they were still on opposite sides, but the funny thing was, he'd had a change of heart. The debate with Marta had pointed it out and removed the importance of buried treasure in favor of laying the past to rest, leaving the spirits alone and moving the town forward.

"I've got a crew coming to help this afternoon, so I'll just leave things as they are." She approached, and without a second thought, he kissed her. "Mmm," she said.

Something as simple as that buoyed his mood right up to the cumulus clouds dotting the otherwise-clear blue sky and helped him forget the magnitude of the meeting they were about to attend.

As they approached the auditorium, the crowd thickened and the noise level rose. Conversations buzzed across the colorful sea of people as Leif and Marta walked down the aisle toward the stage. Lilly and Desi sat in the second row and had saved a seat for Marta. Leif guided her toward them with his hand at the small of her back. Lilly looked up and smiled at them, her gaze dropping to his hand and quickly toward Desi's eyes. Maybe it was the flush on Marta's cheeks or that sparkle when she gazed at him, but the ladies' quick interchange proved they'd noticed. He thought he saw Lilly mouthing, "What'd I tell you?" to Desi, who then cast a knowing smile first at Leif and another toward Marta.

What was with the lady radar? Or was it all his imagination? To put any questions about their relationship to rest, just before Marta stepped into the row of chairs, he reached for her neck, pulled her close and kissed her. The usual electricity flashed in her eyes afterward, and it made him smile from his heart. As Marta edged her way toward the empty seat, Leif engaged first Lilly then Desi's attention, nodded and hinted at another smile before heading to the stage. *That's right, girls, we're an item.* Oh, to be a fly on that auditorium-chair arm for their conversation.

Gerda had dressed like a mayor today in a navy blue suit with a white blouse, offset by a red, white and blue scarf. Her white hair was swept up into a looser knot than usual, and the word *dignified* immediately came to mind. He'd noticed since Desi had come home Gerda had become more stylish, and it probably had to do with her granddaughter's input. He also noticed how Gerda had stepped up to the tough task of taking on the job of mayor, even with this big mess she'd walked into, and she'd earned his true respect for that.

Leif took his seat next to Gunnar. Gunnar's sister, Elke, sat on the other side, and next to her was Ben Cobowa, who looked grim faced. Leif knew exactly where Ben stood on the topic.

Gerda cleared her throat and spoke into the microphone. "I'd like to call this meeting to order. Please take your seats and quiet down."

Surprisingly, the audience quickly responded with muttering and whispers fading to quiet without having to be asked twice. It proved to Leif how important the citizens of Heartlandia took this vote.

Watching from the podium, it became apparent to Leif that there were distinct groups. The Chinook citizens in one section, college students in another, business owners and restaurateurs congregated in a group and the Scandinavian matriarchs and patriarchs assembled in still another section. He cleared his throat as tension gathered there. Today's meeting might turn to chaos regardless of the outcome of the democratic vote. Making sure he could get to Marta and out the nearest door, if necessary, he listened as Gerda concluded her brief but perfectly worded speech. No one had known the vote tally before her speech.

"The vote was very close, but there was a clear majority. Without further ado, Heartlandia has voted and we have listened. Though we won't rush ahead with anything, we will move forward with the plans to explore and possibly dig up the buried trunk, with the intent of disturbing as little burial ground as completely necessary. This technique will soon be explained in the *Heartlandia Herald*."

Leif glanced at Elke and Ben, alarm tightening their eyes.

Cheers and protests erupted; grumbling and excitement all mixed together in a clamorous stew. Certain brows knitted with distress, concern registered on other faces, victory lit up some eyes and gravity darkened features in others. What a mess.

Gerda used a gavel to bang on the podium, but it didn't do any good. Sgt. Norling stepped up, making three harsh claps in front of the microphone, but to no avail. He whistled through his teeth, renting the air. That got some to quiet down, but others still huddled in heated conversations.

A gentleman who looked as if he'd stepped straight off a movie set walked toward the stage. Clearly Native American, he wore a dark suit with a leather bolo tie, expensive-looking boots and enough turquoise jewelry to open his own Southwest attire store. His hair was long and braided in historical Native American fashion. His stern expression promised further discussion on the supposedly closed topic.

Hadn't they already been through this part? The vote had been cast. In his heart, Leif hoped they'd just drop the whole thing. Forget the trunk had ever been mentioned in the captain's journal and move on, but it was too late. Definitely. And he'd been the one to bring the original trunk to the attention of the powers that be. Regret at seeing his town torn apart made him wish he'd never come forward with his findings, but in his heart he knew it was what he'd had to do.

Lilly had set up an interview with Leif for next week regardless of what the outcome would be. Now, with the vote being final, he planned to explain how he intended to identify the trunk and what was inside without actually digging a huge hole. He'd given this possibility a lot of thought. Maybe if the folks understood the technique they'd calm down.

The visitor spoke to Gerda, and afterward she solemnly glanced at Ben and Elke, who were nearby, then she nodded. He stepped toward the microphone. "My name is William Maquinna. I am a lawyer and am here on behalf of the Chinookan peoples of the Clatsop tribe, who wish to maintain the sanctity of their forefathers' burial ground."

"We took a vote, fair and square." One man, three-quarters back in the auditorium, stood and shouted him down, causing good Scandinavian manners to intervene with an outburst of shushing.

The speaker ignored the man. "We maintain this sacred ground is not in Heartlandia's jurisdiction."

"Mr. Maquinna?" Mayor Rask spoke up tentatively. She leaned toward the mic. "We've done our research, and though the Ringmuren delineates the park from the burial grounds, the land does, in fact, also belong to Heartlandia. I'll be glad to share the maps with you." She glanced up at the audience. "Or anyone."

With the speakers at a standoff, the audience got noisy again, and Gunnar called in the nearby increased police presence. There had never been a riot in Heartlandia, and today wouldn't be any different. It wasn't in their genes. But because emotions were running high, having additional police made sense.

Gunnar got a call and, assessing the brewing situation before him, took it. He spoke less than thirty seconds, while Gerda regained the attention of the audience.

"The town monument's been vandalized," he said to Leif as soon as he hung up. "Someone's sprayed paint all over it."

What if Marta's mural got defaced, too? Leif stood, walked off the stage and strode directly to her. "You need to know something," he said, reaching across the first row to get her hand as the crowd continued on in the unruly fashion.

Hustling to get into the aisle, she followed him to the side of the stage. "What's up?"

"Someone's defaced your grandfather's monument."

Anger sparked in her gaze, and her chin shot up with indignation. "Who would do such a thing?"

"Who knows?"

"I've got to make sure no one ruins my work, too. Let's go," she said.

Like a lioness protecting her young, Marta grabbed Leif's hand and led him toward the door at the side of the stage. He didn't protest, though he glanced back at the auditorium, wondering how things would turn out.

"I knew nothing good would come of this buried-treasure business," she muttered as they pushed through the door.

At least she hadn't said *I told you so*.

"Was my grandfather's work ruined?" she asked as they jog walked toward the history quad.

"Gunnar said they'd used spray paint. The sculpture is granite, right?"

She nodded. "I think we'd better bring in some experts for this job."

"Know anyone?"

"I'll ask around."

When they arrived at the half-painted mural, relief rolled over Leif's nerves and across Marta's face. It was just as they'd left it.

Chapter Eight

Over the weekend, Sgt. Norling caught the misguided college students who'd defaced public property. They'd left a note at the scene stating that all history of Heartlandia was bogus. Thanks to Marta's input, Gunnar had called in the National Park Service experts on graffiti removal. The granite sculpture would require a special restorative cleaning agent for porous stone surfaces, applied with natural bristle brushes. Then, to prevent further damage, the cleanser would be removed with potable water using fan-tipped garden hoses.

Just what Heartlandia needed, another town project focusing on their shaky beginnings.

To keep Marta's project safe, Leif built a sliding protective barrier for the entire length of the mural that could be rolled closed and locked each day. His goal was to give Marta peace of mind. Depending on the state of the city once the mural was completed, the college could elect to leave the weatherproof cover in place or take it down.

Grumbling and heated debates continued all over town during the weekend, and the police had to step up their watch, but no fights had been reported. The biggest protestors were the college students, who'd held a peaceful sit-in at the Ringmuren to make their point.

Monday morning before heading to the mural site, Marta read Lilly's article about Friday's meeting, the outcome and the citywide reaction. The *Herald* reporting was evenhanded. The reader couldn't possibly tell whose side she was on, even though Marta knew personally that Lilly was against any intervention on sacred soil. Lilly ended her weekly column asking the question: "Did the students make a good point, even though choosing the stupid method of vandalism to make it? Or is it possible for a couple of new pieces of information— Captain Prince discovering Heartlandia and potential buried treasure in sacred land—to change everything else this town has been built on?"

Now, as Marta painted the college wall, she considered the article. She expected that in the heat of everything going on, there would be an onslaught of responses to the questions posed for weeks to come.

Having done the lion's share of work in the preparation for painting the mural—Marta had used the schematic grid over the smaller version in transferring the painting to scale on the college history quad walls— transferring the project seemed like a breeze. Things were moving along quicker than she'd expected. Most important, she was proud of the results so far. She stood back and smiled at the day's work. The mural looked great, if she did say so herself.

Getting back to painting, Marta called out the next color she needed, and almost immediately Desi handed up the paint to her with a clean brush.

"I don't know what I would have done without your fiancé coming to Leif's house when I was sick," Marta casually mentioned through the respirator mask while feathering dove-colored clouds on top of the cornflower-blue sky.

"He's the most caring man I've ever met."

Funny, Marta thought *she'd* already met the most caring man in all of Heartlandia. Leif.

"You're a lucky woman," she said rather than debate the matter. "When's your wedding?"

"We want to get married the Saturday after Christmas."

"How lovely!" It was quickly approaching Thanksgiving, so that was soon.

"I'd love for you to come."

Wow. Once Marta finished the project and left town, could she handle turning right around and coming back and seeing Leif again, by then her pregnancy overshadowing everything else? Or would it be smart to stay on with Leif that extra month? She forced her attention back to painting rather than think about the possibility. "Please send me an invitation, and if there's any way I can make it, I'll be here."

Maybe that could be her backup plan. Leave, let Leif realize what he'd be missing for a month, then come back and force him to admit he cared about her. After laying down the rules, she'd quickly lost track of the "no strings" part, falling deeper each day for him. But was it reciprocal? She had no clue. In all of their crazy lovemaking, he'd never once uttered anything about her staying on with him. Shouldn't she be glad, because wouldn't that make leaving Heartlandia easier?

"Good afternoon, ladies." Leif's familiar voice threw her out of the confused thoughts.

She turned, saw the world's most masculine man holding a... "Hey. What's that?"

He had a wicker basket in his hand and looked a little awkward. "Lunch. Want to join us, Desi?"

The wise young woman backed off. "Oh, thanks, but I've got class in an hour. I'll just grab something from the cafeteria first."

Marta noticed Leif didn't try to persuade Desi otherwise and liked that he wanted to keep her for himself. As Marta finished what she was working on, Leif put the basket down and talked to Desi.

"Lilly's going to interview me a little later. Should I be scared?"

Desi lifted her brows, her creamy light brown skin glowing in the sun and her chocolate-colored eyes looking playful. "You mean will she put you on the hot seat?"

"Well, since you put it that way, yes."

"Let's just say she has a knack for getting more information than you realize."

Marta sensed Leif needed backup, so she came up behind him and wrapped her arms around his waist. "I'll protect you, baby."

He leaned into her embrace and she automatically relaxed just being near him. He twisted and put his free arm around her shoulders. "Then, I know I'm in good hands."

In a flash, their conversation had shifted from the interview to the moments they'd spent making love just that morning. Come to think of it, her hands *had* worked wonders on him. Waking in the early-morning light, finding each other, they'd brightened the outlook of the day from their bodies touching and tangling together. No wonder she'd been in such a great mood and had accomplished so much already this morning.

Desi stood watching them for a few moments. A soft, knowing smile crossed her full lips. "I'm going to leave you two lovebirds to your lunch. Eric has signed up to help this afternoon. See you tomorrow, Marta."

"Thank you for organizing my crew," Marta said, realizing she already considered Desi a good friend. "I couldn't do this without you guys."

"No problem. Happy to do it. I'm learning so much."

Once Desi left, Leif kissed Marta soundly on the mouth, her open lips both an invitation and a promise for that night. He had that moony haze in his eyes she'd come to love whenever they ended their kisses, their ever-growing attraction buzzing between them. Who needed lunch? She did! She was pregnant and had an appetite like she'd never experienced before. It caused her stomach to growl at the mention of food.

He laughed at the condemning sound. "Good thing I stopped by."

They set up lunch on the grass under a nearby tree not far from the mural so they could keep an eye on it. Unfortunately, it was also not far enough away from the noisy campus and the between-class crowds, but it would have to do.

He'd brought carved-turkey sandwiches, obviously remembering her hesitation to eat deli meat while pregnant because of additives and the slim possibility of getting salmonella. She'd been devouring books on pregnancy each night, and to her surprise, Leif seemed as interested as she was in accumulating the knowledge. He'd also brought pears, apples and blackberries, a carton of milk for her and iced tea for himself. Ravenous from a good morning's work, she ate, thinking contented thoughts, sitting under the peekaboo sun with the man she adored and was constantly turned on by. Life was good.

Perhaps too good.

"You still gonna find me attractive when I'm fat?" she joked, taking a huge bite of sandwich and lightly punching his arm, then just as soon realizing she wouldn't be around when she was really big.

"I'm going to enjoy every minute of helping you get that way," he said with a gleam in his eyes as he handed her the carton of milk.

Oh, God, she could get used to this.

Was he talking about the whole pregnancy or just for while she was here? Did she want to spoil a lovely lunch with a great guy asking about a technicality?

She knew her home was in Sedona, and this was a job she'd been hired to do. It wasn't forever. Hadn't she been the one to lay down their rules for getting together—no strings, just for here and now? And that had seemed to be the final deciding factor for Leif. Everything they'd been enjoying together was icing on the cake, a lovely detour, but it couldn't be permanent.

She took another bite of her sandwich.

Could it?

Desi hadn't been kidding about Lilly. That afternoon, with minimal effort, the petite reporter managed to get Leif to open up about his mixed feelings on digging for treasure in sacred ground. He'd also explained his newly changed plans for going about the job with the intent of disturbing as little earth as possible.

Having pinpointed the one area of concentrated heat with the thermography studies, he planned to use an industrial fiber-optic scope to get a visual of the area. All he'd need to do was drill a three-inch-wide hole sixty to seventy feet deep, fit PVC piping inside for guidance and insert the lit fiber-optic scope to examine the area in question up close. Having made sure of the exact location of the suspected treasure trunk, they'd dig up as little area as necessary to remove it. Or, if there wasn't a buried trunk, they would only have disturbed a few inches diameter of soil—the depth, at the time of the interview, could only be approximated until he actually performed the task.

He realized even this procedure could be a bone of contention with those who opposed touching the burial ground in any way, but he also stressed it seemed the best compromise in this serious matter. And compromise was the bottom line.

Then Lilly dropped a bomb by asking if he'd heard about the Maritime Museum group expedition discovering what seemed to be parts of a sunken ship up the coast of the Columbia River. Speculation was it might possibly be the pirate ship mentioned in the captain's journals.

"Are you serious?" What else could happen in the cluster of baffling revelations?

Eyes big with excitement, she told him everything she knew.

The discovery had happened just that morning, and she'd been on site scribbling notes before coming to interview him. His first thought was, he couldn't wait to get home to tell Marta all about it. His second thought was, thank goodness, this might shift attention from the burial ground and divert some of the heat from his project.

"While I have you here…" Lilly said, her classic almond eyes offset by her borderline punk–style haircut. "I know Gunnar has thanked you, but I wanted you to know how much I love the add-on. Ever since I saw the blueprint, I knew it would be a special house, already was, but the addition, well, wow. Just wow."

Leif smiled—for a writer, she'd gone minimalist—then nodded, filled with satisfaction. "Gunnar knew exactly what he wanted."

"He did. And now that we're engaged, he's given me the okay to make a request."

"You mean I'm not done yet?" he teased, his interest piqued over what might be next.

"Nope." Though in her early thirties, Lilly still had the enthusiasm of a teenager. She handed him a picture of a small Japanese tea pavilion with a pagoda-style roof and wood pillars. It sat in a yard thick with woods, exactly like Gunnar's lot.

"This is beautiful," he said, excited about the chance to build something new and unique.

"I've got all kinds of plans for a teahouse, right on down to the shoji panels and Zen garden. You think you can build this for us? My parents and grandmother would be honored by it."

"Sure. I'd love to."

Lilly hugged Leif. He'd gotten out of practice in the hugging department, but thanks to Marta, he relaxed and enjoyed it. Even hugged back.

"One last thing," Lilly said. "Gunnar and I are having a get-together this Saturday night at Lincoln's Place to celebrate our engagement. We're inviting a few people, and since most of them will be Gunnar's friends, I'd love for you and Marta to come."

"That would be great," he said without hesitation. "Thanks for asking."

Well, how about that? First Marta brings me back from the dead, and now the town counts me in as one of the living.

It felt pretty damn good, too.

On Saturday night Marta emerged from her room looking nothing less than stunning. She'd pulled her hair back into a loose twist and wore extralarge gold double-hoop earrings. She divided a classic-cut white silk blouse and a full-length gold-textured satin skirt with a thick artisan leather belt. Gold Greek-style sandals spotlighted her bright red toenails.

Leif swallowed hard, fighting the impulse to sweep her up and take her straight to his bed. "You look gorgeous."

"Why, thank you. You look pretty damn great yourself."

He'd cleaned up wearing dark slacks and a pale violet dress shirt opened at the throat and with the cuffs rolled to his forearms. He'd even put on his black dress shoes, after searching way in the back of his old walk-in closet to find them.

Marta sauntered over to him and, careful not to mess her hair, he claimed her with a hand on the neck and a tug toward his mouth. They kissed long and tenderly, enough to jumble his brain cells. "You taste great, too," he said, regretfully ending the kiss.

Her caramel eyes looked dreamy and willing to do anything he asked. He loved that about her—knowing she wanted him as much as he wanted her. But she needed time with new friends and he wanted her to be happy. Breaking the moment, he glanced at his watch. "I guess we should go—"

"Or we might get in trouble?"

"You read my mind."

"It's a gift." She gave that saucy, confident expression that always got a rise out of him.

Cliff Lincoln had bought his restaurant after discovering Heartlandia while working as a chef on a cruise ship, and under his hand Lincoln's Place had become the local hot spot. A favorite tourist stop, the town was often overrun by cruise-line guests, pumping much-needed business into local commerce. Tonight, Gunnar and Lilly had taken over the bar area with their private party, though dining was still up and running in the adjacent restaurant.

"Hey, welcome, you guys." Lilly rushed to greet Leif and Marta with a glass of champagne in her hand.

Marta and Lilly hugged hello as Leif looked on smiling.

Lilly wore a cute fluffy-skirted cocktail dress in lavender, with a tight, shiny, sequined top and extra-high silver platform shoes, and she still only came to Gunnar's shoulder. Out of uniform, Gunnar looked rugged, like a younger version of Leif but with a whole lot more muscle mass. The man looked as if he could pull up a tree including the roots with his bare arms.

Heartlandia certainly knew how to grow gorgeous men.

"Help yourself to anything. It's an open bar," Gunnar said, already looking beyond to greet another couple. "Make yourselves at home," he added, moving off.

Leif asked the bartender for a draft beer for himself and club soda with a twist of lime for Marta. Drinks in hand, they roamed the room greeting folks; some were familiar faces and others she'd never seen before. They chatted and listened as someone told a joke that didn't really compute for her, but she laughed politely anyway. Her eyes wandered.

Elke, Gunnar's sister, sat at the end of the bar by herself, and Marta looked around for Ben because she always saw them together and had jumped to conclusions. He was nowhere in sight.

Marta slipped her hand out of Leif's and went over to say hello. "Where's Ben?"

Elke looked puzzled. "I'm not sure."

Feeling she'd put her foot in her mouth, Marta was about to apologize.

"He may stop by later, I think," Elke continued, a finger rubbing the rim of her wineglass.

"I see." Marta had assumed they were a couple since she'd first seen them at the town meetings. They often passed meaningful looks back and forth. At least that was how Marta had interpreted them—meaningful with something more simmering just beneath the surface. Longing? Plus, she could have sworn she'd seen them hold hands once on campus.

"We're not dating or anything, if that's what you're wondering."

Ah, another mind reader. Marta gave a playful grimace topped off with chagrin as she nodded. "I really sensed something between you. Excuse me."

A quick but definite wishful expression passed over Elke's features. "He's a great guy but doesn't socialize much."

Marta made note of Elke dressed very unlike her usual self in a little black dress, actually showing some shoulder and hinting at cleavage. "Too bad he'll miss seeing you like that. I think you look hot."

For a history professor who tended to imitate an old-school librarian in fashion, the change was refreshing, and Marta hoped Ben had the good sense to show up and get an eyeful.

Elke smiled and blushed.

From the corner of her vision, Marta saw an African-American man in a starched white chef shirt and pressed gray slacks, his cook's hat sitting at a jaunty angle. "Is that Cliff Lincoln?"

"Sure is," Elke said, turning her wineglass round and round by the stem. *That Ben better show up.*

Marta had learned all kinds of interesting tidbits about Cliff from her new friends Desi and Lilly. Like the fact that Cliff Lincoln, a Southern chef by nature, had started serving sushi after Lilly had kept hounding him about it. So tonight's table of appetizers not only included crawfish dip, fried green tomatoes, shrimp and grits and hot buffalo wings, but also California and rainbow rolls and assorted raw fish–style sushi bites.

"If you'll excuse me, I'm going to sample the goodies." Being pregnant, Marta avoided the raw fish but discovered something called a punk roll with a tempura-fried green bean at the core, and a hand roll made with a seaweed wrap, vegetables and rice. They were both divine. To her surprise, the fried green tomatoes complemented the other food on her plate.

The bar, filled with friends and a constant stream of cops, both off and on duty, was loud and congested. Marta hadn't been to a party since Lawrence had celebrated his last birthday, and though the atmosphere was more exclusive for that, the camaraderie and goodwill in Cliff's bar was far more enjoyable. But then, her mother's death had put every part of her relationship with Lawrence in a new light.

Thankful to have a smile put back on Marta's face, she noticed Ben Cobowa had managed to sneak in under the radar. As he headed right for Elke, Marta saw the young woman's face light up, and the sight warmed her heart. Maybe she was a mind reader after all.

Desi and Kent arrived a little late, both with a fresh flush to their faces, making Marta wonder what they'd been up to before they'd gotten here.

"Hi!" Desi called out, first hugging Lilly and Gunnar, then finding Marta. "You look gorgeous."

"Thanks. You're looking hot yourself."

Desi's tight red dress hugged her curves in all the right places, and from the admiring look in Kent's eyes, he'd probably been the one to pick it out.

"This little old thing?" Desi teased with an exaggerated Southern accent, then turned in a circle. "I only wear this when I don't care how I look." She'd quoted the sexy actress who'd played Violet from *It's a Wonderful Life* to a T, making Marta laugh.

Desi had told Marta while helping out at the mural that she'd grown up on the road with her mother playing piano bar in a Midwest hotel chain. Desi had also said she'd watched more than her share of old movies. Then they'd gotten into a contest over who could recite the most one-liners from all the classics. It had been a fun way to pass the afternoon painting, but Desi had won, hands down.

Leif wandered over and put his arm around Marta's

waist. Funny how great that simple gesture made her feel. As if she belonged to him. More and more lately, she *wanted* to belong to him, but she figured that was more than she could ask any man while being pregnant. Especially a proud someone like Leif, who'd once wanted his own family but had had the chance taken from him.

Desi's bright diamond engagement ring sparkled in the bar lights, catching Marta's eye. Was getting engaged the latest trend in Heartlandia? For an instant she let herself imagine how it might feel, then on an even greater whim, she pictured her mother's expression, if she were still alive, when Marta showed her an engagement ring of her own.

If you're looking down, Momma, I know how happy that would make you.

Cliff appeared at Desi's side, looking proud to host the engagement party. Desi had told Marta he'd been a mentor and father figure since she'd arrived in town— that he'd encouraged her to stay and even had given her a job. Some people actually thought they were related. They hugged hello.

Lilly rushed up to Cliff, popping some sushi into her mouth. "You did a great job on everything, especially the futomaki."

"What'd I tell you about cussing in public, young lady?" Cliff teased, pride spilling from his large black eyes in making one of the guests of honor happy.

The circle of friends laughed. Marta loved being a part of everything, especially being here as Leif's date.

"What this party needs is some music," Cliff said, shifting back to host mode and before Marta had the chance to go all melancholy. "Desi, you gonna play something?"

She shook her head. "I'm here as a guest tonight, and besides, you'd have to pay me more for private parties."

"Is that so?" He looked at Desi with a father's esteem, and Marta suddenly understood why Desi had asked him to walk her down the aisle in December.

In a few short moments, Latin music carried over the speakers and a handful of couples began to dance. It was a salsa and Marta loved to dance, so she moved her hips to the beat the slightest bit, making her skirt sway this way and that. In an instant, a familiar hand was at her back.

"Want to dance?" Leif said.

Completely surprised by the offer, never in her wildest dreams thinking of Leif as a dancer, she grinned. "Of course!" What could she be getting herself into? No matter how he performed, she'd pretend she loved to dance with him.

Expecting the worst but immediately pleased and dazzled by his smooth moves, Marta's grin stretched even wider. "How'd you learn the salsa?"

"Took some lessons. Sorry if I'm a little rusty."

"You did more than take lessons to dance like this. You're a natural."

"Not that natural. The Danes aren't exactly known for their dancing abilities."

She laughed softly, loving being with Leif, seeing him so much more relaxed than when she'd first met him. Moving with him. Thoroughly enjoying being out with friends in a new town, feeling the camaraderie and general goodwill from everyone. "So what's your secret?"

"Ellen made me take waltz lessons before we got married, and we enjoyed it so much we kept taking lessons.

It kind of became our thing. Worked our way through the Latin dances, and the rest, as they say, is history."

Though he smiled as he swayed his hips to the beat, she waited and watched for that distant look that always followed when he spoke of his wife. Tonight she either missed it or he hid it well. All she could see on his face was joy and sexy blue eyes gazing only at her, undressing her one item of clothing at a time.

Oh, God, this wasn't at all how it was supposed to be when she'd told him they could help heal each other. She'd meant it strictly clinically, not emotionally. He guided her hips outward to the beat and twirled her, then tugged her back to his chest. She draped her arms over his shoulders and, on a high from the fun dance, whispered into his ear. "Now I know why you're such a great lover."

He tilted his head back, eyes bright with a grin. "It's all about the hips, baby."

You got that right. And the passion that drives those hips.

The song ended and quickly morphed into a slow standard, and Leif pulled her close again. She knew, no matter how long she was back in Sedona, she'd never forget his musky leather scent and the strength of his arms whenever he held her. And all the potential she'd never get to see…

Naked. Tangled together. Leif still inside her. They snuggled after sex. Tonight had been particularly passionate. She thanked the hot Latin music they'd danced to all night. The best foreplay in the world.

Completely undone from the climax, she lay limp, breathing shallowly.

His hand came to rest on her stomach, where he rubbed lightly. He hadn't forgotten for a second that she was pregnant, that much she knew. Even if he tried to forget, her belly grew each day, reminding him. *This baby belongs to someone else.* She'd hardly been able to buckle her belt tonight. He kissed her forehead and withdrew, then made a quick visit to the bathroom. Behind the closed door, she heard him hum a happy tune. She'd brought life back into his existence, and he'd helped her forget the blow to her ego from Lawrence. *Lawrence who?*

And she was falling in love with Leif.

It was true. She couldn't deny it another second, even though it was the stupidest thing she'd ever done. Well, that, and wasting five years on a man who would never marry her. Why couldn't a girl listen to her mother?

Sunday evening Marta and Leif worked side by side in the kitchen. She'd prepared an apple crumble ready to go into the oven, and he dazzled her with whipping up a salad, then led her outside while he cooked cedar-plank salmon. He grilled it poolside on the designer barbecue. It was a chilly November evening and she wore her poncho to keep warm.

The dogs cavorted around the yard, eventually wandering over to test the scent from the grill.

"Sit," Leif said. Chip and Dale did as they were told. One yellow and one black Lab sat patiently side by side while he balanced a baby carrot on both of their snouts. "Stay." He stepped away. "Stay." Leif glanced at Marta and grinned; her heart flipped and pulse shimmied. "Staaay." He drew out the word.

Saliva hung in strands from both dogs' mouths, their patience weakening.

"Take it," Leif said, the dogs happily tossing the carrots into the air and, like magic, making them disappear.

Marta clapped with delight, laughing lightly. "You think they even tasted them?" The dogs rushed to her to check if she had a goody for them, too. All they got was a loving pat.

"Who knows, but they'd do that all day if I let them." A satisfied-looking man, Leif lifted the top on the grill to check the salmon. "Originally, when my buddy told me he had two Lab puppies left, I told him I'd take just one. I wanted the yellow dog. But when I went to get him, I saw the two of them rolling around playing, and I didn't have the heart to break them up. I decided they were a package deal and brought them both home. Smartest decision I ever made." He rubbed Chip's ears, then Dale's. "Wasn't it? Yeah."

So the guy had a heart for package deals. Might that give her hope for her own situation?

When the fish was done, he placed it in a dish covered in aluminum. They trekked back toward the house, where a salad and quinoa awaited. It was time to put the dessert into the oven, too. Approaching the kitchen door, she felt a pang of longing that was anything but subtle. It felt like home here. In five years, she'd never come close to this feeling with Lawrence, yet she'd settled for it, telling herself it was the life she wanted. More than likely because her mother kept telling her it wasn't.

She glanced at Leif, his warm smile smoothing over her feelings of loss and discontent as he held open the door, and with a steady gaze he watched as she walked inside. Chip and Dale pushed themselves between them and partially blocked the way, sniffing the air fragrant with cedar and salmon.

"Move it, guys." The dogs obeyed their master, hopefulness in their eyes about what might be in store for them for being good.

"You gonna want ice cream with dessert?" she asked, putting the dessert into the oven.

"Is there any other way to eat apple crumble?" He served a portion of salmon to each of the awaiting plates on the counter.

She opened the refrigerator. "What kind of salad dressing do you want?"

"I like that yogurt avocado stuff."

"Me, too."

Yeah, it felt like home—the kind her momma would have loved for her.

Later, they took a bath together. Leif was already in the tub and Marta slipped into the extrawarm water and settled between his legs. She leaned back against his solid chest, resting her head on his shoulder.

"This feels wonderful," she sighed.

His hands circled her in the sudsy water, finding her breasts and exploring. "You feel great." He nuzzled her neck, steam raising her temperature to match the vapor from the tub.

"Who would have guessed when you picked me up from the airport that we'd become lovers."

He let go a light laugh. "I thought you hated me."

"I didn't know you. I wasn't sure about staying at your house." *I was pregnant!*

His hands wandered to the insides of her thighs, then

up and over her belly and onward to lift her breasts again. She felt him harden behind her. "I'm really glad you did."

She sighed on an inhale as one hand found her folds and cupped her firmly. "It took a lot of convincing to get you here." She arched her back as his hand pressed tighter.

"I've been meaning to tell you how grateful I am." His hot breath over her ear added to the pleasure building inside. "But then, actions always speak louder than words."

"Do you want me?" she whispered.

"More and more each day." He didn't hesitate to answer.

Now his hand worked quickly, and her muscles tightened with the building anticipation and excitement.

"Aah." She sucked in air, soon rigid with need.

"Do *you* want *me*?"

"Yes. You." The word gasped from her lips as he brought her to release. "Only you."

He turned her to face him, and she straddled his lap as he proved again why she wanted and needed him. Only him.

Later, they lay wrapped together under the moonlight.

"You haven't said anything about my job tomorrow," he said.

He'd broached the topic she'd tabled since they realized they were on opposite sides. He was going to dig up sacred ground and she thought it was a horrible idea.

"You know how I feel about it. Nothing good can come from it."

"Okay. We won't rehash the situation. Why ruin a beautiful moment? I just want you to know I'm doing what the town voted to do."

"I understand."

Yeah, they'd drop the subject. Life wasn't always perfect, and this proved it. But in the dark, upset with what tomorrow would bring, Marta smiled toward the ceiling anyway. Remembering the beautifully simple and enlightening story about the dogs Leif had told while barbecuing, she rolled toward him and kissed his cheek. He'd proved with his Chip and Dale story to be a package-deal kind of guy. And why was she not surprised?

"You're an honorable man, Leif Andersen, and I respect that."

"Does that mean you understand about tomorrow?"

"Nope."

There were many more complications to their relationship beyond the great sex. But the biggest question remained—where to go from here? And, being a pregnant lady from out of town who'd talked him into having a just-for-now fling, that topic seemed nearly impossible to bring up.

He'd yet to come to her bed, his deceased wife still cutting a divide between them. She understood the significance, yet tonight they'd been together in the masterbath soaking tub. She'd take that as a step closer in the right direction.

The old, nagging thought of never being able to achieve what her parents had, that once-in-a-lifetime love, kept her wondering in what "right" direction exactly did she want Leif to go. To be her prince, marry her, accept her baby as his? Dreams. All dreams. Foolish notions a mother had once tried to plant in a rebellious girl. Dreams she'd turned her back on all those years ago. Things she should never hope for now.

And yet…

Draped in Leif's embrace, Marta eventually slipped

from a fitful state into near sleep, with one last thought before conking out—if only he could see the package deal waiting in his arms.

Chapter Nine

Monday morning, bright and early, Leif left for the burial ground. The small work crew was meeting him there with the special equipment. Under the first light of day, a surprise awaited him.

"Did they camp out overnight? All weekend?" he muttered as he pulled his truck into the parking lot. No less than two dozen protestors waited at the Ringmuren. He recognized the lawyer from the meeting the other day—what was his name, William Maquinna? Plus several college-aged students he didn't know. Fortunately, Elke and Ben weren't among the group. It would have gotten really weird otherwise.

His guys waited in their trucks for him to take the lead. He didn't blame them—they were here to work, not to answer for their boss. May as well face it head-on.

Leif strode toward Mr. Maquinna. "Good morning,

sir. I understand your concern, and I want you to know that I plan to do as minimal disruption of this land as possible. I explained everything in the newspaper interview and I hope you've all read about my process." He glanced around at stoic faces; only Maquinna nodded.

"One teaspoon of earth is the same as digging up everything," said Mr. Maquinna.

"I hope you don't plan to disrupt the city-approved dig because, if I need to, I'll invite the police up here." Leif, speaking quiet yet firm, making his point as clear as possible, looked deep into the man's eyes, sizing him up. He understood Maquinna's sincerity in representing people long gone.

"And we hope our presence and the spirits of past generations will persuade you to stop." The lawyer stood his ground.

Point taken, but that wasn't going to happen. Nope. Leif needed to get this job done and put it in the past for the sake of everyone in Heartlandia.

After a few moments of silent standoff Maquinna spoke. "We mean you no harm, even though you are the one doing the damage."

Leif realized there was no appeasing the man or his group, and he had work to do, with expensive industrial equipment on loan and a mystery to solve for once and for always. But in his heart he hoped he wouldn't find a buried trunk since that would cause a much bigger excavation than he wanted or planned to do today, or, if he could help it, any other day.

"I don't see it that way, but we'll have to leave it at that." Leif considered offering his hand for a shake, but what if Maquinna didn't take it? The whole situation left a bad taste in his mouth, so he walked off.

Last night, in semisleeplessness he'd thought he'd devised a solution that could put the whole damn thing to rest.

Gravel popped and crunched on broken-down blacktop from tires behind him as another car drove into the parking lot. He turned, and his optimism for getting through this task without incident sunk to his gut. Ben, Elke and *Marta* got out of the car.

He and Marta had avoided this conversation like the apocalypse ever since the town meeting, distracting themselves with more pleasurable things. Like sex. They'd shared a few uneasy words last night but had quickly dropped the subject. Even now he hoped she'd come to support him.

He watched her. She studied him, and he thought he saw empathy in her expression, yet she followed Elke and Ben toward the group of protestors without uttering a word. Last night she'd seemed resigned about him doing this dig and in no uncertain terms made it known she didn't agree. He'd thought the topic had been settled. Hoped it had. They'd agreed to disagree. Now here she was supporting the opposite side, making him feel like crap. Her being here both stung and angered him.

He ground his teeth. *So that's how it was going to be*. Then he whistled to his team to bring the equipment. So much for loyalty. "Let's get this set up."

An eerie sound drew his attention as he continued on. William Maquinna had started to chant. Another man played a simple skin drum and another a wooden flute that looked and sounded like a recorder, sad and primitive. He kept walking, aware that gourd rattles mimicked his every step. Eerie.

He didn't believe in spirits and wasn't going to let

the group freak him out. Not right now anyway; he had business to take care of. Still, the hair on the back of his neck stood on end and he couldn't wait to wrap things up.

As he concentrated on the task at hand, what hurt most was knowing Marta was on the other side of the wall disapproving of his every move.

Well, so be it. He had a job to do.

Marta hadn't felt this queasy since her first trimester. Facing Leif had been gut-wrenching, his disappointment in seeing her obvious. But she had to stand up for what she believed in, even if it drove a wedge between her and the man she was falling in love with.

The similarities between her standoff with her mother popped into her mind. It had ruined their relationship. Did she want to risk that with Leif?

Lilly had arrived not long after she had and was snapping pictures and interviewing the protestors. Then she went around to the other side of the wall to talk to the crew, who promptly asked her to step back from the area. She took pictures anyway.

Marta inhaled a deep breath and removed herself from the group as the tribal music escalated to cries and squeals when Leif's crew made their first dig. The hydraulic device sounded like a giant dentist's drill and overpowered the protestors' wails. She knew Leif was using special equipment, something he called an earth auger, to contain the damage—she'd read the interview in the paper rather than bringing it up and risking another argument at home—and that he planned to dig straight down like they did for water wells. Then they'd check things out with the industrial fiber-optic scope before doing anything else.

The sound of the machinery was far worse than the actual hole they dug. Logically she understood he didn't want to damage the sacred ground, but the thought of disrespecting the land for potential profit didn't sit well with her sense of justice.

She spent the morning sketching faces, being there more as a spectator than a participant, but after a while the intense machinery noise and the high, whining chanting got to her. She needed to get away and remembered that special bench Leif had built for his mother. She walked the length of the park and outward to the shaded area in the woods and pine trees he'd taken her to the first time he'd brought her up here. A shard of light cut straight through the center of some trees and came to rest on the bench. She followed the light to the rugged wooden bench, made from natural planks with small tree branches for armrests and bench legs. The workmanship was distinct and familiar.

As she walked closer, she saw the words carved into the top plank on the backrest of the bench. "In loving memory of Hannah Anika Andersen, who loved her family and these beautiful trees. May her soul rest in peace."

Marta sat on the bench, which seemed to hug her. Leif had wished his mother's soul peace.

Her own mother's face came to mind, as clear as if she were standing right there. *I've got a secret to share, Momma. It took something you'd never approve of to figure it out, too. I'm going to be a mother, and, well, I hope you'll understand that I needed to take this path—the one you never approved of—to finally understand what you wanted for me. The baby has changed every aspect of my life. Turns out I want what you wanted for me all along. A good man. Love. Marriage. A family.*

But like you always said, when we go about things in the wrong way life gets more complicated than it should be. I hated when you told me that, thought all you wanted to do was hold me back, and my desire for independence drove me away from you. I was so determined to prove you and your traditional living wrong that I settled for things I never should have. I tricked myself into believing a modern, sophisticated relationship with Lawrence was everything I wanted, when in my heart I suspected it was only because he wouldn't offer more. I thought high living and jet-setting was good enough. Yet there was emptiness deep down, and I was too proud to admit it. You were right. Lawrence and I used each other. There, I've said it. Are you happy now?

I should have listened to you.

But if I had, my journey may never have brought me here...to meet Leif.

I think you'd like him, Momma. He even built this bench in honor of his mother.

And I never would have come here if I hadn't gotten pregnant. So you see...I wish you peace, just like Leif wishes his mother. I hope I find it, too.

The tribal music got louder, breaking into her thoughts. The carefully molded wood of the bench comforted her, yet desecration of sacred burial ground was occurring. She wiped the tears from the corners of her eyes from thinking about her mother and their unresolved, estranged relationship. Then her thoughts turned back to Leif and the reason she'd come here today.

She knew Leif understood the importance of letting those who have died before us rest. He'd probably go nuts if someone tried to cut down these trees or remove this bench; of course he wouldn't tear up the burial site unnecessarily. She completely trusted his judgment. And him.

In the distance, the drilling stopped, and she assumed it was time to insert the PVC piping and then the industrial fiber-optic scope. She wanted to be near if Leif found anything, even though she dreaded it happening.

After paying respect to a woman she'd never met but one who'd raised a wonderful son and sending special loving thoughts to her own mother, she jogged back to the Ringmuren, wondering where in Heartlandia Ellen's bench was located.

Once back with the group, an announcement from Leif and his crew wasn't forthcoming, though everyone waited silently.

The protest group had thinned out as the morning had worn on and turned to afternoon. Ben was set to work the evening shift, and Elke had an afternoon class to teach, but Marta opted to stay on for Leif's sake. She needed to let him know she was more on his side than he thought. She honored his sense of duty to the city and understood his need for answers. She'd stay here all day if need be and wait for him to finish the job, then she'd ask him for a ride home—that was, if he wasn't furious with her. Again, having a strong sense of the man, she trusted he wouldn't be.

William Maquinna seemed almost in a trance from chanting and singing for so many hours. The drummer and flutist had stopped when the machinery had gone silent. The remaining group stood facing the wall, watching and waiting. Practically holding their breath.

An hour later, Leif emerged from the other side of the Ringmuren covered in dirt, his expression completely impossible to read.

"Our expedition is complete. We've sealed up the three-inch hole we drilled today and replaced every last *spoonful* of dirt, and we will immediately be removing our equipment. Thank you for your patience. We've answered our question and will report our findings to the township committee. There won't be any need for further digging."

The Native American leader began to chant again and the drum, rattles and flute joined in with a lilting sacred melody. From what Marta could tell, the man seemed to be giving praise and asking forgiveness. The insult to the land hadn't been as bad as anyone had expected, and that was at least a small victory for everyone.

A little for this side, a little for the committee, no major harm nor foul, and best of all, the whole messy thing was over. Finally. Hopefully the spirits could forgive.

"I ask for healing of the earth and forgiveness from our ancestors," William Maquinna announced as the last of Leif's equipment was removed and his crew packed up and prepared to leave.

One last quick thought of her mother and whether she had forgiven Marta for stepping out of her life came to mind, followed by a swell of peace. Giving silent thanks, she looked to the treetops, then back at the small crowd.

Many of the gathered group stayed with Maquinna, but Marta set off to catch up to Leif.

So did Lilly. "What'd you find?"

"I have to report to the committee first, then we'll release the findings to the newspaper."

"I understand. Any thoughts?" She looked hopeful.

"I enjoyed the music all day." He gave a closed-lip,

noncommittal smile and Marta knew Lilly would have to back off for now.

Once he got to the truck, Leif turned, as if waiting, and watched cautiously as Marta peeled off from Lilly and approached him. With dirt on his face, dark smudges under his eyes and the dust turning his light hair brown, his blue eyes were more pronounced than ever. Without his saying a word, she understood he didn't hold a grudge about her being here today. She appreciated his tolerant attitude, wished she could be half as accepting of others as Leif was. He opened the cab door for her and she got in, their eyes meeting and melding an instant before he shut her in.

Minutes later, when they'd cleared the park and were halfway down the mountain Leif glanced at her, then back to the road. "It really crushed me to see you there today, you know."

"I'm sorry, but in my own way I was being supportive." She knew he wouldn't like seeing her there, yet she'd gone anyway, couldn't stay away.

"By standing with the other side?"

"Wouldn't I need a hard hat to be on your side?"

"Point taken."

"It's not as if I was chanting or anything."

"Now you're just grasping at straws."

"Sorry. I really didn't want to hurt you. Forgive me." The truth was, since her mother had died, he was the last person on Earth she ever wanted to hurt. "I know you're the kind of man who honors the tasks he gets assigned, even if things get tough. That when you feel committed to something, you see it through."

"That's right. When I start something I want to go all the way with it." He gave her a strange look, and she could have sworn she'd hit on something far more personal between them than a town protest. Now that she'd finally admitted what she wanted to her mother, would he be committed to seeing things through with her, too?

"That music got on my nerves," he said, watching the twists and turns of the winding road.

"And you're machinery got on their nerves."

He loosened up a bit, cracked a smile. "Good."

There wasn't any need to talk or argue anymore. The event was over, so they lapsed into silence again. It was reassuring to know that Leif was the kind of man who liked to finish what he started. Even though, theoretically, she'd been the one to start everything between them.

"I saw your mother's bench again today." She'd skip the part about talking to her own mother for now.

"You did?"

"Yeah, see, I didn't stay with the group the whole time. I sketched." She flipped through her pad as proof. "And I took a long walk. It's so beautiful. You did an incredible job."

"Thank you."

Her heart swelled with feelings and she wanted him to know some of them. "You're a loyal man. Your family must have been very proud of you."

"You didn't know me when I was a teenager."

"Same here. We probably would've hated each other."

"I find that hard to believe. On my end anyway." He dropped hint after hint about her, yet didn't bring up the subject she wanted most to have a conversation about— where they stood. Where did they stand? "Though you would have been way too young for me then."

"I was speaking theoretically. Anyway, if you hadn't

built the college and decided to have someone paint a mural—" *and if I'd never gotten pregnant* "—we would never have met."

"Pretty damn good decision on my part, wouldn't you say?"

She smiled and touched his arm; the sexual spark between them never faltered. "Outstanding."

After a quick shared smile, all seeming forgiven and glances promising more to come, things grew quiet again. It was clear he wasn't ready to talk about "them." Not now, after a taxing day dealing with ancient spirits and chanting protestors and new girlfriends standing with the wrong side.

But there was too much on Marta's mind to keep quiet, so it took all her strength to do so. She'd cut Leif a break for now and change the subject. She could push the man only so far.

She turned toward him, curiosity taking over her thoughts. "What did you find out?"

He chewed his lower lip in thought, then turned his head to her. "That no mystery trunk is worth disrupting a town or a cemetery over." Then immediately he looked back to the winding road.

"What do you mean?"

"I'm telling the committee when we meet tomorrow night that I found a dense deposit of bones, which I did." He stared straight ahead.

"And?"

"There may have been a trunk somewhere around there, too, but since I funded the study, I decided not to go blindly hunting for it, to leave things as they are in respect of the grounds. I won't mention that part—" he pinned her with flashing eyes "—and I hope you won't, either."

Subject closed. He didn't find a trunk, yet he hadn't really tried to find it once he'd discovered the bones. He trusted her with his secret. Now she knew more than ever he was an honorable man willing to do whatever was necessary for the greater good of his town. His study would be inconclusive for a pirate trunk.

He continued to drive, and Marta had yet another reason to love and admire the man. She turned her head and, looking out the window, smiled.

That night, while Leif showered and cleaned up, Marta made a simple meal of scrambled eggs with diced vegetables and cheese, toast and fruit, thinking how domestic she was and smiling the whole time. Leif had put an entirely new spin on the phrase *mi casa es su casa*. She felt completely at home here.

During dinner, choosing to talk about the family bench she'd visited instead of the elephant in the room— the digging at the burial ground—she got a phone call. Seeing who it was, she excused herself and went into the living room to take it. Leif watched her as Chip and Dale followed.

"Marta, it's Manny. How are you?"

Manuel Ortega was the Sedona historian and local quirky TV personality, his specialty being interview vignettes. The town joked and called him the Hispanic version of PBS's Huell Howser, one man with a cameraman and a hand microphone out to discover the state. Ask a question into the mic, then push it into the interviewee's face for an answer, over and over and over. Old school and loads of fun.

"I'm fine. What can I do for you?"

"I've heard about the mural you're painting for Heart-landia, and I want to bring a film crew to interview you."

"Wow, that's a surprise." She'd get to be the one under the spotlight?

"I thought it would be a great angle to be there for the finish. Is anything planned with the city? An unveiling?"

"Good question." She gave a nervous laugh, realizing she didn't have a clue if anything was planned or not. "I mean, I am almost finished, but I don't know about an unveiling or anything."

"Would next week be too soon to come?"

"No. I don't see why not. I've only got one last scene to paint and plan to start that tomorrow."

Leif hadn't *tried* to listen in to Marta's conversation, and it wasn't as though she was hiding anything from him, but she'd started pacing in the other room and one sentence stood out as she passed the large arch separating the living room from the dining room.

"I've only got one last scene to paint."

That certainly hit home. She was almost finished with the mural and would be returning to Sedona sooner than he'd expected. He fought back a spark of panic.

She'd laid down the rules for their relationship—no strings. Yet here he sat, all tangled up in strings since letting go and getting involved with her. Up until now he figured if she'd made the guidelines, she'd have to be the one to change them, but maybe it was time to confront her, see where they stood and if she was anywhere close to feeling the way he did. If so, it was time to come up with some new plans.

The thought of confronting her scared the living daylights out of him. What in the hell was he thinking? He shouldn't even consider changing anything until he was ready to admit he loved her. Did he love her? If he wasn't ready to admit he loved her, how would he be able to open his heart to her child? And even if he was ready to admit his love, would he be ready to be an automatic parent? Hell, could he even be a *good enough* parent for her baby?

Once upon a time, Ellen had believed he'd make a great father. Back then he'd believed it, too, but he was a lot older now.

Standing, he paced, too, his mind spinning with thoughts like plates on poles, but he disguised it by clearing the dishes from the table.

Calm down. He didn't even know if Marta had feelings anywhere near the same as him. She'd made the rules and, as far as he could tell, didn't have any plans to change them. At least she hadn't given him any indication in that regard.

Based on one single sentence indicating the project was almost done, his thoughts had launched out of control. He needed to get a grip, and more important, he needed to talk to someone who might know and understand how he was feeling.

One guy came to mind, a man who'd been through the ringer during and after his divorce. The good doctor, Kent Larson.

He removed his cell phone from his pocket and dialed Kent's number. Before Marta ended her call, he'd already made plans to have breakfast with Kent.

"You won't believe what just happened," she said, rushing into the kitchen to help dry the dishes he'd been washing like a madman. She didn't wait for his response.

"My hometown TV station is going to come and film me finishing the mural. This will be great promo for my art studio and store."

She looked flushed and excited, and Leif's heart sank a little because she also seemed to already have one foot, emotionally speaking, out the door.

Maybe he'd waited too long to tell her how he felt and had already blown it. "That's wonderful. When are they coming?" He fudged his way through his response, doing his best to appear excited for her good fortune. He didn't want to put a damper on her moment to shine.

"Next week."

"Great." Of course he was happy that she was getting some exposure in the media—he wanted her to be successful in her career—but it was the personal part, the going-back-home part—*the leaving-him-behind part*—that ached like a kick to the solar plexus.

The next morning at seven-thirty Leif met up with Kent at the Hartalanda Café in the center of town. Kent was dressed in slacks, shirt and tie for work at his medical clinic. They grabbed a table by the window and ordered coffee right off.

"What's up?" Kent got right to the point.

"I need some perspective and you seem like the right man to give it to me."

"Then I hope I can help."

The waitress brought mugs of hot coffee and took their orders, and Leif sampled the brew before laying his concerns on the line.

"So I've fallen for Marta." He shrugged off the mega confession. "It wasn't supposed to happen, but it did.

She's an incredible woman, and, well, I need some advice."

A lazy smile stretched across Kent's face. "Sounds as though it might be too late for advice."

Leif looked briefly at the ceiling, a sad, halfhearted laugh rolling out of his mouth. "Isn't that the truth?" He put his mug down and played with his fork. "How did you do it? I mean, after your wife left and you met Desi. How did you have the guts to just go for it again?"

It was Kent's turn to give the rueful laugh. "I didn't. Desi got that bright idea, and I resisted from the get-go."

"See, that's why I knew you'd understand."

"My advice is don't be a fool and drag your feet like I did. If you're thinking Marta is a woman you want to be with, go for it."

Leif felt a sheepish expression form on his face. "The thing is, I already have fallen for her, and I'm not sure she's in the same place I am. I mean, she's the first woman I've been with since Ellen, and maybe I got too wrapped up with her or something. Maybe I misunderstood her signals. How can you tell when a lady is into you?"

Kent sat back in his chair as the waitress brought their breakfasts with a benign smile. "Question of the century."

Leif didn't feel particularly hungry, but he made an unenthusiastic attempt to shovel in some pancakes and bacon. "Like I said, she's incredible, and I can't imagine...well, the way we are when we're together..." He put down his fork. "What I mean is, she can't be faking it. You know?"

Kent had his doctor face on. "You've got it bad. Have you told her?"

"Hell no. I've been out of the dating world for so long, I don't know how things work these days. Besides, she seems like such a modern woman, whatever that is."

"I'm not laughing at you," Kent said after smirking. "I know exactly how you feel. Felt the same way. The thing is, Desi was very persistent and, well, I'm a red-blooded guy, so…"

"Yeah, that's not the problem. It's the next part. The 'letting her know how I feel' part."

"Don't do what I did and come off all overbearing and completely unperceptive."

"So how did you find out if she loved you?"

"I tested the waters. Talked about how good we'd be as a couple. How much Steven adored her. That kind of thing. Eventually, she got the point and came around."

"Desi was going to leave town, too, wasn't she?"

"That's what I thought. Turns out she was just waiting for an invitation to stay."

Now, that made sense. Why should Marta stick around if she hadn't been invited and she had a place to go home to? How dense had Leif become during his hibernation?

Leif ate more of his pancakes, thinking about a way to first test the waters with Marta before laying it all out there. Their situation was different from Kent and Desi's because Marta was pregnant. *Wait! That's the test.* The father of her baby hadn't taken any interest. What if Leif told her his honest thoughts about her pregnancy? That he welcomed it. That he'd always wanted a big family. Maybe then he could win her trust and open the door to a long-term relationship. Or maybe he'd better start by just opening the door, see how she responded to that, then move on to the pregnancy.

"Thanks, man. You've helped me put some things into perspective."

"From the look on your face, you seem miserable." Kent had cleaned his plate and topped it off with a long draw from his mug of coffee. "Just let me say that opening up to love again isn't a death sentence. What I found out was it was a ticket back to life. Don't know what I'd do without Desi. Wait. Yes I do, I'd still be a shell. Lonely and miserable."

Leif nodded and took another drink of coffee. He could completely relate to being a shell of a man. It had been his MO ever since Ellen had died.

That night, Leif intended to make sure the committee meeting was short and sweet.

"Before we get started, I have a quick question," he said. "Are there any plans for an unveiling when the mural is finished?" Which it almost was. Even before he'd built the outer protection for the walls, he'd known she needed something better than ordinary ladders, so he'd loaned her a smaller-scale ladder scaffold, which essentially blocked out whichever part of the mural she worked on. Marta had told him she'd taken to leaving the finished portions of the walls behind the barrier he'd built, which hid the entire view, but he knew the mural was just about complete.

Elke spoke right up. "Yes. I've been working with the school administration and head of the art department. We plan a reveal for the college students first, then we'll open it up for a public walk-by. We're just waiting for Marta to give us a tentative date."

"Good. And I assume the newspaper will cover that."

"Oh, you bet. This is a first, and we're all thrilled with what we've seen so far."

For some crazy reason, hearing Elke's enthusiasm made pride well up inside Leif for Marta's accomplishments, even though theoretically he'd only played a small role by sponsoring the project.

"Okay, then, great. I guess we can get on with the purpose of the meeting." He glanced around the table at the six sets of eyes watching him and waiting for his report.

"Here are some of the pictures I snapped with the industrial fiber-optic scope." He took them from the folder and passed them around the table like show and tell. "The white areas are bones. Piles and piles of bones. Elke has examined the photographs and agrees that they prove this area was truly a burial ground. Evidently those bones are what we originally found with the thermography study." He produced a copy of the original map and another of the burial ground, then used a pencil to point to the area being discussed. "Nathaniel Prince's handmade map seemed to point to the same spot, right here, yet this is what we discovered. Now, we could explore other nearby areas, even though there wasn't any indication of anything else in this vicinity under thermography, but it would be a crapshoot and would probably be futile. Oh, and it would really tick off a lot of people, as we've already found out."

Leif knew he would be preaching to the choir for half of the group with his next comment, so he concentrated on the small business and Maritime Museum representatives on the committee. "At the risk of digging wider and deeper without strong evidence for finding anything based on the thermography report and upsetting almost half of the town, I move that we suspend further investigation."

Silence fell over the room, and a few pairs of eyes squinted and re-examined the round photographs as seen through a three-centimeter industrial, fiber-optic camera. After a few more minutes of passing around the results and quiet mutterings, Gerda Rask suggested the committee take another vote.

When he got home that night Marta wasn't there and the house felt cold and drab. He speed-dialed her cell phone.

"Hi!" she said.

"Hey, I was wondering if I should fix a late dinner."

"Actually, I'm with Lilly and Desi and we're in Astoria at their crafter's market. We already ate here."

"Okay." A pang of disappointment drew his attention. "Sounds good." Astoria was the next town over and was noted for the big weekly farmer and crafter market. "I guess I'll see you later, then."

"Most definitely."

Her enthusiastic response took the edge off his original reaction, and he ended the call with a smile.

Chip and Dale needed feeding and a walk, so he had things to keep him busy, but when he came back into the house and ate soup from a can and cheese toast, the empty house felt way too big. How the hell had he lived here by himself for so many years? Did he really want to ever do that again?

He went upstairs, and because the door to the studio was open and he missed Marta filling up his house with life and her freewheeling spirit, he walked inside. How would the room, overflowing with supplies and paint, feel after she left?

A trickle of anxiety worked its way up his spine. He didn't want to think about it. Not yet.

There was an easel facing the largest window and he walked around to see what she'd been painting, other than the mural. His jaw dropped. It was a half-finished portrait of him, smiling like he couldn't remember doing in years—only since Marta had come into his life had he started up again. Chip and Dale were sketched in the background, waiting their turn to be made immortal. A small photograph was tacked to the wood of the easel. It was him, on the day when he'd first taken her to the Ringmuren, the day he'd also shown her his mother's memorial bench.

Was this a going-away gift? Something to remember her by?

Leif loathed the sound of *remember* and *her* in the same sentence.

The soup he'd just eaten must have had too many tomatoes in it, because his stomach had suddenly turned sour.

If she left, he should at least be prepared with a parting gift of his own. But what?

A little after nine, Marta let herself in. Leif had on the evening news while he carved a small piece of teak wood. He quickly folded the towel over his lap and hid the figure he'd started under the chair, then clicked off the TV when she stepped into the room.

Looking happy and invigorated, she approached with a wide smile and some small bags. She bent and kissed him. He savored the kiss. Who knew how much longer he'd get them?

"How'd it go?" he asked.

"We had fun. Look." She wiggled the dangling bead and stone earrings from her lobes. "I got these and several pairs more from this supertalented jewelry maker."

"Nice. I like them."

She sat on his lap and ruffled through the bags, soon finding what else she'd hunted for. "I got this for you."

She handed him a necklace.

"Very nice. What is it?"

She cuffed his shoulder playfully. "It's a moon-mask necklace." She held it before his face by the thick leather strings so he could see it better. "It's made of abalone shell and carved wood."

As the pendant hung and shifted in the lamplight, he was taken by the changing colors and designs from the amazing seashell. It was enclosed by a delicate wood carving, with a funny moon face superimposed over the abalone, making the moon look as though it was ready to blow out a big wind onto the earth.

"That's really nice. Thank you. But you do realize I don't wear necklaces."

She undid the special leather knot and slipped the necklace over Leif's head. "You do now. When I saw this, I had to get it for you. It's made by a Chinook artist. He said the moon is a prophet with the desire to make the world a better place. I'm not saying you're a prophet or anything, but you make the world a better place. You build beautiful homes and colleges. Places where people can grow and be happy. So I said, 'Marta, you've got to buy this for Leif.'" She laughed insecurely, like a young girl, yet seeming so delighted with herself and the fanciful gift she'd given him.

"I like it." Her gesture touched a tender spot inside. "Thank you very much."

She rested her head on his shoulder and sighed. "I'm glad you like it."

They stayed quietly like that for a few moments, resting peacefully, and as his one hand skimmed her arm, Leif mindlessly fingered the handcrafted pendant with the other, wondering if this might be a second going-away gift from Marta. The portrait being the first, and this one, a predeparture gift. Now that he had a clear vision of what he wanted to make for her, plus a new project that just jumped to mind—a cradle—he'd better get moving on that carving so he'd have time to tackle the second.

With the insecure thoughts upending his peace, and because the right words hadn't come, he had a sudden need to take her to bed and make love to her, to prove how he felt about her. And as Kent had strongly advised him, there was no time like the present to get his point across.

Chapter Ten

Right there on the living room floor, on the rug in front of the fireplace—a rug he'd always thought of as useless until this perfect moment—Leif's desperate need to be inside Marta rushed things along. He stripped her and just as quickly undressed himself, leaving his new necklace in place so she'd notice.

With roaming hands reveling over the velvet softness of her skin, the feel of her breasts and abdomen, he used his mouth to make love to her. He opened her and made her ready for him. From all signs, she was as frantic for him as he was for her. Naked except for her new earrings, she looked like a seductive muse. His personal work of art.

He dazzled her with his tongue in all the best places, and when he settled between her legs, she dug into his hair, placing him just so.

He glanced up, and her silky olive-toned skin was slick with sheen. "You're so beautiful."

"So are you," she whispered.

Eager to please, he took her to the limit with his mouth, then, shifting upward, making eye contact before kissing her, he thrust inside, skydiving nearly straight off the cliff. First their bodies crashed together with need, but soon they found their rhythm and rode the flood of sensations on and on and on to the edge. Lingering there barely long enough to catch a breath, they fast-forwarded to whiteout bliss.

When he'd recovered, he lifted her from the thick and fuzzy area rug on the hardwood floor and carried her up the stairs to his bed.

Sweaty and spent from sex, they cuddled in bed under ribbons of full moonlight. Leif inhaled Marta's scent— sex, sweat and cinnamon spice—wondering when she left if he would ever forget her fragrance or the taste of her.

While they'd made love he'd noticed her baby bump had become more pronounced. Could the pregnancy grow that much from one week to the next? Was it crazy to wish the kid was his?

Now fascinated with the growth, his hand wandered to her belly and rubbed lightly. Remembering his conversation with Kent that morning, he thought maybe it was time to test the waters on their relationship.

"What are your plans after the mural's done?" His hand went still on her pregnant tummy.

She sighed. "I've got so much to catch up on back home. And no one knows I'm pregnant yet, so I suppose I'll have to deal with that. I should make a special trip to Phoenix to tell my father, too."

He went onto his elbow and looked square into her eyes. "Just so you know, if you want to stick around for a while, the door's always open here." There, he'd said it. And now he held his breath. The thought had occurred to him on several occasions, yet he hadn't had the nerve to approach the topic until Kent had told him he needed to. If he got a positive response, he'd mention the baby.

Her breath went still, a cautious look formed in her eyes. "Thank you," she said, locking the now questioning gaze onto his. "Sometimes I wish things could be different."

He searched her eyes, trying to figure out the meaning of *sometimes*.

"Sometimes? Like when you're being logical or realistic? Sometimes when you want to run away from it all, or sometimes when you think about sticking around Heartlandia?" *Or sometimes when you think you might be falling in love?* The way he'd meant it and the way he felt.

"All of the above."

He swallowed and pulled her close.

Maybe *sometimes* was a sign she was changing her mind, and that was all he could ask for now. In that case, patience was what he needed.

Yeah, too bad things weren't different, but... "They could be."

She pulled back from the hug, and from the corner of her eye she gave him an odd glance. "Could be? What could be?"

"Different. Things could be different."

"With the wave of a wand? Oh, I wish I believed in fairy tales."

Marta was an independent woman, unafraid to take on whatever life gave her. That was the impression she'd given him from the start. Under challenge in his personal life, Leif had withdrawn from the living; he'd curled into a ball and emotionally shut out the world…until Marta had forced him out. Marta, however, was a survivor. She didn't need him or anyone to make her complete.

Yet…sometimes. He held her tighter, wishing he could read her mind, still too unsure to say, "Why don't we give it a try?" How lame was that when *try* was the weakest word he knew? A person either did things or they didn't. The last thing she needed from him was a limp-wristed try. No. She deserved much better. "Is that how you see us, a fairy tale?"

"Strange woman shows up in town, pregnant, meets a prince of a guy…and they lived…" She flopped onto her pillow, back of hand to forehead. "Happily."

It had been her idea for them to get together—no strings. She'd made it very clear. And until he had more to offer than a good-hearted *try*, he'd have to honor that. "Sounds like a good story to me."

"As the saying goes—" she glanced wistfully at him "—we'll always have Heartlandia."

She's gone cynical. I already sound like a memory.

"And the door will always be open." His body ached for hers. How much longer would she be around to love? He reached out and found her, as heat and sparks and electricity arced over, around and through them, and he did the one thing they both perfectly understood—he made love to her again.

In the dark, after giving her body completely and un-hesitatingly to Leif, Marta couldn't get her hopes up. Leif had taken a huge risk by inviting her to stick around. It blew her mind. And she'd played it down. True, what he'd said had been a major step in the right direction, but there was so much farther for him to go and their time together was running out. He'd taken her offer of "just for now" to heart, even offered to extend it. But she was giving up on those open-ended relationships now, and she'd promised her mother.

The baby had to come first from now on.

But hadn't Leif proved the other night, with his Chip and Dale story, to accept package deals?

If only he could see the package deal waiting in his arms.

Even though she'd been the one to lay down the rules, it would have to be up to him to change "just for now" into forever, the three of them. Because she couldn't and wouldn't set herself up for more heartbreak. Leif would have to be the one to reach out to her; this was his turf. He'd invited her to stay on, but what about the baby?

Each day she found herself more and more open to the possibility of staying with Leif. He'd been the one to suffer the most from love and losing. She had to consider that and respect his reluctance to love again. She might be pregnant, but he had the biggest risk to take by opening his heart. And his invitation was a huge step in the right direction.

Truth was, as bold a facade as she wore, she couldn't take a second rejection for her and the baby. It would break her spirit, and more now than ever, her baby would need a completely strong and capable mother if it was to be just the two of them. She'd be the sole provider, and that was why Manny's TV interview would be so important to her career away from Lawrence. Out on her own. Without a benefactor. Completely independent.

Hers and Leif's was a delicate situation. If she wasn't

pregnant, things could be different; they could be long-distance lovers, take things as they came. But she'd had a long talk with her mother. Maybe it was her turn to let her secret thoughts be known—that she was in love with him and expected more than "the door's open."

Why not tell him now?

"Leif?" she whispered.

Leif had drifted off to sleep. Deep sleep. She wasn't surprised after the vigorous effort he'd put into making love…twice. She smiled and lifted her head, then studied his face, having already memorized all the lines and angles. She painted his portrait from a photograph, but when her job was done, before she left Heartlandia, if he let her go, she wanted to be able to paint him perfectly again…from memory.

Manny Ortega made a big splash entry onto the college campus in his Sedona TV news van the Monday after Thanksgiving. The "La Cucaracha" horn honk nearly threw Marta from the scaffolding. She was putting some finishing touches on the panel depicting the town monument her grandfather had sculpted.

After her heart settled and she figured out who it was, she waved.

The van came to an abrupt stop and the short and wide Manny popped out from the passenger side. *"Buenos dias, muchacha. Que paso?"* His normally curly hair was cropped close to his head.

"Hi. How are you?" She cleaned her hands, took off her mask and climbed down from the ladder scaffold. They hugged like old friends, though they were only acquaintances back home. She hitched her thumb over her shoulder. "So what do you think?"

"Wow, this looks beautiful. You'll have to paint one for Sedona. I know the perfect spot."

"To be honest, I prefer painting on canvas, but this has been a great experience." She'd worn loose-fitting overalls in the hopes of playing down the pregnancy during the interview. Tongues would wag soon enough back home; she didn't need to rush the gossip along just yet.

"Don't say another word until we get set up. Save all your thoughts for our interview, okay?"

"Sure."

It took another half hour for Manny and the camera guy to prepare. In the meantime, Desi utilized the brawn of a couple of the college football players who'd volunteered to help slide back all of the barriers from the rest of the mural. Since the town-monument vandalism, she'd taken to leaving the rest of the mural covered, even when she worked on the newest panel.

"Wow, this is something, *mujer.*" Manny stood, arms akimbo, gaping at all of her hard work, making her feel proud of the effort. "Let's pan out from right here," he said to his partner, using his thumbs and index fingers to make a frame and looking inside. Back to business, he spent a couple of minutes discussing the best shots and deciding where Marta should stand and what lighting was best. As they discussed the interview, Marta and Manny slipped easily into speaking Spanish, the language her grandmother had taught her, and once everything was settled, before she realized it the tape was rolling and she needed to switch back to English again.

Halfway through the interview a figure moved through the gathering group of curious onlookers. She recognized Leif immediately. She glanced at him and he gave a friendly wave. Unable to do more, she blinked and nodded while answering Manny's latest question.

"What's going to be your next project?" Manny asked, then moved the microphone toward her.

Having a baby?

"Well, a certain Sedona representative suggested I paint another mural for my own hometown." Trying her best to be personable for the interview, she teased.

Their interchange went on for several more minutes as he asked her to explain the meaning of each portion of the panel. Then he threw her a curveball.

"So what will you paint for Sedona?"

"Wow, I'll have to give it some thought. Is that a real offer?" She grinned.

"As a matter of fact it is. I've been given the go-ahead to tell you a secret donor has funded the town mural for Sedona. What do you think?"

"I can't believe it!" Her hands flew to her cheeks. "How exciting."

The camera moved in close, and from Manny's ear-to-ear grin, he couldn't have looked happier with her reaction. She'd faked it, though. The questions swirled in her head, and it took extra concentration to focus on the interview again. After a few more questions and answers the interview ended, and boy was she glad. Having never been through anything like this before, she was worn out and stressed. One thought in particular nagged at her.

Was Lawrence behind this new offer, still trying to keep her under his thumb? If so, she'd never consent. Knowing who funded the mural would have to be included in her contract.

Marta glanced up, searching for Leif in the group of onlookers.

But he was nowhere around.

They'd shared a wonderful Thanksgiving with Gerda, Desi, Kent and his son, Steven. But Leif hadn't again broached the subject of her staying on after the mural again or becoming part of her package-deal condition. She couldn't very well force the topic. It was a good thing she hadn't told him she loved him. Opening his life to a ready-made family would have to be completely up to him. Because he was an honorable guy, she didn't want to influence his thinking and have him do the right thing on her behalf, like accepting a package deal when all he really wanted was the lady.

She'd spent the entire Thanksgiving weekend painting the mural undisturbed by students, other than the ones who'd volunteered to help. Because Gunnar had had some time off from the police department, he and Leif had worked nonstop on Lilly's teahouse.

These were good times. Thriving times. Yet their relationship had seemed to come to a standstill. Great sex, sure. The door had been left open for extending that, but there'd been no talk about the real future.

"I'm staying at the Heritage Hotel," Manny said after they finished the interview. "Why don't you join me for dinner tonight?"

Marta knew Manny's wife of thirtysomething years from the artist guild and understood him to be a proud grandfather, so she knew this wasn't a come-on. He was simply asking her to dinner.

A part of her wanted to run it by Leif, which seemed absurd for an independent woman, but there it was. He'd sneaked into her life on yet another level. "That'd be fun. Thanks."

After Manny and his cameraman broke down their

equipment and left, Marta couldn't concentrate to paint anymore and the day was only half-over. When the students Desi had assigned showed up for their after-lunch detail, she asked them to help her put things away and cover the mural with Leif's barrier on wheels.

Who would fund a mural in Sedona? She hoped it wasn't Lawrence and prayed it wasn't Leif trying to get rid of her. She wasn't ready to go home to Sedona, to face the people who didn't even know she was pregnant yet. And the last person she wanted to ever see again was Lawrence.

After her talk with her mother, she couldn't very well leave Heartlandia without being straightforward and letting Leif know how she felt about him.

Filled with confusing thoughts, restless and anxious, she took a short walk to think things through. More firm than ever, the only way she'd consent to paint a mural in Sedona was if Lawrence had nothing to do with it.

She bought some juice at the student store, then noticed a sign with an arrow pointing toward the Memorial Rose Garden. It was on the main path, and having a hunch, she followed it. The path soon forked, one way toward the English department buildings, the other toward the hillside. It was an easy choice, because that was toward the rose garden.

The campus was built on rolling slopes with commons all around and a beautiful view of the Columbia River off in the distance. She sipped her juice, never getting tired of looking at that river. Wandering farther and farther from the buildings, still following the arrows, she got lost in her thoughts. What if Leif funded the Sedona project as an easy way to let her go? What would she do then? Soon overcome with amazing scents—fragrant roses—she dropped that line of insecure thinking and found herself at the secluded garden on the outermost portion of the college.

And there she saw it—a beautifully carved wooden bench. Unlike the other two across town, this one was ornate and girlie. It was also a swing hanging from a rustic and sturdy frame made entirely from tree branches.

The abundance of roses scented the air, almost burning her nostrils, or maybe it was the rush of emotion fizzing through her body on seeing the swing. Walking solemnly toward the bench, she sensed an almost sacred aura around it. This was Ellen's. Leif had built and put it here with every ounce of love he possessed. She stepped closer to read the fancy calligraphy carved on a plaque resting atop a varnished tree-stump pedestal. "In memory of Ellen Andersen, the love of my life. Never to be forgotten."

The words hit like a kick behind the knees. Marta needed to sit down but didn't dare sit on Ellen's bench. She rushed away, toward the granite water fountain, leaned over for a drink as her own tears spilled into the water, then found a standard metal bench to recover.

One specific early conversation with Leif came to mind.

"How come you've never—" She'd ventured to ask a question that hadn't mattered nearly as much then as it did now.

Somehow, he'd known exactly what she was asking. "Remarried?"

It had turned out she wasn't the only one who could read minds and cut people off midsentence. "Because I can't imagine ever replacing her. I don't see how anyone can ever measure up. No woman wants to settle for replacement status."

Marta finally hoped for the love of her life, the kind of love her parents shared, but Leif had already found and lost his. She was pregnant with another man's baby, yet she had the crazy notion that a man like Leif, as loyal and devoted as they came, could see her for what she was—a woman in love with him. Someone willing to venture into a new life together. With him. If he was open to it.

From the start Marta must have come off as a seductress to Leif, preaching free love without strings. She wouldn't deny it was about time the man lived again, and she took pride in being a part of his reawakening. But only looking for a distraction to ward off the sting of Lawrence's rejection at the time, she hadn't bargained on falling for Leif. Now the big question was, would he take a chance on loving her and the baby, or was he even capable of it?

She glanced over her shoulder at the magnificent swing, the huge reminder of what stood between her and Leif, then looked down at her stomach, the other growing reminder why the odds were stacked against them.

Leif drove and drove. He had to keep moving, to occupy his mind, or his thoughts would eat at him. Marta had been happy and charming during the interview. Full of life and hope. Hell, she already had a job lined up back home. Why in the world would a bright light of a woman like that want to tie herself down with a ghost like him?

She'd practically had to pry him out of his rut, but damn if dangling sex like a carrot hadn't finally done the trick. Was that all that it was to her? And there was nothing wrong with that if it was. He was the jerk who'd projected emotions into the mix. They'd had a great thing going, the two of them, but he'd slipped up, let something that was never supposed to happen again occur—he'd fallen in love. Keeping it quiet was a cop-out, and now he'd have to tell her and take the consequences because he had to know one way or the other how she felt about him before she left. But the biggest question of all was, did he have the nerve to love again when life was a gamble and no one, not even Marta with her mind-reading ways, could predict what the future held? Did he have the strength to deal with losing love again?

Why did he feel as if he'd just been punched?

He drove in circles around a small park, then on to the houseboat section of town as he made plans on how and when to tell her how he felt. He couldn't call himself a man if he didn't. By his calculations, because the big reveal was planned for Monday next week, she'd be out of here by early December. Which gave him exactly this weekend to make his move.

His cell phone rang. Only then did he realize he'd been driving around aimlessly for a couple of hours. The dogs hadn't even complained.

"Leif? It's Marta. Listen, Manny Ortega has asked me to join him for dinner tonight, so I wanted to give you a heads-up."

He did his best not to sound disappointed. After all, she was a freewheeling, independent woman who didn't need a sad sack of a guy dragging her down. "Hey, that sounds great. Have a good time."

Well, he could check off tonight.

Maybe he better wait until after the big mural reveal before he announced how he really felt about her. The last thing he wanted to do was compete with her painting. Or come off like a jealous, crazed lover. When Leif finally came clean with his feelings, he wanted Marta's undivided attention.

In the meantime he had the night to get busy with his carving for Marta—a chunk of teakwood that had mysteriously taken on a life of its own. Then he'd get to work on the crib. It was actually a good thing she wouldn't be home tonight because he had so much to do.

Hours later, Leif lay in bed unable to sleep. It was almost one and Marta hadn't come home yet. He trusted her when she'd explained that Manny was a friend from her hometown. But what bothered him was how obviously she missed home. Manny had asked her to dinner and she'd leaped at the chance.

He heard the front door open. The dogs stirred and lightly whined. "It's okay, guys." The three of them lay quiet and listened as steps came up the stairs.

Leif's heart stuttered with disappointment when he realized she'd gone on to her own room.

The next morning felt like going back to square one, day one. Leif met up with Marta in the kitchen, a tentative smile on her face.

"Good morning," she said, already dressed in her work overalls. "I'm going to have to spend the rest of the week working like a madwoman on all of the finishing touches to the mural."

"I'd offer to help, but I promised Lilly I'd work on her teahouse and get it done before her parents come to visit for New Year's."

"I understand."

He found a sponge and wiped up some crumbs on the counter. "Got home late last night."

She nodded. "We got carried away with gossip from back home." She poured cereal into a bowl, cut up a banana on top and added milk. "The crazy man wants to stay on and film the reveal and interview some of the locals." She spooned a bite and crunched. "Also, I asked Manny to help me put my shop for sale or lease since he has so many connections in Sedona. From now on I just want to concentrate on painting."

"When are you planning to leave?"

"My flight is a couple of days after the unveiling."

He poured coffee from a curiously quivering carafe. She'd already bought her ticket home, even though he'd invited her to stay on awhile. "So soon?"

She touched his back; he turned and found her unsure gaze concentrating on his eyes. "I have a lot to take care of back home. It's been building up ever since I've been here. I can't dump all the responsibilities on my assistants. And I need to see my own doctor—not that I don't appreciate Kent's doing the obstetrical care."

"I understand." At least he was *trying* to understand. There was that lousy word again. It really was useless because no way, with all the *trying* in the world, did he understand. Not by a long shot.

How had things morphed so abruptly into this awkward, giant step back to the beginning? He took her hand and gently rubbed the palm with his thumb. "I missed you last night."

Her eyes cast downward. "It was late. I didn't want to wake you."

Something had changed between them, and he was clueless. "You wouldn't have."

Her thick lashes lifted, and those mink-warm eyes gazed earnestly into his. "Come sleep in my bed tonight."

His thumb stopped circling the meat of her palm. Why the sudden test? He shut down. Went still. "Not sure I'm ready."

"Why not, Leif?"

His knee-jerk reaction was to say, "You know why," but he bit it back. A long silence stretched on as she searched his eyes for an honest answer. One he wasn't prepared to give. He ground his molars tightly together while the elephant sat smack in the middle of the room.

Ellen.

Marta deserved an answer.

"I guess I'm still not ready to go there." *To love and lose, to withstand gut-wrenching pain, emptiness so deep I can't breathe. Not knowing how to go on living.*

She canted her head as if his words hurt her ears. "I see."

Disappointment lingered in the kitchen like a stale coffee. She'd tested him. He'd failed. He wasn't prepared to make the leap. Would he ever get over the loss that came with love?

But they both had obligations and work to do. He couldn't deal with the major issue still keeping them apart in a two-minute conversation on the go in the kitchen, especially when Marta seemed to already have one foot back home in Sedona. Already half-gone.

"Will you be home tonight?" Like a fool in love, he still craved her company, but he let her remove her hand from his.

"I plan to be."

"I'll grill something for dinner."

"Okay."

Civil, and sad. They went about their day independent from each other.

That night Marta apologized to Leif over the phone. Manny had asked her to take him to Lincoln's restaurant, saying he wanted to experience the nightlife in Heartlandia. Desi had even agreed to play the piano, even though it wasn't the weekend. Manny planned to film the scene for his show, too.

The truth was, Marta had been asking Leif to take her there for weeks, especially after the engagement party. Leif had figured he had plenty of time to take Marta, and honestly, he liked keeping her all to himself. Turned out he was wrong about having all the time in the world, and his selfishness had come back to kick him in the teeth.

Marta didn't ask Leif to join them, and it cut deep.

"I won't be late," she said over the phone.

"Stay out as long as you want," he said, meaning to sound perfectly fine with her enjoying herself without him, but it didn't come out anywhere near the way he'd meant. The only positive point out of the situation that night was he got a lot of work done on the cradle.

After sleeping in her room the rest of the week, obviously knowing Leif wouldn't go there, on Sunday Marta asked him to help with the final stage of the mural.

Because it was a cloudy morning, he wore a sweatshirt and she a bulky fisherman's sweater she'd bought from a knitting store in town. They bought takeout coffee, one high octane, the other decaf, and croissants from the local bakery, though Leif didn't have much of an appetite. From the way Marta picked at her croissant, she didn't, either.

"Elke got the bright idea to hang a huge curtain over the mural and to rig up a way to draw it up for the reveal. We bought all of this inexpensive material yesterday, enough to cover every inch of the walls. I'll need you to take down the barrier for good."

"What about the risk of someone defacing the mural?"

"Elke has arranged for school security tonight."

"But what about in the future?"

"We agreed it's a painting meant to be shared with all, not kept locked away."

As if on cue, Elke and Ben arrived by car, apparently having the same idea as Leif and Marta from the looks of takeout coffee cups and a bag in their hands.

"Hi!" Elke said, excitement brightening her face.

As they greeted each other, several more people arrived to help with the day's project, padding the distance ever expanding between them.

For the next several hours Leif and Ben broke down the sliding wood barrier. Elke and Marta used the scaffolding and held panel after panel of the sky-blue shiny polyester material in place as a male student used an industrial-strength stapler to tack it to the wood trim.

Afterward, several students from the theater arts and set design classes stitched the panels together and rigged up a way to raise the curtain using triple-braided cord every five feet. Someone explained to Leif the technique they'd used was makeshift Roman shade, whatever that meant. Leif nodded and pretended he understood. The end result was a scalloped valance accentuating the beautiful mixture of colors in Marta's rich and masterful mural, and Leif was impressed with the resourceful students.

The group applauded at the first rehearsal, and Leif snapped a panoramic picture on his phone, making sure to include Marta standing on the sideline, a burst of pride sharpening her gorgeous smile. Then he walked over and waited his turn to hug her.

"This is so fantastic," he whispered over her ear, loving the way she felt, intensifying how much he'd missed holding her. She held tightly, too.

Because of the group gathered around, Leif only kissed Marta lightly, but her lips seemed to welcome his. At least it was something. They all ordered fast food for lunch as they worked on the finishing touches, and by the time they'd finished and arrived home, it was dark.

Marta was exhausted, excited and a nervous wreck about Monday.

After a light dinner, Leif brought her some herbal tea—her favorite stress-relief chamomile blend—and a couple of oatmeal cookies where she sat in the living room.

"Thank you," she said, glancing up from her laptop computer.

He kissed the top of her head instead of her mouth, which was where he wanted to kiss her. "Anything I can do?" He hoped she'd catch his double entendre.

"Are you good at writing speeches?"

Well, that had fallen flat. He laughed softly, ruefully. "No. But if you need help relaxing I've got a few ideas." Not above trying to make his point a second time, he went for the obvious.

With every cell in his body he wanted her, but for the past week she had given him no hint of a sign that she wanted him.

As expected, she didn't respond to his less-than-subtle suggestion about making love to ease her tension, but she continued to stare at the computer screen, typing, deleting, *tsk-tsking* and typing more. Loss sneaked into his life like an insidious vapor, sucking the air out of him one breath at a time.

He couldn't very well carve with her in the room, so he went to the garage and put the finishing touches on the cradle, sanded it and prepared to stain the wood the color of Marta's eyes—walnut. He racked his brain trying to figure out how he and Marta had gotten derailed. What had happened? Had he wanted too little? Had she wanted more?

He'd tested the waters, like Kent had suggested, letting her know the door was open for her to stay on. But he hadn't mentioned the baby and, damn it, he should have.

Days had gone by, they'd started sleeping in separate rooms and in a few more days she'd be gone.

He worked furiously on his project and got lost with his own style of art, then was surprisingly happy with the outcome. Next he wanted to get back to the hand sculpture, to start sanding if he hoped to complete and stain it before she left, but not tonight. It was late and he still had to walk the dogs. Tomorrow was a big day for Marta and he needed to be there with his full support.

After caring for the dogs, he went back into the house to find Marta had gone to her room for the night. Instinct told him to go in, climb in the bed with her and hold her all night, but the nagging sense of being shut out stamped down his true desire. She obviously considered that the safe zone. One big question came to mind: When had their "just for now" turned to "is this the end?"

Monday morning, Marta dressed in a long colorful skirt with a white blouse and loose beige jacket to disguise the pregnancy. She wore a pair of silver earrings she'd bought at the craft fair and, on a whim, decided to leave her hair down with an ivory-colored comb holding one side back.

When they met up in the kitchen, she saw that Leif had put on a tweed sport coat, white button-down shirt and a new pair of jeans. Her pulse fluttered, admiring how handsome he looked, how rugged. When she noticed he wore the moon-face necklace on the outside of his shirt, she kissed his cheek.

"You ready for this?" he asked. "Your big day."

"Not nearly enough."

"The mural is beautiful. It's perfect. What are you worried about?"

"Artist insecurity, I guess. We depend on what others think of our work. I have to make a living."

"Realistically all it takes is one person who believes in you."

One person with a lot of cash. The sincerity in his eyes touched her soul, but she had to stop him from saying one more word. He'd said the door was open to stay on, but she was through with benefactors with benefits. "Been there. Done that, Leif. All I got was pregnant." She couldn't open the door to dependence again. She needed to stand on her own two feet. To prove to herself she could do it before she could be worthy of a good man's love.

"About that…" he started.

As he spoke, she inadvertently glanced at her watch. She was running late. "What? I'm sorry, Leif. I wish we had more time to talk now, but we've really got to get going."

She saw his eyes go dark, then shut down. Realizing she was the cause of that look hurt like a knife to the heart, but the clock ticked on.

He quickly recovered and, gentleman that he was, opened the back door for her to step outside first. The dreary weather from yesterday had moved on, leaving a clear, sunny, late-autumn sky, though her outlook as far as Leif was concerned felt socked in with heavy gray clouds. He opened her door and helped her up into the truck cab, then walked around to the other side. Marta took out her laptop and brought up her speech, anything to get her mind off how badly their love affair had turned out. First she'd wanted more from him, now he wanted more of her. Which, because of time constraints, she couldn't give. Another lesson to be learned: no-strings affairs were bogus. They didn't exist. Someone always got hurt. What a lousy idea she'd had. *Yes, Momma, I get it. Remember?*

He started the car and they drove off toward the college.

Since discovering Ellen's bench, Marta understood that Leif had found his one true love early in life and he'd lost her. Maybe in his mind that could never happen again, and Marta couldn't compete with a dead woman. With a setup like that, she'd never come close to being first place in his heart—hadn't he warned her about that when she'd first come on to him?—and the realization had taken her aback. So she'd stayed away from Leif the past several nights.

The question was, could she settle for being a not-quite-good-enough replacement for a dead wife? The answer was no. Even her mother would have approved of that decision.

And she hadn't even touched on the ramifications of being pregnant with another man's baby and how that would affect any long-term relationship with Leif. Theirs was a far too complicated relationship to work out in the short time left.

Yet was she crazy to still hope for his love? Her parents' brand of love.

A tiny voice far, far in the back of her mind whispered yes, so no matter how much she wanted to do otherwise, she'd continue to sleep in her guest room, waiting for Leif to show a sign he'd worked through that barrier... until she left for good.

When they arrived at the college, Leif bussed her lips and smiled. "You're going to knock them dead."

God, the man was ripping out her heart with kindness. "Thank you." She wrapped her arms around his chest, and her clutching at his back was from loss, not nerves.

He held her close and lightly rubbed her back. "Relax, they're going to love you."

Will you love me, Leif? "Thanks." She let go, stood straight, fluffed her hair and smoothed her jacket. "How do I look?"

"Beautiful. As always." His tender smile nearly sent her flying to the sky.

"Thank you. I'll never be able to thank you enough."

She turned and started to walk toward the podium and thought she heard him mumble, "I can think of several ways."

A large crowd had gathered on the sprawling lawn near the history quad. The shiny blue curtain sparkled under the glare, and excitement for the big reveal was palpable. Her nerves ratcheted up another notch.

Gerda explained how things would work and offered her a chair. As she waited, her thoughts returned quickly to Leif.

Today, as she had every day since finding Ellen's

bench, she'd go on with her life, concentrating on what was best for her, her baby and her career. She pasted a smile on her face as her heart pounded and she watched the theater arts students lift the curtain from her mural with only a tiny glitch in the form of one uncooperative rope and panel. They fixed it amazingly fast and hoisted the curtain the rest of the way. The large crowd, including the mayor and the police and fire department chiefs, broke into applause, and she could have sworn she heard scattered gasps of delight. The gratification was bittersweet considering what she stood to lose with Leif.

After the extended applause died down, Mayor Rask introduced her.

Marta used the small portable computer to bring up her speech, though she knew it by heart.

"First off, please forgive me, I'm an artist, not a public speaker." She inhaled, attempting to quell her nerves.

"Earlier this year, when I heard about Heartlandia's quest to find a mural artist to tell your story, I didn't think I stood a chance. I mean, I tend to paint huge canvases, but I'd never painted a whole mural before. But since I was looking for a change in my life, I challenged myself and submitted my name anyway. As they say, no risk, no gain. When the committee found out my grandfather was the artist who sculpted your town monument, they took a closer look at me and my body of work.

"With the guidance of Professor Elke Norling, I've told your history through art. All I can say is, the experience has been life changing. True, we had a little hiccup when I first arrived almost three months ago and the news broke about your town first being discovered by a pirate…" She paused as she heard an uncomfortable titter ripple through the crowd, then continued, "But I incorporated that precipitating incident into my mural and quickly moved on."

She looked up and smiled, her eyes immediately finding and settling on Leif. He smiled encouragingly, though she thought she detected pain in his expression.

"As many of you may already know, this project would have been scrapped without the determination of one man, Leif Andersen. Without his wholehearted belief in the mural, and in me, as well as his financial support, we'd have no reason to celebrate today. Without him, we'd be staring at blank beige stucco walls. He is the visionary who built this college, who wanted art on the walls. I was just the lucky person to get to do the job. And to be honest, that was all it was to me when I first arrived, just a job. But through Leif, I discovered there was so much more here. I hadn't merely been hired—I'd been welcomed and adopted by the town, and he set out to prove it by opening his home to me and by introducing me to so many of you. He shared the best views with me. He introduced me to the sacred spots, the Ringmuren, the burial ground, his parents' memorial benches. Did you know that though several miles apart, there is a straight view from his mother's to his father's bench? I just discovered that with binoculars the other day. And in the Memorial Rose Garden right here on campus there is a touching and beautiful homage to his wife. These are the special memories I will take with me. He taught me to see your town through the love in his eyes. Through Leif, I've gained a new family, and now I've fallen for you, Heartlandia."

Watching for his reaction, she saw his head dip and his eyes cast downward. Maybe she'd taken it too far—she'd practically admitted she loved him—but she wanted the town to know what a great man he was, how much this campus meant to him, how he deserved their thanks and respect. And she wanted him to know she understood how much he loved his wife. That she finally understood that kind of love was irreplaceable.

"So I'd like to publicly thank you, Leif." Surprised by the rush of emotion, Marta said the words with a fluttery voice. She cleared her throat. "Thank you for your vision and for giving me the opportunity to open my heart to the wonderful people of Heartlandia. A part of me will always remain here." She gestured toward the mural to the right of her.

"Thank you! And thank you, Heartlandia."

Applause, cheers, even Manny's silly "La Cucaracha" van horn chimed in to the celebration. Marta was stunned by the acceptance. Gerda stepped back behind the podium and gave Marta a hug, told her the mural was beyond her greatest expectations, then posed with her as Lilly took a photograph for the newspaper. She'd promised Lilly an interview in the afternoon and also agreed to be around for the next two days as the mural was opened to the general public. And she would leave for home on Wednesday.

Elke had gotten the bright idea to make extralarge postcards for keepsakes and for the cruise ship and bus tourists who regularly visited Heartlandia. Elke had also suggested Marta autograph the first hundred to hand out as keepsakes of the event right after the unveiling. Manny headed straight for her with microphone in hand, no doubt ready with more questions.

There wouldn't be a moment to steal to be with Leif, to tell him she finally got it, that she loved him anyway. And if one day he felt ready to go all in again, she'd be waiting.

[faint show-through text from reverse page, illegible]

Chapter Eleven

After Marta's speech, when everyone swarmed her, Leif spotted Kent in the crowd on the college campus and made a beeline for him. "You got a minute?"

"Sure. What's up?"

"Everything has backfired. I need some serious help."

Kent looked around the busy campus. "Want to go to the rose garden to talk?"

That stopped Leif cold. The rose garden? The very place Marta had just let on she knew about. The place where he'd pledged his undying love and devotion to his wife until his own death.

May as well face it.

"Sure. Why not?" Why not walk straight into the fire…because if he wanted Marta for the rest of his life, he'd have to deal with what held him back once and for all. And it had to be quick because she was leaving on

Wednesday. What with everything going on today, it would be a wash. That gave him one day, Tuesday, to convince Marta to stay.

They entered the rose garden and sat on the opposite side because there was no way Leif could have this conversation sitting on Ellen's bench. In his heart, though, he knew she'd understand. Hell, she'd told him to move on in that dream, hadn't she?

Once he had Kent's undivided attention and Leif homed in on why he'd brought Kent here, he opened up.

"So I tested the waters with Marta, let her know I was open to her staying on with me as long as she wanted."

"You said that?"

"Well, not in so many words, but I'm pretty sure I got my point across."

"Did you bring up the baby? Are you open to that, too?"

"Uh, no, but wouldn't she know that?"

Kent smiled. "Good try. So now you have to say everything out loud. Don't leave any chance for doubt. Oh, and you have to prove it, too."

Listening to Kent, Leif realized he'd been pretty damn vague. He hadn't even brought up the baby. Oh, man, he hadn't been anywhere close to direct.

"How in the hell am I supposed to prove it?"

Kent had a perplexed look on his face, as if asking, "Seriously, dude, you don't know how to do that?"

"You have to tell her you love her and the baby and you want her to stay."

The words set off a cold burst right in the center of his chest. *Man up, Andersen. It's for the woman you want to spend the rest of your life with.* "That's easy for you to say."

"I'm not saying it's easy, but it's what you've got to do."

Leif understood. If he wanted to be a part of the living again, he had to be willing to take a big risk.

They shook hands, and after Kent left, Leif went to Ellen's swing and stood staring.

You know I love you and I'll never forget you, but I've been so lonely since you've been gone. I had a dream where you told me it was okay to move on, to live my life, and now I've found someone I want to be with. He glanced up at the trees, hands on his hips. *I never saw this day coming because I'm scared to death feeling this way.* He gingerly sat on the swing, inhaled the fragrant roses, thought of his deceased wife's sweet face. *You'll always be a part of me, babe. You turned me into a man, made me the grown-up I am. The thing is, I can't go on wishing you were still alive. I can't keep hiding behind that god-awful pain when I lost you as an excuse never to love again. Nothing is certain in life, but I think you'd be the first to kick my butt into gear, right? If I want to love again, I've got to risk the pain that comes with it. There's no getting around it. You taught me to be a man, and now I've got to act like one. No offense, but I'm done being a ghost. I know you'd want this for me, too.*

He sat quietly in the garden on his wife's memorial bench, letting the peace of the moment shower over him. *Remember how much we wanted children? Well, I've got a chance to be a ready-made father, and as scary as that seems, I want to take it. You think I'll be a good dad?* A light breeze whisked past his cheek. It felt like a kiss and gave him chills. Sitting still for several more minutes, pondering how his life had changed for the better since a certain artist had showed up in town, he decided to go after what he wanted most. Marta.

Leif went home, changed his clothes and threw a

change in his backpack, loaded up the dogs and everything he'd need to finish his carving and drove to his dad's favorite camping spot at Fogarty Creek State Park. He'd take tonight, a night when Marta was booked to the hilt with activities, to plan his action. There was no way he'd let her leave town without knowing he loved her and he wanted to be a part of her and her baby's lives.

It was almost nine when Marta finally made it back to Leif's place. A light was on in the kitchen, and a simple note lay on the counter. "Gone camping. See you tomorrow. Be here. Leif."

Her optimistic attitude deflated. With only a couple days left before she went home, he'd chosen to go camping. What kind of message was he sending? What about spending time with her?

She worried her lip and pushed her hair back. Did she mean anything to him? She'd made so many mistakes, being the one to withdraw first, then expecting him to notice and come after her. How infantile was that? She'd expected too much too soon from a man who'd lived like a recluse for three years. He'd come a long way in the short time they'd been together, yet she expected more because she'd had a change of heart where love was concerned. How could the guy possibly keep up?

She shouldn't have said that part about Ellen in her speech today; that had probably pissed him off royally. Plus, she'd dodged him for several nights, using Manny as an excuse, and she'd sent him back into hiding…and he'd gone camping. Man, she'd really blown it.

She dialed his cell phone but it went straight to voice mail. "Come home. Please" was all she said.

Upset and tired yet restless and, worst of all, resigned,

she went upstairs. Glancing around her room, she decided to occupy her time in the big empty house breaking down what little she wanted to take from the studio and packing up her bags. Tomorrow was going to be another big and busy day, and who knew when she'd find time to prepare for her trip home otherwise?

She missed Leif with every breath. With each item she packed, anxiety grew inside. She had to tell him she loved him before she left. No more dancing around the borders on that. He was the best man she'd ever met, and he deserved to know that.

For the next several hours, Marta cleared out her drawers and closet, working furiously to distract herself but doing a terrible job. Weepy and confused, she continued filling two of her three suitcases, even taking them downstairs and hefting them into the trunk of her rental car in readiness, assuming she'd be driving herself to the airport on Wednesday. All she had left was her overnight bag and the clothes she intended to wear tomorrow and on the day she left town. The closet and drawers were empty, and she tucked away what remained in the bathroom for easy access. For all intents and purposes, her room was clear. Then she crashed on the bed, lonely, craving Leif with every thought but, thanks to the pregnancy, exhausted and in great need of sleep.

Tuesday morning, Leif packed up bright and early and drove straight home without even eating breakfast. He'd thought everything through and made his plans; now he couldn't wait to see Marta, to tell her he loved her and he wanted her here with him for the rest of his life.

Sure, he'd understand if she needed to make a trip home to put things in order and settle any unfinished business. Hell, he was a modern-day man, so he'd even understand if she went back to paint a mural for Sedona... as long as her place of residence was with him.

When he pulled into his driveway it was noon, and her rental car was gone. Good. He wanted to clean up, shave, shower and set up a few things before he saw her.

An hour later, he'd transformed from grungy to best dinner-out clothes. And he didn't mind saying so himself that he smelled damn sexy, too. He set about fixing up the living room, getting some logs ready for starting a fire when she got home and putting the completed carving, now wrapped and tied with a bow, on the coffee table. The cradle would be a surprise once he got her attention with everything else. It waited with one big pink and blue bow in the entry closet. He even brought down what was left of the candles he'd lit the first night they'd made love. Oh, and chocolate. He needed to make a run to the sweet shop in town for the best and most delicious Swiss chocolate to give Marta. He'd offer her sparkling non-alcoholic cider instead of champagne, too, so he needed to buy that to prove she and the baby were foremost in his thoughts. Wouldn't his second gift to her prove that?

And after he'd told her he loved her, the best way to prove he'd made the final leap over his fear of loving her all the way was to make love to her on his old bed in his old room. The room she'd tried to lure him back to but he'd refused, proving how scared he still was. He'd finally figured it all out sleeping under the stars. And today he wouldn't let her shut him out. He'd evolved and was ready to face his fears, embrace her and the baby, and she needed to know it without a doubt.

He rushed to the linen closet to find the best and sexiest sheets he owned. He'd change the bed and maybe set a couple of candles in there, too, then surprise her when he took her to bed.

His ear-to-ear grin plummeted to his chin when he opened the master bedroom doors. The drawers were askew, closet empty—even her suitcases were gone.

She'd already gone.

Hell, he hadn't gotten to say goodbye. To tell her he loved her. He dropped to a knee, his breath kicked out of him. He glanced through suddenly blurred vision at the emptiness and groaned.

She hadn't so much as left a note.

But her flight was scheduled for tomorrow. He was supposed to take her to the airport, just like the day he'd picked her up. Where in the hell did she go?

She still had to be in town. And if she was still in Heartlandia, he'd find her.

Panic setting in, his pulse beating rapid-fire, Leif catapulted out of the room and took the stairs like an indoor twister. He broke outside, sprinting to his truck.

Turning the ignition, he wondered if he was doomed to be alone forever. His parents had died early, his wife far too young, so he'd gotten used to being alone. But not anymore! He threw the truck into gear, drove like a maniac and fishtailed out of his driveway. Life was too short to live alone. He didn't want another moment to go by without Marta.

Kent's logic had clicked last night in the camp as he slept in his old pup tent. The reward for letting go and loving again would be much greater than any potential loss. Yet here he was already at the "loss" part and hating every second. He didn't want to be an old lonely man. He wanted to live and love, have a family. He'd defeat the gnawing fear this time around.

His heart was opened wide and there was more than enough room for both Marta and the baby. If she'd only have him. That was supposed to be his job today, to convince her beyond all doubt that they belonged together. All three of them. Now all he had to do was find her.

First he'd call the car rental to see if she'd returned the car. He pulled over to make the call, fumbling his way through finding the number.

With a sigh of relief he hung up. The car hadn't yet been returned. She still had to be in town. His brain was all jumbled. He hadn't been thinking clearly. Idiot. He called her cell. It went directly to voice mail.

"It's Leif. I need to talk to you. Call me, okay?"

For the next hour he drove like a madman all over town, up and down the main streets, searching for her and the rental car. She wasn't at the college, either. He called Lilly's cell. It also went directly to voice mail.

"This is Leif. Do you know where Marta is? Call me."

He drove to the train station on a crazy whim, thinking she might be there. Yeah, his brain cells were shot through and through with panic and fear; his actions didn't make much sense, but it was better than sitting still, twiddling his thumbs doing nothing and losing her. There was no sign of Marta at the train station, either. He'd started grasping at anything, anyplace, driving in circles.

On the verge of giving up, of admitting defeat, he pulled out of the art-supply parking lot, thinking of heading up to the Ringmuren, and spotted a police car. Gunnar Norling was driving. He honked and sped to catch the police sergeant.

Gunnar noticed him and pulled over. Leif jumped out

of his truck and strode toward Gunnar's car, where the cop had already gotten out.

"Have you seen Marta? She's gone. Didn't leave a note, and I can't find her anywhere. Her cell's turned…"

"Lilly and Desi are hosting a baby shower for her."

He stopped in his tracks. "A baby shower?"

Gunnar grimaced. "You know she's pregnant, right?"

"Of course I do." Leif understood he looked like a madman, but he wasn't stupid.

"They're having it early since she'll be leaving tomorrow." Gunnar glanced at his watch. "Should be over by now, though."

He felt completely out of the loop, but what could he expect when he and Marta had essentially quit communicating the past few days? Then the news dawned on him. She hadn't left town! She was still in Heartlandia. He still had a chance.

Like he'd been given a second start and was reenergized because of it, Leif sprinted back to his crazily parked car. "Thanks, man!"

"Drive carefully." Gunnar laughed the words.

Leif peeled out, hitting the highway like a race-car driver, figuring the most logical place to go was home.

Marta couldn't believe the sweet gesture her two new friends had made. They'd invited her to lunch, then surprised her with the baby shower. They'd also invited a handful of ladies from town, each someone Marta had quickly come to care about. Gerda Rask, Elke Norling, two art students she'd taken under her wing while painting the mural. Though Cliff Lincoln had offered his banquet room for the shower, he'd also stuck around and became their private host for the afternoon, seeing to their every need like a doting father.

Over coffee and cake, Desi filled her in on her true love story with Kent. It occurred to Marta that when love was right and meant to be, it was okay to trust and depend on someone else. Necessary, even. Desi was definitely a better woman for it and still remained independent and able to follow her dreams. It was time to quit hiding behind that fear of a "benefactor" keeping her under his thumb. The only thing that mattered was *who* the benefactor was and if he was the right man. And Leif definitely was. When he'd asked her to stay on, he knew she was a package deal. She and the baby had both been invited.

Desi's story gave Marta hope she would find the same balance and happiness for herself.

Hadn't she already without realizing it?

Desi followed Marta home to help carry in all of the wonderful baby gifts she'd received and would have to make arrangements to ship home. One more item to add to her goodbye list. When they got there, a pang of disappoint shot through Marta when she realized Leif's car still wasn't home. Would he really stay AWOL on their last day together?

There was so much she needed to tell him, to make him understand. She loved him and wanted to be with him…if he'd have her.

Heartsick that he would let her go without a proper goodbye, she unlocked the front door and they went inside.

"Looks like someone's got some plans," Desi said when they rushed by the living room and she noticed the special setup.

Marta's hopes cautiously crawled out of the doldrums as she inspected the room. "I wonder what that is." She pointed to a box, definitely bigger than a ring box, with a huge bow.

"Let's get these boxes upstairs so I can clear out. I don't want to ruin any surprises, you know?" After Desi put the last package on the perfectly made bed, she hugged Marta.

They stared at the candles strategically placed around the room. Desi gave a mischievous smile and Marta got chill bumps on her arms. Leif had been in here, making plans.

"Maybe we better put the gifts over there." Desi pointed to the overstuffed lounger in the corner.

After they moved everything, Desi smoothed out the bedspread and winked. Then she left the room. "I want details, lady. Details!" She giggled as she went down the stairs, and a few seconds later Marta heard the door close tight.

What a great group of people her new friends were. Heartlandia felt more like home than Sedona, and the thought of leaving tomorrow made her chest ache. She glanced around her bedroom, which lifted her spirits. What was Leif up to?

To distract herself from her hopes getting too high, she went into the art studio and packed the unfinished portrait of Leif inside a large transport box. She planned to ship it home, finish it and bring it back to Leif in case he let her leave—another one of her last-ditch backup plans.

The back door slammed. "Marta! Marta!"

It was Leif, and he sounded desperate. Her pulse quivered and her breath got all screwy. "Up here." She could barely find the air to call out.

Rapid-fire feet pounded up the stairs. She opened the studio door, joy rushing into her veins. There he was, disheveled but really well dressed and wearing an urgent, earnest expression.

"Don't go. Stay with me. Please."

"Leif, I…"

"I love you."

He loves me? Her head went swimmy, and she tried to focus. "What about the baby? Wait. What? You love me?"

He stepped closer, took her hand, tugged her near. "I love every part of you, and that includes the baby." His eyes brightened, if that was even possible. "Wait. We've got to do this right. Come downstairs with me."

Pulling her along, he guided her downstairs to the living room. "Sit, sit." He put her in the plush wingback chair closest to the fireplace. Next he turned on the gas and lit the already assembled logs, then popped up and flipped a switch on the wall. Slow classical string music filtered through speakers hidden in the corners of the room.

"Oh, wait!" He rushed to the kitchen, opened the refrigerator door and came back with a bottle of chilled and sparkling apple cider. The glasses were already on the coffee table, but he didn't open the bottle or pour anything.

"I've made some gifts for you," he said, reaching for the pretty package with the maroon bow and handing it to her. He hovered over her as she opened it with shaky hands.

"Oh, Leif, this is beautiful. Did you carve it?"

He nodded. She turned the small sculpture this way and that, admiring the two figures melded together, one taller, the smaller one clearly pregnant with a baby outlined and etched inside the swell. She'd planned on being two against the world, but Leif's family idea felt far more appealing. She glanced up at him, tears blurring her vision. "Thank you."

"You're welcome, but wait, there's more." He dashed to the closet and pulled out the baby cradle.

Marta gasped. "Oh, my God, that's beautiful."

"I want both of you here with me."

Tears brimmed on her lids as he bent and hugged her. "When the baby's born, I'll carve his or her name right here."

"It's so beautiful. You've outdone yourself."

He dropped to one knee and took her hands in his.

"Please stay with me." The dogs had edged their way into the area, one butting him in the back, the other nudging her knee for a pat. "Stay with *us*. I love you. Make my life complete again."

She leaned into his arms, held him as if he'd disappear if she let go. "I love you, too." They kissed like the first time, fiery with passion and longing. God, she'd missed making out with him.

Then he stood and invited her to dance with him, and she joined him, gently swaying to the slow and quiet waltz.

"You deserve to hear the whole story," he said, one arm snug around her lower back, the other palm holding her hand. He kissed her fingers, then continued, "How you scared the hell out of me with your beauty and talent. I thought you were the most sophisticated woman on the planet and couldn't imagine you'd find anything about me appealing."

She couldn't resist kissing his cheek, then pressed hers next to his.

"But you kept chipping away at me." He spoke gently over her ear. "You came on so fast. How was I supposed to figure it all out? It was like some voodoo serum or something. I started feeling things. Dreaming about things. Wanting things. With you. I wanted you.

"And you were wise enough to already know that." He pulled back to look into her eyes. "Thank you."

"My pleasure."

"You tortured me, making it all sound so easy, so doable. Just for now. We can heal each other." He kissed her forehead. "You did heal me, Marta. Put feelings back into my heart. Thank you for not giving up."

Tears brimmed and threatened to spill over Marta's lids again. She had given up that very afternoon, and now he'd proved why she never, ever should have doubted him.

"That's why I want you to stay. Be with me. Let me be your home base. Let me give you and the baby a home. Let me love you from now until forever. I need you to tell me I can do that."

There was no doubt in Marta's mind that Leif knew how to love for eternity, that when he mated, he did it for life. That he was also a package-deal kind of guy, and he'd just offered everything to her. Well, almost everything. "Please do."

"Then, marry me." He said it with certainty, as though there was no doubt and she should make her decision right that instant.

Her breath got stuck in her windpipe; she was afraid to move, to jinx it, to lose this moment, but the guy needed and deserved an answer. She'd once put him on the spot and waited for him to act, and now things were the other way around.

She held his face with trembling fingers and looked deep into the blue depths of his eyes, the eyes of the man she loved with all of her strength and hope. "I was afraid you'd never ask me to stay, but I never dreamed of this. Yes. I want to marry you."

After another long and satisfying kiss, he took her hand and, forgetting about the cider and chocolate, walked her up the stairs and straight to her bedroom, then closed the door behind them.

Chapter Twelve

Two and a half years later...

It was a cloudy, blustery March day in Heartlandia.

"Gabriella needs a sweater," Marta called from the newly finished wraparound front porch—the two-year anniversary gift to her from the greatest husband in the world. From here, they could sit in the high-backed rocking chairs designed and handmade by Leif and watch sunsets and the Columbia River sparkle far off in the distance. They loved their sunsets together.

Leif played with their daughter as he loped in slow motion to catch her. The toddler giggled and ran away on the wide green lawn until she fell down.

"I got you!" Leif, acting like a huge monkey, chased after her, then swept her up from the ground.

"No! No!" Using her favorite word these days, Gabby halfheartedly fought her father.

"Mommy says you need a sweater, kitten. Aren't you cold?"

"Nooo!"

Leif pretended to eat her stomach, growling and laughing at the same time, then threw her over his shoulder like a bag of protesting potatoes.

"No, no, no, no."

Nothing meant more to Marta than to see Leif with her daughter. Their daughter. He'd married her before she'd delivered, giving Gabriella his last name and heart, sight unseen, and had never looked back. From the love and attention he gave, the child may as well have his blood running through her veins.

Leif made it to the porch railing, smiling up at her. "How're you feeling?"

"Fat," Marta said, rubbing her back and displaying her growing belly through the form-fitting top over leggings. "I just got a call from Kent."

"Everything okay?" He carefully put the sweater on Gabby, even though she squirmed like an octopus.

"Got the results of the amniocentesis back."

His eyes lit up. "And?"

"The baby's healthy."

"And?"

"I thought you didn't want to know the sex. Weren't you the one to turn your head during the ultrasound?"

"Maybe I lied."

"What kind of example is that for our daughter?"

He laughed. "Men are allowed to change their minds." Gabriella had settled down a little, as if knowing the importance of her parents talking about the new baby coming. He rushed up the steps and joined Marta there, tugging her near and kissing her. "I want to know. Especially if you do."

She decided to play it coy to draw out this wonderful moment. "I suppose it could be considered cruel and unusual punishment to expect me to keep a secret for four more months."

He kissed her again. "I'd hound you day and night. Tell me."

She put her hands together and pressed them to her lips, as if praying. "Okay. So remember those names we were tossing around last week?"

"Yes, now come on, you're driving me crazy." He tickled her sides, making her laugh. "How can I engrave the name on the cradle in time if you don't tell me?"

"You do have a point."

"Girl or boy?" He came at her with tickle fingers again.

She skipped aside to avoid more friendly torture. "It's a boy!"

He went still. "We're having a son?"

Delighted with the sudden over-the-moon expression on Leif's face, she laughed more. "That's generally what boy babies are called."

"Gabby, you're going to have a little brother! Isn't that fantastic?"

"Yay, fastic!" the child chimed in, clapping as if she'd just made a potty all by herself. "But I wanted a doggie." She pouted out her lower lip.

Leif looked at Marta with his usual she-says-the-cutest-things gaze, pride and love rolled together and welling in his eyes. Marta's vision blurred, taking in the two most important people in her life, one hand rubbing the ever-growing next addition to their family.

Her mother had a term for times like these. She called

them *golden moments*, and standing on the porch, gazing at her husband and daughter as they cheered for the coming baby, Marta decided this qualified for the greatest golden moment of her life.

That was, *after* that September day when she'd found and soon enough fell in love with Leif Andersen.

* * * * *

For a long, still moment their eyes held.

The intensity of his gaze reminded her of Mitch as a student, determined to understand the subject she was helping him to master. Back then he'd been reading a page in a poetry book; right now it felt as if he was reading her face as his gaze searched her eyes, her mouth.

In turn she explored his face. His chiseled face. His strong jaw. The knowing glint in his green eyes framed by those too-expressive eyebrows. And his mouth, which lifted to a half-smile that gave a promise of pleasure and that made her own lips part expectantly, her breath quicken.

Her eyes locked with his and a thrill of anticipation tingled through her.

Mitch Bailey was about to kiss her. And she was going to kiss him right back.

FROM PARADISE...
TO PREGNANT!

BY
KANDY SHEPHERD

All rights reserved including the right of reproduction in whole or in part in any form. This edition is published by arrangement with Harlequin Books S.A.

This is a work of fiction. Names, characters, places, locations and incidents are purely fictional and bear no relationship to any real life individuals, living or dead, or to any actual places, business establishments, locations, events or incidents. Any resemblance is entirely coincidental.

This book is sold subject to the condition that it shall not, by way of trade or otherwise, be lent, resold, hired out or otherwise circulated without the prior consent of the publisher in any form of binding or cover other than that in which it is published and without a similar condition including this condition being imposed on the subsequent purchaser.

® and ™ are trademarks owned and used by the trademark owner and/or its licensee. Trademarks marked with ® are registered with the United Kingdom Patent Office and/or the Office for Harmonisation in the Internal Market and in other countries.

Published in Great Britain 2015
by Mills & Boon, an imprint of Harlequin (UK) Limited,
Eton House, 18-24 Paradise Road, Richmond, Surrey, TW9 1SR

© 2015 Kandy Shepherd

ISBN: 978-0-263-25143-2

23-0615

Harlequin (UK) Limited's policy is to use papers that are natural, renewable and recyclable products and made from wood grown in sustainable forests. The logging and manufacturing processes conform to the legal environmental regulations of the country of origin.

Printed and bound in Spain
by CPI, Barcelona

Kandy Shepherd swapped her fast-paced career as a magazine editor for a life writing romance. She lives on a small farm in the Blue Mountains near Sydney, Australia, with her husband, daughter and a menagerie of animal friends. Kandy believes in love at first sight and real-life romance—they worked for her!

Kandy loves to hear from her readers. Visit her website at www.kandyshepherd.com.

To my husband, James, for the trip to Bali and the
answers to my endless questions about
"The Beautiful Game."

CHAPTER ONE

ZOE SUMMERS KNEW she wasn't beautiful. The evidence of her mirror proved that. *Plain* was the label she'd been tagged with from an early age. She wasn't *ugly*—in fact ugly could be interesting. It was just that her particular combination of unruly black hair, angular face, regulation brown eyes and a nose with a slight bump in the middle added up to pass-under-the-radar plain.

After a particularly harrowing time in her life, spent at the basement level of the high school pecking order, she'd decided to do something about her unremarkable looks. Not a makeover, as such—rather, she'd aimed to make the best of herself and establish her own style. Now, at the age of twenty-seven, Zoe Summers was known as striking, stylish and smart. She couldn't ask for more than that.

As a consequence of her devotion to good grooming she'd spent some time every day of her vacation on the beautiful tropical island of Bali in the spa of her luxury villa hotel.

Back home, fitting in beauty treatments around running her own accountancy and taxation business could be problematic for a self-confessed workaholic. Here, a programme that included facials, exfoliation, waxing, manicure and pedicure fitted right in with her mission to relax and replenish. And all for less than half the price of what it would cost in Sydney.

Late on the fourth and final afternoon of her vacation, she lay face-down on a massage table in the spa and let the masseuse work her skilled magic on the tight knots of tension in her shoulders. *Bliss.*

As she breathed in the soothing scents of sandalwood, frangipani and lemongrass her thoughts started to drift. She diverted them from anything to do with her business and the decisions she still had to make. Or from the very real concern that her cat had gone on hunger strike at the cat boarding place.

Instead she pondered how soon after her massage she could take a languorous swim in the cool turquoise waters of the hotel's lagoon pool. What to choose for dinner at one of the many restaurants in Seminyak. Should she buy that lovely batik print sundress in the nearby boutique? Or the bikini? Or both? The price tags bore an astonishing number of Indonesian rupiah, but in Australian dollars they were as cheap as chips.

She sighed a deep sigh of contentment and relaxed into that delicious state somewhere between consciousness and sleep.

When the massage table began to vibrate she thought at first, through her blissed-out brain, that it was part of the treatment. But then the windows rattled and the glass bottles of scented oils and lotions started to jiggle and clank. When the bottles crashed to the stone floor she jumped up from the table in alarm.

She knew before her masseuse's cry of, 'Earthquake!' what was happening.

It was an effort to stay on her feet when the floor moved beneath them like the deck of a boat on choppy waters. No use trying to hold on to the walls, because they seemed to flex inward. The masseuse darted under the protection of the wooden table. Zoe did the same.

She cowered with her knees scrunched up to her chest, heart pounding, swallowing against a great lump of fear, her hand gripping tightly to the girl's—she didn't know who'd grabbed whose hand first, but she was grateful for the comfort. The room shuddered around them for what seemed like for ever but was probably seconds, stopped, then shuddered again.

Finally everything went still. Cautiously, Zoe inched out from under the table. She nearly gagged on the combined scent of spilled aromatherapy oils. When the masseuse told her they had to head to an emergency meeting point she nodded, too choked with anxiety to actually reply.

She wanted to get out into the open ASAP. But she was naked—save for the flimsy paper panties she'd donned for the massage to protect her modesty—and her clothes and sandals were in an inaccessible closet. She snatched up the white towel that had covered her on the massage table and with clumsy, trembling fingers wrapped it around her, tucking it in as securely as she could. In bare feet, she picked her way around the shards of broken bottles on the floor, grabbed her handbag and followed the masseuse outside.

Still reeling with shock, Zoe hurried along the tropical plant-lined pathway that led from the spa to the main building and pool area of the hotel. To her intense relief there didn't appear to be a lot of damage. But her fear didn't dissipate. Once before disaster had struck from nowhere, changing her life for ever. Who knew what she could expect here?

During her stay she hadn't taken much notice of the other guests. Each villa was completely private, with high walls around it and its own lap pool. Now she was surprised at the number of people gathered for an emergency briefing in the open courtyard outside the reception area. She was the only one in the crowd to be clad in just a towel, but other people were in swimwear or wearing assorted hastily donned garments.

Could she get to her room? If she was going to die she didn't want it to be in a white standard-issue hotel towel.

The other guests were terrified too. She could see it in their grim faces, hear their concern in the murmur of conversation in several different languages.

The hotel manager took the floor to reassure them that the tremor was low on the Richter Scale of seismic activity. He told his guests that electricity had been knocked out but that the hotel emergency generators would soon kick in and it would be business as usual. There was no need to panic.

But what if there were aftershocks?

The manager's reassuring words did little to make Zoe's rapid heartbeat subside or her hands less clammy. It was time to get out of here, before any other disaster might strike. She'd seen the sights. She'd wound down. She'd been pampered from head to toe. Now she was anxious to get home.

She was just about to ask the manager if the airport was open when a man spoke from several rows of people behind her.

'Is there a tsunami warning?' he asked.

The word 'tsunami' was enough to strike renewed fear into Zoe's heart. But it wasn't the thought of an imminent tidal wave that kick-started her heartbeat into overdrive, it was the man's voice. Deep, confident, immediately familiar.

Mitch Bailey.

But it couldn't be. There must be lots of Australian-accented male voices in Seminyak. The west coast town was a popular vacation playground for Australians. Besides, it was ten years since she'd last heard that voice. She must be mistaken.

'No tsunami warning,' the manager replied to the man. 'There's no danger.'

'What about aftershocks?' The man asked the question she was too paralysed by fear to ask herself.

It sounded so like him.

'Not likely now,' said the manager. 'It was a small tremor.'

Zoe risked a quick glance behind her to identify the owner of the voice.

And froze.

It was Mitch Bailey, all right—right up at the back of the room. He was instantly recognisable: green eyes, dark blond hair, wearing a pair of blue checked board shorts and nothing else. His tanned, well-honed chest was bare. The blood drained from her face and her mouth went dry.

He was as handsome as he'd been at seventeen. *More handsome.* His face was more chiselled, more lived in, and his dark blond hair was cut spikily short—much shorter than when she had known him. He was tall, broad-shouldered, but lean, with well defined muscles. Then he'd been a suburban high school heart-throb. Now he was an international soccer star, who regularly topped magazine lists of 'The Sexiest Men Alive'.

She quickly turned back and ducked her head. *Dear heaven, don't let him recognise her.* He was part of a past she had chosen to put well behind her. She couldn't let him see her.

Zoe thought back to the first day she'd met him. Grieving over the death of her parents, in an accident that had also injured her, she'd been removed from her inner city home and her laid-back, no-uniform high school and dumped mid-term by her disapproving grandmother—her father's mother—into an outer suburbs school where she'd known no one and no one had seemed to want to know her. The uniform had been scratchy, uncomfortable and hideous—which was just how she'd felt during her time at Northside High.

Her first sight of Mitch Bailey had been of him surrounded by girls, with his girlfriend Lara—blonde and beautiful, of course—hanging possessively onto his arm. Zoe had kept her head down and walked past. But a burst of chatter had made her lift her head and she'd caught his eye. He'd smiled. A friendly, open smile born of his place as kingpin of his social group. He'd been a jock, a sports star—the most popular of the popular boys.

He hadn't needed to smile at nerdy *her*. But he had, and it had warmed the chill of her frozen heart even though she'd been unable to manage more than a polite stretching of her lips in return.

Later they'd become sort of friends, when he'd had a problem she'd been able to help him with. But the last time she'd seen him he'd been so unforgivably hurtful she'd shrivelled back into her shell and stayed there until she'd got out of that school. Now she had no desire to make contact again with anyone from that place—least of all with him.

She tensed, her eyes darting around for an escape route, then realised her panic was for nothing. No way would he recognise her. She looked completely different from the unhappy seventeen-year-old he'd befriended all those years ago. But she kept her eyes to the ground anyway.

She wanted to ask the manager about the airport as she was due to fly back to Sydney the next morning. But she didn't want to draw attention to herself. If she'd recognised his voice, Mitch might recognise hers. It was unlikely, but possible. She kept her mouth shut just in case.

The manager had said it was okay for the guests to return to their villas. That was where she was headed—pronto.

As other people started to ask more questions Zoe inched to the edge of the group. Not meeting anyone's gaze, and as unobtrusively as she could, she edged away towards the pathway that led to her private villa. Once there she could order room service for the rest of her stay, to make sure she didn't bump into Mitch Bailey.

Please, please don't let him be anywhere around when she checked out.

She quickened her pace as she got near the pathway.

'Zoe?'

His voice came from behind her and she started. She denied the reflex that would have had her turning around. Instead she kept her head down and kept walking, hoping against hope that he wouldn't call her name again. *Let him think he'd been mistaken.*

Mitch had noticed the dark-haired girl wrapped in a white towel as soon as she'd come into the courtyard. What red-blooded male wouldn't? The skimpy towel barely covered a sensational body.

It was knotted between high, round breasts and fell just to the top of slender, tanned thighs. Might it fall off at any moment? And, if so, was she wearing anything underneath? He'd been lying by his pool when the earthquake had hit. What had *she* been doing to be clad only in a towel?

But he'd thought no more about it as the girl had found a place near the front of the group of guests who had gathered to hear the charming Balinese hotel manager explain the ramifications of the earth tremor.

Mitch had been to Bali before, and knew small tremors like this weren't uncommon. He'd appreciated the manager's well-meant reassurances. But still, he'd asked the question about the tsunami because it didn't pay to ignore possible danger. Mitch was the kind of guy who liked to anticipate and prepare for the next move—'reading the play', they called it in soccer. There was a prominent sign on the beach warning people what to do if there was a tsunami warning. Therefore he'd needed to ask about it.

At his second enquiry the girl in the towel had turned briefly, to see who was asking the scary questions. Recognition had flashed just briefly before she had hastily turned back round.

He was used to that these days. Strangers recognised him as being an international soccer player. Or from the endorsements for designer menswear and upscale watches he'd posed for—the advertisements were on billboards even here in Bali. This woman might be a young mum who wanted him to sign her child's soccer ball. Or a fan with much more than signing on her mind.

He narrowed his eyes. The thing was, she had also seemed familiar to him. Her eyes had only caught his for a split second but there had been something about the expression in them—anxious, in a pale, drawn face—that had tugged at his memory. He'd met so many people over the last years, but he couldn't place her. He'd dredged his memory with no luck.

But then she'd hotfooted it away from the group of guests. He'd admired her shapely behind, swaying in that tightly drawn towel as she'd headed for the pathway that led to the private villas. Once she was gone he'd probably never see her again, and would be left wondering who she could possibly have been.

Then he'd noticed the slight, almost imperceptible limp as she'd favoured her right leg. It was enough to trigger memories of a girl he'd known for a short time in high school.

'Zoe!' he'd called.

She'd paused for a moment, her shoulders set rigidly. Then continued to walk away.

Now he pushed his way to the edge of the row of people and took a few strides towards her to catch up.

'Zoe Summers?' he asked, raising his voice.

This time she stopped and turned to face him. For a long moment their gazes met. Mitch was shocked to realise she had recognised him and yet had chosen to walk away. He was swept by conflicting feelings—the most predominant being shame. It was what he deserved after the way he'd treated her all those years ago.

'Mitch Bailey,' she said, head tilted, no trace of a welcoming smile. 'After all this time.'

'I knew it was you,' he said.

Her expression told him a kiss on the cheek, a hug, even a handshake would not be welcome. He kept his hands to his sides.

She looked much the same. More grown-up, of course. But the same sharp, intelligent face. The same black hair—only shorter now, and all tousled around her face. The piercings she'd sported so defiantly at school had gone, leaving tiny telltale holes along the top of her right eyebrow and in her nose, and there was just one pair of discreet gold studs in her ears instead of multiple hoops.

There was something indefinably different about her. Perhaps it was her air of assuredness. He didn't remember that. Back then she'd emanated a miasma of misery that had made other adolescents uncomfortable around her. The 'keep away' glower hadn't helped either. He'd considered himself privileged to have discovered the amazing person behind it all. Until he'd blown their friendship.

'I didn't think you'd recognise me,' she said.

He'd forgotten what an appealing voice she had: mellow, slightly husky.

'You mean you hoped I wouldn't.' He'd intended his words to sound light-hearted, but they came out flat.

She shrugged. 'I didn't say that. It's been years.'

He swallowed uncomfortably. 'Strange way to meet again. In an earthquake.'

'A "tremor" the management called it,' she said with a wry twist to her lips. 'Playing it down so as not to freak out the tourists.'

'Whatever name you give it, it scared the daylights out of me.'

She reacted with a raising of her perfectly shaped black eyebrows. 'Me too,' she said, with the shadow of a smile. 'I thought my end had come. Still think it's a possibility.'

'Where were you when the quake struck?'

'Having a body massage down at the spa.'

Where she must have been naked. So that was why she had only a towel wrapped around her.

Mitch willed his eyes to stay above her neck. Before today he'd only ever seen Zoe in a shapeless school uniform. He hadn't taken much notice of her body back then— it was her brain that had interested him. Besides, he'd had a girlfriend. Now he realised what great shape Zoe was in—in her own quiet way she was hot.

'Where were *you* when it hit?' she asked.

'Just about to dive into my lap pool. Then I noticed the surface of the water shimmering, which was kind of weird.'

'That must have been scary.' She shuddered as she spoke.

'Yeah. It was.'

'So much for relaxing in a tropical paradise,' she said, with a bravado that didn't hide the shadow of unease in her eyes.

She clutched her towel tighter to her. Mitch refused to let himself imagine what might happen if it slid off.

An awkward silence fell between them. Zoe was the first to break it. 'I'm going to head back to my villa,' she said.

'How about I come with you? Who knows what we'll find when we get back to our rooms.'

Her response was more of a cynical twist than a smile, but it was nonetheless attractive. 'Thank you, but I don't need a big strong man to protect me. I'm quite capable of looking after myself.'

'I'm sure you are,' he said. 'But I... Well, I don't really want to be on my own if we get any aftershocks.'

He wasn't afraid to admit to vulnerability. Just never on a football pitch.

'Oh,' she said.

For the first time she seemed flustered.

'You're not...you're not with someone?'

'You mean a girlfriend? No. What about you? Are you on your own?'

'Yes,' she said, with no further explanation.

He glanced down at her hand. No wedding ring. Though that didn't necessarily mean no man in her life. 'I'd like to catch up, Zoe. Find out what you've been doing in the last ten years.'

She paused. 'I don't need to ask what you've done since we last met,' she said. 'You're quite the sporting hero. The media loves you.'

He shrugged. 'Yeah… That… Don't believe everything they dish up about me. But seriously, Zoe, I'd really like to spend some time with you.'

Zoe looked up at him and her heart gave a flip of awareness. Mitch Bailey. Still the same: so handsome, so unselfconscious, standing before her in just a pair of swim shorts that did nothing to hide the athletic perfection of his body. So full of the innate confidence that came with the knowledge that he had always been liked, admired, wanted. So sure she'd want to spend time with him.

And she'd be lying to herself if she said she didn't.

He was the best-looking man she'd ever met. Had been then—still was now. She couldn't deny that. But all those years ago she'd seen a more vulnerable side of Mitch that had endeared him to her before he'd pushed her out of his life. Had it survived his stardom? It was difficult to resist the chance to find out.

'I'd like to catch up too,' she said lightly. 'After all, it isn't every day an earthquake brings long-lost school buddies together.'

He didn't seem to remember the circumstances of their last meeting. It had been a long time ago. Devastating to her at the time. Insignificant, it seemed, to him.

Had she had a crush on him back then? Of course she had. A deeply hidden, secret, impossible crush. He'd been so out of her league she would have been relentlessly mocked if anyone had found out.

'Great,' he said with a smile.

If she didn't know better, she'd think it was tinged with relief.

'The manager said it was business as usual. We can order drinks. I don't know about you, but I could do with a beer.'

'Me too,' she said.

And the first thing she'd do before she spent any more time alone with Mitch Bailey would be to put on some clothes.

CHAPTER TWO

ZOE'S VILLA HAD suffered minimal damage from the tremor—just a few glasses she'd left out had smashed to the tiled floor. Still, it was a shock—a reminder of how much worse it could have been. Might yet be.

She wanted to clear up the broken glass. But she felt awkward dressed only in the towel and she still felt very shaky. For every piece she picked up, she dropped another.

Mitch insisted he do it for her. Thanking him, she escaped into her bedroom and pulled closed the door that divided the room from the living area. The villa was like a roomy one-bedroom apartment, with all the external doors folding back to access the enclosed courtyard and private lap pool.

Her heart was thumping like crazy. Residual fear from the earthquake? More likely the effect of being in close proximity to Mitch Bailey.

She hadn't *stalked* him over the years. Not that. But when a boy she'd gone to school with had shot to fame she wouldn't have been human if she hadn't read the magazine stories, watched the television interviews, cheered for him when he'd been the youngest ever player in the Australian Socceroos team for the World Cup.

All the while she'd been getting on with her life—first

studying, then working, dating, and only ever thinking
about him when the media brought him to her attention.

Now he'd been thrust into her life again. And she was
clad in a towel, with no make-up on and her hair all mussed
up with massage oil.

Hastily she pulled on a sleekly cut black bikini, then
slid into a simple sleeveless dress in an abstract black-and-
white print. It fell to just above her knees. The humid tropical heat made anything else uncomfortable. She pulled
a brush through her hair and slicked on a natural toned
lipstick.

Did she want to look her best for Mitch? Her 'best' involved twenty minutes in front of a mirror with a make-
up kit and heated hair tongs. She shouldn't be worried
about how she looked now; he'd seen her at her worst ten
years ago. She shuddered at the memory of what she'd
looked like back then. The mono-brow. The bushy hair.
The prone-to-eruption skin.

But still, she wished today she could look her usual
polished, poised self. Her best self. There was no deny-
ing she'd feel more confident with straightened hair and
more make-up. But she didn't want to waste time fussing
over her appearance when she could be catching up with
Mitch. Who knew when she'd see him again—if ever?

He'd switched on the television in the living area and
was watching the screen when she came back out of her
bedroom.

'The manager was right—there's minimal disruption,'
he said. 'Seems like Bali gets small tremors like this quite
often. But the risk of aftershocks is real.'

Aftershocks. She knuckled her hand against her mouth
to suppress a gasp; she didn't want to appear too fearful.
Not when Mitch seemed so laid back about the risk.

He switched off the TV and turned to face her. Had he

grown taller since she'd last stood so near to him? They were both in their bare feet. He seemed to stand about six-foot-one to her five-foot-five.

Six-foot-one of total hotness.

Mitch was an elite sportsman in his prime, and he had celebrity status with as many fans as any actor or musician.

Her proximity to his bare chest was doing nothing to slow down her revved-up heartbeat. If she'd had a T-shirt big enough to stretch over all those muscles, she would have offered to lend it to him. But wouldn't it be a crime to cover that expanse of buff body?

She wanted to take a step back, but didn't want to signal how disconcerted she felt by said buff body being so close to her. Instead she stood her ground and forced her voice to sound controlled and conversational.

'So this region sometimes gets harmless tremors? That didn't stop it from being frightening, though, did it?' she said. 'I huddled under the massage table, making all sorts of bargains with myself about what I'd do if I got out safely.'

'What kind of bargains?' he asked.

'Spend more time with friends and less at work. Give more to charity.' She shrugged. 'Stuff that wouldn't interest you.'

His eyes were as green as she remembered them, and now they looked intently into hers. 'How do you know they wouldn't interest me?' he said, in a voice that seemed to have got an octave deeper.

A shiver of awareness tingled through her. *Sexiest man alive, all right.*

'Our lives are so different. It's like we inhabit different spaces on the planet,' she said.

'What do you think is my space on the planet?'

'Spain? I believe you play for one of the top Spanish teams. I've never been to Spain.'

'I live in Madrid.'

'There you go. I still live in Sydney. Fact is, the air you breathe is way more rarefied than mine.'

'I don't know if that's true or not. We're both staying in the same hotel.'

'My booking was a last-minute bargain on the internet. Yours?'

He smiled. The same appealing, slightly uneven smile he'd had at the age of seventeen. 'Maybe not.'

'That's just my point. You're famous. Not just for being a brilliant football player but for being handsome, wealthy, and photographed with a different gorgeous woman on your arm every time you're seen in public.'

And they were all tall, blonde and beautiful clones of Lara, back in high school.

'That's where you have an unfair advantage over me,' he said. 'You've read about me in the media—seen me on TV, perhaps. That's not to say what you've seen is the truth. But I know nothing about what's happened to you since we were at Northside High.'

'Because we occupy different space on the planet,' she repeated, determined to make her point. 'I went to another school after Northside, but I was still in Sydney. Away from school I hung out in the same clubs and went to the same concerts as other kids our age. But our paths never crossed again.'

'Until now,' he said.

'Yes. It took an earthquake to shake us back into the same space.'

He laughed, and she had to smile in response.

'You've still got a quirky way of putting things. Seriously, Zoe, I want to know all about you,' he said.

His words were flattering, seductive. Not seductive in a sexual way, but in a way that tempted her to open up and confide in him because he sounded as though her answer was important to him. That *she* was important to him. Even aged seventeen he'd had that gift of being totally focussed on the person he was addressing.

She realised it was highly unlikely she'd see Mitch again after today. He would go home to Madrid; she would fly back to Sydney. There was also a chance that a bigger earthquake might hit and the whole resort area would be wiped out. It was unnerving in one way—liberating in another.

'How about we get that beer and then we can talk?' she said.

'About you?'

'And you too,' she said, finding it impossible not to feel flattered. 'I'd like to hear about your life behind those media reports.'

'If that's what you want.'

'I'm warning you: my life story will be quite mundane compared to yours.'

'Let me be the judge of that,' he said.

'There are beers in the mini-bar,' she said. 'I've been on an alcohol-free detox since I've been in Bali and sticking with mineral water. Not that I drink a lot,' she hastened to add.

'I think getting out of an earthquake unscathed is reason enough to break your fast,' he said, heading towards the fridge.

He brought out two bottles of the local Indonesian beer, took off the caps and handed one to her.

'Let's take them out near the pool,' she said, picking up one of the remaining glasses to take with her. The ceiling fans were circulating air around the rooms, but the air-conditioning didn't appear to be back on yet. Besides, it felt too intimate to be alone in here with Mitch, and the king-sized bed was too clearly in view.

It was only a few steps out to the rectangular lap pool, which was edged on three sides with plantings of broad-leaved tropical greenery. Two smart, comfortable wooden sun loungers with blue-striped mattresses sat side by side in the shade of a frangipani tree. A myriad of pink flowers had been shaken off the tree by the quake onto the loungers and into the water. The petals floated on the turquoise surface of the pool in picture-perfect contrast.

In different circumstances Zoe would have taken a photo of how pretty they looked. Instead she placed the beer bottle and the glass on the small wooden table between the two loungers. She flicked off the flowers that had settled on one lounger before she sat down, her back supported, her legs stretched out in front of her. Thank heaven for all that waxing, moisturising and toenail-painting that had gone on in the spa yesterday.

She felt very conscious of Mitch settling into the lounger on her right. His legs were lean, with tightly defined muscles, his classic six-pack belly hard and flat. Even she knew soccer players trained for strength, speed and agility rather than for bulky muscle. Come to think of it, she might know that from hearing him being interviewed on the subject at some stage...

These villas were often booked by honeymooners, she knew. The loungers were set as close as they could be, with only that narrow little table separating them. Loved-up couples could easily touch in complete privacy.

She had never touched Mitch, she realised. Not a hug. Not even a handshake. Certainly not a kiss. Not even a chaste, platonic kiss on the cheek. It just hadn't been appropriate back then. Now she had to resist the urge to reach out and put her hand on his arm. Not in a sexual way, or even a friendly way. Just to reassure herself that he was real, he was here, that they were both alive.

She and Mitch Bailey.

He swigged his beer straight from the bottle. The way he tilted back his head, the arch of his neck, made the simple act of drinking a beer look as if he was doing it for one of those advertisements he starred in.

He was graceful. That was what it was. Graceful in a strong, sleek, utterly masculine way. She didn't remember that from the last time she'd seen him. Off the football field he'd been more gauche than graceful. At seventeen he hadn't quite grown into his long limbs and big feet. Since then he'd trained with the best sports trainers in the world.

Yes, he inhabited not just a different space but a different planet from her. But for this time—maybe an hour, maybe a few hours—their planets had found themselves in the same orbit.

Mitch put down his beer. 'So, where did you go when you left our school?' he asked. 'You just seemed to disappear.'

Zoe felt a stab of pain that he didn't seem to remember their last meeting. But if he wasn't going to mention it she certainly wasn't. Even now dragging it out of the recesses where her hurts were hidden was painful.

She poured beer into her glass. Took a tentative sip. Cold. Refreshing. Maybe it would give her the Dutch courage she so sorely needed to mine her uncomfortable memories of the past. She considered herself to be a private person. She didn't spill her soul easily.

'I won a scholarship to a private girls' boarding school in the eastern suburbs. I started there for the next term.'

'You always were a brainiac,' he said, with what seemed to be genuine admiration.

Zoe didn't deny it. She'd excelled academically and had been proud of her top grades—not only in maths and science but also in languages and music. But if there'd been such a thing as a social report card for her short time at Northside she would have scored a big, fat fail. She'd had good friends at her old inner city school, an hour's train ride away, but her grandmother had thwarted her efforts to see them. The only person who had come anywhere near to being a friend at Northside had been Mitch.

'I had to get away from my grandmother. Getting the scholarship was the only way I could do it.'

'How did she react?'

'Furious I'd gone behind her back. But glad to get rid of me.'

Mitch frowned. 'You talk as though she hated you?'

'She did.' It was a truth she didn't like to drag out into the sunlight too often.

'Surely not? She was your *grandma*.'

Mitch came from a big, loving family. No wonder he found it difficult to comprehend the aridity of her relationship with her grandmother.

'She blamed me for the death of my father.'

Mitch was obviously too shocked to speak for a long moment. 'But you weren't driving the car. Or the truck that smashed into it.'

He remembered.

She was stunned that Mitch recalled her telling him about the accident that had killed her parents and injured her leg so badly she still walked with a slight limp when she was very tired or stressed. They'd been heading north to a music festival in Queensland; just her and the mother and father she'd adored. A truck-driver had fallen asleep at the wheel and veered onto their side of a notoriously bad stretch of the Pacific Highway.

'No. I was in the back seat. I...I'm surprised you remember.'

He slowly shook his head. 'How could I forget? It seemed the most terrible thing to have happened to a kid. I loved my family. I couldn't have managed without them.'

Zoe shifted in her seat. She hated people pitying her. 'You felt sorry for me?'

'Yes. And sad for you too.'

There was genuine compassion on his handsome famous face, and she acknowledged the kindness of his words with a slight silent nod. As a teenager she'd sensed a core of decency behind his popular boy image. It was why she'd been so shocked at the way he'd treated her at the end.

As she'd watched his meteoric rise she'd wondered if fame and the kind of adulation he got these days had changed him. Who was the real Mitch?

Here, now, in the aftermath of an earthquake, maybe she had been given the chance to find out.

CHAPTER THREE

WERE THERE ELEPHANTS in Bali? There were lots of monkeys; Mitch knew that from his visit to the Ubud area in the highlands.

He'd heard there were elephants indigenous to the neighbouring Indonesian island of Sumatra that had been trained to play soccer. But he would rather see elephants in their natural habitat, dignified and not trained to do party tricks.

Whether or not there were elephants on Bali, there was an elephant in the room with him and Zoe. Or rather, an elephant in the pool. A large metaphorical elephant, wallowing in the turquoise depths, spraying water through its trunk in an effort to get their attention.

Metaphorical.

Zoe had taught him how to use that term.

The elephant was that last day they'd seen each other, ten years ago. He'd behaved badly. Lashed out at her. Humiliated her. Hadn't defended her against Lara's cattiness. He'd felt rotten about it once he'd cooled down. But he had never got the chance to apologise. He owed her that. He also owed her thanks for the events that had followed.

Zoe hadn't said anything, but he'd bet she remembered the incident. He could still see her face as it had crumpled with shock and hurt. He mightn't have been great with words when it came to essays, but his words to her had wounded; the way he'd allowed her to be mocked by Lara had been like an assault.

Now Zoe sat back on the lounger next to him, her slim, toned legs stretched out in front of her. He didn't remember her being a sporty girl at school. But she must exercise regularly to keep in such great shape. It seemed she hadn't just changed in appearance. Zoe was self-possessed, composed—in spite of the fact they'd just experienced an earthquake. Though he suspected a fear of further tremors lay just below her self-contained surface.

'I want to clear the air,' he said.

'What...what do you mean?' she said.

But the expression in her dark brown eyes told him she knew exactly what he meant. Knew and hadn't forgotten a moment of it.

'About what a stupid young idiot I was that last day. Honest. I didn't know that would be the last time I'd see you.'

Mitch was the youngest of four sons in a family of high achievers. His brothers had excelled academically; he'd excelled at sport. That had been his slot in the family. His parents hadn't worried about his mediocre grades at school. The other boys were to be a lawyer, an accountant and a doctor respectively. Mitch had been the sportsman. They could boast about him—they hadn't expected more from him.

But Mitch had expected more of himself. He'd been extremely competitive. Driven to excel. If his anointed role was to be the sportsman, he'd be the *best* sportsman.

The trouble was, the school had expected him to do more than concentrate on soccer in winter and basketball in summer. With minimal effort he'd done okay in maths, science and geography—not top grades, but not the lowest either. It had been English he couldn't get his head around. And English had been a compulsory subject for the final Higher School Certificate.

His teenage brain hadn't seen the point of studying long-dead authors and playwrights. Of not just reading contemporary novels but having to analyse the heck out of them. And then there was poetry. He hadn't been able to get it. He hadn't wanted to get it. It had been bad enough having to study it. He sure as hell hadn't been going to write the poem required as part of his term assessment. He *couldn't* write a poem.

Zoe Summers hadn't been in his English class. No way. The new girl nerd was in the top classes for everything. But during a study period in the library she'd been sitting near him when he'd flung his poetry book down on the floor, accompanied by a string of curses that had drawn down the wrath of the supervising librarian.

The other kids had egged him on and laughed. He'd laughed too. But it hadn't been a joke. If he didn't keep up a decent grade average for English he wasn't going to be allowed to go to a week-long soccer training camp that cut into the school term by a couple of days. He'd been determined to get to that camp.

The teenage Zoe had caught his eye when he had leaned down to pick up his book from the floor. She'd smiled a shy smile and murmured, 'Can I help? I'm such a nerd I actually *like* poetry.'

Help? No one had actually offered to help him before. And he'd had too much testosterone-charged teenage pride to ask for it.

'I'll be right here in the library after school,' she'd said. 'Meet me here if you want me to help.'

He'd hesitated. He couldn't meet her in public. Not the jock and the nerd. A meeting between them would mean unwanted attention. Mockery. Insults. Possible spiteful retaliation from Lara. He could handle all that, but he had doubted Zoe could.

His hesitation must have told her that.

'Or you could meet me at my house after school,' she'd said, in such a low tone only he could have heard it.

She'd scribbled something on a piece of paper and passed it unobtrusively to him. He'd taken it. Nodded. Then turned back to his mates. Continued to crack jokes and be generally disruptive until he'd been kicked out of the library.

But he had still needed to pass that poetry assignment. He had decided to take Zoe up on her offer of help. No matter the consequences.

Her house had been just two streets away from his, in the leafy, upmarket northern suburb of Wahroonga. Their houses had looked similar from the outside, set in large, well-tended gardens. Inside, they couldn't have been more different.

His house had been home to four boys: he still at school, the others at universities in Sydney. There'd been a blackboard in the well-used family room, where all family members had chalked up their whereabouts. The house had rung with lots of shouting and boisterous ribbing by the brothers and their various friends.

Zoe's house had been immaculate to the point of sterility. Straight away he'd been able to tell she was nervous when she'd greeted him at the front door. He'd soon seen why. An older woman she'd introduced as her grandmother had hovered behind her, mouth pinched, eyes cold. He'd never felt more unwelcome.

The grandma had told Zoe to entertain her visitor in the dining room, with the door open at all times. Mitch had felt unnerved—ready to bolt back the way he'd come.

But then Zoe had rolled her eyes behind her grandmother's back and pulled a comical face.

They'd established a connection. And in the days that had followed he'd got to like and respect Zoe as she had helped him tackle his dreaded poetry assignment.

'I want to explain what happened back then,' he said now.

Zoe shrugged. 'Does it matter after all this time?' she said, her voice tight, not meeting his eyes.

It did to him. She had helped him. He had let her down.

'Do you remember how hard you worked to help me get my head around poetry?' he asked.

'You were the one doing all the work. I just guided you in the right direction.'

He slammed down his hand on the edge of the lounger in remembered anger. 'That's exactly right. You made me use my own words—not yours. It was unfair.'

'What…what exactly happened in the classroom that day?'

'The teacher had had the assignment for a week. So I was on edge, waiting to see if I'd passed or not. By then it had become something more than just wanting to go to the soccer camp. She handed out the marked essays, desk by desk. She saved mine for last.'

'You should have easily passed. By that time we'd spent so much time on it—you really understood it.'

'I thought I'd understood it, too. She got to my desk. Held up the paper for everyone to see the great big "Fail" scrawled across it. Told the class I was a cheat. Read out my grade and added her comments for maximum humiliation.'

The look on that teacher's face was still seared into his memory.

Before he'd studied with Zoe he would have made a

joke of it. Clowned around. Annoyed the teacher until she'd kicked him out of the classroom. But not that time. He'd deserved better.

'What happened?'

'I snatched the paper from the teacher's hand and stormed out.'

'To find me lurking outside in the corridor. Pretending I was waiting for a class to start in the next room. Ready to congratulate you on a brilliant pass. Instead I got in your way.'

He noticed how tightly she was gripping on to her glass. No wonder. He'd vented all his outraged adolescent anger and humiliation on her. It couldn't be a pleasant memory.

'Instead I behaved like a total jerk.'

'Yeah. You did. You...you thrust the paper in my face. I can still see that word written so big in red ink: "Plagiarism".'

'She thought I was too stupid to write such a good essay. And I took it out on you.'

He'd yelled at her that it was *her* fault. Told her to get out of his way. Never talk to him again. Had he actually shoved her? He didn't think so. His words had been as effective as any physical blow.

He'd seen her face crumple in disbelief, then pain, then schooled indifference as she'd walked away. She'd muttered that she was sorry—she'd only been trying to help. And he'd let her go.

Worse, a half-hour later he'd encountered Zoe again. This time he'd been hanging near the canteen, with his crowd of close friends and his girlfriend, Lara. Zoe had obviously been startled to see them. Startled and, he'd realised afterwards, alarmed. She'd immediately started to turn away, eyes cast down, shoulders hunched. But that hadn't been enough for Lara, who hadn't liked him studying with another girl one little bit.

'Buzz off, geek-girl,' Lara had sneered. 'Mitch doesn't need *your* kind of help. Not when he's got *me*.'

Then Lara had pulled his face to hers and given him a provocatively deep kiss. Her girlfriends had started to laugh and his mates had joined in, their laughter echoing through the corridors of the school.

He'd just kept on kissing Lara. When he'd finally pulled away Zoe had gone. It was only later that he'd realised how he'd betrayed her by his silence and inaction.

That had been ten years ago. Now she smiled that wry smile that was already becoming familiar. 'Teenage angst. Who'd go back there?'

'Teenage angst or not, I behaved badly. And after ten years I want to take this opportunity to say sorry. To see if there is any way I could make it up to you.'

Digging deep into feelings she'd rather were kept buried made Zoe feel uncomfortable. She found it impossible to meet Mitch's gaze. To gain herself a moment before she had to reply, she put her glass down onto the table and tugged her dress down over her thighs.

'We were just kids,' she said.

Though Lara's spite had been only too grown up. And the pain she'd felt when Mitch had ignored her hadn't been the pain of a child.

Truth was, the episode was a reminder of a particularly unhappy time in her life. She'd rather not be reminded of how she'd felt back then. That was why she had tried to avoid Mitch earlier on, when she'd first recognised him.

'I was old enough to know better,' he said.

Now she turned to face him. 'Seriously, if you hadn't

always been popping up in the media I would have forgotten all about what happened. I'm cool with it.'

He persisted. 'I'm *not* cool with it. I want to make amends.'

She wished he would drop it. 'If it makes you feel any better, my experiences at Northside made me stronger—determined to change. No way was I going to be that miserable at my new school. I decided to do whatever it took to fit in.'

'Your piercings? Which, by the way, I used to think were kinda cute.'

'Gone. I wore the uniform straight up—exactly as prescribed. Put the "anything goes" lifestyle I'd enjoyed with my parents behind me. Played the private school game by their rules. I watched, learned and conformed.'

And it had worked. At the new academically elite school she hadn't climbed up the pecking order to roost with the 'popular' girls, but neither had she been one of the shunned.

'Was it the right move?'

Again she was conscious of his intent focus on her. As if he were really interested in her reply.

'Yes. I was happy there—did well, made some good friends.'

One in particular had taken the new girl under her wing and helped transform the caterpillar. Not into a gaudy butterfly, more an elegantly patterned moth who fitted perfectly into her surroundings.

'I'm glad to hear that. But I want you to know I feel bad about what happened. I want to right the wrong.'

Zoe shrugged, pretended indifference, but secretly she was chuffed. Mitch Bailey apologising? Mitch Bailey maybe even grovelling a tad? It was good. It was healing. It was—she couldn't deny it—*satisfying*.

'Consider it righted,' she said firmly. 'Apology accepted. You were young and disappointed and you took it out on the first person who crossed your path.'

'I tried to find you,' he said.

'You did?' she said, startled. That he'd remembered the incident at all in such detail was mind-boggling.

'After the soccer training camp I went away on vacation with my family. When I got back to school you weren't there. I went around to your house. Your grandmother told me you didn't live there any more. I thought she was going to slam the door in my face.'

'Sounds like my grandmother.'

'Remember how she always made you leave the door open and patrolled outside it? I felt like a criminal. Did she think I was going to steal the silver?'

'She was terrified you'd get me pregnant.'

Mitch nearly choked on his beer. He stared at her for a long, astounded moment. *'What?'*

Zoe waited for him to stop spluttering, resisting the temptation to pat him on that broad, muscular back. She probably shouldn't have shared that particular detail of her dysfunctional relationship with her grandmother.

She felt her cheeks flush pink as she explained. 'I told her we were just friends. I told her you had a girlfriend. That the only thing going on in that room was studying.'

Not to mention that Mitch Bailey wouldn't have looked at her as girlfriend material in a million years.

'Why the hell did she think—?'

'She wasn't going to let me—' Zoe made quote marks in the air with her fingers '—"get pregnant and ruin the future of some fine young man" the way my mother had ruined my father's. You counted as one of those fine young men. She knew of your family.'

How many times had her grandmother harangued her

about that, over and over again, until she'd had to put her fingers in her ears to block out the hateful words?

Mitch frowned. 'What? I don't get it.'

Thank heaven back then her grandmother hadn't said anything to Mitch about the pregnancy thing. She would have been mortified beyond redemption.

'It sounds warped, doesn't it? I didn't get it either when I was seventeen. I thought she was insane. I'd adored my parents. They'd adored each other. But Mum was only nineteen when I was born. Because my father dropped out of his law degree my grandmother blamed my mother for seducing him, getting pregnant on purpose and ruining his life.'

'Whoa. You said your life story was *mundane*.' He paused, narrowed his eyes. 'And she transferred the blame to you, right?'

'Yep. If I hadn't come along her son would have got to be a lawyer.'

'And he wouldn't have died?'

'Correct.'

'That's irrational.'

'You could say that.'

'Yet she gave you a home?'

'Reluctantly. She couldn't even bear to look at me. I look like my dad, you see. A constant reminder of what she had lost. But she felt she had to do the right thing by her granddaughter.' In spite of herself a note of bitterness crept into her voice. 'After all, what would her golfing friends have thought?'

'Did you have any other family you could have gone to?'

'My mother's brother, whom I love to pieces. But as he has a propensity to dress in frocks sometimes the courts didn't approve of him as guardian to a minor.'

Mitch laughed. 'The lawyers must have had fun with

that one.' He sobered. 'No wonder you were so miserable back then.'

The rejection by her grandmother had hurt. There had been no shared grief. No comfort. Just blame and bitterness. 'I did something about it, though,' she said.

'What could a kid of seventeen have done?'

'My new best friend at school—who incidentally is still my best friend—had a mother who was a top lawyer. She helped me get legal emancipation from my grandmother. There was compensation and insurance money from the accident that got signed over to me. I was able to support myself.'

He whistled. 'That was a tough thing to do. Brave too.'

She shrugged. 'My new life started then.'

'You had worse things going on than a teenage me ranting at you…'

She met his gaze. 'What happened with you hurt me. I won't deny it. I…I valued our friendship. It was a beacon in the darkness of those days.'

Mitch swore low and fluently.

She waited for him to finish. 'It's history now. I appreciate your apology. And I don't want to hear one more word about it.'

'Just a few more words,' he said, with that engaging grin.

'I can't imagine what more there is to be said,' she said, her lips twitching into a smile in response. 'But okay. Your final words. Fire away.'

'I was sent to the principal to be punished for my plagiarism. She was new that year and didn't know me. When I explained she listened. Turns out I had a mild form of dyslexia that had never been diagnosed. I got help. My grades picked up. Not just in English, but all my subjects. I could have gone to university on my Higher School Certificate results if I hadn't chosen to play soccer instead.'

'Mitch, that's wonderful news!'

Her instinct was to reach out and hug him. With every fibre of her being she resisted it. She could not trust herself to touch him.

But while *she* thought touching was not on the agenda, Mitch obviously thought otherwise. He reached out and put his hand on her shoulder. 'I have a lot to thank you for, Zoe,' he said.

His hand was warm and firm on her bare skin and she had to force herself not to tremble with the pleasure of it.

She had to clear her throat before she could reply. 'Not me. The principal. Yourself. That's who you should thank.'

He let his hand drop from her shoulder and she felt immediately bereft of his touch. That attraction she'd felt for him at seventeen was still there, simmering below the surface.

'I'm determined to thank you, whether you acknowledge your role in the outcome or not,' he said. 'The least I can do is buy you dinner.' He looked at his watch. 'An early dinner?'

That threw her. She'd assumed once they'd sorted out the problems of the past he'd be on his way. 'Here? Now?'

'I don't think it would be a good idea to go into Seminyak so soon after the quake. Too dangerous.'

'I...I was going to order room service,' she blurted out.

'I was going to suggest the hotel restaurant. But I might get recognised. And I don't want anyone else intruding on our reunion celebration. Room service is a great idea. Your villa or mine?'

'Uh... H-Here would be good,' she stammered. *Reunion celebration?*

Had the earthquake knocked her off that massage table

and she'd hit her head? Was she hallucinating? Or in some some kind of coma?

Her and Mitch Bailey, having dinner *tête-à-tête* in the seclusion of a luxurious private villa in Bali? Maybe she'd wake up and find herself back in the spa, sprawled amid the debris with a big fat headache.

But if it *was* a dream, or a long-ago fantasy come true, she was going to enjoy every second of being with Mitch. Who knew what tomorrow might bring?

She swung her legs off the side of the lounger. 'I'll go get the room service menu.'

CHAPTER FOUR

MITCH RECLINED ON HIS lounger and watched Zoe as she walked into the living area. He couldn't keep his eyes off the way her hips swayed enticingly under the body-hugging dress. Somehow he doubted that seductive sway was intentional. He'd seen enough of the type of woman who turned on the sex appeal with seduction in mind to know the difference.

No. Zoe had a natural, unconscious sensuality. The fact that she seemed unaware of it made her only more appealing. *Zoe Summers. Who would have thought it?*

He couldn't get over the difference in her. It wasn't that he'd found her unattractive as a teenager. There'd been something quirky and rebellious about her that he'd liked. But now…now she was sexy as hell. Sparky and feisty too. He was finding it fascinating to discover the woman she'd become. Was grateful to the twist of destiny that had flung them together.

She headed back towards the pool, waving a cardboard folder. 'I had to hunt for it, but I've got the room service menu.'

Mitch swung his legs from the lounger so he sat on the edge. 'Let's take a look.'

'It's the same food as the restaurant. I've eaten there a few times. It's good.'

Menu in hand, she hesitated near his lounger. He patted the seat next to him. Cautiously she sat down, being so careful to keep a distance between them that it made him smile. Again she tugged down her dress to cover her thighs. But that only meant the neckline of her dress slid down, revealing more than a tantalising glimpse of the swell of her breasts.

Surely he would have noticed if she'd had a body like that back at school?

'What's for dinner?' he asked, shuffling a little closer to her until her scent filled his senses. 'Any recommendations?'

'I don't know what you like,' she said.

Of course she wouldn't. Despite that briefly opened window on a shared past, he and Zoe were strangers.

'What are *you* going to order?' he asked.

'Something not too spicy,' she said. 'The curries don't agree with me.'

'Bali belly, huh?' he said. 'Happens to the best of us. But you survived?'

Zoe pulled a face. 'I'll spare you the details,' she said. 'I seem to be over it now, but don't want to risk a relapse.' She handed over the menu. 'I'm going to stick with the *ayam bakar*—I've had it before with no...uh...ill effects.'

Mitch read out the description of her chosen dish. 'Organic chicken pieces marinated in a special blend of Indonesian spices, grilled, and served with a lemongrass salsa. Sounds good.'

'It's absolutely delicious. I want to learn how to make it when I get home.'

'You like cooking?'

She nodded. 'I wanted to have cooking lessons while I was in Bali but I've run out of days.'

'Next time,' he said.

She bit her lip and paled at his words, paused for a long moment. 'Yes,' she said finally. 'Next time.'

Mitch cursed himself for his insensitivity; he'd already suspected she was only masking her fear.

Would there be a next time? Or another earthquake? Maybe a tsunami?

Despite the manager's reassuring words Mitch knew there was a risk the entire resort would be wiped out by breakfast. But he tended towards optimism in his view of life. Not so Zoe, he suspected.

She'd lost her whole family when disaster had hit from nowhere. No wonder she was frightened. He wanted to take her in his arms and reassure her that there was a low statistical risk of any more serious danger. But he sensed she wouldn't welcome it. He sensed a 'hands off' shield around her.

'Y'know, I'm not really that hungry,' she said in a diminished voice.

She twisted her hands together. To stop them trembling, he guessed.

'You do realise it's highly unlikely anything else is going to happen?' he said gently.

Her chin rose. 'I know that.'

'There's no need to be frightened.'

'Who said I was frightened?'

'I thought that was why you'd lost your appetite?'

'No. I...' She met his gaze. 'Maybe I *am* a little frightened,' she admitted.

'Let's order for you anyway. You might get hungry later.' He scanned the menu. 'I'm hungry right now.'

'You were always hungry,' she said, with a weak smile that tugged at the corner of her mouth.

Her lovely, lovely mouth.

'Back then, I mean.'

'Your granny mightn't have been so nice, but she made good cookies.'

Zoe nodded. 'Baking cookies with her is one of the few nice memories I have of her. She liked having a boy to cook for. I realise that now.'

'Is she still around?'

Her lips tightened. 'I guess so. I don't know and I don't care.'

'I don't blame you,' he said. Not after the way she'd been treated by someone who should have cared for her. Hearing about the old woman's pregnancy fear for Zoe had given him the creeps.

She nodded and quickly changed the subject. 'Anything on the menu appeal?'

This was the first time he'd eaten at the hotel apart from breakfast. He'd spent most evenings with friends who owned the most fashionable beachfront nightclub in Seminyak. 'I'm going for the Balinese mixed seafood.'

Zoe had to shift a little closer to him to read the menu. Her scent was fresh, tangy, with an underlying sweetness. Much like her personality, he suspected.

'That looks good,' she said. 'Healthy.' She looked up at him. 'I guess you have to watch everything you eat?'

'All the time. When I'm training or before a game I carb-load. On vacation I stick with lean protein and vegetables.'

'I eat healthily too,' she said. 'But as I'm far from a professional athlete I also make room for chocolate.'

'I can't remember when I last ate chocolate.'

From the time when he'd first started playing for Sydney soccer clubs his diet had been overseen by a nutritionist. It was all about discipline. Discipline and constant self-denial.

'You want to order dessert?' he said, flipping the menu to the appropriate page.

'Why not? The mini chocolate lava pudding with lychee ice cream might be good for my nerves.'

He liked her self-deprecating attitude to her fears. 'That's as good an excuse as any,' he said. 'Fruit salad for me. I've spent a season on the sidelines. I have to be at my peak when I start intense training again.'

She glanced at his right knee. So she knew about the incident when two opposing players had slammed into him and his anterior cruciate ligament had snapped.

'Australia's most famous knee...' she said.

Mitch found it disconcerting that Zoe was so aware of the details of his life while he knew so little about hers. He doubted he'd ever get used to the scrutiny he endured as a celebrity athlete. Even his knee had become public property.

'I wouldn't say "most *famous* knee",' he said, laughing it off.

'How about most notorious knee?' she said, her head tilted to one side, teasing.

'Notorious knee? I like that.'

Most painful knee was more like it. Both in terms of the actual injury and also in the way it had lost him a season of play. The memory of being carried off the field came flooding back. The agony. The terror that he wouldn't be able to play again. The months of rehabilitation and physiotherapy that had followed. The effort to get himself back to peak fitness after the weeks on crutches.

'I don't see a scar,' she said, her eyes narrowed.

'No scar,' he said. 'Three small incisions for keyhole surgery have left tiny marks. That's all.'

For a moment he was tempted to place Zoe's hand on

his knee and let her feel the punctures. Not a good idea. He found her way too attractive to be able to trust himself.

'Is it healed now?' she asked.

'Good as new.' He wouldn't admit to anyone his niggling fear that once he was back in the game his knee would betray him again. His sporting life would be over if it did.

'There was talk that your injury might force you to retire,' she said.

'No way,' he said vehemently.

This exact injury had brought other great players' careers to a skidding halt. He wasn't going to let it end *his*.

It would take something more catastrophic than a cruciate ligament repair for his manager, his fans *or* himself to allow him to consider giving up. At the age of twenty-seven he was in his football prime. He cursed the six months it had taken him to achieve full recovery. Now he had to get back out there on the field and prove he could play better than ever.

Soccer was his life.

Zoe drew her dark brows together. 'So, why are you in Bali?'

'I was visiting family in Sydney, then decided to have a break here on the way back to Madrid. I met up with a mate who has a surf gear business. Another runs a big nightclub.'

'When do you go back?'

'Who knows how the earthquake has affected the airlines? But I'm scheduled to fly to Singapore then back to Madrid the day after tomorrow.'

It was May. He would hurl himself into intense training immediately he got back. Pre-season games started at the end of June. He needed those 'friendly' games to test his knee and get back into top form before the season proper commenced. The first games for La Liga—the Spanish league—started at the end of August.

'What about your flight?' he asked Zoe.

'I fly out tomorrow morning, if all goes well.' She crossed her fingers.

'I guess the airlines will keep us informed,' he said.

If all goes well.

He didn't repeat her words—didn't want to bring her fear to the fore again.

There was an awkward pause that she rushed to fill. 'Do you like living in Madrid?'

'Madrid rocks. An Aussie boy from the north shore of Sydney living in one of Europe's great cities never tires.'

All true. But he hadn't admitted to anyone how lonely he could get there, despite the buzz of playing for one of the world's best teams. He had friends on the team, of course, but there were also some big egos to deal with—and the truth was they were in competition with each other as well as the opposing teams.

He wasn't about to admit to that downside now. Zoe had flitted into his life again and he was very careful of what he said to people except his family and his closest friends—careful of who he let in to his private world. You never knew who would talk to the press. Or misrepresent his words on social media. Or post a compromising selfie.

'Do you speak Spanish?' she asked.

'Enough to get by.'

Mitch decided the conversation had centred too much around him. He was way more interested in her.

'Me muero de hambre.'

Zoe laughed—a low, husky laugh that hadn't changed at all since she was a teenager. She'd grown into that sensual, adult laugh.

'You're dying of hunger. Did I get that right?'

'You speak Spanish?' He knew so little about her—wanted to know more in this accelerated getting-to-know-you situation they found themselves in.

'Hablo un poco de español,' she said, with an appropriately expressive shrug.

'You speak a little Spanish,' he translated.

'And a little French, and a little Italian, and a few phrases in Indonesian that I've learned in the last few days.'

'You've travelled a lot?'

'So far most of my travel has been of the armchair variety. I'd *like* to travel a lot. I'd love to be fluent in different languages. I'll study more some day—when I'm not so busy working.'

Of course she would. Zoe had been so smart at school. And she'd grown up into a formidable woman. Formidable and sexy. How very different from the women he usually dated. From nowhere came the thought that Zoe Summers would be a challenge. The kind of challenge it would be pleasurable to meet.

'I have no idea what work you do,' he said.

'I have my own accountancy and taxation advice company.' She paused. 'Yeah. I know. *Boring.*'

'I didn't say that,' he said.

She pulled a face. 'I can see the thought bubbles wafting around your head.' She made a series of little quote marks in the air as she sang the words in a clear contralto. '"Boring. Boring. Boring."'

He laughed. 'Wrong. My thought bubbles are "Clever Zoe" and "Intelligent" and "Entrepreneurial".'

'Oh,' she said. 'They…they're great thought bubbles.'

'But don't ask me to sing them as I'm totally tone deaf.'

She laughed. 'I'm grateful—both for the thought bubbles and for sparing me the singing.'

'You couldn't call it singing. There isn't a musical bone in my body.'

'Not a singer and not a poet?' She smiled. 'Seriously, though, my clients are anything but boring—'

'And neither are you boring,' he said.

She flushed pink, high on her cheekbones. He would have liked to trace the path of colour with his fingers, then move down to her mouth. Her lovely mouth, with the top lip slightly narrower than the bottom lip, giving it an enticing sensuality.

'That's nice,' she said simply.

'Tell me about your clients,' he said. 'I'm intrigued.'

'I specialise in working with creative people.' Her face softened. 'People like my parents, who were hopeless money-managers. Charming. Talented. My father played guitar. My mother's instrument was her voice. But they were feckless with money.'

She stopped.

'That was way more information than you wanted.'

He leaned closer to her. 'No, it wasn't. Tell me more. I'm interested in what you do.'

She backed away—so slightly he might have thought he'd imagined it if he hadn't been so focused on her. He found it intriguing to have her nervous of him. He was used to women who were unabashed—blatant, even—in expressing their desire for him.

'Shall we order the food first, if you're so hungry?' she said, her words tumbling out in a rush. 'I know the manager said it was business as usual, but the kitchen might not be up to speed after the quake.'

Mitch's empty belly told him that was a very good idea. But he wasn't going to let her get away for long with changing the subject. He was fascinated by her—wanted to make the most of the hours they were fated to spend together.

'Okay,' he said.

She got up from the lounger. 'I'll phone it through.'

Mitch got up too, and took the menu from her. 'No. I'll order. They can bill the meal to my room.'

She went to snatch it back. 'It can be billed to my room.'

He held on firmly to the menu. When she tried to take it he held it above his head. 'In the rarefied space where I dwell, I pay for dinner.'

Zoe bristled at his comment. She liked to be independent. 'Please at least let me pay for my own meal,' she said.

'No,' he said, in a firm, forceful way that brooked no argument.

It was a gracious gesture on his part, and it would be crass of her to argue. 'Okay. Thank you. I'll—'

She was going to say she'd pay next time, but of course it was highly unlikely she'd be having dinner again with Mitch Bailey. Further earthquakes or not.

Mitch headed to the phone to order the meal. His back view was breathtaking: broad shoulders tapered to a swoon-worthy butt, then long, strong legs. No wonder his fans went crazy over him. Lost in admiration, she felt a tad light-headed herself.

She observed the way he walked, with the confident easy strength of a man at the peak of physical perfection. There wasn't the slightest indication that he favoured his right knee in his athletic stride. She prayed the knee was now strong enough to help him soar right back to the heights of the success he craved.

'You were right—the meal will be around an hour,' he said when he returned.

'Lucky we ordered when we did, then.'

Mitch didn't sit back down on the lounger. 'It's hot. How about cooling down in your pool?'

It *was* hot—and humid—and suddenly Zoe wanted more than anything to dive into the water. Perspiration prickled on her brow and her dress clung stickily to her back. But the pool wasn't very large. It seemed too intimate to be sharing it with him. Maybe she'd spent too long admiring his rear view. Then again, sitting outside was starting to get uncomfortable—despite the shade of the frangipani tree.

Mitch didn't hesitate. He strode to the edge of the pool and dived in with an arrow-perfect dive and barely a splash.

He swam the length of the pool underwater, his tanned, perfect body spearing through the turquoise depths. When he emerged his hair sat sleek and dark against his head, and his broad shoulders and chest glistened with drops of water caught in the late-afternoon sun. Zoe caught her breath at how handsome he looked.

'Come on in!' he called with the engaging grin that had appealed to her so much all those years ago.

Still she hesitated. Usually she wouldn't think twice about slipping off her dress and diving in. But the very act of taking off her dress in front of Mitch paralysed her. It seemed like... Well, it seemed like a striptease—as if she were displaying her body for his delectation. But it would seem ridiculous to go inside when she already had her bikini on underneath.

She compromised and turned away, angling her body for minimum exposure to Mitch. Then slid her dress up and over her head, tossing it onto the lounger.

She was aware of Mitch's gaze on her. Of the admiration in his eyes. It disconcerted her. She wasn't afraid to be seen in a bikini. She worked hard to stay slim and strong. And her fashionable bikini was quite modestly cut, in a retro style reminiscent of a swimsuit from the nineteen-fifties. But she was suddenly aware of how its very design drew attention to her breasts, her hips. In the past Mitch had seen her as a nerd, a geek. She doubted he'd even noticed she was female. Not with tall, curvy Lara always in tow, staking her claim on Mitch at any opportunity. Not that she'd needed to—Mitch had only had eyes for his blonde girlfriend.

But now... Now Mitch had noticed she was female. It was in his narrowed eyes, in the way his head was tilted to the side as he watched her.

And she liked it.

CHAPTER FIVE

ZOE LIKED THE way Mitch didn't hide his appreciation of the woman she'd become. She liked the easy way she could talk with him. She liked having him back in her life, even if only for these few hours. No way would she let that be ruined by feeling awkward or self-conscious. That kind of negativity had been left far behind her, in the corridors of Northside High.

He was the most beautiful man she was ever likely to meet—and not just in appearance. Scratch the surface of the mega sports star, the billboard model, the oestrogen magnet who had female hearts in a flurry all around the world, and the Mitch she'd liked so much when she was seventeen was still there. Even more confident and self-assured, but still Mitch.

Thanks to a random shifting of the tectonic plates beneath the earth's crust she'd been gifted this time before they each went back to their lives on opposite sides of the world.

She took a few swift steps to the edge of the water and waded in. Although a more than competent swimmer, she didn't want to risk an embarrassing belly flop in front of one of the world's elite athletes.

Zoe gasped and squealed at the initial coolness of the water, then welcomed it. With slow, easy strokes she swam from one end of the pool to the other. On her return lap she found herself very close to Mitch—so close their bodies actually nudged in the water: thigh against thigh, hip against hip. His body was strong, hard, muscular.

A shiver of pleasure ran through her at the contact. Had he noticed? Hastily she pushed away through the water to swim another lap.

He must be so used to women fawning all over him. That would *not* be her. She was determined to seem friendly, but not too friendly. No groupie-like grasping for attention from Mr Sexiest Man Alive for her. Much as she might yearn for it.

Her laps completed, she stood facing him in the shallow end of the pool, the water up to her waist

'That was a good idea. So refreshing.'

'It's not a huge pool, but it works,' he said.

No doubt he was staying in one of the larger, more luxurious villas the size of a house at the other end of the resort.

'This pool's only meant for two,' she said, breathless more from her proximity to him than from the vigour of her swimming. 'These villas are popular with honeymooners, I believe.'

She was suddenly heart-stoppingly aware of the utter privacy afforded by the high wall and the tropical trees and shrubs that grew above it, the solid, ornately carved wooden gate. A couple could frolic without a stitch on in this pool and no one would know.

'I booked in to this place because I wanted privacy,' Mitch said. He looked down to the bare third finger of her left hand. 'Why are you here on your own?'

'Because I want to be,' she said, careful to keep her voice matter-of-fact. 'May is a good time to take a break before all the end-of-financial-year mayhem in the final weeks of June.'

No need to mention that she'd needed to get away on her own to escape the fallout of a relationship break-up.

'That wasn't what I meant,' Mitch said with a slow grin. 'I wanted to know if there was a man in your life.'

'Oh,' she said. It was a reasonable question but she felt flustered by it. As if he'd been reading her mind. 'No,' she said. 'Not…not any more.'

'That surprises me,' he said.

She was aware of his appreciative gaze taking in the swell of her breasts over the top of her bikini bra, her bare shoulders and arms. She sucked in her stomach.

'There was someone. But…but I broke up with him a month ago.'

'Were you meant to come here with him?' He gestured around him. 'To this "couples' paradise"?'

'We were talking about Thailand. This was a last-minute booking.'

He nodded. 'Yeah, you said.' Mitch's green eyes narrowed. 'So you came to Bali to nurse a broken heart?'

'No.' She sighed, looked down at the water where it rippled around them. 'More likely I…I broke *his* heart.'

'I didn't take you for the heartbreaker type,' Mitch said.

Zoe slowly shook her head. 'I didn't think I was the heartbreaker type either. I've had my share of dating hurt, but it's not pleasant to be the one dishing it out. I'm not proud of it. He was a wonderful guy.'

'But not wonderful enough to go on vacation with?'

She met his gaze. 'Not wonderful enough to marry. We were talking about taking a vacation together. Then he turned it around to talk of a honeymoon.'

'And you ran scared?' Mitch said.

'I don't know about being scared. I just didn't feel the same way he did.'

She was beginning to wonder if there was something

wrong with her that at the age of twenty-seven she still didn't want to commit to a man. This recent proposal was the second one she'd turned down. But she wasn't going to share that with Mitch.

'You're not interested in marriage?' he asked.

'Of course I am. One day. And I'd like to have a family. But not now. Not to him—nice as he was. I didn't feel strongly enough to make that kind of commitment.'

The conversation was taking on a more personal slant than she cared for. But the shock of the earthquake, the surprise of seeing Mitch again, had loosened her inhibitions about talking about her love-life—or lack of it.

'Fair enough,' he said.

'I won't compromise. When I get married it will be because I'm head over heels in love and know it will last for ever.'

His brow raised. 'Okay…'

She laughed. 'You're looking at me as if you can't believe I said that.'

'I was surprised,' he admitted. 'I took you more for the practical, pragmatic type.'

'Because I'm an accountant with a business degree?'

'Who knew that underneath the number-crunching and the bean-counting there beats the heart of a romantic?'

Zoe tried not to sound defensive. 'Maybe it *is* ridiculously romantic of me, but I want the kind of love my parents had. They adored each other. I won't settle for less.'

'Admirable,' he said.

'But over-idealistic?'

'I didn't say that.'

'Just raised your eyebrows and let me think it?'

He grinned. 'I didn't realise my eyebrows were so expressive.

'You'd be surprised what your eyebrows reveal about you,' she said.

Mitch waggled his eyebrows. 'What are my eyebrows saying now?'

Zoe paused to think up a sassy reply—only to be hit by a splash of expertly aimed pool water.

'Hey!' she spluttered, wiping water from her eyes with the back of her hand. 'What was that for?'

His eyes crinkled in amusement. 'You didn't read my eyebrows quickly enough, did you? They were challenging you to a water fight.'

'Challenge accepted,' she said without further hesitation. 'This is war.'

Laughing, she angled around him, shooting sprays of water with the edge of her hand as she struck the surface. Laughing too, he retaliated faster, harder, until the spray was constant between them. Defence became attack; attack became defence.

As Mitch pulled his arm way back, for a powerful splash she couldn't hope to deflect, Zoe ducked and swam underwater to the other end of the pool before resurfacing.

'Hah! Retreating from the battlefield,' said Mitch.

'A tactical move to regroup my energies,' Zoe said breathless, laughing, pushing back her wet hair from her eyes.

Mitch raised his hands above his head. 'I surrender,' he said, with that big, endearing grin that had made him the darling of the women's magazines.

It wouldn't take much for her to surrender to him.

With just a few strokes of his strong, sinewy arms he had reached her. He wasn't the slightest bit out of breath.

'Why don't I trust that surrender one little bit?' she said, moving back in the water so she could feel the edge of the pool at her spine.

'Because I learned the game fighting dirty with my three brothers in our backyard pool,' he said, stopping just a pace from her.

'Let's call it a draw, then, shall we?' she said. Her heart was pounding—not from exertion, but from his closeness: the muscled breadth of his chest, the washboard abs.

The utter male perfection of him.

'I'm a competitive guy. I don't give in too easily.'

She didn't know whether the towering conquest in his stance was real or part of the game. Her heartbeat skipped up a further gear.

She met his gaze for a long moment before replying. 'I'm a diplomatic woman. I'm thinking of ways we can end this peacefully.'

Oh, she could think of several ways that she'd never dare put voice to.

He laughed. 'Seriously? How can I argue against that? I really am conceding.'

'Can I trust you?' she asked playfully.

He held out his hands, palms up in supplication. 'You can trust me, Zoe,' he said.

Other words unspoken hung in the air. Trust had been an issue in their brief, shared past. But he had redeemed himself by apologising for the incident that had ended their youthful friendship.

This was just a game.

The silence was broken by the loud crowing of a rooster coming from a few buildings away.

'The final word comes from Mr Rooster,' Zoe said.

Mitch scowled. 'Darn bird. He crows morning, noon and night.'

'He must have quite the harem of hens to keep happy.'

'It's not a sound I hear in the heart of old Madrid.'

'Or me in Balmain, in inner Sydney.'

'You live in Balmain?'

She nodded. 'In a converted warehouse on the waterfront, overlooking Mort Bay.'

'I played the Balmain Tigers in junior club. They were a good team. Beat 'em, of course.'

'You really are competitive, aren't you?'

'Only winners are grinners,' he said, and although he was smiling his words rang true. 'In my game you can't afford to be anything else.'

'An attacking midfielder. That's what I've seen you described as. It sounds aggressive.'

Zoe had seen him play on screen: swift, superbly balanced, relentless and graceful all at the same time. No other player had caught her attention. She'd thrilled at the TV commentator's praise for Mitch. While she didn't know a lot about soccer, she'd got what the commentator had meant when he'd said Mitch had the vision to split a defence with unerringly accurate passes perfectly weighted to gift his teammates with scoring opportunities. No wonder his team wanted him back.

His jaw set. 'You have to be aggressive to win, Zoe. Tactical and ruthless.'

'And you're all about winning?'

'The game is *everything*.' He emphasised the word so there was no missing his message.

'And in your personal life?'

'What personal life?' he joked, but his eyes were shadowed and serious.

He had quizzed her about *her* love-life; she had a few questions of her own.

'You were with Lara for a long time,' she said.

Again, she didn't want him to think she'd been stalking him. But Mitch's hometown girlfriend had attracted lots of media attention—both in Australia and overseas. Lara had only got blonder and more glamorous as she'd grown up. The golden couple had been all over the media, and Lara had become the queen bee of the contingent of footballers' wives and girlfriends the media nicknamed WAGs.

'We had our ups and downs,' Mitch muttered.

Zoe wouldn't have been human if she hadn't felt a small degree of satisfaction when she'd seen Mitch had finally split with Lara. Much as she'd put that incident at school behind her, Lara's maliciousness had been impossible to forget. She'd been the meanest of the mean girls. *Mitch deserved better.*

'I'm sorry,' she said, willing her voice to sound sincere.

Mitch shrugged and water slicked off his broad shoulders. 'Don't be. We broke up and got back together so many times. It was never going to work.'

From his carefully schooled expression and even tone of voice Zoe sensed there was more to it than Mitch was saying. That was okay. It was none of her business.

'No one special since?' She thought of the parade of Lara look-alikes who'd featured briefly on Mitch's arm.

He turned to scoop up a palm frond that had fallen into the water and tossed it out onto the courtyard, his back rippling with sculpted muscle. 'I don't have time for someone special. Date someone more than a few times and they start thinking it's more than a casual thing.'

Who could blame the poor girls for wanting more with a man like Mitch?

'You must get women flinging themselves at you all the time.' *But what a way to get your heart broken.*

He shifted and looked uncomfortable. 'Football groupies and over-eager fans come with the territory,' he said. 'What's more difficult is meeting genuine women not blinded by money and fame.'

'I can see that, but—'

He cut across her. 'But that's irrelevant right now. My personal life is on hold. Indefinitely. I've got something to prove. There's no room in my life for relationships. Not now. Not for years.'

'You're focusing on success and nothing is going to distract you?'

'That's exactly right,' he said. 'I'm glad you understand. Women usually think they can change my mind.'

'The hopes of all those fans shattered!' she said with mock mournfulness.

'And you breaking hearts all the way, let me remind you.'

'If you put it like that...'

'Putting it like that makes us both single,' he said, his deep voice a tone deeper.

'Yes,' she murmured through a suddenly choked throat.

For a long, still moment their eyes held. The intensity of his gaze reminded her of Mitch as a student, determined to understand the subject she was helping him to master. Back then he'd been reading a page in a poetry book; right now it felt as if he was reading her face as his gaze searched her eyes, her mouth.

In turn she explored *his* face. His chiselled face. His strong jaw. The knowing glint in his green eyes framed by those too-expressive eyebrows. And his mouth, lifted to a half-smile that gave a promise of pleasure that made her own lips part in anticipation, her breath quicken.

Her eyes locked with his and a thrill of anticipation tingled through her.

Mitch Bailey was about to kiss her. And she was going to kiss him right back.

CHAPTER SIX

MITCH HAD BEEN aching to kiss Zoe ever since she'd joined him in the pool. But just as his lips grazed hers, just as her lips parted under his, just as she uttered a delicious little moan of surprise and need, an Oriental-sounding chime came from the carved gate to the villa.

'Room service!' called a cheerful voice with a lilting Balinese accent.

Mitch stilled. Zoe looked up into his eyes. He saw echoed in hers the same frustration he was feeling at being thwarted in their first kiss.

For a long moment they stood motionless in the water, his mouth still claiming hers, her hands resting on his shoulders in silent agreement to pretend they weren't there.

The doorbell chimed again.

Mitch muttered a curse under his breath. Then he pulled Zoe closer and kissed her hard. She wound her arms around his neck and kissed him back with equal passion. Heat ignited between them so fast he was surprised steam wasn't rising from the water.

Damn the room service timing.

With regret he let her go, then pulled her back for a final swift kiss. If she could see his thought bubble now it would give her the promise torn from him. *Later.*

'Come in,' he called to the waiter on the other side of the gate, his voice hoarse.

Reluctantly he let Zoe go, supporting her when she seemed to stagger in the water. When she'd regained her balance he swam to the edge of the pool, then turned back to check she was okay.

The sight of her wading out of the water made him suck in a gasp of admiration. *She was awesome.* With both hands she pushed her wet hair from her face, so it was slicked behind her ears and flat to her head. The severe hairstyle emphasised the angular, unconventional beauty of her face. That black bikini concealed more than it revealed, yet he found the very subtlety of it tantalising. Zoe was smart, fun, *different.* He couldn't remember when he'd last bantered and laughed like that with a woman.

He flung a blue-striped beach towel around his shoulders and handed her one as she got out of the pool. 'It's an improvement on the white one,' he said in a low voice.

'Anything would be an improvement on that,' she said, her voice not quite steady as she wrapped the towel around her.

The smiling young waiter, dressed in the version of traditional garb that formed the staff's uniform, carried in a large silver tray. He placed the tray on the outdoor table and, with a flourish, lifted the lids that covered the plates.

'*Terima kasih*—thank you,' Zoe said to the waiter with her vibrant smile.

Her teeth were perfect—even and white. Had she worn braces at school? Mitch couldn't be sure. He was racking his brains to try and remember everything about her back then.

Their dinner was presented with simple Asian elegance. No one would know it had come from a kitchen suffering the after-effects of an earthquake. Deliciously spicy smells wafted from the tray and Mitch's stomach rumbled. But hunger of a different kind was foremost in his mind.

He echoed Zoe's thanks to the waiter, tipped him generously, and watched impatiently for the high, ornate gate to close behind him.

Finally he was alone again with Zoe, in the total privacy of the villa. It seemed suddenly very quiet. He was aware of the faint lapping of the water against the sides of the pool; the rustle of birds settling for the night in the surrounding trees. He swore he could even hear the fizzing of the bubbles in the mineral water Zoe had ordered. A faint smell of incense wafted across from the nearby Hindu temple, to mingle with the aromas of their dinner and the sweetness of frangipani blossom.

Mitch found he had to clear his throat to speak. 'Dinner is served,' he said, with a mock bow.

'So I see. It smells amazing. I…I'm suddenly hungry again.'

There was an edge to her voice—as if she were trying too hard to make conversation. She tugged at the knot that kept the beach towel secure between her breasts.

'The waiter has gone,' he said. 'You can ditch the towel.'

'I'd rather keep it on,' she said.

'Because it's so cold?'

Although it was starting to get dark, it was still hot, the air thick and humid.

'I feel more comfortable covered up,' she said, not meeting his eyes.

'Zoe—'

'Mitch—' she said at the same time.

'Back then—'

'In…in the pool—' she stuttered.

'When we—'

She raised her eyes to meet his. 'I don't think it should happen again. The...the kiss, I mean.'

'I didn't think you meant the water fight,' Mitch quipped.

She smiled and her shoulders visibly relaxed. 'I enjoyed the water fight.' She flushed high on her cheekbones. 'I...I enjoyed the kiss.'

'I'm glad to hear that.' He couldn't keep the irony from his tone.

'But...'

With a sinking feeling, Mitch had known there was a *but* coming.

'But, considering the circumstances, I think we should stick to...to being friends.'

Mitch felt intense disappointment with an overlay of relief. He suspected Zoe wasn't the kind of girl for a one-night fling. And right now that was all he could offer with his life the way it was. He'd hurt her in the past. He certainly had no wish to hurt her now.

'You're right,' he said through gritted teeth.

Of course she was right—much as he might wish otherwise, much as he ached for her to continue that kiss.

'Just friends.'

'Thank you,' she murmured.

But he wanted her.

This urgent desire for her had come from left field. He hadn't looked at Zoe in that way when they'd been teenagers, much as he'd liked her. He'd been with Lara, and he'd prided himself on being faithful even then.

But now he was single, and the sway of Zoe's hips, the swell of her breasts, her lovely mouth and her husky laughter was driving him crazy with want. However, he knew it would be better for her if he held back and didn't act on that desire. Better for him too. He didn't want to carry another burden of guilt away with him when they said goodbye.

'So we'll treat that kiss as the spoils of our water battle in the swimming pool?' he said, forcing his voice to sound light-hearted.

'In which both sides triumphed,' she said, with a sigh that sounded halfway between relief and regret. Which only made him want her more.

Oh, yes, a kiss from Mitch was a prize indeed.

Zoe's head was still spinning from the impact of Mitch's brief but passionate possession of her mouth. His lips had only been on hers for such a short time, but the joy of it had been seared into her soul.

If a kiss felt like that what would making love with him be like?

She pushed the thought far, far away into the deepest recesses of her heart.

Had she always wanted this? Her body pulled close to his? The taste of him? the touch of him? The sheer bliss of being with him?

That teenage crush had never gone away.

It was only one kiss. But it had awakened a desire for him so powerful it would have led to more than a kiss. And she couldn't deal with that. Not when he'd made it so clear that there was no room for a woman in his life. Not when, once this brief alignment of their planets was over, they'd go back to their different worlds. *She would probably never see him again.* Her desire for him was as impossible as that deeply buried crush had been so long ago.

'No need to look so woeful,' he said.

He pulled her into a hug. She hesitated at first, then relaxed into his arms. Her head rested on his shoulder and he stroked her hair. She closed her eyes, the better to savour the utter pleasure of his hands on her.

'It's not our time, not our place,' he said. 'But I'm glad we met up again, Zoe Summers. I'm pleased to count you as a friend.'

'Me too,' she said, wishing she could stay in his arms longer, knowing it wasn't a good idea. Her in a bikini, him in his swim shorts—full-body, bare skin contact. While her mind was telling her to pull away her body was clamouring for more.

'Let's enjoy our dinner,' he said. 'Then I'll go back to my villa. Because I can't guarantee I won't kiss you again.'

Zoe blinked down hard on a sudden smarting of tears. 'Good idea. I...I mean bad idea. I mean *wise* idea.'

She pulled away from his hug, feeling bereft of his warmth, his strength, and forced her voice to sound cheerful and matter-of-fact when inside she was a churning mess of conflict.

It would be only too easy to tell him to stay. But then, when they went their separate ways, she would have to live with it—and that might throw her right back into those high school feelings of unworthiness she'd worked so hard to shake off. Her life was settled, steady, sure—dull compared to his.

She could never be part of Mitch's world.

She tucked the beach towel around her a little more firmly. *'Usted debe ser hambre,'* she said in her best Spanish accent.

'Now that you mention it, yes, I am starving,' he said. He took her hand and led her to where the waiter had set up their dinner table, with two chairs facing opposite each other. 'Let's make the most of this meal.'

Zoe did her best. The *ayam bakar* with lemongrass salsa was one of the best chicken dishes Zoe had ever enjoyed.

But she managed only a few half-hearted bites, pushing it around her plate. Mitch, on the contrary, ate heartily. By not eating was she trying to postpone the moment dinner was over? If so, what did that mean *he* was doing?

He pushed his plate away with a satisfied sigh. 'The food in Madrid is amazing, but this fish is up there with the best meal ever.'

'It looked really good,' she said, struggling to make polite conversation.

'But you've hardly touched yours,' he said.

'I'm not really hungry,' she murmured, the knot in her stomach tightening.

'Why don't we wait a while before we eat dessert?' he said.

'Good idea,' she said.

Anything to postpone the time when they had to say goodbye.

Darkness had fallen, but the sensor-driven lights hidden in the greenery and at the edge of the pool had been switched on. The scene was peaceful and beautiful.

'This time last night I was watching the sunset on the beach,' Mitch said.

'Me too,' she said.

She wished he hadn't evoked the memory of it. Standing on the endless stretch of the dark Seminyak sand, watching the magnificence of the sun sinking into the sea, had been the only times she'd felt lonely on this solitary vacation. To know Mitch had been somewhere on the same beach somehow made it worse.

He got up from his chair.

'Let's sit over here,' he said, heading towards the loungers.

He dragged away the small table from in between and pushed the loungers together. When he'd sat down he patted the lounger next to him. It was an invitation she could not resist.

Mitch put a friendly arm around her. She relaxed against his shoulder, breathing in the clean, male scent of him, storing up the memory of it to relive next time she saw him on television, playing the game he loved so much on some international soccer pitch, where tens of thousands of spectators watched him in the flesh.

How would she be able to bear it?

At that precise moment the rooster chose the occasion for another of his raucous, triumphant cries, which lifted her from her maudlin thoughts.

'Trust him to have the last word,' she said.

Both she and Mitch laughed.

But the laughter froze in her throat as she noticed the still turquoise surface of the swimming pool start to shimmer—as if a giant hand had picked up the concrete edge and shaken it.

CHAPTER SEVEN

LAUGHING AND FOOLING AROUND with Mitch had distracted Zoe from the danger of a possible aftershock. Now her fear came rushing back as powerfully as a possible tsunami.

The loungers she and Mitch were reclining on started to shake. The plates, knives and forks and glasses from their unfinished feast clattered together. Zoe shrank against Mitch, paralysed with terror. The whimpering that echoed in her ears came from her.

'Under the table—now,' Mitch urged, and he helped her roll off the lounger and crawl to the table. He pushed her under first, then squeezed in with her, putting his arm around her to pull her tight to him.

Was this it—the big one?

Every so often she had nightmares about being in the car when the truck had hit them. Of struggling in and out of consciousness with an agonising pain in her leg. Paramedics talking to her in soothing tones with an edge of pity they hadn't been able to suppress. No one answering her questions about her parents. The eventual dreadful knowledge that she would never see them again.

She was usually successful at pushing thoughts of her loss to the dark shadows at the back of her mind. Not so now.

Earlier today something with the potential to wipe out

her world had again come from nowhere, completely out of her control. Now it was threatening her again.

She burrowed her face against Mitch's shoulder, grateful for his comfort, his strength, for the soothing reassuring sounds he was making as he stroked her back.

'You'll be okay. I think it's only a tiny tremor,' he repeated.

As it happened, he was right. It was probably only seconds rather than minutes before the tremor subsided.

For a few long moments she stayed in Mitch's protective embrace as the resort settled again.

'Do you think there'll be another tremor?' she asked, her voice muffled.

'Difficult to say,' he said. 'If anything catastrophic had happened—like a tsunami warning—we would have heard alarms by now.'

'That...that wasn't too bad.' She lifted her head to meet his gaze but was reluctant to move out of the comforting circle of his arms, the illusion of safety under the table.

'I think it's safe to come out now,' he said with that disarming smile, but he made no effort to move away from her.

'Thank you,' she said, mildly ashamed of her reaction. 'I never thought I'd dive under a table twice in one day.'

She'd always prided herself on her level-headedness. *But she had been afraid.*

She eased away from his arms and crawled out from under the table while Mitch did the same, then stood next to him as they looked around them. Except for a further scattering of frangipani blossoms and a new palm frond on the surface of the pool, now still again, there had been no damage. The rooster was going crazy—but then he did tend to sound off at this time of evening.

But what if it hadn't been that way?

What if she and Mitch had been injured? What if she'd never seen him again not because he'd gone back to Madrid but because he…?

She couldn't bear even to think through the rest.

Or what if another quake came during the night and…?

You could never be certain of tomorrow.

'You okay?' he said.

She nodded. 'You?'

'Fine. It was nothing compared to the last one. Though it did jolt me.'

'I'm glad you didn't go back to your villa.'

'Me too,' he said. 'I would have been in a state without you to hold on to.'

He was being kind, uttering the self-deprecating words for her sake. She knew that. It was she who had fallen to pieces. Not him. He hadn't been afraid. Not for a moment. He was just trying to make her feel better.

That seemed to be Mitch all round. Sexiest man alive. Star athlete. Fun. And kind. In short, the most wonderful man she had ever met or was ever likely to meet. *Mitch was unique.* And not just because of the way he looked or his skill with a ball.

The earthquake had dropped him into her life again and shaken the way she thought to its very foundations. Nothing could be the same.

Suddenly everything became very clear. She did not want to be plagued with regrets. This might be the only chance she ever had to be with Mitch.

She couldn't let him go back to his villa.

She turned to face him and clutched his arm so hard he winced. Her heart was thudding so loudly she was surprised he couldn't hear it, and her mouth was dry.

'Don't go tonight, Mitch. Stay with me.'

His eyes seemed to darken to a deeper shade of green. 'Zoe, are you sure?'

She tilted her face to his, twined her arms around his neck and kissed him. He seemed surprised, and paused for just a second before he kissed her back. His lips were warm and firm and exciting beneath hers and she explored the way he tasted, the way he felt. Mitch hugged her to him as he deepened the kiss so it escalated into a passionate meeting of mouths, tongues, teeth.

Desire for him rushed through her—urgent, demanding, insistent. *She wanted him and she wanted him now.*

It wasn't about the earthquake—that was just a facilitator. It was about *him*. If she'd bumped into him at sunset on the beach she would have wanted him. If she'd chanced upon him in a bar in Seminyak and they'd got chatting she would have wanted him.

She was realistic. Mitch obviously went for stunningly beautiful girls like Lara—blonde and glamorous. She, Zoe, hitting average on the looks scale, was never likely to capture Mitch Bailey's attention. But here, now, she had.

She'd wanted him at seventeen and hadn't been able to have him. Now she was going to take what she wanted. Even if it was for only one night.

She broke the kiss and pulled away, panting and breathless. 'I…I think we should go inside.'

'It's completely private here—look at the height of those walls.'

'Wh…what about helicopters?'

Mitch's brow rose, bemused. 'Helicopters? Why would you worry about *helicopters*?'

She felt a little foolish. 'I don't know. Your world is so different to mine. But I thought—'

Mitch laughed, but it was laughter free of mockery.

'I'm not so famous that I'm harassed by paparazzi buzzing overhead in helicopters.'

'Just being sure,' she said. 'I would hate to see a blurry photo of us on the internet, with a reference to myself as the "mystery brunette" seen making out with Mitch Bailey in his luxurious Bali villa.'

'Not going to happen,' he said.

'You're sure of that?' she said, with more than a touch of worry.

Mitch trailed a finger along the curve of her jaw, sending a jolt of awareness through every pleasure receptor in her body. 'What happens in your villa stays in your villa,' he said. 'I don't want publicity either.'

'I'd still be happier if we went inside,' she said.

The walls were high, but she *would* prefer to be behind closed doors with Mitch, safe from any curious eyes.

'Just one thing before we go,' he said.

He picked up a frangipani blossom and tucked in behind her ear, making it a caress.

The gesture undid her. Who knew Mitch could be so romantic?

'Thank you,' she said with a slow smile. 'I love the scent.'

'And a second thing…'

He reached over and undid the knot that secured her beach towel so it fell to the ground.

Zoe in his arms. Zoe kissing him. Zoe wanting him to stay with her.

There was nothing he wanted more.

But, much as he ached to pick her up and carry her into her bedroom, Mitch knew he had to slow things down.

For all Zoe's sassiness and smarts, Mitch sensed a vulnerability about her that had not lessened since he'd known her as a recently bereaved seventeen-year-old. The foundations of her life had been yanked out from underneath her. This earthquake had shaken them some more—and he didn't just mean literally.

He wanted to take up her invitation. But he wanted her to be sure what she was letting herself in for. He could not damage her further.

As soon as they got inside the villa Zoe tilted her face to his. Her flawless skin was flushed, her brown eyes luminous with desire, and her lips were parted on a half-smile that was so seductive he caught his breath. Laughing that low, husky laugh, as though she knew her power over him, she pulled him to her for another urgent kiss.

When the kiss threatened to get out of control he broke away, smoothed her hair—drying now into a dark mass of waves—from around from her face, and secured the flower behind her ear. He liked the way it looked there—exotic, sensual. Then he cupped her face in his hands, looked deep into her eyes.

He had to clear his throat to speak. 'Before we go any further we have to be sure. This is all there can be for us. Tonight.'

She laughed a husky, strangled laugh. 'Tonight might be all we ever have. We could wake up to find ourselves floating out to sea.'

'There's that,' he said. 'But—'

She put a finger to his lips to silence him.

He moved it away, then slipped his fingers through hers and firmly held her hand by her side.

'This has to be said.'

He was trying to be the sensible one here, when all he could think of was how much he wanted Zoe.

She made a pretend pout, which astounded him, and had him fighting the temptation to kiss her again.

'I don't want to waste any more time talking,' she murmured.

He groaned. Did she know what she was doing to him? He gave in to temptation and planted a quick kiss on her lovely mouth. But that was it until they'd got this sorted. He wanted her—but he did not want her hurt.

'You're amazing, Zoe. Gorgeous. Fun. Smart as ever. A surprise. But there's no room for a serious relationship in my life. Not for years. Not until I'm thirty. Maybe thirty-five. I was at the top of my game when I got injured. I have to prove myself all over again. I can't afford…emotional entanglements.'

She shook her head and made a little murmur of impatience. 'Can't you see I'm not looking beyond tonight? The world as we know it could be wiped out—I want to take the chance for us to be together while we can. You were wonderful when you were a teenager and you've grown into a wonderful man. All the qualities you had then are still there, and more. I want to spend this night with you. No matter what tomorrow might bring.'

'Thank you,' he said, moved by her words.

Back then, he realised, she had seen potential in him that others hadn't; only Zoe had recognised him as more than a good-looking jock.

'I could say the same about you.'

There was a wistful edge to her smile. 'Thank you. But, as I said earlier, we live on different planets. I'm not expecting more from you than this one night.'

He started to say something but she put her finger across his mouth again.

'I want you. But I wouldn't want a relationship with someone in the public eye—a man who belongs to his fans, not one hundred per cent to me. I'd be miserable with someone who travels the world while I'm left at home, torturing myself with thoughts about the women who might be throwing themselves at him. I'm a private person. I don't want the world to know me because of the man I'm with. I…I could never be a WAG.'

Though her words made absolute sense, he found them more than a touch insulting. That *was* his life. And it was the best life a guy could have. *It was all he wanted.* For him it wasn't about the kudos, the fame, the money. It was about the game.

'That's a lot about what you *don't* want,' he said. 'Now let's hear what you *do* want, Zoe.'

She pulled one of those faces he found so appealing. 'We've established it's ridiculously romantic of me, but one day I want a real, for ever kind of love.'

'Like your parents had?'

She nodded. 'Not just for me, but for my children. I had the happiest childhood you can imagine. It was erratic. We moved from one shared household to another. From one failed venture to another. And at the age of ten I knew how to lie to a debt collector. But I was secure in the love my parents had for each other and for me. I want to love and be loved on that scale. I…I think I value it so much because it was wrenched away from me.'

'And that happened not long before I first knew you.' He felt a surge of anger against his younger self, who had hurt her at a time when she hadn't needed more hurt added to her burden.

'When you first knew me I was like a…like a creature who had been wrenched from its cocoon way too soon and thrown into the harsh reality of life with a grandmother who resented me.'

Mitch realised his parents also had a good marriage. They argued. There was noise and fireworks. But they were happy, and they'd raised well-balanced, successful sons. It was a fine goal to aspire to. *Just not yet.* Marriage right now would seem like a trap.

'I guess that's what I want too, one day. But not now.'

He'd made a lot of sacrifices to get where he was. Since he'd left school he hadn't had what most people would call a 'normal' life. Giving up any thought of a permanent relationship was another sacrifice he was more than happy to make. But if he could have Zoe for tonight—for one night—that would be something very special.

She looked up to him. 'Mitch, you asked me what I really want…'

'Yes. And you told me.'

'I told you what I want for the future. Ask me what I want for *now*.'

'I'm asking you,' he said, his voice hoarse with need.

Her eyes were huge and her mouth quivered. 'I want *you*, Mitch. Just you.'

He could not resist her any longer.

With a groan, he lifted her up to sit on the edge of the countertop. She wound her arms around his neck, her thighs gripping his waist as he held her to him. He kissed her mouth, deep and demanding, then pressed urgent, hungry kisses down the smooth column of her throat as she arched her body to his.

He hoped his kisses would transmit everything he couldn't say about how glad he was to be with her on this night, when they didn't know what they might wake up to the next hour, the next day. He kissed her and kissed her and kissed her—until kissing was no longer enough.

Zoe was woken by the soft, insistent buzzing of her mobile phone to let her know there was a text message for her.

For a moment she didn't know where she was. She blinked against the early-morning light filtering in through the louvered doors. Heard that noisy rooster greeting the dawn.

She was in Bali. Still alive. With Mitch.

Mitch.

He lay beside her on his back, the sheets rumpled around his hips, his arms flung above his head in total relaxation. Her breath caught at how beautiful he was. *Beautiful* wasn't a word she'd normally use to describe a man, but it fitted Mitch. His smooth skin was gilded by the sunlight, his face rough with golden stubble she wanted to reach over and stroke. But she didn't want to risk waking him.

Her heart gave a huge, painful lurch at the thought that she would most likely never see him again. But if she'd woken up alone this morning she would have always regretted it.

Cautiously, so as not to disturb him, she reached over to her phone and slid the buzzer off. It was a message from the airline. Her plane back to Sydney was on schedule. She needed to be at the airport in two hours. That just gave her time to have breakfast with Mitch. To say goodbye.

No.

She couldn't bear that.

This kind of situation was a first for her. She could only imagine how awkward and embarrassing it would be to face him. Last night with Mitch had been perfect. She wanted to keep its perfection encapsulated in her mind for ever. Not sullied by awkward goodbyes, murmured promises they both knew would never be fulfilled.

Besides, she rationalised, the Ngurah Rai International Airport at Denpasar was sure to be bedlam because of the earthquake and its aftershock. She wanted to make sure she got on that plane and out of here; she didn't think she could cope with another tremor.

She looked back at Mitch, breathing deeply and evenly in her bed. They'd both got what they'd needed from each other at a time of threat and uncertainty. Comfort. Reassurance. *Sex.*

Oh, yes. Sex such as she'd never imagined. Sex that had seen her soaring to unimaginable heights of pleasure with Mitch. Again and again. Then again, when they'd woken some time after midnight, turned into each other's arms, laughed at the fact that they could still want each other after all the satisfaction they'd already given each other, and once more made love.

Afterwards they'd crept outside to the courtyard in the moonlight and polished off their abandoned desserts—even her melted ice cream—whispering and stifling their laughter when Mitch had threatened to crow out loud like a rooster.

They'd finally gone to sleep entwined in each other's arms.

Now, she supported herself on her elbow as she admired him for the last time—his handsome face, his finely honed athlete's body. In repose, his features looked much as when she'd first met him as a teenager, but layered now with the strength and character of a successful man.

For a fleeting, heart-wrenching moment she wished that things could be different.

She could so easily fall in love with Mitch.

She acknowledged the thought before she pummelled it, vanquished it, shoved it away into the furthest corner of her heart, never to be acknowledged again.

She slid out from the sheets as silently as she could. Mitch murmured in his sleep, threw out an arm across her abandoned pillow. She stilled. Held her breath. Waited a heartbeat, then another. But he didn't wake up.

She crept to the bathroom, then haphazardly flung her

stuff into the wheeled carry-on bag that was her only luggage. She regretted the lack of the batik bikini; she should have bought it when she saw it. She tugged a brush through her hair...decided to put on her make-up at the airport.

As quietly as she could she checked the closet, the bathroom, the hooks behind the bathroom door for anything she might have left behind. Before she slid on her shoes she tiptoed into the bedroom for a final silent farewell to the special man who had brought her body alive with so much pleasure last night.

She could not resist bringing her face to his and pressing a butterfly-light kiss on his beard-roughened cheek.

'Thank you,' she whispered.

Her heart caught at his sleepy murmur in response, at his faint smile. But he was still asleep.

She filled her memories with one final look at him. Then she turned and walked out through her hotel room, past the still waters of the pool, where three pink frangipani blossoms floated on the surface, and through the ornately carved wooden gate that led to the outside without looking back.

Mitch woke to bright sunlight that made him screw his eyes up against it. *Zoe*. Memories of the night he'd spent with her came flooding back.

'Stay with me,' he murmured, still half asleep.

He rolled over, seeking her, wanting to pull her close. He could smell her scent on his pillow, on *him*. But he was alone in Zoe's king-size hotel bed, the sheets next to him crumpled and cold.

Fully awake now, he strained to hear if she was in the shower. But the door to the adjoining bathroom was open and no one was in there.

'Zoe?' he called.

He swung himself out of the bed.

'Are you there?' His voice echoed in the empty still-ness of the room.

Then he noticed the closet door, ajar so he could see where a row of empty hangers swung. A drawer had been left slightly open.

Naked, he padded out into the living area. He looked through the sliding glass doors to the empty pool area. Plates and glasses lay haphazardly on the round table where they'd left them after their post-midnight snack.

Then he noticed the stack of Indonesian rupiah near the telephone. *'For the maid—thank you,'* was written in a bold, slanted hand on a piece of hotel notepaper.

She was gone.

He sank onto the sofa, stabbed by a feeling he couldn't put a name to. Loss. Regret. *Loneliness.*

The pain of it made him double over, his elbows on his knees, his head cradled in his hands. *Zoe.* What an amaz-ing woman. Last night had been like nothing he'd ever experienced before. Her lithe, slender body. Her generous mouth. Her laughter. Her warmth. Her wit. The thought-fulness and tenderness that was innate to her.

Zoe.

He wanted to roar out her name so she could hear him wherever she was—at the airport, on the plane. Hear him and come back to him.

But that couldn't be.

He had a difficult road ahead of him. Starting over. Fighting for his place in every game. Proving to the nay-sayers that his knee injury had not relegated him to the status of a once great player.

He could not be distracted by a woman. And Zoe would be a major distraction. She was a for ever kind of woman—

and for ever was a long way away from him. She deserved more than what he had to give.

The game. *The Beautiful Game.* That was the important thing.

A woman he could love—that had to come later.

CHAPTER EIGHT

Two months later

ZOE WAS STANDING by her desk, checking that all the documents she needed for that morning's important meeting in the city were loaded on her tablet. She was concentrating hard, but at the back of her mind she was aware of her senior accountant, Louise, chatting with someone at the external door to the office.

Her business—The Right Note: Accountancy and Tax—occupied the ground floor of a converted warehouse, part of a complex in Balmain. Zoe's living space was on the mezzanine level above.

She hoped the person at the door wasn't a client, hoping for an unscheduled appointment. That was the trouble with a client base drawn from musicians, writers, artists and entertainers—their idea of time didn't always match hers.

A glance at her watch told her she had time to catch the 9:15 a.m. ferry for the twenty-minute ride from Balmain into the city—but not a lot to spare.

She'd come to a crossroads with her business, and today's meeting with a potential buyer might help her decide which path to take. She needed to be at her most alert for the appointment—not flustered from being late. Louise would have to deal with the client.

Then Louise was by her side, her face flushed with excitement. 'Zoe, you've got no idea who's at the door, wanting to see you. *Mitch Bailey.*'

Zoe was too taken aback to do anything but stare at Louise.

'You know—the soccer player—the really hot one,' Louise added, her intonation implying that any red-blooded woman who didn't know who Mitch Bailey was needed her head read.

Zoe felt the blood drain from her face. Her heart started to hammer and a wave of nausea threatened to overwhelm her. Her hand went suddenly nerveless and her tablet started to slip from her grasp.

Louise caught the tablet and placed it on Zoe's desk. 'That's how I'd react if Mitch Bailey came to see me,' she said in a low, excited tone. 'He's even better-looking in person. Those eyes really are the most amazing green. And his smile... *Wow!*' Louise paused when she didn't get any reaction. 'Are you okay, Zoe?'

Zoe nodded. Cleared her throat. 'Of course I'm okay,' she choked out, in a reasonable facsimile of her normal speaking voice.

Mitch was here?

Louise nattered on. 'Do you think he's come to see us as a client? Someone might have recommended us to him. He wouldn't say. Just wants to see you. He's in the waiting area.'

Zoe cleared her throat. 'I...I'll see him.' She dragged in some deep, steadying breaths.

Mitch.

What was he doing in Sydney? What was he doing *here*?

As far as she knew Mitch was in Madrid, but her information wasn't up to date. On her return from Bali she'd found it impossible to stop thinking about him. Reliving over and over again the magical hours they'd shared at the villa. Every day she'd scoured the press for mentions of him, checked his official social media pages.

Ultimately she'd found it too distracting, too painful.

One night—that was all it was ever going to be. Mitch had made it very clear that there would be nothing more than that between them. An interlude with no future.

After a week she'd made a conscious decision—for her sanity's sake—not to check up on him, never to read the sports pages of the newspapers or watch the sports reports on television.

For all that, she hadn't been able to stop the dreams of him, of them together, that came to haunt her sleep. But she had nearly succeeded in putting him behind her—their time in Bali had been relegated to a bittersweet memory. And now he was here. It hardly seemed real.

Her hand went automatically to smooth her hair, and she pressed her lips together to ensure her lipstick was smooth.

'Don't worry about that. You look great,' whispered Louise, her eyes alight with curiosity.

Zoe hadn't confided in Louise or any other friend what had happened between her and Mitch in Bali.

'I wasn't worrying—' Zoe started to say, then stopped. Of *course* she was worrying about how she looked. *Mitch was here.*

Zoe wanted to sprint into the waiting area but forced herself to a sedate pace. She shouldn't read anything into this. Not after two months. Maybe Mitch was seeking some help with a double tax agreement with Spain. Or some other accountant-type advice.

She pasted a professional smile to her face. But her smile froze in stupefied admiration when she saw him. Mitch. Wearing a stylish tailored charcoal suit that emphasised his broad shoulders and strong, graceful body. He looked as if he'd stepped down off one of his billboards. The sexiest man alive was here in the waiting area of her company. And after the night they'd spent together she knew only too well how much he deserved that label.

Warm colour rushed into her cheeks when she realised it was the first time she'd seen him with clothes on—or more clothes than a pair of checked swim shorts.

Mitch seemed to freeze too, and she was conscious of him taking in every detail of her appearance. Thank heaven she'd taken extra trouble to look her best for the meeting. She was wearing a fitted deep pink designer suit—on sale at a bargain basement price but still designer—with slick black accessories. And she'd been up at the crack of dawn to make sure her hair and make-up were perfect.

She thought she'd got close to the image she wanted to portray to the management of the bigger firm—professional, but with a creative edge. To Mitch she hoped she appeared self-assured and independent. The kind of woman who took it completely in her stride when she was suddenly confronted by a man she had made love with two months ago. Without any communication whatsoever in between times. A woman who never cried into her pillow when she woke from her dreams of him.

She started to speak but had to clear her throat in order for the words to come out. In truth, she wasn't sure what to say. The last words she'd spoken to Mitch had been interspersed with sighs and murmurs of pleasure as they'd made love.

'Mitch—this is a surprise,' was all she could manage.

'Zoe.'

He took a few steps towards her and halted. She realised with a start that he seemed uncertain of his reception from her.

Her first impulse was to fling herself into his arms—that was where she wanted to be more than anything. But she wasn't a person who generally acted on impulse—unless an earthquake prompted her to do so, that was.

Instead she greeted him with a polite kiss on the cheek.

He held her briefly to him. Even that close contact was enough to send her senses skittering into hyper-awareness. Of his scent. His hard strength. The warmth of his body.

As he released her she stepped back and almost tripped on her stiletto heels. So much for seeming nonchalant, as if his presence didn't bother her at all.

'I was in Sydney and decided to look you up,' he said.

'How did you—?'

'Know where to find you? It didn't take advanced detective work to find an accountancy firm in a converted warehouse at Balmain.'

'Clever you,' she said, glad beyond measure that he had taken the trouble to track her down, uncertain as to his reason for doing so. 'But *why* are you in Sydney? Is it your knee?'

Mitch shook his head. 'My father had an accident.'

Zoe's hand flew to her mouth. 'I'm so sorry. Is he—?'

'He's fine. But I had to fly out to make sure for myself. I got here yesterday.'

He'd been in Sydney a day and she'd felt no awareness of him, had no 'Spidey-sense' knowledge that he was nearby. But then why should she? He was a one-time friend who'd become a one-time lover. That was all.

She was aching to ask him why he had come to see her, but instead took refuge in polite conversation.

'What happened to your dad?'

'He took up cycling—became a MAMIL.'

'You mean a Middle-Aged Man in Lycra?'

'That's the one. He went head over heels over his handlebars. Thankfully not in the path of any traffic. But he dislocated his collarbone, broke an arm and cracked a few ribs.'

'Ouch.' She shuddered in sympathy for the man she'd never met. 'Poor guy. Is he in hospital?'

'He's back home now. Complaining about having to stay in bed and making my mother's life hell.'

'But she must be so glad he's okay?'

His eyes crinkled in fond amusement. 'Of course she is.'

'Do your parents still live in Wahroonga?'

He nodded. 'In the same house I grew up in.'

The Bailey house was just a few streets away from her grandmother's house, where she'd spent such a miserable time. Since her return from Bali, Zoe had checked up on her grandmother. She was still alive, also still living in Wahroonga. But Zoe felt no desire to get in touch. Her life there seemed such a long time ago. The only good thing about that time had been Mitch.

'How long are you in Sydney for?' she asked, and immediately wished she could drag back the words. She didn't want him to think she was fishing for a chance to see him. But then again, he'd sought her out...

'I fly out tomorrow.'

'A short visit?' Her carefully modulated words masked her disappointment.

'Enough time to take you out to dinner.'

She swallowed hard. 'You mean tonight?'

'Are you free?'

Her pride didn't want him to think she was immediately available for a last-minute date. But she didn't want to play games. Especially not when the prize was an evening with Mitch. She couldn't lie to herself. Pride lost the battle.

'Of course I'm free,' she said.

Back in Madrid, Mitch hadn't been able to get Zoe out of his head. Her laughter, her passion, her vivacious face and gorgeous body had kept invading his thoughts.

He'd thrown himself into training. But still he'd thought of her. He'd dated other women. But each date had been hours wasted as in his mind he compared the poor woman—no matter how beautiful and charming— unfavourably with Zoe.

It had irked him. He didn't *want* to be distracted by thoughts of her. He didn't know why she'd slipped so thoroughly under his skin. Was it because *she'd* left *him* that morning two months ago? Left him and not made any effort to get in touch?

Yes, they'd agreed not to contact each other. But women had a tendency not to believe him when he told them he couldn't get involved. He'd had a few holiday flings before. With beautiful women who had recognised him and wanted to take whatever Mitch Bailey had to offer. He had always been the one to leave them to wake alone in their hotel room. And, when they'd tried to get in touch, to politely make it obvious that they were wasting their time.

Not Zoe. She'd left a note for the maid, but not for him. Was it a sense of unfinished business that bothered him? That made him unable to forget her?

He'd had no intention of seeing her when he'd unexpectedly come to Sydney. But he'd found himself looking her up—just out of interest, he'd told himself.

This morning he'd been on his way to a meeting with his Australian agent in the eastern suburbs. Somehow he'd detoured west to Balmain and down the narrow streets to this complex of converted warehouses. Now he'd asked Zoe out to dinner.

It was insanity. He should not be nudging open a door that should be kept firmly shut. Nothing had changed since Bali. There was still no room for Zoe or any other woman in his meticulously planned life. Yet here he was. And regretting it already.

Because the polished businesswoman standing before him wasn't the Zoe he remembered from their time together in Bali. That uninhibited Zoe had had tousled hair, worn no make-up, and had looked quite at home in nothing but a plain white towel—or nothing at all.

This Zoe—Corporate Zoe—was strikingly attractive in a very different way. The tailored, form-fitting suit and high heels, the shorter hair cut in an artfully layered style, the perfect make-up—all screamed candidate for Businesswoman of the Year. Not the girl who'd given as good as she'd got in a no-holds-barred water fight. Or in a big bed among tangled sheets under the slow flick of a ceiling fan on a steamy tropical night.

'Dinner tonight it is,' he said.

Though now he'd seen her he wondered if it was such a good idea.

In Madrid, he'd kept thinking about the connection they'd shared. A connection that had gone way beyond the physical and was like none he'd ever felt with a woman. But had it just been a holiday fling spiced by peril, the urgency of danger? Would they now struggle to find common ground?

'I'll look forward to it,' she said in her characteristic husky voice.

In any other woman he would find that voice an affectation. But Zoe's voice had had the same deep timbre at seventeen. Then it had seemed at odds with her schoolgirl persona. Now she'd grown into it—a sensual adult voice that sent awareness of her as a woman throbbing through him.

'Have you got anywhere in mind?'

He didn't. It had been a spur-of-the-moment decision to track her down. It would make him late for his meeting with his agent. Not that the agent would care. He made enough from his cut of Mitch's local earnings to put up with tardiness from his star client. Still, Mitch had called ahead to alert him. He believed in professional behaviour at all times.

He hadn't got as far as thinking about a restaurant. To see Zoe again, to see if she was still the woman who'd haunted his thoughts for two months, was all he had thought about.

'I'm going to be flat out all day so I'll look forward to dinner,' she said. 'I have a really important meeting with a company that—' She squealed. 'The ferry! I'm going to miss it! Be late for the meeting!'

Her face was screwed up in panic. Suddenly she looked more approachable. More like the Zoe he knew—or thought he knew.

'Let me drive you,' he said. 'To the city?'

'No. I mean yes. The meeting *is* in the city. But peak-hour morning traffic will be too heavy; I'll still be late. A ride to the ferry stop would be helpful, though.'

'Can do,' he said. 'I'm parked in your car park.'

'How did you get past the security guard?'

He grinned.

Her lips lifted in a half smile. 'Of course. You're Mitch Bailey. Why did I bother to ask?'

She turned rapidly on her high heels, dashed out of the room, and returned seconds later with a stylish leather satchel flung over her shoulder.

'Let's go,' she said.

Walking more briskly than he'd imagine anyone else could in those heels, she took off across the wooden dock at the harbourside front of the building, past the small marina and around to the car park.

He pressed his key fob and lights flashed as the doors unlocked on the innocuous mid-range sedan he'd rented for the few days he was in Sydney. It wasn't the type of car people would expect Mitch Bailey to drive, which was exactly why he'd chosen it. Choose a top-of-the-range European sports car like the one he had back in Madrid and he'd be inviting attention he didn't want.

So far he had evaded anyone outside his family and close circle of friends knowing he was back in Sydney. And Zoe too, of course. Where did she fit in? Friend? Lover? He found it impossible to categorise her.

She broke into a half run to get to the car and flung herself into the front passenger's seat after he'd opened the door for her. The car was suddenly filled with her energy, with her warm, heady scent—immediately familiar.

As he steered the car out of the car park she apologised for the rush. 'One of the bigger accounting firms has approached me to buy my business. My meeting this morning is with them.'

'That sounds impressive.' It didn't surprise him at all to hear she was doing well in the corporate world.

'It's flattering—that's for sure. They think I've tapped into a niche market they want a part of.'

'You don't sound one hundred per cent enthusiastic.' Since when had he been able to read her voice?

'I am and I'm not. They propose that my company would be absorbed by them as a specialised division, with me as the manager. But I worry that the vital personal touch might get lost if I lose control. My clients are an eccentric bunch and they could get scared off—even see my move as a betrayal. But I could help more people, expand the business to other states where there's a need for it.'

'It's a big decision.' He liked the way she was considering her clients—not just the potential gain for herself.

'There's pros and there's cons. I'll go in there this morning with an open mind.'

'You can tell me all about it tonight. I'll be interested to see what happens.'

As they spoke Mitch drove as fast as he could around the steep, narrow streets of Balmain, one of the oldest inner western suburbs of Sydney. The streets were lined with quaint restored nineteenth-century terrace houses and historic shop fronts. The area suited Zoe.

He turned into Darling Street and headed down towards the water. Ahead was the ferry terminal, framed by a view of the Sydney Harbour Bridge on the other side of the harbour.

'Thank heaven,' Zoe breathed when they saw the ferry was still docking. 'I wouldn't have made it without you.'

'You wouldn't have been late if I hadn't distracted you.'

'I'm glad you distracted me,' she said, tucking her satchel over her shoulder.

Mitch didn't know whether to read that as flirtatious or as a mere statement of fact. She was giving nothing away. Was she happy to see him or not? Had Bali meant anything to her?

She started to open the door before the car was completely stopped, then scrambled out. 'Gotta dash.'

She paused, half out and half in the car, revealing a stretch of slender leg that Mitch could not help but appreciate.

'I live on the floor above the office. Pick me up at seven-thirty tonight.'

'Right,' he said.

He reached out and put a hand on her arm. She stilled, and for a moment he thought she might shake his hand away from her.

'Good luck with the meeting,' he said. Had she thought he was going to say something else?

'I might need it,' she said, moving away. 'Thanks for the ride. See you tonight.'

She headed down to the ferry, which was now loading people across the gangplank. Commuting by ferry was an attractive part of Sydney living, he'd always thought.

The sight of her shapely back view in the bright pink suit as she broke into a half run down to the ferry was very appealing. She might be a different Zoe from the one he remembered from their time together in Bali, but she was just as hot in that subtly sexy way he'd found impossible to forget.

Which Zoe would he see tonight?

CHAPTER NINE

MITCH SAT ACROSS from Zoe at the harbourside restaurant he had booked for their dinner. He was not usually a man who found himself tongue-tied in conversation with a female companion. But tonight he was scraping around for something to say.

He and Zoe had already exclaimed over the spectacular view—the restaurant was situated on the north side of the harbour, right near the north pylon of the Sydney Harbour Bridge—and together they had marvelled at the sight of the lit-up ferries and pleasure boats criss-crossing the darkened waters of the harbour. They'd commented on the swimmers braving the winter to do laps below them, in the black-marked lanes of the Art Deco-style North Sydney Olympic Pool. And they'd each said how fond they were of the big grinning face that marked the entrance to Luna Park, the harbour-front amusement park next door.

Trouble was, that elephant was back. It was sitting below them, in the pale blue waters of that big swimming pool, looking up at them, taunting them. He and Zoe had spent the night together two months before, had shared the fear of possibly losing their lives, and yet neither of them had mentioned it. They were just acting as though they were old acquaintances catching up, skimming the surface with dinner table talk.

This morning he'd seen Corporate Zoe. Tonight he was with Sophisticated Zoe, stylish in a simple purple lace dress that covered her arms and chest but revealed glimpses of her creamy skin, the enticing curves of her breasts through the gaps in the lace. Her hair was slicked back smoothly to her head and she wore long drop earrings that moved when she turned. She was striking, elegant, self-assured.

Heads had turned when they'd walked in to the restaurant together—and they hadn't been looking at him. But he wanted the Zoe who'd turned *his* head wearing nothing but a skimpy white towel.

He remembered the flower he had tucked behind her ear that night in Bali—a prelude to the intimacy that had followed. Next morning he had found it, crumpled on her pillow. Never would he admit to anyone how he had scooped it up, wrapped it in a tissue from the bathroom and taken it back to Madrid with him.

He picked up the menu. 'Perhaps we should order?'

'Good idea,' she said.

'The menu looks good. Are you hungry?'

How inane was this conversation? He was flying back to Madrid the next day. The way this was going it didn't seem likely he would get a chance to talk to Zoe about anything important—let alone anything intimate.

He resisted the temptation to glance at his watch.

'Not excessively,' she said. 'I don't know that I've ever got over the Bali belly.'

At last—a reference to their recent shared past. He hoped the elephant was appeased.

'You're still feeling unwell?'

'Off and on.'

He frowned. 'That's a worry. You should get it checked out. You might have caught a tropical bug. They can have long-lasting consequences.'

He thought about telling her the story of his teammate who'd picked up a parasite through his bare feet in some country or other, but decided that was hardly dinner date conversation.

Zoe sighed. 'I know. I should go to the doctor. It's just I've been run off my feet at work—it's our busiest time of the year. All I do is work, work and more work.'

And date? Had she been going out with other guys? Had she found dating as unsatisfactory as he had?

The thought of her with another guy had tortured him back in Madrid. Had the ex-boyfriend come sniffing around? If he, Mitch, had had Zoe in his life he wouldn't have let her go easily.

Mitch gripped the side of the menu. *He had let her go.* He had made love to her all night and then just let her go.

Had he seriously expected he could just fly into Sydney, show up on her doorstep and everything would be as it had been in Bali? He gritted his teeth. She wouldn't be independent, feisty Zoe if she just fell back into his arms. This was up to him. Unfinished business or not.

'Promise me you'll get to the doctor as soon as possible?' he said.

She smiled. 'I promise. Thank you for your concern.'

Their eyes met across the table. To his relief, he saw genuine appreciation in hers. That was at least a step up from guarded politeness.

'Good health is important,' he said. 'As I know only too well.'

'Your knee,' she said. 'I keep meaning to ask about it. Is it holding up?'

'So far, so good. I'm back to match fitness. Let's hope it stays that way. I've still got a lot to prove.'

'And your father?' She laughed, and her laughter had

a nervous edge to it. 'No different from this morning, I guess. Sorry. Dumb question.'

'It wasn't a dumb question. He gets grumpier by the hour. Hates being inactive.'

'Did you get your interest in soccer from your dad?'

This wasn't how he'd pictured his reunion with sexy, passionate Zoe. Talking about his father. But if that was the way it was going he might as well throw his grandfather in too.

'Dad liked to kick a ball around. But it was my grandfather who really got me into soccer.' He smiled. 'Grandpa is English, and he would hate to hear me refer to football as "soccer".'

Zoe tilted her head attentively and her earrings swung. He wanted to reach over and still them. But would his touch be welcome? Her 'hands off' shield was very much in place.

Mitch realised that this evening might not go as he'd anticipated. After their meal was served he might get a polite brush-off and a cool kiss on the cheek like the one she'd given him this morning. He wasn't used to that. It stymied him.

'I didn't know your family was English?' she said.

'My father was born in England and grew up there. In his twenties he came out to Australia on a gap year—only they didn't call it that in those days—met my mother here and stayed. We lived in north London, near my grandparents, for a year when I was eight. My grandfather got me hooked on soccer then. He used to take me to games...got me on a local team. He played for a London team himself when he was young. He lives and breathes the game.'

'He must be so proud of you now.'

'Not proud of me playing for a Spanish team. In fact he's disgusted.'

'Why don't you play for an English team?'

'I did. But a Spanish team bought me.'

'*Bought* you? Like a commodity?'

'I guess you could put it that way.'

'I know so little about the game.' She smiled. 'If an old schoolfriend hadn't become a soccer superstar I'd know even less.'

'Just ask if there's anything you'd like to know,' he said.

An old schoolfriend? He wanted to be so much more than that to her. Passionate, playful and sensual—that was the Zoe he remembered from Bali. He couldn't settle for just friendship after she'd been all that to him. But then he couldn't offer her a relationship either.

In that regard nothing had changed since they'd last met in Bali. He could *not* let himself be distracted from his game by Zoe or any other woman. *He just couldn't.*

Last year he'd been briefly involved with a woman who had been too temperamental for his taste. When he'd broken it off with her there had been scenes, threats, confrontations—until he'd been forced to take out a restraining order against her.

It had been during that time when he had suffered his knee injury. Had the stress caused him to miss that split-second warning that two opposing players were headed towards him, clearly with the intent to take him out? He believed there was a good chance it had. It wouldn't happen again.

'Why do they call it "The Beautiful Game"? It sounds so...so *romantic*,' Zoe said.

His grandfather had often used the term, and had explained it to him many times as a kid. 'It's because the game is beautiful in its simplicity. It's not loaded with complex rules. If you have a ball you can play anywhere. Kids in their back yards or on dusty streets all over the world...

highly paid players on a perfectly groomed pitch. It's an intelligent game—an individual's game as well as a team game. They say the first person to officially call it "The Beautiful Game" was the great Brazilian footballer Pelé.'

Mitch paused, conscious that he sounded as if he was preaching.

'I don't want to bore you…'

'You're not boring me at all. I can see how much you love your game. I admire your passion. No wonder it comes first with you.'

There was a hint of the Bali Zoe's teasing in her smile.

'Even if you *are* bought and sold like a racehorse.'

Zoe obviously had no idea of the money that changed hands at the top level of soccer. It wasn't the huge deal in Australia that it was in Europe, where players' incomes were splashed all over the press. Even he'd been astounded at the amounts that had poured into his bank account since he'd made it to the top. And that didn't include the sponsorship and endorsements his agent was always negotiating.

He was glad Zoe didn't seem to have any interest in his income. Lara had been only too aware of every possible euro, pound and dollar that might come his way. It had been a bitter realisation that Lara had been more in love with the money and the spotlight than she had been with him.

Ultimately she'd pressed for marriage—to secure that income, he'd believed. That had resulted in their final split—and a pay-out from him to stop her selling the story of their relationship to the media. To be fair to Lara, she'd stuck to the deal. It hadn't come as a shock when she'd taken up with another player not long afterwards.

Since then he'd steered clear of women he suspected of being interested not in the real Mitch Bailey but in his image and wealth. There were plenty of them around. Star footballers could be a target for the unscrupulous.

The waiter came alongside their table and asked if he could take their order. Mitch quickly chose white fish and steamed vegetables in a lemon yogurt sauce. Zoe ordered a cheese and spinach vegetarian dish, explaining that she had lost her taste for meat since she hadn't been feeling well.

The conversation dwindled to virtually nothing. The elephant in the pool below was wallowing in the shallow end and spraying water through its trunk all over the swimmers. But neither he nor Zoe seemed able to call it to heel.

Zoe pleated the edge of her linen napkin, drew her finger around the edge of her water glass, played with her dangly earrings. She must be feeling as uncomfortable as he was. This was untenable.

Mitch reached across the table and stilled her hand with his. He looked into her eyes for a long, still moment.

'Zoe, I wish I could see what was in your thought bubbles,' he said. 'Because we're not making any headway talking and I don't have much time.'

Zoe gripped his hand in deep, heartfelt relief that Mitch had found the courage to say what she had been too knotted with nerves to say. He'd been so formal, his conversation so stilted—unless he was talking about soccer—that she'd feared the connection they'd shared in Bali had been completely severed. That she'd never see again the Mitch she'd shared both danger and ultimately pleasure with in the seclusion of her villa back in Seminyak.

'My thought bubbles?' she said, knowing her voice sounded shaky but unable to do anything about it except follow her words with a nervous laugh. 'Please don't ask me to sing them, because there's a guy over there with a cell phone who seems a tad too interested in us.'

In fact it looked as if the onlooker was about to snap a photo of them. Zoe withdrew her hand from Mitch's, kept her hands firmly on her lap.

'No need to sing,' Mitch said, with the disarming smile that struck straight to her heart.

He looked so impossibly handsome in that dark suit. She could still hardly believe he was here with her in Sydney. Her pulse quickened at the thought of what the evening might bring.

She took a deep, steadying breath. 'Okay. My thought bubbles say: "Apprehensive". "Awkward". "Curious".'

'"Curious"?' he said, his head tilted to one side, his eyes narrowed.

'Curious as to why you looked me up when you'd made it so clear you didn't want anything ongoing between us.'

'Fair enough,' he said. 'What about "awkward"?'

Under cover of the tablecloth overhang Zoe wrung her hands together. 'I'm anxious that I'll say the wrong thing—I'm second-guessing every word. I'm over the moon that you're here, but I don't want to appear too glad to see you in case…in case you think I'm wanting more from you. You made your agenda for the future very clear.'

'Which explains "Apprehensive"…' said Mitch.

She nodded, unable to speak through a sudden lump of emotion. She blinked against unwelcome, mortifying tears. 'Yes,' she forced herself to say.

'My thought bubbles are pretty much the same,' he said slowly. 'I'm worried that we seem like strangers to each other.'

'Exactly,' she said. 'And I don't know what to do about it.'

Mitch leaned across the table. 'I thought about you a lot when I was back in Madrid, Zoe.'

'I…I thought about you too.' She didn't want to give too

much away. Such as the fact she still awoke from dreams of him to find herself in tears.

'We didn't get to say goodbye in Bali.'

There was accusation in his voice and affronted pride in his eyes.

Zoe realised that Mitch, the celebrity sportsman, was not used to being left by a woman. Not in those circumstances. She hadn't meant to take the upper hand by creeping out of the villa without awakening him to say goodbye. It had saved her an awkward moment. Mitch might be used to such no-strings encounters. She was not.

'It seemed better that way,' she said, finding it difficult to meet his eyes. 'We'd agreed it…it would only be for that night.'

'When I woke up and you weren't there I was gutted.'

'It…it was difficult to leave you, but it would have been worse to face you. I…I had never been in that situation before. I didn't know how to deal with it.'

She'd sobbed in the taxi all the way to the airport. Then huddled into her seat on the plane for the entire six-hour flight home to Sydney, desperately trying not to sob some more.

His mouth twisted wryly. 'Severing all contact between us seemed the right thing at the time. When I got back to Madrid and had time to think, it seemed all kinds of wrong. I wanted to get in touch. But I thought that wouldn't be fair on you. My situation hadn't changed.'

'I wanted to contact you too. But I…I didn't want to seem like a…like a groupie. I…know you're probably plagued by them.'

Mitch's so-expressive eyebrows rose. 'Don't ever think that. You are nothing like that. Not that I've had anything to do with groupies, and nor am I criticising them, but I see what goes on.'

'Each to his own,' she murmured, glad that Mitch had distanced himself from that aspect of his fame. But still... She couldn't believe their one night in Seminyak had been the first no-strings incident for *him*. He was idolised by women.

'You're smart, gorgeous, funny. I couldn't stop thinking about you.'

On the surface, those words should have sounded romantic. But Zoe detected an undertone of annoyance— even anger. It was as if she were some unwelcome prickly thorn, pressing into his consciousness. She wasn't at all sure she liked it.

She swallowed hard. 'I...I couldn't stop thinking about you either,' she said. 'I tried, though. I really tried. Otherwise I would have gone crazy. I purposely avoided the sports pages, the international sports news. That's why I got such a shock to see you this morning. I had no idea you were in Australia.'

'I was going crazy in my own way, trying to find out what *you* were doing. You've got such rigid privacy settings on your social media.'

'You tried to stalk me on social media?' Zoe tried to suppress her laughter so it didn't attract attention. 'Imagine...Mitch Bailey stalking me—I'm flattered.'

'I wouldn't say "stalking" you,' he said, with what she took to be more affronted pride. 'More...attempting research into your comings and goings. And failing dismally—courtesy of your firewalls.'

'I told you...I'm a private person.' She looked sideways at the guy on the other table with the camera phone. His attention was now on his meal, not on Mitch, thank heaven.

'Did you date other guys?'

The directness of Mitch's question stunned her. But she didn't have to search for an answer. 'No. I didn't want to.'

How could any other man have compared to Mitch? Trouble was, no other guy she'd met in the meantime had attracted her. That night in Bali had shown her what it could be like between a man and a woman. Not just the lovemaking. It had also been about the shared laughter, the joy, the connection that to her had been so much more than physical.

She wanted Mitch but he could not offer her what she needed—commitment, love. One day she'd meet someone who could offer her more than one night in his busy schedule. She had no intention of putting her life on hold for Mitch Bailey.

No matter that just sitting opposite him at a restaurant table was thrilling her in a way being with any other man never had. No. She hadn't even looked at another man in the last two months.

His relief was palpable. 'Good,' he said.

Zoe gasped. His reaction was a bit rich. What did he mean, *'good'*?

He had no rights over her personal life. They'd made no commitment—hadn't even exchanged contact details. She was free to date whom she darn well pleased. The fact that she hadn't met anyone who came anywhere near him was beside the point.

She wanted to say something but bit her tongue. It was an unexpected bonus to see Mitch again. She didn't want to ruin it by being combative. What was the point?

'What about you?' she said.

He shrugged. 'I went out with a few women.'

Jealousy—fierce and unexpected—stabbed her so hard she flinched. She couldn't bear to think of him with someone else. And that was crazy, considering the nature of their relationship. Not that you could even call it a relationship. Heck, you couldn't even call it a *friendship*. She couldn't find a label to paste on whatever it was with her and Mitch Bailey.

She didn't say anything, just raised an eyebrow. While she churned inside with jealousy.

'It was a disaster,' he said. 'I kept comparing them to you and they fell short. I gave up on dating.'

What was she meant to infer from that? 'Oh...' was all she managed to choke out, with her jealousy somewhat appeased.

For a long moment their eyes met. But if she was searching for more she didn't find it. His gaze was guarded.

'It's good to see you, Zoe.'

'It's good to you, too,' she said.

'There's something there...more than friendship,' he said.

A secret thrill that he had acknowledged it pulsed through her. 'So what are we going to do about it?' she asked eventually. 'Fact is, I still live in Sydney and you still live in Madrid.'

'And that isn't going to change,' he said. 'For all the reasons I explained to you before. But we could keep in touch on the internet.'

'You mean I'd have to let down my firewalls for you?' she said, in a feeble attempt at humour.

'Yes. You'd have to let me scale those walls.'

Did she detect a note of triumph in his voice? Mitch liked to win. *For what purpose?*

She found herself pleating her napkin again. 'Will you be back in Australia any time soon?'

It would be torture to wait months and months to see him.

'It's not likely,' he said. 'Not until next year, when the season ends. Playing league football is more than a full-time commitment.'

'That…that's a long time.' How could they possibly maintain anything resembling more than a casual friendship on that time scale?

'Are you planning a trip to Europe any time soon?' he asked.

She shook her head. 'I'm not sure…'

She'd blown her vacation budget with the Bali trip. There was no spare cash for an expensive trip to Europe, and she didn't believe in paying for vacations on credit.

'That's a shame. You could have visited me in Madrid,' he said. 'I have a very nice apartment in old Madrid. You'd like it.'

'I…I'm sure I would,' she said. 'I'd like to see Spain some day. That would give me an incentive to study Spanish again.'

Would it be worth a credit card binge to see Mitch in Madrid? Excitement started to bubble up at the prospect.

'Let's think about how we can make it work,' he said. 'I have a full schedule of training, then pre-season matches in England, France and Italy before the season starts the last week in August. We could fit in a visit when I'm playing at home? That is if it coincided with your trip?'

Zoe was about to engage seriously with Mitch about what might be a good time for her to visit Madrid if she happened to be travelling to Europe—and then it hit her.

Mitch wasn't actually *inviting* her to visit him. He wasn't putting himself out in any way. Such a trip would be all about her running around the world to meet him at his convenience. For *what*? A bootie call? If she just happened to be in the neighbourhood? He was hedging his bets in a major way.

She swallowed down hard against a sudden bitter taste in her mouth. There would be no trip to Madrid for her to chase after Mitch in the hope of spending time with him. In her book, old-fashioned as it might be, the man did the chasing.

Before she could explain this to Mitch the waiter arrived at their table with their food and proceeded to describe in detail the meals they'd ordered. She put down her napkin— by now pleated to a narrow strip—and thanked the waiter.

She looked at the food on her plate—beautifully cooked and presented. But she didn't feel like eating. As the aroma of the food filled her nostrils a wave of nausea overtook her. Mitch was right. She needed to check out this recurring illness. Or was it disappointment that was making her feel like this?

Mitch picked up his fork. 'You haven't told me how your meeting went today with your potential purchaser?'

Zoe was grateful for the change of subject. She pushed her food around her plate with her fork. 'They made me a generous offer,' she said. 'Set out some attractive if constricting terms and conditions. We talked about expanding my specialised service into other states.'

'And...?'

Zoe shrugged. 'I'm still not convinced. I'm a very independent person—used to running my own show. I'm not sure how I'd take to being at the beck and call of a boss.'

'I believe that,' said Mitch. 'So, how did you leave it with them?' He seemed genuinely interested.

'I told him I'd consider it. In the meantime I talked with my friend Louise, who works with me. I've been thinking of bringing her into the company as a full partner. She'd have to *buy* in, of course. Then we could think of expanding. We already spend quite a bit of time commuting to Melbourne, to service the clients we have there.'

'You're very ambitious,' he said, and she appreciated the admiration in his voice.

'Yes,' she said. 'That's one reason I'm seriously considering the offer. Perhaps I can move higher in a bigger firm than I could on my own. It's all worth considering.'

'You've got a big decision to make. It will be interesting to see what you decide to do,' he said. 'Be sure you let me know.'

Was he just saying that? Did he really want to stay in touch?

'Yes…' she said non-committally.

'We've both come a long way since we were seventeen,' he said, his brows drawn thoughtfully together. 'Me where I am—you with your own business.'

Startled, she looked up. 'I guess we have.'

'We've both still got a long way to go,' he said.

She knew his career was all-important to him, and he'd made it very clear that he'd put his personal life on hold. But she aspired to more than business success. Success for her also meant a fulfilling personal life one day. That lifetime love she aspired to—and a happy family life.

With a wrench to her heart that was almost physical she realised it would never happen with Mitch—no matter the strength of her feelings for him. By the time he reached a stage when he wanted to settle down she would be long in his past.

CHAPTER TEN

Mitch predicted almost to the minute the time when the guy with the camera phone Zoe had been keeping her eye on would make his way to their table: after he and Zoe had finished their main courses and the waiter had removed their plates.

Mitch knew from the guy's respectful attitude and the phone held so visibly in his hand that it wouldn't be a problem. But Zoe's eyes widened in alarm.

He remembered what she'd said about being a private person. Even a casual friendship with him opened her up to possible confrontations with the paparazzi.

'Mitch, I'm a huge fan—so is my son,' the guy with the camera said. 'Could I have a photo with you, please?'

'Of course,' said Mitch, looking around for the waiter.

'I'll take the photo,' said Zoe, jumping up from her seat.

Full marks to Zoe. That was one way of avoiding being in a photo. Maybe he didn't need to worry too much about her coping with any possible publicity.

She took the guy's phone and made a fuss of posing Mitch and his fan.

'Thank you,' the guy said to Zoe. 'Can I get one of me and you two together now?'

'I... I...' Zoe stuttered.

'Of course,' said Mitch.

'It's for my wife,' his fan explained. 'She didn't like Lara one little bit and will be happy to see you with such a lovely young lady.'

Again Mitch was struck by how public his life had become. It was highly improbable that this man's wife had ever actually met Lara. The woman just hadn't liked the Lara she'd seen in the media.

'Zoe is an old friend of mine,' said Mitch, 'and she is indeed lovely.'

Zoe was obviously too stupefied to object. Mitch called the waiter over to take the photo. That would save both him and Zoe from any unflattering 'selfie'.

After the fan had gone happily on his way Zoe turned to him. She shuddered. 'Do you have to put up with that all the time?'

'I'm never rude to a fan. He was a good guy. We made his evening—his wife and son will be chuffed.'

'I found it disconcerting, to say the least,' Zoe said, in a tone so low it was nearly a whisper. 'Especially what he said about Lara.'

She looked nervously around her, as if there might be a photographer at every table. Fact was: there could be. Everyone with a smartphone was a potential paparazzo these days. But that came with the turf. Mitch had learned to deal with it.

'C'mon—let's leave if it's making you uncomfortable,' he said. 'We can grab a coffee somewhere else, if you'd like.'

'There are a few nice cafés around here,' she said. 'We could walk along the boardwalk by the harbour.'

'Good idea. We can work that dinner off.'

Not that she'd eaten much.

She hesitated. 'I…I won't end up on some gossip website, will I? You know—"Mystery brunette on harbourside stroll with visiting soccer star"?'

Mitch thought about her helicopter fears back at the villa in Bali. She was right—they did exist on different planets. Zoe was so unlike Lara, who would have been preening at the thought of being in the spotlight.

'That guy? Highly unlikely,' he said. 'He'll show the photo around to the other parents at his boy's soccer club though, I'll bet.'

Although freedom from other, less scrupulous people, who cashed in on opportunistic amateur shots, he couldn't guarantee. But he'd seen no one suspicious tonight. No one would imagine he'd be in Sydney when he should be in Europe, playing 'friendly' matches to warm up for the season to come.

But he'd had to see if his father was okay. And then there was Zoe. He'd be kidding himself if he denied that he'd leaped at the opportunity to see Zoe.

Now he realised that if at the back of his mind he'd hoped meeting with her again would leave him cold—would rid him of his attraction to her—then he'd been totally mistaken. She was even hotter than he'd remembered. There was nothing he wanted more than to take up where they'd left off in Bali.

Of course Zoe tried to pay her share for the dinner. He'd anticipated that, and had already settled the bill when Zoe came back to the table after going to the ladies' room.

'I insist on paying for the coffee, then,' she said, with that already familiar stubborn tilt to her chin.

Yes, Zoe was *very* different from the other women in his orbit.

They walked out of the restaurant into the narrow back street of Milson's Point. It was a typically mild Sydney winter night, but Zoe wrapped her arms around herself and shivered. She reached into her purse and pulled out a filmy scarf she wrapped around her shoulders.

'I can't imagine *that* will keep you warm,' he said.

'I'm fine,' she said, with an edge to her voice, not meeting his eyes.

'No, you're not, you're shivering,' he said. 'Come here.'

He pulled Zoe into his arms and held her very close, until her shivering stopped, and finally she relaxed against him with a small sigh, her head resting against his shoulder Mitch didn't know whether to interpret that sigh as relief or defeat.

He closed his eyes, the better to savour the sensation of having her close. He inhaled the sharp sweet scent of her—a Balinese blend of lemongrass and jasmine, she'd told him when he'd asked—that brought back heady memories of that brief, intense time they'd spent together in her villa.

This. This was what he'd longed for back in the echoing emptiness of his apartment in Madrid. He should not be letting himself feel this. But he heaved a huge sigh of relief that she made no effort to break away from him.

'Warm now?' he asked, his voice a husky rasp.

'Yes,' she murmured against his shoulder.

She pulled away, but remained within the circle of his arms, her own arms around his waist.

She looked up to him. 'Thank you.'

Her face was in semi-shadow, her earrings glinting in the reflected light from the illumination of the giant grinning face of the entrance to Luna Park that loomed behind him. The sounds of carnival music and kids screaming on rides travelled on the still air.

'What next, Zoe?' he asked.

Her eyes told him that she knew he wasn't talking about the direction of their walk.

'Whatever we both want,' she said slowly.

She lifted her mouth to him. He didn't hesitate to accept the invitation. He bent his head and kissed her. But his kiss was brief and tender—he was as aware as Zoe of the possibility of interested eyes on them.

'I've been wanting to do this all day,' he said.

'Me too,' she said, a catch to her voice.

A taxi drew up and a noisy group of people got out, obviously heading for the restaurant. Zoe turned away from his embrace. As if by silent consent he took her arm and they headed away, to leave the restaurant behind them.

He walked beside her down the steep steps near the giant smile at the entrance to Luna Park to reach the harbour walk that ran by the harbour's edge, from Lavender Bay to Milson's Point. Despite the mildness of the night there was a hint of a breeze blowing off the water.

As they reached the boardwalk Zoe shivered again, and pulled the flimsy excuse for a wrap tighter to her. 'I don't know why I didn't wear a coat,' she said.

Mitch didn't hesitate to put his arm around her and pull her to his side. To hell with the possibility of cameras. He and Zoe weren't the only couple strolling along the boardwalk with their arms around each other. They would just blend in. He wanted her near him.

It had been such a long time since he'd lived in Sydney, and he found himself caught up in the magic of Sydney Harbour on a calm, clear night. He blocked the thought that being with Zoe was part of the magic. He could not allow himself to think that. Not when he was leaving tomorrow. Not when he didn't know when he would see her again.

In silence, they walked past the Art Deco façade of the pool and under the arch of the bridge. He didn't know whether the silence was companionable or choked with words better left unsaid.

Once they reached the eastern side of the bridge he

and Zoe paused and leaned on the cast-iron railing to look across the water to the Opera House, its giant white sails lit up with a beauty that was almost ethereal.

'Do you think you'll ever come back to live in Australia?' Zoe asked.

He shrugged. 'Maybe. I don't know. Sydney will always be home. But for the foreseeable future Europe is where I want to be.'

At the age of twenty-seven he saw that future stretch way ahead of him, exciting with possibilities. He was cautiously optimistic about his knee. Who knew how far he could go?

'Tell me again when you have to go back to Madrid? It really is tomorrow?'

'Yes,' he said.

The single word seemed to toll like a warning of impending doom.

Zoe was looking ahead at the view so he couldn't see her face. But he felt her flinch.

'So…so we only have tonight,' she said, again with that little catch to her voice that wrenched at him.

'Yes,' he said. 'I fly out in the afternoon.'

A big harbour cruiser went by and a blast of brash music shattered the tranquillity of the scene. Did Zoe like that kind of music? Probably not. He realised how much he didn't know about her. How much he wanted to know. One day, perhaps…

'I wish it wasn't such a long way between Australia and Spain,' she said wistfully.

It remained unspoken between them that it wasn't only the twenty-two-hour flight that separated them. His need to prove himself over and over without distraction stood in their way. Mitch liked Zoe. *Really* liked her. But he couldn't let that liking and his attraction grow into anything deeper. This wasn't the time for him. No matter how he might find himself wishing it could be different.

'Me too,' he said. 'But even if we lived closer I still couldn't promise anything more than—'

'Friendship with benefits?' she said.

He followed her gaze as she looked down into the dark green water of the harbour. Small waves from the cruiser's wash were smashing against the sandstone supports of the railing.

'Very occasional benefits,' she added, in a tone so low he scarcely caught it.

Put like that, it sounded so callous.

With his fingers, Mitch tilted her chin upwards so she had to meet his gaze. 'Zoe, I wish it could be more. Who knows what could happen in the—?'

'Future?' she said. She reached up to silence him with her finger on his mouth, as she had done before. 'Let's not talk about the future.'

The thinly veiled sadness in her eyes made his resolve waver. 'Who knows? One day...' he said.

Slowly she shook her head. 'It seems to me we can only take this one day at a time. So we'd better make the most of the hours we've got left.'

'Agreed,' he said.

He hoped her idea of a wonderful way to fill the hours coincided with his. Alone. Private. Clothes optional.

'How long since you've been to Luna Park?' she asked.

He paused, surprised at the question. 'Years and years,' he said.

'Me too,' she said. 'Not since I was at uni. The noise and music coming from there sounds fun. Let's walk through before we go and find a coffee shop.'

Mitch was too startled to reply. It was hardly *his* idea of making the most of the hours they had left together.

'Sounds like a plan,' he said, with an effort to sound enthusiastic.

'We can just walk around and look,' she said.

His parents had taken him and his brothers to Luna Park when he was very young. Then it had been closed for years, and he hadn't revisited it until he was a teenager. He'd taken his training so seriously that amusement parks hadn't been much on the agenda. Besides, Lara had looked down her nose at what she'd thought was a plebeian form of entertainment.

'That could be fun,' he said.

He took Zoe's hand in his as they walked along the harbour back towards the bright lights and clashing noises of Luna Park. She looked up at him and smiled, and he smiled back.

Holding hands with Zoe. Who would have thought something so simple, so everyday, would make him feel so…? He thought hard about what this feeling was. *Happy.* Being with Zoe made him feel happy.

As they walked under the big grinning face into the entertainment park he gave it a mental salute.

CHAPTER ELEVEN

ZOE HAD NO IDEA why she'd suggested going to Luna Park with Mitch. Panic, perhaps? Prolonging the inevitable? What she really wanted was to be alone with him, somewhere quiet and romantic.

But she was struggling with the 'friends with occasional benefits' scenario. She wanted Mitch with a deep, yearning hunger—a craving. It was impossible to stop sneaking glances at him to admire his profile, the shape of his mouth, the set of his shoulders. She found everything about him exciting. The thought of the sensual pleasures they had shared made her shiver with remembered ecstasy. But she balked at the idea of being his occasional lover.

Bali had been different. The circumstances had been extraordinary. She'd believed there would be only the one time. That she would be able to put their encounter behind her almost as if it had been a dream. It hadn't been easy to forget him. And now he was back in her life, but on very uncertain ground. It might be commonplace for a celebrity sports star to do the 'occasional lover' thing. Not so for an ordinary girl with dreams of a once-in-a-lifetime love. A girl teetering on the edge of falling in love with him.

Walking hand in hand with Mitch like any other couple strolling along the harbour walk on a mild Thursday evening felt so *right*. She loved the feel of his much larger hand enfolding hers, the way their shoulders nudged, the subtle intimacy. As if they were meant to be together.

But tomorrow he would be on his way to Madrid again. And she would be left with perhaps the comfort of an occasional phone call. She had no illusions. Once he was again immersed in his game she would not be at the front of his mind.

Luna Park was chaotic and fun. It was the perfect distraction from the hollow feeling of loss Zoe felt at the thought of Mitch flying back to Madrid the next day. Her spirits had lifted as soon as she was surrounded by the bright lights, music and carnival atmosphere.

Set right on the harbour, surrounded by some of the most expensive real estate in Australia, the old-fashioned fun fair operated in the evenings during school vacations despite the protests of its well-heeled neighbours. Zoe supported its right to be there—the Sydney icon had existed since 1935, built on land that had been the construction site for the building of the Sydney Harbour Bridge.

For many older Sydney-siders the place was loaded with nostalgia. Zoe's maternal grandmother had brought her here a few times by ferry when she was a little girl—it was one of her only memories of her as she had died when Zoe was seven.

She sometimes wondered how different her life would have been if *that* grandmother had been alive when her parents had died and she had been put into *her* care.

Once through the entrance, she and Mitch were surrounded by rides and sideshows on both sides.

She looked around and laughed. 'Just watching the rides is making me feel dizzy.'

'They're fast and furious, all right,' said Mitch. 'What do you want to ride first? The Wild Mouse rollercoaster?'

What had she got herself into? Zoe pretend to cower, but her fear was real. 'Uh...I'm actually terrified of it.'

Mitch couldn't mask his disappointment. He looked longingly upwards to where the brightly painted carriages rattled at great speed along the tracks. Excited squeals and shrieks rang out every time a carriage swung around.

'I didn't take you for such a wimp, Zoe,' he said, but the way his eyes crinkled and he squeezed her hand let her know he was teasing.

She looked up at him. 'I have a confession to make. When it comes to rides I *am* a wimp. When I'm on something like the Wild Mouse, screaming, it's not from excitement but from genuine fear.'

'You *have* to be kidding me?' he said, raising his expressive eyebrows. 'A fun fair is all about exhilaration and terror and regretting that last hot dog you ate. Why did you bring me here if you weren't prepared for the screaming? Does that mean we don't even get to go on the Hair Raiser?'

He waved his arm towards a ride where strapped-in riders were raised up high in the sky, only to be plummeted back to earth at a frightening pace, screaming all the way.

To Zoe's eyes it was terrifying. She pulled a repentant face. 'Sorry. You wouldn't get me up on that thing in a million years. It would be an amazing view of the city, up so high, but I'd have my eyes tightly shut and wouldn't see a thing. I'd forgotten how scary these rides are.'

'So we're only going on *girly* rides, are we? Don't expect me to ride with you on that wussy carousel.' Mitch glowered, but ruined the effect with a smile that insisted on breaking through his frown.

'Actually, I rather like those pretty ponies. Sure you wouldn't join me on one? Safe and sedate—just how I like it.'

Safe and sedate? There was nothing safe or sedate about the way she felt about Mitch…

Mitch crossed his arms across his chest. 'No to the painted ponies. You will never, *ever* get me on one of those things.'

'I love the giant slides. Or I could challenge you on the dodgem cars?'

'Now you're talking,' he said.

They only had to wait a few minutes for the next dodgem session. Zoe liked the way Mitch wasn't the least bit self-conscious about lining up with a crowd of mainly teenagers. Looking around her, she saw she wasn't the only woman in a dressy dress and heels.

'Shall we share a car?' she asked as they got ready to run and claim one.

'I want one of my own,' he said.

Once Zoe was strapped into her bumper car and the music started she stepped on the accelerator too hard—and crashed her rubber bumpers straight into Mitch's car.

'Gotcha!' she called, smiling.

'A challenge?' he said, assuming a racing driver's position behind the wheel, his expression deadly serious. 'We're talking professional, here. I drive to win.'

'You're on,' she said. 'I drive to destroy.'

As they took to the circuit and thumped and bumped their electric cars into each other, and the surrounding cars, Zoe started to laugh. By the time the session came to an end she was paralysed by giggles.

Mitch helped her out of her car. 'That was so much fun,' she said as her giggles subsided.

'You were determined to thrash me,' he said.

'And I did,' she said.

'I would dispute that. I counted the bumps and I came out ahead.'

'Oh, really?' she challenged. 'How many bumps?'

'I was five more than you. Do you concede defeat?' he said, grinning.

'I wasn't counting, so I have to believe you,' she said, narrowing her eyes in mock anger.

'That said, I'll allow that you were a worthy opponent.'

'I just wish I'd thought to count the bumps—I'm sure I came out on top.'

'I enjoyed it,' he said. 'Kids' stuff, but fun.'

'The thing is,' she said, 'I don't think I ever acted that childish when I was a child.' She tucked her arm through his. 'C'mon—let's try another ride.'

They wandered through the fun fair until Zoe stopped at the Laughing Clowns sideshow.

'I was so scared of these things when I was little,' she said.

A row of motorised vintage clown heads with open mouths moved from side to side, ready for people to throw small balls in the hope of winning a prize.

'You seem so fearless, Zoe, and yet you have all these hidden fears,' Mitch said.

He rested his hand on the back of her neck and the casual contact sent shivers of awareness coursing through her.

'Not so hidden,' she said. 'Lots of people are frightened of clowns. There's even a name for it—coulrophobia. I still don't like them.'

He leaned in closer. 'What else are you frightened of, Zoe?' he asked in an undertone.

Of falling in love with you and getting my heart pulverised, she thought, but she would never put voice to that.

She forced her voice to sound unconcerned. 'Earthquakes, of course. But we've been there—done that.

Nothing much else—what about you?' she said. 'Snakes? Spiders? Sharks?'

He shook his head. 'I wouldn't go out of my way to encounter any of those, but I'm not scared of them.' He paused. 'I…I fear failure.'

She stared at him, too surprised at his admission to speak. 'But you're so successful,' she said eventually.

'You're only as good as your last game,' he said. 'Failure on the world stage isn't a pretty thing.'

'So if you don't come back fighting this season, with your knee fixed, you'll consider it failure?'

He stilled and went silent, and Zoe sensed his thoughts had turned inwards.

'Yes,' he said, after a long pause.

The single word was a full-stop to the thought and she knew there was nothing further to be said.

Mitch looked at the clowns, challenge in his stance. 'I'm not scared of *these* things. I'm going to beat 'em,' he said with confident arrogance. His eyes narrowed as he assessed the clowns' state of play before taking out his wallet.

The young guy behind the counter explained that Mitch needed to get five balls into the clowns' mouths—each clown varying in points scored. Mitch paid for and took the balls. Then he focussed his gaze, took aim and, one at a time, shot all five balls into the gaping mouths of the clowns.

Zoe clapped her hands together, doing a little dance of excitement. 'Well done!'

'Not bad,' said Mitch, with studied nonchalance.

It was nothing—absolutely nothing—compared to his achievements in soccer, but she was there with him and that made it special to her.

Would she ever be able to come to Luna Park again without him? There would be memories everywhere.

The sideshow attendant handed over a bright blue teddy bear as Mitch's prize. But Mitch pointed to a little white stuffed dog, wearing a miniature Aussie-style hat.

'That one, please,' he said. He turned to Zoe and handed it to her. 'For you,' he said. 'To remember what fun we've had this night.'

Zoe took the toy and clutched it to her, ridiculously pleased. Unwelcome tears stung her eyes. She swallowed against a sudden lump in her throat. 'Th...thank you. It's very cute.'

Did he have to remind her how fleeting their time together was?

Before Mitch had a chance to say anything more, a thirty-something man who had been standing behind them, waiting his turn for the clowns, turned to Mitch. 'That was awesome, mate.'

Mitch nodded in acknowledgement of the praise. 'Focus is what it takes,' he said.

Zoe could see recognition dawn in the man's eyes before a big grin split his face.

'As Mitch Bailey knows only too well!' he said. 'Mitch, you're meant to be in *Spain*.'

He reeled off an impressive list of European fixtures in which Mitch's team was scheduled to play. Then he pulled out a crumpled flyer for a restaurant.

'Can I get your autograph?'

Mitch obligingly autographed the piece of paper, then shook the man's hand. As the man walked away he looked back over his shoulder to Mitch several times, grinning. Zoe didn't have to be able to read his thought bubbles to understand the man's delight in having met his idol.

The full weight of Mitch's responsibilities to his fans seemed to settle on her shoulders. She began to comprehend his determination that nothing could come between his return to top form. Not her. Not any woman. But she refused to let it suppress her spirits.

Tonight was hers.

Mitch looked down at Zoe. Her face was flushed, and strands of her dark hair had come loose from its severe style to waft around her face. Laughter still curved the corners of her mouth and her eyes shone.

He reached out and smoothed the errant hair back into place. He had never wanted her more.

'Thank you,' she murmured. 'I must look a mess.'

'You could never look a mess,' he said. 'You look like a woman who's faced a mighty dodgem battle and won through.'

She was breathtaking. Attractive, yes, but also vibrant, smart and straightforward. Zoe Summers was unlike any other woman he'd met.

Something deep inside him seemed to turn over as he looked into her eyes. When they'd been battling with so much fun, intent on the dodgem car circuit, he'd been struck by how effortlessly they got on together. There were no games, no pretence. It had taken him back to their water fight in the pool in Bali—how much he'd enjoyed that too. And that was on top of how superlatively they'd got on in bed.

It struck him what it was that drew him so strongly to her—she grounded him. He knew she didn't give a toss about his money or fame. She'd been on his side when they were teenagers. He firmly believed she was on his side now. He could be himself with her, in a way he couldn't with anyone else outside his family.

Her idea to come to Luna Park had been inspired. She'd relaxed, and so had he. He could think of no other place he'd rather be right now than here with her.

Not even Madrid.

That was a dangerous thought.

He had to block it.

If he wasn't careful this woman could change his life. And he did *not* want to deviate from the path he had set himself.

All he had with Zoe was tonight. He'd better remember that.

'Time to go?' she asked.

'Yes,' he said. 'We can drive to a coffee shop.'

'Or have coffee at my house?' she said.

Coffee or something more? He just wanted to spend time with her, no matter how it might end up.

'Great idea,' he said.

'Let's go, then,' she said. 'Before more of your fans realise Mitch Bailey is in town.'

He took her hand and led her out of Luna Park, striding so fast she had to ask him to slow down, breathlessly reminding him that she was wearing high heels.

He slowed his pace on the steep stairs up to the narrow street where he'd parked the car. Then, in the shadows the streetlights did not illuminate, at last he kissed her—fiercely, possessively—and she kissed him back with equal fervour.

CHAPTER TWELVE

ZOE DIDN'T EVEN MENTION coffee when they got back to her place. Mitch didn't give her the chance to. He made sure she scarcely had time to draw breath between urgent, drugging kisses. He was too conscious of the hours, the minutes, the seconds ticking by until he had to say good-bye to her.

She didn't protest. Laughing, breathless, she took him—stumbling as they tried to walk and kiss at the same time—through the reception area, where he'd waited for her that morning, past an office and into a large living room. She fumbled with light switches, missing half of them with unsteady fingers, so they could see where they were going.

Between kisses he registered that the room was all industrial chic, with soaring ceilings, open beams, rough old brickwork and wide hardwood floors. Further through was another living area with sleek modern furniture. Open metal stairs led to a mezzanine that Mitch assumed was her bedroom. The east-facing wall comprised floor-to-ceiling industrial windows that framed a night-time view across Mort Bay to Goat Island.

But he was too busy feasting his eyes on Zoe to bother with the view, no matter how spectacular.

Still kissing, they landed on the white sofa, laughing as their limbs tangled and tripped them. A large slumbering tabby cat yowled its protest at their occupation of its sofa and shot off towards the kitchen.

Mitch found the zipper of Zoe's purple dress and tugged it down over the smooth skin of her shoulders. Her scent filled his nostrils: warm, womanly, arousing. Her curves, soft and lovely, moulded to his chest, her thighs pressed to his. *At last.* This was what he had been wanting for two long months. *Zoe.* There had been no other woman in between.

He shrugged off his jacket as she divested him of his tie and fumbled with fingers that weren't steady at the small buttons on his shirt.

A pulse throbbed at the base of her neck and he bent his head to press a kiss there. She clutched at his shoulders with a murmur of pleasure deep in her throat that sent his senses into overdrive. He broke the kiss. Pulled back. Her eyes were unfocused with passion, her mouth swollen from his kisses.

'Zoe, are you sure?'

All Zoe could think of was how much she wanted Mitch. Her heart was frantically doing cartwheels; her body was pulsing with desire. He was irresistible. And she didn't want to resist him for a moment longer.

Just one more time. Please. Just one more time with this once-in-a-lifetime man.

She was going into this with eyes wide open, not prompted by fear or anything other than the overwhelming need to have Mitch with her while she had the chance. *One last time.*

'I'm very sure,' she murmured, not even wanting to waste a minute on words when she could be touching instead of talking.

She wound her arms around his neck to kiss him again,

parted her lips for his mouth, his tongue, and felt the slide of her dress over her hips as it fell to the floor.

Zoe awoke several hours later. Somehow she was up in her mezzanine bedroom. How…?

She blinked to bring herself to full consciousness. Memories of Mitch carrying her up the stairs to the bed after they'd made love on the sofa filtered through. They'd made love again and she'd fallen asleep in his arms, her head pillowed on his chest, feeling the thud, thud, thud of his heartbeat reverberate through her being as she'd swallowed the words she'd longed to utter: *I love you, Mitch. Don't leave me, Mitch.*

Now she was alone in the bed and she could hear him softly padding around the room. His clothes must be downstairs. She should get up. Go down with him. Watch him as he dressed to leave her and go back to his life that had no room for her. But she couldn't expose herself to that particular form of torture. Instead she drew her knees to her chest and curled her naked self into the tiniest ball possible.

'Zoe? Are you awake?'

She heard his hoarse whisper but she was too weary for words. For platitudes. For promises made in the aftermath of passion and not likely to be kept.

'Mmm…' she murmured, pretending to be asleep.

She felt him stand over the bed. 'I have to go back to my parents' house, Zoe, to pick up my stuff, say goodbye to them. But I'll call around to see you on the way to the airport—around ten. We can say goodbye properly, swap contact details.'

He waited for her answer.

'Okay,' she murmured, hoping she sounded convincingly sleepy.

But when he leaned over to kiss her on the cheek she

lost it. Lost all dignity, lost all pride and clung wordlessly to him until he gently unwound her arms and lowered her back onto the bed.

'See you in a few hours,' he whispered, kissing her again before he left.

She held herself rigid in the bed as she listened to him move around downstairs, heard his footsteps walk through the office, the quiet slam of the door closing behind him, the sound of his car disrupting the stillness of the night.

After he'd gone Zoe lay there for a long time, unable to sleep, her thoughts churning round and round. *She couldn't deal with this.* Couldn't allow herself to be picked up and put down at a man's whim.

She wasn't a cool girl—could never be a cool girl able to handle a casual relationship with aplomb. Underneath her stylish clothes and smart haircut she was still Zoe the nerd who longed to be loved.

She didn't want to engage in some battle of the sexes scenario. But it did appear that men were able to make love to a woman—make it seem special and memorable—and then walk away without a backward glance.

As Mitch had done to her in Bali. And had just done again. And she, to save her pride, her heart, had pretended that it didn't hurt.

But to a woman—*this* woman, anyway—it was more difficult to separate sex from emotion. From love. She couldn't just write off an intimate connection like the one she'd just shared with Mitch as a mere physical fling.

She'd been dumb enough to fall in love with him. All he wanted was no-strings fun while she wanted to be bound by ribbons of love and commitment to the man she gave her heart to.

Mitch wasn't that man. He'd made that very clear, much as she might long for it to be otherwise. The lovemaking they'd shared last night had meant nothing to him, though he'd made sure she enjoyed it to the fullest. She'd gone into it willingly. Did not regret it. But she deserved more than Mitch was prepared to give.

Friends with benefits didn't do it for her—no matter how spectacular the benefits.

If Mitch came to see her as promised, later this morning, she would make all the right noises. The *Let's keep in touch*, the *I'll look you up when I'm next in Europe*, the *I hope to see you next time in Sydney*, conversation. But after he left she would wipe Mitch from her mind, from her heart.

At last she dozed off into a fitful sleep. When she awoke again, to early-morning sunlight filtering through the blinds, it was like a repeat of the dreams of him she had suffered since Bali: waking to find she was alone after all. Only this time she could still see where the sheets had twisted around his body, inhale the scent of him, feel the imprint of him on her. He had been only too real.

She got out of bed, staggered with sudden dizziness and a wave of nausea. Coffee. That was what she needed.

She clung to the railing as she made her way down the winding metal stairs that led from the mezzanine to the living area. There was no trace of Mitch left—not even a lingering scent.

Then she saw the toy dog Mitch had won for her, propped on the coffee table. Mitch had joked that he didn't want it watching them and turned its back to them.

Zoe took the few steps over to the coffee table, hugged the fluffy toy to her and let the tears come.

CHAPTER THIRTEEN

An hour later Zoe yawned and stretched as she let herself out of her front door. The coffee had done nothing to quell the nausea—in fact just a sip had made it worse. She'd been lucky enough to get a cancellation for an early-morning appointment with her doctor in Balmain village. It was a crisp, sunny morning and she'd decided to walk.

Even after eating only a few bites of her meal last night she'd awoken feeling unwell again. It was annoying to feel like this when she was so used to perfect health. If, as Mitch seemed to think, she had picked up some long-lasting exotic bug she needed to get it fixed. Or maybe it was stress. Or a food allergy. Half the people she knew these days seemed to have some kind of food intolerance.

Then again, maybe it was caused by heartbreak.

She didn't have to wait long to see the doctor. Straight away, Zoe told her how she'd got food poisoning the first day she'd been in Bali and hadn't seemed to get over it. She was astounded when, after listening to her recital of tummy-twisting woes, her doctor suggested she take a pregnancy test.

Zoe shook her head. 'It couldn't be that,' she said. 'I'm on the pill. We were careful. It was only one night.'

Her doctor gave her a reassuring smile as she handed

over a pregnancy-testing wand and directed Zoe to the medical practice's bathroom. 'It's a good idea to rule it out for sure.'

Zoe had thought she'd felt fear when the earthquake had hit. But that fear was nothing to what she felt in the privacy of the medical centre's bathroom. She had to wait three endless minutes before she dared to look at the result panel of the testing stick. One thin pink line meant she *wasn't* pregnant. Two pink lines meant she *was* pregnant.

She thought her eyes were blurring when she saw two distinct pink lines. Pink lines as deep in colour as the suit she'd been wearing the day before. She closed her eyes and opened them again, but the two lines were still there. She shook the device, in the hope that it might shake back down to one line, like the mercury in a thermometer. But the two pink lines were still there, glaring at her.

This couldn't be.

Those thin pink lines were turning her life upside down more than any earthquake.

Too numb to move, she stayed a long time in the bathroom. Eventually the practice nurse knocked on the door and asked if she was all right. She staggered back down to the doctor's consulting room, holding on to the corridor wall for support.

'You okay?' her doctor asked.

'Not really,' she said. 'It says I'm pregnant. That's not possible. I…I don't *feel* pregnant.'

But when she really thought about it maybe she did. The off-and-on nausea. Her aversion to certain foods. The inexplicable craving for oranges she'd put down to a need for vitamin C. A tendency to be over emotional, which was not like her at all. And when she'd dressed last night, in that gorgeous purple dress she'd bought just before she went to Bali, she'd been surprised when it had seemed tighter across the bust than she'd remembered.

But her brain refused to accept the possibility.

'Don't I need a blood test to be sure?' she asked.

'The test you've just taken is extremely accurate,' the doctor said. 'But just to be certain I'll ask you to hop up onto the bed so I can examine you.'

Zoe moaned under her breath. Could the day get any worse?

'You're definitely pregnant,' the doctor said, after a series of palpations. 'About eight weeks along, I'd say.'

She was eight weeks pregnant.

It seemed impossible. But the timing was spot-on.

'The sickness you're feeling should start to ease soon, as your hormones settle down,' the doctor said.

'How could this have happened? We took precautions.'

'No precautions are one hundred per cent effective,' the doctor said. 'My guess is that your digestive upset in Bali negated the effectiveness of your pill. Put simply: it wasn't absorbed—it didn't work.'

Zoe squeezed her eyes tight shut. This couldn't be true.

When she opened them it was to see the concerned face of her doctor.

'You have...options...' the doctor said.

'No.' Zoe was stunned by the fierce immediacy of her reply. 'No options. I'm keeping it.'

She couldn't bring herself to say *the baby*. Not yet. Not now.

Mitch's baby.

'The father...?' the doctor probed discreetly.

'We're not...not in a relationship,' Zoe replied. 'I...I'm in this on my own.'

She hardly heard another word as the doctor handed her a bunch of pamphlets. Talked of blood tests. Nutrition advice. Referral to an obstetrician. Choice of hospital. Antenatal classes. Nothing really sank in. This couldn't be happening.

She was going to have a baby in February.

It took her twice as long to walk home as it had to get to the medical centre. Her feet felt leaden and it seemed as if she was walking through dense fog. The more she thought about being pregnant, the more complicated the situation got.

She dreaded telling Mitch. He'd made it so clear he wasn't ready for commitment—certainly not for a family. *'Not until I'm thirty. Maybe thirty-five.'* His words echoed in her head over and over.

Then worse words seeped into her thoughts like poison. Her grandmother. *'I won't have you getting pregnant and ruining the future of some fine young man the way your mother ruined my son's.'*

In Bali she'd told Mitch what her grandmother had said. Was that how Mitch would see it? Would her getting pregnant ruin *his* future? It would certainly change it.

Her breath caught on a half-sob. *Not as much as it would change hers.*

Would he think she'd tried to trap him? That she'd demand money? Even marriage? *The oldest trick in the book.* She couldn't bear to think he would believe that of her.

Imagine if the press got hold of it. How sordid they would make it look. A one-night stand. A holiday fling. A scheming woman. It would not reflect well on him.

Mitch's career was all-important to him. He'd been so clear that he couldn't have distractions at this vital stage of his career. What could be more of a distraction than an unplanned baby—with its mother a woman he was only just getting to know?

A mother. She was going to be a *mother*.

From nowhere came a fierce urge to protect her baby. *Her baby*. This baby would be wanted. Would be loved. This was far from the way she'd dreamed of starting a family, but it had happened. She was strong. She was independent. She could do this on her own.

By the time Zoe got back home she'd made her decision. She would not tell Mitch she was pregnant.

Mitch had an early breakfast with his parents, feeling sad to say goodbye to them while his father was still in a cast and a sling and so obviously in discomfort. But that was another price he paid for his international career—being so far away from his family.

His mother had been determined to drive him to the airport. Much as Mitch loved his mother, he had been equally determined that she would be staying home in Wahroonga. He wanted to drive himself, so he could detour to Balmain and see Zoe one last time before he flew out to Madrid.

As he drove his rental car into Balmain, Mitch realised he was excited—heart-pounding, mind-racing excited—at the thought of seeing Zoe, even for only an hour. He had never felt like this about a woman. Always the game had been first and foremost—his emotions and energy channelled into his relentless drive to the top level.

Realistically, now was not the best time to get involved, to be thinking there might be some kind of future with her. But his attraction to Zoe was as out of his control as the earthquake had been. He had to ride with it.

Their night together had shifted something in his thinking. On the drive back to his parents' house he had found himself wondering if Zoe could play a part in his life.

Could she be a support rather than a distraction? Would having her with him in Madrid be less of a distraction than *not* having her there?

Because deep in his gut he knew Zoe was important. *Very* important.

One thing was for sure: he had to see her again, and see her again as soon as possible. Being back in Madrid would be easier if he knew he would be seeing her as soon as they could make it happen. He wanted to make a definite arrangement for her to come and visit as quickly as she possibly could. Her first-class airfare paid by him, of course.

On his third knock, Zoe answered her door.

As a footballer, Mitch was good at reading other players' intentions. Some commentators saw his skill as uncanny. He believed it was because he had been blessed with a well-developed subconscious antennae that picked up on the slightest variations in body language.

But he didn't need more than a basic knowledge of body language to know that something was wrong. Zoe looked washed out and drawn; her hand braced against the doorframe didn't look steady. His first thought was that she was ill.

'Mitch,' she said, offering her cheek for his kiss, but her greeting wasn't over-burdened with enthusiasm—and certainly not with passion.

He swallowed his dismay. Last night she had been so responsive in his arms.

Today she was wearing skinny black jeans and a loose black top that swamped her slender frame. It drained the colour from her face, making the contrast of her red lipstick appear garish. Her eyes seemed shadowed and dull.

He drew back. Searched her face. 'Are you okay?'

Her gaze slid away from his. 'Just tired. It was such a late night last night.'

Worry for her coursed through him. Fatigue. Illness. *Please don't let there be something seriously wrong with her.*

'You look unwell,' he said, more bluntly than he'd intended.

'I actually went to the doctor this morning,' she said.

'And? Did he test you for tropical bugs?'

'It's not a tropical bug. It's...it's... She's testing me for food allergies.'

'That's great. Not great that it could be an allergy. But great you didn't bring something home from Bali with you.'

Zoe choked, and then started to cough. He patted her on the back until her coughs subsided.

'I'm okay now,' she said.

He frowned. 'I don't like the sound of that cough.'

Her smile was forced. 'There's nothing to worry about. I...I'm not sick.'

Mitch wasn't convinced.

She turned on her spike-heeled black boots. 'It's cold out here. You'd better come in.'

The shiver that went through him had nothing to do with the weather.

Mitch followed her through into her living room. The view was, indeed, as spectacular as he'd thought it would be last night.

'This is a wonderful space,' he said, looking around him.

For the first time she smiled, but it was a wan imitation of her usual smile. 'It is wonderful, isn't it? I get it for a very good rent.'

For the first time Mitch felt an intimation of fear. Was

she having second thoughts about them keeping in touch? He regretted not telling her last night that she was so much more to him than a 'friend with benefits'. They'd vaguely discussed her visiting him in Madrid. But nothing concrete. He wanted to remedy that this morning—before he left for the airport.

He looked over to the sofa, where they'd made such passionate love. The cat was firmly ensconced once more, curled up in a ball. It opened one yellow eye, inspected him, and went back to sleep.

'No one working today?' he said. 'Except the mouse-catcher, there, of course.'

His joke about the cat fell flat.

'Louise and our office manager are on a course. I cancelled all my appointments because…'

He wanted her to say it was because he was going to call by and she wanted privacy. But he had a sinking sensation that wasn't what she was going to say.

'Because…because I wasn't feeling well,' she said.

She didn't wait for a reply from him, but turned away so all he saw of her was her black-clad back. Then she spun round to face him. She crossed her arms in front of her chest, seemed to brace her shoulders.

'I can't do this—with you, I mean,' she blurted out. 'I've thought about it. Not knowing when I'll see you again. Being a…a part-time lover. Sleeping with you with no kind of commitment. It's not me. It…it can only lead to heartbreak—for me, anyway. Why pretend otherwise?'

Mitch was too astounded to answer for a moment. 'I don't get it. Last night we talked about you coming to Madrid.'

'Did we? I don't recall a definite invitation. Just *Drop in for a bootie call if you happen to find yourself in Europe*.'

'Zoe, I didn't meant that.'

But that was exactly what it would have sounded like to her. He cursed under his breath.

'Last night we were kidding ourselves that we could keep something going. But all the barriers are still there and...and they're insurmountable.' Her voice broke.

'I don't agree,' he said. 'We can—'

She put up her hand in a halt sign. 'Don't say it. I've made up my mind. In any case, even if you *were* offering more than friends with benefits, I couldn't deal with the public attention. For a private person like me it would be hell.'

'But last night—'

She spoke over him. 'We...we need to get on with our own lives. I'm sorry, Mitch.'

Her words sounded rehearsed. Was this why she was tired? Had she been up since he'd left here, practising how to dump him?

He fisted his hands by his sides. 'I'm surprised. And disappointed.'

And angry as hell.

'I've thought about it a lot since...since last night.'

'So that's it? It's over between us before it even started?'

Dumbly, she nodded, her eyes bleak.

'Then there's nothing further to be said.'

He turned and walked out. She made no effort to stop him. If she'd been able to read his thought bubbles all that would be visible would be dark, thunderous clouds.

Mitch was so churned up he was scarcely aware of how he got out of Balmain and on the road to the airport.

What in hell had gone wrong? He couldn't believe Zoe had had such a complete turnaround of feelings.

But he couldn't *make* her feel what he felt—make her

see what a good chance they had of something special if they both worked at it.

He had to put her behind him.

It wasn't as if he'd be short of feminine attention once he got back to Madrid.

Oh, yes, there were plenty of eager women around for a player of his standing in La Liga. He was only alone by choice.

But none of them was Zoe.

His hands clenched tightly to the steering wheel. As he drove towards the airport his thoughts spun around and around, unable to make sense of his confrontation with her.

It hadn't seemed right. There had been something about her. She'd seemed…*cowed.* The thought of her face brought back a flash of memory. The way her shoulders had been hunched over, the way she'd kept her eyes to the ground. She'd been like that Zoe he'd wounded long ago in high school.

But he'd done nothing to hurt her this time.

Something else had happened. Something she was hiding from him—for a reason he couldn't fathom.

As he neared the industrial area of Mascot, home to Sydney's Kingsford-Smith Airport, he was still puzzling over what he might have missed.

He thought about her doctor's diagnosis. How could the doctor know straight away that Zoe hadn't contracted a tropical disease? There would have to be tests—tests that would take days to come back from a pathologist.

The more he thought about it, the more he was convinced something was seriously wrong. Something Zoe was determined to hide from him.

Twice before she'd left him with unfinished business. The first time when they'd been teenagers. The second in Bali, after a night of passionate lovemaking. There wouldn't be a third time.

He still had a few hours until he had to check in for his flight.

He swung the car around and headed back to Balmain.

CHAPTER FOURTEEN

AFTER MITCH WALKED OUT Zoe was in such a state of shock she couldn't think straight. She immediately began to worry if she had done the right thing in concealing her pregnancy from him.

She hadn't just concealed it—she had *lied* about it. She had out-and-out lied to Mitch by telling him she was being tested for food allergies to explain her symptoms.

Zoe smothered a semi-hysterical laugh. She wasn't very good at deception. She'd always prided herself on her honesty. Mitch must think she was at best unbalanced; she didn't dare think what he might call her at worst. The confusion, hurt and barely suppressed anger on his face at her ill-thought-out words had distressed *her*. Heaven knew how awful it had been for *him*.

She had decided not to continue their friendship before she'd gone to the doctor. But she'd had no intention of blurting it out to him this morning. She just wouldn't have answered his texts, replied to his emails, until he'd got the message. She'd wanted to avoid a messy confrontation.

But that had been before she knew she was pregnant.

She paced the length of the apartment—back and forth, back and forth—totally at a loss to know what to do, until she began to feel dizzy. It seemed surreal that in the space of a few hours her world had been turned so totally upside down, leaving her staggering and disorientated—way worse than after the earthquake.

She'd discovered she was pregnant, and she'd lost Mitch when she'd only just found him.

Finally, when she truly thought she might topple over from a crippling combination of fatigue and angst, she sank into the sofa. Einstein, her dark tabby cat, looked at her with baleful eyes but allowed himself to be hugged tight.

'What am I going to do?' she asked the cat as she stroked him.

The rhythmic motion on his soft fur was soothing to both of them. She often talked to her cat; he was a great listener. It didn't matter that he only answered with the occasional meow that she fancifully imagined to be a reply.

'I'm going to have a human kitten, Einstein, and I don't know how I'm going to cope.'

Her words echoed through the empty space, emphasising her aloneness. Einstein just purred.

In some ways she identified with the cat. He'd been a disreputable-looking stray, hanging around the warehouse complex car park. With patience and cans of tuna she'd tamed him. Once she'd established that he didn't belong to anyone she'd adopted him.

She and Louise had called him Einstein because, as Louise had put it, 'He's a genius cat to have found *you* to dance attendance on him.'

Einstein was as fiercely independent and self-sufficient as Zoe liked to think she was. After all, she was the girl who had emancipated herself from her grandmother aged just seventeen. She'd put herself through university on her own. Got admitted as a chartered accountant. Established her business by herself.

She'd become very good at solving problems without

seeking help. But she was totally unprepared for a surprise pregnancy and for bringing up a baby on her own.

Suddenly she was overwhelmed by a fierce longing for her mother. A woman desperately needed her mother with her at a time like this. And her father too. He would have given her good advice on what to do about Mitch.

Should she have told Mitch she was pregnant? Presented it as an issue they needed to look at together? After all, they'd made this baby together. Did he have a right to know he was going to be a father? Was it the wrong thing to do to keep him out of the picture? Should she tell him and make it clear she would make no demands on him—financial or otherwise?

Zoe clutched her head with both hands against the throbbing of an impending headache. Conflicting thoughts and questions she could find no answer to were banking up in her brain and banging to be let out.

She glanced at her watch. It seemed like for ever, but Mitch hadn't been gone long. If she was quick she could catch him on his mobile phone and ask him to come back. Or meet him at the airport.

She didn't have Mitch's number.

They hadn't actually exchanged phone numbers or addresses. There'd been no need to as yet. They'd planned to swap all their contact details this morning, if things had gone differently.

Could she get hold of his number from somewhere? Maybe look up his parents and call them? What kind of reception would she get from his mother? A strange young woman, calling to get her famous soccer star son's personal phone number so she could tell him she was pregnant? As if *that* would happen.

She didn't even have a clue about which airline he was flying with. And no airline would divulge passenger details to tell her if he was booked on their 2:00 p.m. flight to Madrid. If she wanted to talk to him she would have to scurry around the terminal, trying to find him. No way could she bear to do that. If he were flying first class he'd go straight to a private lounge anyway.

It seemed she'd missed her chance to tell him face to face that she was pregnant.

If she decided to tell him at some time in the future she would have to try and contact him in Madrid. Maybe she could find out who was his agent or his manager and get a message to him through them. *Yeah, right.* They'd think she was a groupie or a stalker—or worse.

What a mess she'd made of this.

But she'd had her reasons for not telling Mitch and they'd seemed valid at the time. For the moment she'd stick with them.

Louise would have to be told, though, when she got back at lunchtime. They were good friends as well as work colleagues. Her pregnancy would have implications for the business. It would affect the possible buyout and her plans for expansion. Nothing they wouldn't be able to work through, though. Women got pregnant and managed their careers all the time.

It was Mitch who was her concern.

She sighed and yawned—exhausted, overwhelmed, and weary beyond measure.

'Move over, Einstein,' she said to her cat, so she could stretch out on the sofa beside him.

As she settled herself next to the purring cat at last she allowed herself to think about her baby—the new little person she would be bringing into the world in February. Would she/he look like her and Mitch? Her black hair with his green eyes?

Or a little boy or girl who looked just like Mitch.

She smiled at the thought and put her hand protectively on her still flat tummy. But as she drowsed into sleep she thought about how delighted her mother and father would have been to be grandparents and her smile melted into tears.

Zoe was awoken by an insistent buzzing. She struggled through layers of sleep to recognise it as the front door buzzer. *Please don't let it be a client*. She couldn't even face a delivery person, let alone some number-befuddled artiste who'd got themselves into a huge mess with their tax reporting or their quarterly Business Activity Statement.

Right now she couldn't cope with someone spilling a shoebox full of scrappy invoices and receipts all over her desk and begging for help. Usually she'd see it as a challenge, and be delighted to assist. But today it would be the befuddled leading the befuddled.

She moved a protesting Einstein and swung herself off the sofa. Once on her feet she staggered, and had to steady herself against a sudden light-headedness. With clumsy fingers she pushed her fingers through her hair and rubbed under her eyes for smeared mascara.

'Coming!' she called.

It seemed to take for ever to reach the door, and Zoe took a deep breath before she opened it. She thought she was hallucinating when she saw Mitch standing there. She wiped her eyes with the back of her hand and looked again. But he was still there, as billboard-handsome as ever but with his face set in unfamiliar grim lines.

Mitch.

Joy filtered through her shock to warm her heart. *He'd come back*.

'You're…you're meant to be at the airport,' she managed to choke out.

He didn't explain but rather launched straight into tight-lipped speech. 'Zoe, you obviously have your reasons for saying what you did this morning. But I'm not leaving until I know the truth.'

'I...I wanted to... I didn't have your number and...'

The words seemed to stall in her throat. She stared at him until the lines of his face seemed to go fuzzy. Her hand flew to her mouth. She felt flushed, light-headed, nauseated. She clutched at the doorframe. For the first time in her life she was going to faint.

Zoe felt Mitch catch her, lift her into his arms, cradle her to his chest. She could hear his voice as if it were coming from a long way away.

'Zoe... I've got you, Zoe.'

He carried her to a chair in the waiting area and forced her head between her knees. She was aware of his hand, warm and reassuring on her back.

'Breathe,' he said, his voice coming back into normal range. 'Breathe in and out, slowly and deeply. You told me you've done yoga. Use your yoga breathing.'

She did as he instructed until the fog cleared. But it was an effort to lift her head.

'Slowly,' Mitch said. 'Lift your head slowly.'

He handed her a paper cup of water from the cooler.

'Just sip it,' he said.

Obediently, she took a few sips of the cold water.

He hunkered down in front of her, his green eyes narrowed. 'Are you going to tell me what's going on?'

Not here. Not now. Not with her at such a disadvantage. She needed her thoughts to be clear.

Weakly, she bowed her head and didn't answer.

'So there *is* something?' he said gruffly.

She nodded.

'I knew it,' he said.

'I…I'm sorry about…this morning…the way I….' She couldn't force the words out. She swallowed hard but it didn't make it any better.

'How long since you've eaten?' he said.

'Last night…I think.'

'When you just nibbled at your dinner? You didn't have any breakfast?'

She shook her head. 'Nothing. I thought the doctor might want to take blood for tests. I didn't want to have to go back another time, so I decided to fast so I could have the tests done straight away.'

It had seemed a good idea at the time. Then, after her visit to the doctor, food had been the last thing on her mind.

'What have you got in your refrigerator? I'll make you something to eat.'

'There's some bread in the freezer. Some toast, maybe?'

'You stay here and keep sipping on that water. Whatever else might be wrong with you, it's my bet you're dehydrated.'

She heard him rattling around in the kitchen. Soon the smell of toast wafted towards her. Suddenly she was starving. But she took Mitch's advice, leaned back in the chair and kept sipping water.

Within minutes he returned, with a plate holding two pieces of wholewheat toast, cut into squares. 'I think you should eat it dry until you see if you can keep it down. Just nibble on it to start with.'

He was so kind. She flushed. What if she didn't keep it down? How humiliating would *that* be in front of Mitch?

But she did keep it down. And she started to feel better. Stronger. Who knew? All she'd needed was some food.

'Thank you so much, Mitch, for looking after me. I feel fine now.' She wasn't used to being pampered—found it difficult to accept it.

'And, from that coolness in your voice, you think you're dismissing me and that I'm going to go away. Not happening. I told you—I'm sticking with you until I get to the bottom of what's going on.'

He'd come back to her.

It changed everything. She would have to pick her moment to tell him the truth. He was every bit as wonderful as she'd thought he was. And more. She would not find it easy to tell him she'd lied to him about something so important. That he was going to be a father.

Mitch was relieved to see the colour return to Zoe's cheeks, the light come back to her eyes. She'd given him a fright by fainting. But it was nothing he couldn't handle. It wasn't uncommon for a player to pass out from the sudden pain and shock of an injury.

Why she'd fainted was what he was determined to know. And why she'd behaved the way she had earlier this morning. It didn't make sense.

At the back of his mind was still the suspicion that there was something very wrong and she was trying to protect him from a painful truth. That was the kind explanation. What he knew for sure was that she was concealing *something* from him.

He didn't give up easily—he would never have got to where he was if he had. He wasn't going to give up on Zoe. Or leave her here to suffer by herself. She had no family. Was so fiercely independent that she wouldn't ask for help from anyone.

He needed to catch that plane and get back to Madrid.

But he'd left her on her own once before, in a corridor at a high school. In all conscience he couldn't to it again.

Who was he kidding? He felt more for Zoe than he ever had for a woman. It would nag at him if he left her—if he didn't look out for her. She awoke in him a deep, almost primeval urge to protect her. He would stay with her, no matter the cost to him.

'You said you'd cancelled your appointments for the day. Is that still the case?' he asked.

She nodded.

'Today's Friday. I assume you don't have any business plans for the weekend?'

'No.'

'Social engagements?'

'None to speak off.'

'Good.'

'What do you mean, "good"?'

'Because I'm taking you away. Somewhere you can get the rest you so obviously need. Somewhere we can talk. Talk until there's no more pretence or prevarication between us. I just need to make a few calls.'

She gripped the arms of the chair. 'You're taking me away? What the heck do you mean by *that*?'

He waved his hand around to encompass her office, the living area, the view to the harbour. 'This isn't working for us. The city. Being in Sydney. It's some kind of barrier. I thought we'd breached it last night. Got back to how we were in Bali. But obviously not.'

'No,' she said softly, looking somewhere near her feet.

'I'm not letting you go without a fight, Zoe. If it were at all possible I'd fly us back to Bali. But that can't happen. So I'm going to take you somewhere else.'

She looked directly up at him. 'You're kidnapping me, Mitch?'

'You could call it that.' She sure as hell wasn't going to get away from him.

Zoe smiled. It was a watery smile, but a smile just the same. 'I think I like the idea of being kidnapped.'

She pushed herself up from her chair. He took her elbow to support her.

'Please don't faint on me again,' he said. 'When your eyes rolled back in your head I thought—'

Those same brown eyes flashed indignation. 'My eyes did *not* roll back in my head.'

'They did.'

'They did not. I would have felt them if they had.'

'Okay, they didn't,' he said, unable to suppress a grin. 'They just...tilted a bit.'

'I don't know whether to take you seriously or not.' She shuddered theatrically. 'That would be such an unattractive look. I wouldn't want you to think of me as an eyes-rolled-back kind of girl.'

'Now I don't know whether to take you seriously or not,' he said.

'You'll never know, will you?' she said, with a challenging tilt to her chin.

She was cute. Very cute. And he was relieved to see a spark of *his* Zoe back again. But he wanted so much more than just a spark. He wanted the Zoe he'd been with in Bali. The Zoe he'd developed feelings for and didn't want to let go.

She frowned. 'But what about Madrid? Shouldn't you be back there? I'm worried that—'

'Let *me* worry about that. I can stretch my absence until Monday. I have to fly out tomorrow evening, come what may, but I'm going to keep you locked up in my kidnapper's lair until tomorrow afternoon. We either sort things out—'

'Or...?'

'Or we say goodbye for good.'

She stood very still. He could hear the ticking of the large clock on the wall behind him, the ding of incoming emails on the computer in the next room, even the faint slap of the water against the wooden piers below the building.

'Okay,' she said at last. 'But I hope you don't intend to gag and bind me and throw me in the back of your car?'

He laughed. She looked so washed out, her eyes shadowed, but that Zoe spirit was still there. 'I wouldn't dare,' he said.

'So...where are you taking me?'

'I can't take you to Bali, so I'm taking you to Palm Beach.'

Her face brightened. 'Palm Beach? I *love* Palm Beach. Even though I've only ever been there a few times. Even though it's winter.'

'There's a heated pool at the house.'

'I've never been kidnapped before. So what do I pack...?'

'Casual...comfortable. Something warm. It can get chilly by the sea. Oh, and walking shoes.'

Those sexy little boots wouldn't do for long walks on the beach.

He made a few calls on his mobile phone—one of which was to postpone his flight back to Madrid. He had to admire the efficiency with which Zoe packed her small red overnight bag and flung on a black-and-white-checked coat. In less than ten minutes she was ready.

'What about the cat?' he asked.

'I've left a note for Louise. She'll look after him.'

'I'm glad we don't have to take him with us,' he said.

She looked up at him. 'Would you really have brought Einstein with us?' she asked.

'Einstein? You call your cat *Einstein*?'

'Long story. I'll tell you later.'

'Yes. I would have brought Einstein with us if I'd had to. I don't mind cats.'

She went very quiet again. 'We haven't even established whether we like dogs or cats yet, let alone—'

'We can talk about that on the way down to the beach,' he said. 'Though, for the record, I love dogs and I like cats too. We had both when I was growing up. Not having a dog or a cat around the place is one of the things I miss, living in Spain.'

But they didn't get a chance to talk about dog and cats, or favourite movies or their taste in music, let alone the reasons Zoe had stonewalled him earlier this morning.

Because almost as soon as he'd driven the car out of Balmain and over the Anzac Bridge, heading north to the Harbour Bridge, Zoe had fallen asleep.

CHAPTER FIFTEEN

ZOE WAS ANNOYED with herself to find she had slept for most of the one-hour drive to Palm Beach—the most northern of Sydney's northern beaches. Her time with Mitch was so limited, and she didn't want to waste a minute of it.

But by the time her eyes had started to flicker open they had already driven past every one of the long, sandy beaches and the surrounding suburbs that lay between Manly and Palm Beach.

By the time her eyes were fully open they were on Barrenjoey Road, with the blue, boat-studded waters of Pittwater on their left, and cruising into Palm Beach. She barely had time to notice the handful of shops and restaurants that formed the hub of this exclusive, resort-like suburb as they flashed past.

Zoe didn't know how many times she'd heard Palm Beach referred to as 'the playground of the rich and famous'. When Hollywood celebrities jetted into Sydney in the summer it was often to stay in luxurious beach houses owned by themselves or their billionaire Aussie friends up here on the Barrenjoey Peninsula. Real estate was prized on this strip of land that jutted out into the sea, bounded by the surf beach on one side and the calm waters of Pittwater on the other.

Still feeling a tad drowsy, she allowed herself the luxury

of watching Mitch as he drove. He made even an every-day thing like driving a car look graceful and controlled. Both hands were firmly on the wheel as he concentrated on the road ahead. She noticed he wore one of the expensive watches he endorsed in an advertising campaign. He'd told her he only endorsed products he believed were of the best quality and design. His face—already so familiar to her—was set in such a serious expression. Designer sunglasses masked his eyes.

She wished she could see his thought bubbles. Was he looking ahead to a future—if his knee continued to hold up—as an elite athlete at the top of his field?

He was a determined, driven man who had made his thoughts about not settling down until he was in his thirties very clear. And yet it appeared he was serious about wanting her as part of his future in some way—he wouldn't have turned around at the airport otherwise.

But it wasn't just about *her* now—or even about *him*. They'd made a baby together. The way he'd looked after her when she'd fainted gave her cause to think that despite his celebrity status he was not the kind of man who would deny his own child. *He would make a good father.* It would be up to her to make sure he played some role in their child's life.

'That trip went fast,' she said, trying out her voice and finding it to be back to normal. She had never, ever fainted before.

'The lady awakes,' Mitch said, giving her a sideways glance.

Zoe remembered waking up next to him in Bali, after a night of sensual pleasure. How wonderful that time together had been—as it had been last night. She longed to be something more in his life and not to have to say goodbye in the morning. Would it ever happen?

'I missed the whole drive down. I wish you'd woken me up,' she said.

He smiled. 'So you could quiz me about my preference for dog over cat?'

'Something like that.' She'd planned to segue into his thoughts on having kids.

'You obviously needed the sleep,' he said. 'Feeling any better?'

'Much better,' she said, stretching her limbs as best she could in the confines of the car. 'Thank you.'

'We're nearly there,' he said.

'So I see.'

It was a magnificent winter's day, the sky cloudless, the sea a deep blue.

'It's ages since I've been down here. I'm a city girl—I don't stray over the bridge too often.'

'We came down here for a couple of vacations when I was a kid and I loved it. A friend of my parents had a house here.'

'Nice,' she said.

Now the road ran parallel to the surf beach that stretched to the Barrenjoey headland at one end and Whale Beach at the other. Even on a weekday in winter there were people swimming, and others in wetsuits, riding boards or paddling surf kayaks out into the breakers.

She opened her window to enjoy the salty air.

'We lived in Newtown,' she said. 'My parents weren't much for the outdoor life. They were arty, musical, and preferred to hang out in coffee shops rather than on beaches. Though when I was older I went with friends to the eastern suburbs beaches, like Bondi and Coogee. That was... that was before I moved to Wahroonga.'

'I was always a north shore boy. I learned to surf here, how to handle a surf kayak. My brothers were older than me—they taught me.'

'Knowing you, you probably overtook them at it your first day in the water.'

'Yeah. That's how it happened. They weren't too happy, having their kid brother beating them so quickly. But that was the way it was in my family. I was the brawn—they were the brains. And that's how it's played out. Just like my parents planned—they got a doctor, a lawyer and a banker.'

'And one of the best sportsmen in the world,' she reminded him.

'They appreciate that—don't worry. They're very proud of my success. They always supported me in anything I wanted to do,' he said.

'But why did they pigeonhole you?' she said, indignant on his behalf.

'They recognised our aptitudes early on, I suppose.'

'You've got plenty of brains. I know that for sure. You even ended up writing a halfway decent piece of poetry for that last essay.'

'You mean the essay that got the big red "fail"?' he reminded her.

'I don't know how that awful teacher could have thought you had plagiarised that poem,' she said.

'You mean because it was so very, very bad?'' he said with a grin.

'It wasn't bad. She just didn't appreciate the analogy between scoring goals in a soccer game and goals in life. It was wonderfully rich in similes and metaphors and—'

'And more similes and metaphors, and a whole heap of words I didn't understand. It was *bad*, Zoe,' he said. 'Admit it.'

'It didn't have to be a masterpiece to get you a pass,' she said. 'I liked it, and that's that.'

He glanced sideways at her. 'Thank you for your loyalty. I didn't deserve it.'

She put up her hand in a halt sign. 'No need to go there again.'

She wondered how loyal he would feel towards *her* when she told him she was pregnant.

'I got a place to study engineering at the University of New South Wales. Did I tell you that?'

'You didn't—that's fantastic. You must have done well in the final exams.'

'I had no intention of taking up the place, of course,' he said. 'To play football was all I'd ever wanted to do since my grandfather took me to my first game at White Hart Lane in London. I applied to university just to prove I could get in.'

At the south end of the beach Mitch turned off and swung into a street a few hundred metres back from the water. He pulled up in the driveway of an elegantly simple house, rising to two storeys, all whitewashed timber and huge windows. It was surrounded by perfectly groomed tropical gardens. In an area of multi-million-dollar houses, it fitted right in.

'Is this your parents' friends' house?' Zoe asked. 'It's fabulous.'

'No, it's mine,' he said simply.

'Oh,' she said, not attempting to hide her surprise. Mitch hadn't mentioned owning property of any kind. But then she hadn't asked.

He opened her car door and went around to swing out both her small bag and one of his own.

'This house looks like a very posh kidnapper's lair,' she said.

'I don't think you'll object too much to the conditions of captivity,' Mitch replied with a smile.

They took a small glass-fronted elevator from the garage to the second floor. Zoe stepped into an airy, spacious living room that opened out through folding glass doors to a deck and an infinity edge swimming pool. Beyond that was a magnificent view of the sea, right up to the Barrenjoey headland, filtered by a stand of the tall cabbage palm trees that gave the area its name.

She turned to Mitch. 'Can you forgive me if I can't come up with anything more than *wow*?' she said. 'Except maybe *wow* again? I could look at that view all day.'

'I bought the house for the view.'

'The house itself isn't too shabby either,' she said.

The interior looked as if it had been designed by a professional, in tones of white with highlights of soft blue and bleached driftwood. Large artworks with abstract beach and marine life themes were perfectly placed through the room. It was contemporary and stylish, straight from the pages of a high-end decorating magazine. And yet there were homey touches everywhere—like a shabby-chic old pair of oars, a glass buoy covered in ancient knotted rope, tiny wooden replicas of fishing boats—that took away any intimidating edge.

What an idyllic place for children.

She slipped off her coat. The sun streaming through the windows made it superfluous.

'The house is awesome, isn't it?' said Mitch. 'I bought it with all the furniture included when the market was down, for a very good price.'

Zoe's money-savvy brain recognised that he'd got a good deal by buying at the right time. But around here a 'very good price' would still measure in the multi-millions.

Great. Just great. Mitch must be very wealthy. Wealthier than she'd thought he must be. And, from her experience with her clients, the wealthier they were, the more protective they were of their money—and defensive against people they suspected of wanting to take a bite out of it.

Like a girl who got pregnant on a holiday fling and came looking for a pay-out.

She forced the negative thought to the back of her mind. If she wasn't to tie herself up in knots of anxiety again she had to trust in Mitch that he wouldn't believe she'd had any other motive that night in Bali than to be with him. No matter what else he might come to believe when she told him about her visit to the doctor.

'Let me show you around,' Mitch said.

He took her for a quick tour. The kitchen seemed to be stocked with every appliance and piece of equipment possible. The bathrooms were total luxury. Each of the four bedrooms had ocean views.

Mitch took her overnight bag to the master bedroom, with its enormous bed and palatial en-suite bathroom. 'I'm putting your bag in here,' he said.

She stilled. 'And where are you putting yours?' she asked.

'That's up to you,' he said.

Whatever happened here in this beautiful house, whatever transpired with Mitch, she didn't want to sleep in a different bedroom from him.

'Put your bag with mine. Here. Please.'

The bedroom opened up onto a balcony. While Mitch went to get his bag she stepped out onto the balcony, breathed in the salt air. A flock of multi-coloured lorikeets took flight from the orange flowering grevillea that grew next to the pool. This truly was a magnificent place.

Mitch placed his bag next to hers and came up behind her on the balcony. He put his arms around her and pulled her back to rest against his chest. After a split second of hesitation she let herself relax against his solid strength. She felt safe, secure—and terrified.

This. Mitch. His arms wrapped around her, his breath

stirring her hair, his powerful body close. It was what she wanted. Now. And in the future. She was terrified that would never happen. Not when he discovered how dishonest she'd been with him.

That she was pregnant.

Mitch held Zoe close, relieved she hadn't pushed him away. He didn't want to let her go. Out of his arms—out of his life. They had twenty-four hours to sort out whatever was troubling her. He just hoped it was something he could work with—or solve for her.

He wanted her with him.

The more he was with her, the more he realised that a 'now and then' relationship wouldn't satisfy him for long. What he felt for her couldn't be blocked or passed or sent off the pitch.

'A good substitute for Bali?' he asked as they both looked ahead at the view.

'Oh, yes,' she said. 'It must be glorious in summer.'

'One day, maybe, I'll get to see it in summer. Usually I don't even get back to Australia for Christmas.'

'So you bought the house as an investment?'

'An investment for now. A home for later. When my football career is over.'

He hated to say those words. Right now he couldn't bear even to think about a life without playing.

'Is that inevitable?'

'It's a young man's game. I've still got good years ahead of me.' If the knee stood up to it. And if he didn't suffer any other serious injuries. 'But, yes. It will end.'

'What do you plan to do? Afterwards, I mean?'

Mitch liked it that Zoe didn't seem to realise he would never have to work again. He'd been careful with invest-

ments and he would continue to be. That was where banker
and lawyer brothers came in handy.

'I was bored witless while I was recuperating,' he said.
'I had a good look into some of the injury prevention de-
vices for sportsmen. Shin guards, ankle wraps, mouth
guards. That kind of thing. I reckon they could be better.
I'm looking into that.'

'Sounds good. You'd still be involved in sport.'

'But that all seems a long way away, Zoe. I don't want
to think about it too much. I'm concerned about the now,
not the future.'

'Of course,' she murmured, her voice subdued.

The change in her tone signalled a warning. They had
limited time. He had to try and recreate the atmosphere
that had brought them together in such a spectacular way
back in Bali at her villa.

'I can't promise roosters.'

'Just parrots?' she said.

'Or Indonesian food,' he said.

'Or earthquakes?' she added.

Mitch could think of various ways he might make the
earth move for her, as he had last night. He could carry her
right now to that big bed behind them in the bedroom. But
first he had to find out why she had behaved the way she
had this morning. After the fun they'd had at Luna Park,
after the lovemaking they'd shared, he still wondered why
she had dismissed him so coldly.

'However, there *is* a swimming pool—that's bigger and
better than the one at the villa.'

'With colder water?' she said pretending to shiver.

He looked over to the sparkling blue pool. There was
no elephant in residence. Both he and Zoe knew what had
to be tackled.

'The water should be heated up enough to swim,' he said. 'Not quite the same as Bali, but warm enough.'

'It's the most beautiful pool—I've never swum in a wet edge pool before. Are you sure I won't drift over the edge?'

He laughed. 'There's a ledge below. It's quite safe. Anyway, I'm here to catch you if you get into trouble,' he said.

'Are you, Mitch?' she said, in that tremulous voice that worried him.

She went to ease away from him but he hugged her tighter. 'Of course I am.'

They stood without speaking for a long moment.

Zoe broke the silence. 'So. The pool. Do you leave the heating on all the time?'

'The pool is solar-heated. But there's a gas-fired booster. I called the manager this morning and got her to switch it on.'

'You have a manager?'

'She looks after several of the properties here for absentee owners. My family use the house too. And sometimes I let it out to carefully vetted guests.'

'That makes sense. If the house is earning income you can get tax benefits too.'

'Of course you *would* know that,' he said. 'I also got the manager to stock the fridge with basics.'

'I was wondering about that. I wasn't sure what kidnappers did about feeding their victims. And it's been a while since that toast. It must be lunchtime.'

'Some of the restaurants here do delivery service. I asked the manager to pick up their latest menus.'

'So we can get room service? Like in Bali?'

'Yes,' he said. 'We can order lunch now.'

Zoe twisted in his arms so she faced him. He refused to let her go.

'Mitch, before we order lunch, and definitely before I get into a bikini, there's something I have to tell you.'

Mitch held his breath. *What was coming?*

She looked up at him, her eyes huge in her wan face. 'I'm pregnant.'

CHAPTER SIXTEEN

MITCH COULD NOT BELIEVE what he was hearing. *Zoe was pregnant?* He gently pushed her away from him. Stared at her as if he she were a stranger as he tried to process what she had just told him. Then the reality of it hit him. He cursed loud and hard.

How had he let this happen? He had trusted her. What an idiot he had been to lose control in Bali. Not to take absolute charge over contraception. What the hell had he got himself into?

Damn. Damn. *Damn.*

She didn't say another word, just stood on the veranda facing him, the glorious view stretching behind her. He knew she was nervously waiting for his response, but he was too shocked to say anything. Nothing in his twenty-seven years had prepared him for this moment. He cursed again.

He didn't know a lot about pregnant women—in fact he knew virtually nothing. He hadn't been in Australia when his nephews—the children of his oldest brother and his wife—had been born.

But some of the cards began to fall into place. Sickness, fainting, fatigue—all symptoms of a worrying serious illness. *Or a pregnancy.* What a blind fool he'd been.

'You're pregnant? And you didn't tell me?'

She flinched at the harshness of his voice but he didn't care. He'd been so careful to protect his future. Now a moment's lust, a moment's carelessness, had thrown everything off course.

She didn't look any different—still slim. But when he thought about last night he remembered that her breasts had seemed larger. He'd appreciated that. It must be a symptom too.

'I only found out myself this morning,' she said.

Her bottom lip was quivering, and she looked near to tears, but she met his gaze fearlessly. She gripped the veranda railing so hard her knuckles showed white.

'This morning? When you went to the doctor?' Strangely, he believed her.

'Yes. I got the shock of my life,' she said. 'I wasn't expecting it at all.'

He looked again at her slender figure in the tight black jeans. 'You're absolutely sure you're pregnant?'

She nodded. 'There's no doubt. The doctor gave me a test and examined me.'

Zoe pregnant.

He was struggling to get his head around it.

'But how did it happen?' He realised what a stupid remark that was the second the words were out of his mouth. He and Zoe had made love with passionate intensity all through that sizzling tropical night two months ago.

Through her misery, a spark of *his* Zoe emerged. 'The usual way,' she said. 'You know—basic biology.'

'But we were careful. You're on the pill.' He ran a hand through his hair in frustration. He should have taken care of the contraception.

'I know. But the doctor told me the pill doesn't work if it's not absorbed. And the Bali belly meant it didn't get digested. So no protection.'

It was the first time Mitch had seen Zoe so downcast; her lovely mouth set tight, her face strained, her eyes shadowed.

'So your illness wasn't an illness at all?'

'The initial food poisoning, yes. But once I got back to Australia it was what's called morning sickness.' Her mouth twisted wryly. 'Or, in my case, sometimes all-day sickness.'

Percolating through Mitch's shock was real anger. He'd been worried half-crazy about her. Driving back from the airport earlier, he had been imagining her with a serious, possibly fatal illness. What angered him was how dishonest she'd been.

He'd been stupid. She'd lied.

He made no effort to mask his anger. 'So when did you intend to tell me you were pregnant?'

He doubted she was even aware she was wringing her hands together. 'I...I didn't know how you would react. What...what you'd think of me.'

'You were going to let me fly back to Madrid without a word? What was I going to get—a lawyer's letter, demanding maintenance?'

She cringed from him. 'No! I was in shock. I was... frightened.'

Mitch took a step towards her. 'You were *frightened*? Frightened of *me*? What did you think I would do to you?'

Her face crumpled. 'I didn't know. I was so shocked. Trust me when I say it never entered my head that I could be having a baby. I didn't want you to think I...I'd tricked you into...into some kind of commitment. Or that I expected anything from you. I know how important it is to you to be...unencumbered. A baby certainly doesn't figure anywhere in your plans.' Her chin rose. 'It didn't figure in mine either.'

A baby. The actual word 'baby' hit him. Pregnancy was one thing. Baby was another. The reality was that Zoe was bearing a child—*his* child. Realising that sent Mitch into a deeper state of shock.

He and Zoe were going to be parents.

'Did you *ever* intend to tell me that I was going to be a father?'

He a father. Zoe the mother of his child.

The thoughts were so shocking, so unexpected, whirling around his head.

'Yes. No. I didn't know what to do.'

'You lied to me, Zoe. You said your sickness was caused by food allergies.'

'It was the first thing I could think of that might sound plausible. I didn't want you going back to Madrid worrying about it. Not when I know how extremely important the next few months are for you.'

'You're damn right about that,' he said.

Her chin tilted. 'I don't expect anything from you, Mitch. Not money. Not support.' Her mouth twisted bitterly. 'I know I'm nothing to you except a casual bedmate. If I ever thought anything else this sure as heck proves it.'

She headed for the bedroom, pushing past him. She picked up her red bag.

'I assume I can get a taxi from here? I'll walk down to the surf club to wait for one.'

He took a step towards her. 'Zoe—stop.'

She put a hand up to ward him off. 'Don't come near me,' she said, her voice as cold as her eyes.

She was leaving him again.

He grabbed her arm. She went still.

'Touch me again, Mitch, and I'll have an assault charge on you so fast your head will be spinning.'

He stared at her, shocked. How had it come to this?

After all they'd shared last night? What had happened to his plans for her to become part of his life? He'd been wrong to react the way he had.

She turned and walked away from him, her back ram-rod-straight. But he could see her shoulders shaking.

As she left the room the enormity of what he'd done hit him. Zoe hadn't planned this. She'd tried to save him worry. He cared for her. *She was having his child.* And she was walking out of his life. A life he'd begun to hope she could share with him.

He took the strides necessary to reach her. 'Zoe. Stop. I'm sorry. I was out of order, speaking to you in that way. It was a shock. But I was wrong to react like that.'

She turned back to face him, her lips set in a tight line. 'I want nothing from you, Mitch.'

'But what about the baby?'

'There's just one thing. For his or her sake I'd like you to acknowledge the child as yours. To play a role in its life.'

The truth slammed into Mitch and left him reeling. *He wanted Zoe. He wanted the baby.*

'Zoe, I really am sorry. Please don't walk away. It was an accident, but we're in it together. *My* child. *My* responsibility. You don't have to go through this by yourself.'

To his intense relief she put down her red bag.

No way was he going to 'play a role' in his son or daughter's life. He was going to be a father. A *good* father. Like his father had been to him. And his grandfather before him.

'When is the baby due?'

'February, the doctor said.'

The reality of it hit him with full force. Something akin to anticipation, even a stirring of excitement, began to infiltrate his thoughts.

'My parents will be beside themselves,' he said. 'Especially my mother—she's desperate for more grand-children.'

'You...you'd tell your *parents*?' Zoe's eyes were huge with trepidation.

'Of course I'll tell my parents. This isn't just about you and me, Zoe. Not any more. This will be the next genera-tion of my family. A Bailey grandchild. A Bailey great-grandchild. A niece or nephew. A cousin. In my family our child will be a reason for celebration—not commiseration.'

Zoe shook her head in seeming disbelief. She put her hand on her belly in an age-old gesture of protection that shot straight to Mitch's heart.

'I...I'm still coming to terms with this. That we've made a little person.'

'You're thinking about what your grandmother said, aren't you?'

That mean old witch had a lot to answer for, the way she'd treated her hurting, vulnerable granddaughter. She wouldn't be getting her claws into *his* child, that was for sure.

Mutely, Zoe nodded.

'This baby won't ruin my life,' Mitch said. '*You* are not ruining my life. We're twenty-seven—not seventeen. Our careers are established. We've got more than enough money.'

Zoe had no idea just how much money.

'All true,' she said.

But Mitch could sense a big Zoe *but* coming up.

The more he thought about this baby, the more he thought it wasn't such a disaster. He wanted Zoe. He had to look after her and the baby. They had to be with him.

'Zoe,' he said. 'Come here.'

He held out his arms to her. Her eyes widened but she took the few steps needed so he could draw her into his arms. He held her tight, close to his heart. He allowed relief to flood through him. She was okay. Not ill. Not terminal. *Pregnant with his child.* He would look after her. He would protect her.

'I'm not angry. Not any more,' he said. 'I'll admit it was a shock. But this child is our responsibility. We need to get married as soon as possible.'

Zoe froze in Mitch's arms. She pulled away. Looked up at him. 'Get *married*?'

Mitch drew his brows together. 'Of course, get married. You're pregnant.'

He sounded so certain, so matter-of-fact.

Problem solved. Let's get on with it.

Not a word about love.

Could you actually feel a heart breaking? That must surely be the explanation for the sudden pain that stabbed her somewhere in that region.

During those long, sleepless hours this morning, when she'd decided to end things with Mitch, she'd allowed herself a single moment to dream of the impossible. She'd let herself fantasise that Mitch would fall in love with her the way she'd fallen in love with him. That their planets might end up permanently aligned.

Her pregnancy had put paid to those dreams.

Those ever-present tears started to sting her eyes again but she fiercely blinked them back. *Darn hormones.*

'Just because I'm pregnant it's no reason to get married,' she said.

Mitch's frown deepened. 'Of course it is. I'm old-fashioned, Zoe. I want us to be married before you have the baby.'

She broke away from him, turned, looked blindly out at the view. Then spun back to face him.

'Mitch, I appreciate your gesture. It's honourable of you. Gentlemanly. But I can't marry you.'

'I don't get it. You're having my child. I want it to have my name. I want us to be together when he or she is born. To bring our child up together. Give him or her a good life.'

'That's impossible.'

He shrugged. 'There'd be some logistical problems—I acknowledge that. You'd have to come to Madrid to live with me. I can't live here. Not now. Not yet. But I know you want to travel, learn European languages, so I hope you won't mind that. We'd have to sort something out with your business... You could even bring your cat if you wanted.'

The pain in her heart intensified. She wanted to be with Mitch in Madrid more than anything—but not like this.

'No, Mitch. I can give my child a good life here in Sydney. But I want my child to know his or her father. I want you to be involved. Maybe...maybe when our baby is older he or she could spend time with you in Madrid, or wherever you end up living. It should be possible to have some kind of shared custody, if that's what you want. I don't know... I haven't had time to think it through.'

If only it could be different—him, her and their baby together.

Mitch's mouth set in a hard line. For the first time she saw the toughness, the aggressive strength she knew must be there for him to have got where he was in his ultra-competitive world.

'I don't agree,' he said. 'A child needs both mother *and* father, and I want to be a father to my child.'

'You *can* be a father, Mitch. I would encourage you to have a relationship with our child. I...I just don't want to get married.'

How it hurt to say that. *To lie.*

'Why, Zoe? Surely it's the only answer.'

Slowly, she shook her head. 'Mitch, I don't think I'm getting through to you.' It was difficult to keep her voice steady and reasoned. 'Don't you remember what I told you in Bali? I only want to get married if...if I'm head over heels in love.'

'I remember,' he said slowly.

The love was there on her side. There was no doubt about that. She'd been in love with him when she was seventeen—a hopeless, unrequited love. And it had been ignited again in Bali, she now realised.

'The man I marry has to love me in the same way. I...I can't settle for less. Not...not even to give my baby its father's name.'

'But, Zoe, I *do* love you,' Mitch said.

Her poor wounded heart soared. But she yanked it firmly back to the ground again.

'Mitch, you don't have to say that. It doesn't change things.'

Mitch took her by the shoulders, his voice low and urgent. 'Zoe, I'm not just saying this. I *love* you. Why do you think I came back this morning? Brought you down here? You know I'll get a hell of a fine and a reprimand from my club for not being on that plane to Madrid, for missing a game.'

'You're missing a *game*? But, Mitch, that's so important to you. Your knee—your—'

'Not as important as you, Zoe. When I drove home from your place last night I was determined you'd come and visit me in Madrid as soon as you could. Once you were there, I might not have been able to let you go. I'm asking you to marry me now. Most likely I would have asked you to marry me when you came to Madrid.'

'But it... But... I want to believe you, but it seems so sudden.'

'Does it?' He tilted her face so she was forced to meet his gaze. 'I wasn't completely honest with you in Bali.'

She shrank back from him. 'What do you mean?'

'I left out part of my story about when we were at school together. When I came back from soccer camp I kept looking out for you at school because I wanted to say how sorry I was for the way I'd behaved. But that wasn't all. I missed you. *Really* missed you. School wasn't the same without you. I missed our talks. I missed the way we laughed together. The way you believed I was so much more than anyone else thought I was.'

'I still think that,' she murmured, not expecting an answer.

'When I went round to your grandmother's place and she told me you wouldn't be coming back I was gutted. I got moody—bad-tempered. Lara didn't like it. "What's the matter with you?" she taunted me. "Were you in love with that geek girl?"'

Zoe felt herself blush for her seventeen-year-old self. 'Surely she didn't say that?'

'She'd hit on a truth I hadn't recognised until she put voice to it. It all made sense. I *did* have feelings for you— feelings I hadn't acknowledged. That's why I missed you so much. I snapped back at Lara. Denied it. I realised then why she'd been so mean to you. She was jealous. She'd seen how it was with you and me from the get-go.'

'I can't believe this,' Zoe said, slowly shaking her head. She wanted to believe it. But it seemed surreal.

'Believe it,' said Mitch. 'My first break-up with Lara was over you.'

'But you got back with her. Stayed with her for years, on and off.'

'You weren't around. I was seventeen. Lara was persuasive. What can I say?' Mitch said with a rueful grin.

'So how do you explain what happened in Bali?' she said, still reeling from what Mitch had confessed.

'You caught my eye straight away. I thought you were hot even before I recognised you.'

'Really?' she said, pleased. It didn't hurt a plain girl's ego to hear that she'd caught Mitch Bailey's eye.

'You were wearing a towel that scarcely covered your amazing body. Of *course* I noticed you.'

'I don't know what to say to that,' she said. 'I was terrified the towel was going to fall off.'

'I was hoping the towel *would* fall off.'

'Mitch!' she said with mock indignation, and laughed.

'I thought I was long over you. That my feelings for you had been a teen thing. I was glad to see you and to be able to put things straight. That was all. I didn't expect to fall in love with you all over again.'

'And...did you?' She couldn't control the tremor in her voice.

He nodded with a smile that set her heart racing. 'But I didn't realise how hard I'd fallen until I was back in Madrid. I tried to deny it. *Man*, did I try to deny it. The timing wasn't right. Like the timing of this baby isn't right. But we can't control that, can we? Life can have a way of making up our minds for us.'

'My getting pregnant, you mean? Or...or you falling in love?'

'Both,' he said. He cupped her face in his strong, gentle hands. 'What about you, Zoe? Could you fall in love with me?'

The look of mingled hope and expectation in his eyes made her knees feel weak and shaky.

'Oh, Mitch, I'm already in love with you.'

'Head over heels?'

'So head over heels I feel dizzy. I had a crush on you

at school, but I never dreamed it would be reciprocated in any way.'

'It was such a long time ago. We were kids.'

'But the emotions were real,' she said slowly. She thought back to those hours she'd spent with Mitch in the privacy of her villa. 'I…I think I fell in love with you during our water fight.'

'I can't pinpoint when. It was just…*there*,' he said. 'And everything changed. I tried to tell myself it was just a vacation thing. Reaction to fear of the earthquake. All that. Then when I saw you in Sydney, looking so hot in that pink suit, I knew the attraction was genuine. But you were so glamorous, so contained—so unlike the Zoe I'd known in Bali. I wasn't sure it was the same person.'

'I was terrified of saying the wrong thing. It took a while for us to relax with each other.'

'Yes,' he said. 'Until I wiped you out on the dodgems.'

'I'm glad we worked it out,' she said, hoping he could tell the depth of her feelings for him.

At last he kissed her, his mouth warm and possessive and tender.

Kissing a man you loved, who loved you, who wanted to spend his life with you, felt so different from the other kisses she'd shared with Mitch. Just as exciting, just as sensual, but taken to a new level by love. She wanted Mitch's kisses for the rest of her life. Never anyone else's.

There never had been anyone else, she realised. This was true love—first love.

And they were going to have a baby. A little boy or girl to bring more joy and love into their lives.

She pictured a little boy who looked just like Mitch, kicking a soccer ball around with his father's skill and talent. Or a little girl doing the same thing. A little girl with her dark hair and—

She broke the kiss 'Mitch, one little thing...'

'Yes?' he said.

'You know how you didn't recognise me at first?'

'It didn't take long. You were still the same Zoe. You just looked a bit different. Your hair, your—'

'My nose. I had a nose job when I was twenty-one. I thought I should let you know that. Just in case the baby... Well, the baby won't inherit this expensive new nose. The old one is still there, lurking in my genes. With a horrid bump in the middle.'

Mitch laughed. He gently stroked down her nose with his finger. 'This is a very nice nose. But I never even noticed you had a bump in it before.'

He kissed her again, deep and slow. She looked over his shoulder at that big, imposing bed. It would only take a few steps to take them there.

Mitch broke away from the kiss. His breathing was heavier, his eyes a shade darker with desire.

'So, will you marry me, Zoe?'

She didn't hesitate. 'Oh, yes, Mitch. *Yes.*'

They kissed for a long, long time. Then Mitch started to walk her back into the bedroom.

She broke the kiss to murmur against his mouth. 'Do you want to know what's in my thought bubbles?'

'Yes,' he said.

'No words. They're just filled with beautiful rainbows of joy,' she said.

CHAPTER SEVENTEEN

The following June

ZOE LEANED FORWARD in her VIP seat in the president's box of the Madrid stadium, where the final game of the Spanish La Liga season was being played at the home of Mitch's club. They only needed to draw to win the league and become the champions—the most sought-after of honours.

Mitch was below on the pitch, playing the toughest and most important game of his career to a packed stadium of nearly one hundred thousand spectators.

She could only imagine how it had felt for him as he had run through the players' tunnel onto the pitch to be greeted by the mighty collective roar of the fans. The game was being beamed worldwide by satellite to millions more fans—maybe billions.

Mitch, the only Australian, had become a star in a star-studded team. Over the course of the season that had been a test of his injured knee, he had scored ten goals in a total of twenty-seven league games—the best of his career.

But now the vast stadium was silent as, in the dying seconds of the game, her husband lined up to take the free kick that would decide the outcome of the game against his team's closest rival.

Five of the opposition's players had lined up to form

a wall, each of them with their hands cupped over their nether regions for protection against a possible hit by the ball.

At any other time Zoe would have found that action amusing. But not now. Her fingernails were digging into her hands so hard they were drawing blood, but she didn't notice.

All she was aware of was Mitch as he took the free kick and curled the ball up over the heads of the players in the wall and into the top corner of the net. It was a breathtaking demonstration of his skill that left the goalkeeper helpless.

Goal!

Zoe jumped up from her seat, fists pumping in the air, as she cheered for her husband. He had scored an equalising goal to clinch the title for his team. *They'd won the league!* Mitch's team were now the champions—the most important title for any major club.

The crowd erupted into a deafening roar of approval.

On the large-screen monitor she saw a close-up of Mitch's face, his expression one of triumphant ecstasy, his grin huge. He acknowledged the crowd's cheers and pulled off his team shirt, leaving his perfectly sculpted chest bare as, arms outstretched, he ran a victory lap in only his shorts and long white socks. He looked breathtakingly handsome and the fans went delirious.

Then he was overtaken by his jubilant teammates in a great show of hugging and back-slapping that culminated in the players throwing their grinning coach above their heads in the air.

Part of the gig of being married to a soccer star was that Zoe had to share his bare chest with the world. There were internet video channels dedicated to just that—shots of Mitch with his shirt off. But she had to deal with it, knowing that while Mitch might be public property to his fans he came home to share *her* bed and enjoy the private family life they cherished. He had never given her cause not to trust him implicitly.

She looked down to where baby Isabella still slept in the carrycot by her feet, oblivious to her famous daddy's triumph.

Zoe's heart seemed to flip over with love for her daughter. Mitch called her the most beautiful baby in the world. With her mummy's dark hair, her daddy's green eyes and straight nose, she was very pretty. Her sweet nature and bright ways made her a joy to have in their lives. If she would just learn to sleep through the night Bella—as she was already called—would indeed be perfect.

It remained to be seen if she would grow up to be the soccer star her father predicted she would be.

In the next seat to her Amanda Bailey, Mitch's mother, wiped away tears of pride in her youngest son. She looked dotingly on her only female grandchild.

'The little pet didn't stir—even with all that commotion,' she said.

Zoe met Amanda's eyes in a perfect communication of shared joy. From being initially wary of Zoe, Amanda had become the best mother-in-law Zoe could ever have imagined having.

Even though they had at first questioned the haste of their son's wedding plans, Mitch's parents had come up trumps in helping them organise the ceremony and reception at short notice.

The ceremony had been perfect—held in the small chapel of an ancient monastery just outside of Madrid. Her dress, from a leading Spanish fashion house, had been exquisite in its simplicity and style—and cleverly cut to disguise the growing presence of baby Isabella.

Zoe had hoped for an intimate reception, but with

Mitch's fame that had not been possible. But it, too, had been perfect, with all his family and friends there. Mitch had flown over a number of her friends too, as their guests.

Louise, who was doing a brilliant job of steering The Right Note to further success as a full business partner, had been among them. She had moved into the Balmain apartment and taken over Einstein's care, as both she and Louise had agreed that he wouldn't have been happy with a move to another country. Louise had brought with her to the wedding a card signed with Einstein's pawprint that had made Zoe both laugh and cry.

When the time had come Amanda had insisted on flying to Madrid to be with Zoe and Mitch in the days after Isabella's birth, to help out. In an unobtrusive, loving way she had given her the help and support Zoe knew her own mother would have given her as she, in turn, had learned to be a mother.

Amanda had flown back to Australia once Zoe was managing motherhood on her own. Now she was back to watch Mitch's big game.

In marrying Mitch, Zoe had gained not only an adoring husband but also a warm, welcoming extended family that had filled the painful gap left by the loss of her own parents. It was an outcome she hadn't ever dreamed of.

Now she and Amanda looked again to the monitor, to see Mitch being interviewed on the pitch by a gaggle of sports media representatives. He switched effortlessly from English to Spanish in his replies, and Zoe was pleased with herself for being able to understand the Spanish. She had fitted right into life in Madrid and could happily converse with most people.

The main commentator for one of the big sports networks was interviewing Mitch now. Her husband's beloved face filled the screen.

'You've come back from your knee injury in spectac-ular form, Mitch,' the interviewer said. 'And I hear talk that you've been nominated as Footballer of the Year. Is this your greatest moment?'

Mitch looked directly into the camera. 'Yes, it's the greatest moment of my career,' he said, in that deep, fa-miliar voice. 'But the greatest moment of my life was when my beautiful wife, Zoe, agreed to marry me, followed by the birth of our precious daughter, Isabella.'

Zoe stared at the screen long after Mitch had finished the interview. She knew he would be with her as soon as he could, and it wasn't long before she heard murmurs among the other guests in the VIP area that let her know he was on his way.

Dressed now in his team tracksuit, and wearing a medal on a ribbon around his neck, Mitch headed towards her, politely accepting the congratulations being showered on him but making it clear that he had eyes for only one per-son—his wife.

He swept her into his arms and hugged her close. Cam-eras flashed, but Zoe didn't care.

'We did it,' he said.

'*You* did it. I just cheered,' Zoe said. 'It was your vic-tory.'

'It was *our* victory,' Mitch corrected her. 'I could never have done what I did this season without your love and support. Having you by my side has made all the differ-ence. Thank you, wife.'

Mitch and his team had won the grand prize today. But Zoe knew the greatest prize of all was the love of her hus-band—and *she* had won it.

* * * * *

MILLS & BOON®

Regency Vows Collection!

If you enjoyed this book, get the full Regency Vows Collection today and receive two free books.

2 BOOKS FREE!

Order your complete collection today at
www.millsandboon.co.uk/regencyvows

0615_MB512

MILLS & BOON®

The Thirty List

At thirty, Rachel has slid down every ladder she has ever climbed. Jobless, broke and ditched by her husband, she has to move in with grumpy Patrick and his four-year-old son.

Patrick is also getting divorced, so to cheer themselves up the two decide to draw up bucket lists. Soon they are learning to tango, abseiling, trying stand-up comedy and more. But, as she gets closer to Patrick, Rachel wonders if their relationship is too good to be true…

Order yours today at
www.millsandboon.co.uk/Thethirtylist

MILLS & BOON®

The Chatsfield Collection!

2 BOOKS FREE!

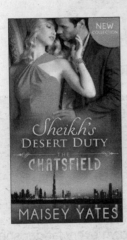

Style, spectacle, scandal…!

With the eight Chatsfield siblings happily married and settling down, it's time for a new generation of Chatsfields to shine, in this brand-new 8-book collection! The prospect of a merger with the Harrington family's boutique hotels will shape the future forever. But who will come out on top?

Find out at
www.millsandboon.co.uk/TheChatsfield2

CHATSFIELD_PROMO_BK

MILLS & BOON®

The Sharon Kendrick Collection!

1 BOOK FREE!

Passion and seduction….

If you love a Greek tycoon, an Italian billionaire or a
Spanish hero, then this collection is perfect for you.
Get your hands on the six 3-in-1 romances from the
outstanding Sharon Kendrick. Plus, with one book
free, this offer is too good to miss!

**Order yours today at
www.millsandboon.co.uk/Kendrickcollection**

415_ST_10

MILLS & BOON®

Why not subscribe?
Never miss a title and save money too!

Here's what's available to you if you join the exclusive **Mills & Boon Book Club** today:

✦ *Titles up to a month ahead of the shops*
✦ *Amazing discounts*
✦ *Free P&P*
✦ *Earn Bonus Book points that can be redeemed against other titles and gifts*
✦ *Choose from monthly or pre-paid plans*

Still want more?
Well, if you join today we'll even give you
50% OFF your first parcel!

So visit **www.millsandboon.co.uk/subs**
or call **Customer Relations on 020 8288 2888**
to be a part of this exclusive Book Club!

SUBS_2014

MILLS & BOON®

Cherish™

EXPERIENCE THE ULTIMATE RUSH OF FALLING IN LOVE

A sneak peek at next month's titles...

In stores from 19th June 2015:

- **The Millionaire's True Worth** – Rebecca Winters *and*
  His Proposal, Their Forever – Melissa McClone

- **A Bride for the Italian Boss** – Susan Meier *and*
  The Maverick's Accidental Bride – Christine Rimmer

In stores from 3rd July 2015:

- **The Earl's Convenient Wife** – Marion Lennox *and*
  How to Marry a Doctor – Nancy Robards Thompson

- **Vettori's Damsel in Distress** – Liz Fielding *and*
  Daddy Wore Spurs – Stella Bagwell

Available at WHSmith, Tesco, Asda, Eason, Amazon and Apple

Just can't wait?
Buy our books online a month before they hit the shops!
visit www.millsandboon.co.uk

These books are also available in eBook format!